Some men don't know they're there,
if they can't see themselves reflected in a lover's eyes.

If they aren't there, they need never be real, never take chances, and are free lock themselves away with their obsessions. But then they meet someone, a special man in whose eyes they become real, solid—and hot. That man gets past their walls, stops them in their flight from a sordid past, and who pushes them into their dreams... In this volume, ForbiddenFiction presents six of E.E. Grey's stories about men reaching beyond the limits of their fears and becoming real, in love.

Reaching Out

E.E. Grey

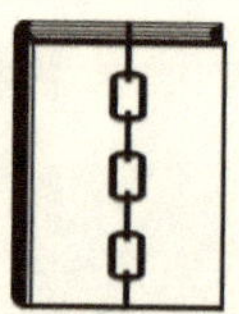

ForbiddenFiction
www.forbiddenfiction.com
an imprint of

Enspire Publishing
www.enspirepublishing.com

REACHING OUT

A ForbiddenFiction book

Enspire Publishing
Hayward, California

CREDITS
Editor: D.M. Atkins, James L. Wolf, Lon Sarver, and Rylan Hunter
Cover Designer: Siolnatine
Cover Photo Credits: Adapted from photo by Lopolo at Shutterstock.
Inside Cover Designer: D.M. Atkins & Soilnatine
Inside Photo Credits: Photos by Studio-54-foto, Derek R. Audette, Dnf-style, Norman7, Choreograph, & Mystock88photo at Dreamstime, and LanaLanglois at Pixmac. Photo by igordutina, creatista, Natlit, imagerymajestic & keeweeboy at Pixmac Additional photo editing by Siolnatine. Photo by MaxWolfe at Flickr
Production Editor: Kaye O'Malley
Proofreading: Blue Sapphire, JhP323, lil.fireffly, and Kailin Morgan

SKU: EEG-1.100012-01 FFP
ISBN: 978-1-62234-349-2

Published in the United States of America

DISCLAIMER

This book is a work of fiction which contains explicit erotic content; it is intended for mature readers. Do not read this if it's not legal for you.

All the characters, locations and events herein are fictional. While elements of existing locations or historical characters or events may be used fictitiously, any icit erotic content; it is intended for mature readers. Do not read this if it's not legal forresemblance to actual people, places or events is coincidental.

This story is not intended to be used as an instruction manual. It may contain descriptions of erotic acts that are immoral, illegal, or unsafe. Do not take the events in this story as proof of the plausibility or safety of any particular practice.

Such content should not be read as a depiction of the desires, opinions, or fetishes of the author or the staff of ForbiddenFiction.com.

Contents

Cigarette Burns

Cigarette Burns

The fog seems to press in around him, misting his jacket and the mess of unruly blond hair that falls into his eyes as he stares at the dark and dirty pavement below his feet. He tugs at the tips, dyed black only because he's too lazy to re-dye the rest or cut it off. The cigarette between his fingers smolders gently, the red tip bright against the darkness of the alley.

Fucking bars that don't let you smoke inside, is the only thing he's thinking as he raises the cigarette to his mouth and takes a long drag.

Shivering, Maddox releases the tip of his hair and stuffs his hand in his pocket, hunching his shoulders as if trying to sink into the brick wall behind him. He should go back inside, but there's nothing for him there. There's nothing for him out here either, just the slow burn of his cigarette and the flickering streetlamp a few feet away.

It's not that late out, barely midnight, but he's had more than a few drinks already. Honestly, he thinks he deserves it after the shit he's gone through lately. Despite the tingling warmth in his fingers, the rest of him is still cold as he takes another drag and sniffs from the way his nose is starting to go numb.

The mist settles decidedly in his hair and on the shoulders of his black jacket as he leans back against the brick wall, contemplating going back inside or just going to a liquor store and continuing the party on his own. It's not as if he has anyone to disappoint at this point aside from himself.

Flicking the cigarette away and watching it fizzle out in a puddle, he pulls out another and lights it slowly. The flame from his lighter dances in the darkness then disappears in a small click as he shuts it off and stuffs the lighter in his jeans' pocket.

A few people are walking down the street beyond—Maddox can hear them—and they seem to slow as their eyes pass over the alleyway with him hunched in the darkness.

He knows he doesn't look presentable, with his hair a fucking mess and the jagged edge of a tattoo peeking out from under his collar. There are bags under his hazel eyes and he hasn't showered in three days, but who's counting anyway? He smells like stale cigarettes now with a hint of cheap beer, and he's not even sure when the last time he changed his shirt was. What did it matter anyway? It isn't as if there is anyone to impress.

He can still hear Joel in his head, his pompous voice filling him as he tells him there's someone else, it's over and he's leaving.

"It's not you, Maddy. Well, actually it is. Sorry."

It's the 'sorry' that haunts him the most (and maybe the 'Maddy' too. He fucking hates that nickname). It hadn't been sincere in the least, and Maddox hadn't felt at all bad about accidentally dropping Joel's iPhone in the toilet five minutes later.

He knows he shouldn't be so upset about it considering how the last few months have gone, but Maddox is mad; at Joel and at himself. How could he not have known that Joel was fucking cheating on him for two months? He'd been so much happier, and it wasn't as if they'd been having sex at all. Seven months down the drain on an asshole like that. It makes him want to smash something that belongs to Joel or drown his sorrows in alcohol. He's chosen the latter, mostly because Joel had taken his things when he'd left two days ago.

Huffing to himself, and he can even see his breath now as it gets later and colder, Maddox sucks in the sweet nicotine of his cigarette. It's been months since he's had one, all because of Joel. He doesn't fucking care anymore though. He'd given up a lot for Joel and he's tired of it. At least with Joel gone he can finally be himself again, without the extra effort of trying to quit smoking or actually keeping the apartment clean. What pisses him off most is that despite how much he tried to change, in the end, it wasn't enough. Maybe he should never have bothered in the first place.

Pulling his sleeves down over his hands, Maddox raises the cigarette to his mouth again. He wishes he was drunker than he is; wishes he didn't have to think about any of this. He can't even remember what he did before he met Joel. It seems so long ago now.

There's a noise down the alley, the sound of the bar door opening and someone stepping out. Maddox should really go home or at least somewhere warm like back inside, but he doesn't even care enough to get out of the cold at this point. Instead, he tongues his cigarette and shrinks back against the wall as someone comes his way.

It's a guy that had been in the bar. He was there when Maddox arrived, but he hadn't paid him much attention. He doesn't look cold in his own jacket and jeans. He stops a few feet from Maddox, sweeping back his dark brown hair out of his eyes and glancing down the alley as if waiting for someone.

Maddox ignores him, scrunching up further. He's still got half a pack of cigarettes to go through if he feels like it. He can do anything if he feels like it now. The thought should be liberating, but it just makes him angrier.

"Hey, can I bum a cigarette?"

The guy is next to Maddox now, hair falling back in his big, dark eyes. He's a few inches shorter than Maddox but built thicker with his square shoulders, the shape echoed in his jaw. He's got his hands stuffed in his jacket pockets now and he rocks back on his heels for a second as Maddox contemplates him.

Without a word, Maddox pulls out his crumpled box and taps out a cigarette, handing it over to the guy. The guy doesn't ask for a light, pulling a lighter from his back pocket instead.

Maddox's hair is damp and he can feel the mist on the back of his neck too now, colder when the breeze picks up down the alley. He fights back a shiver and takes a drag of his cigarette, eyes half on the guy next to him now.

The guy is decently attractive, he thinks, eyes flitting over his face, from his crooked nose to his pale, pink lips closed around the end of the cigarette. His hair is cut messily, like he did it himself, uneven lengths on different sides, too long in the front. He watches the guy's tongue dart out to wet his lips as he takes the cigarette away and leans his head back against the wall.

It's been too long, Maddox thinks. He watches the guy and wonders what it would take to get him to go down on him. He doesn't even know if the guy is interested in other guys, but it never hurt to ask. He can't bring himself to, though, and he looks away. No one would want to with him anyway; Joel had made that perfectly clear.

His cigarette is almost finished and he's just thinking about grabbing one last beer before going home to see if there's anything left of Joel's to break when the guy beside him shifts, shoving his hair out of his eyes again with a rough hand. When Maddox looks over he finds the guy watching him intently. It doesn't make him nervous or excited or anything. He's lost all ability to care. If apathy was a religion he'd be a god.

"Long day?" the guy asks.

Maddox scrunches up in his jacket in the cold, staring down at his cigarette instead. It's almost burned down to his fingertips but he doesn't smash it out yet.

He doesn't reply to the guy either. He doesn't need to reply. He's not going to spill his sob story to some random stranger he met in an alley between the trash cans and the stray dog rooting in the corner. It's pathetic enough that he even cares about all of this. He doesn't need to relive it again.

The guy moves first, turning towards Maddox as Maddox fingers his cigarette and wonders how much penalty there would be to break the lease on his apartment. Every fucking thing in it reminds him of Joel and how much of an asshole he really is.

"Hey," the guy says and Maddox glances at him, thinking he sees a flash of silver in the guy's mouth, maybe a tongue piercing. "You want to get another drink?"

Maddox pauses. He thinks maybe the guy is coming on to him, but maybe he's also hallucinating. It's been seven months since he's done this, even talked to another guy with sex as a possible outcome. In a way it had been nice, not having to guess, knowing he'd have someone to go home to. That had all been a joke.

"No," he mutters, finally replying to the guy, using his voice for what seems like the first time in days. It's rough from all the cigarettes, scratchy and low.

The guy isn't insulted, licking his lips again before raising the cigarette and taking a drag. Maddox watches him, watches the way his tongue flicks out first, dragging over his bottom lip. He hasn't been with anyone in months, and it's not like it would take much to get him going at this point.

"You wanna fuck then?" the guy asks, plain and simple as if asking for another cigarette. His eyes are big and dark (interested) in the flickering light of the streetlamp and Maddox watches him shove his hair back again, casually, as if he's said nothing out of the ordinary.

As blunt as it is, Maddox just contemplates it for a minute. He doesn't know this guy at all, and neither of them has even really expressed interest, but Maddox is a little drunk, and he's sure he could get into it.

The guy, on the other hand, takes a step towards Maddox, eyes roaming over his collarbone and the tattoo peeking out there. It's the look in his eyes, dark and purposeful, the flicker of something more than just a passing interest, as he meets Maddox's, that sends the first shiver down his back that's not due to the mist pressing in around him.

The guy's mouth curves slightly as he watches Maddox, fingers playing with his cigarette. "What do you say?" he asks, tongue flicking out to wet his bottom lip again.

Maddox feels something in his chest sort of seize up at the question, but he doesn't want to know why. He can do anything he wants now, and that includes fucking random guys he meets outside of bars.

"Okay," he says finally, stubbing out what's left of his cigarette on the wall behind him. The crumpled butt drops to the wet pavement. His fingers are cold and he pushes his hands into his pockets as the guy's mouth curls into a smirk and he nods towards the end of the alley.

Maddox doesn't reply but steps away from the wall and the guy joins him, rough fingers brushing against the bit of exposed skin at his wrist. His glance slides sideways, eyes on the guy's mouth, the way his hair is already back in his eyes. They don't need to speak as their eyes meet again and

Maddox doesn't question his decision for a second as they leave the alleyway together.

They go to Maddox's apartment because it's closest, and, for the first time in three days, he's not thinking about Joel. He's not thinking of the cruel way he'd just said, 'By the way, I've been fucking someone else for two months.' He's thinking about the guy next to him, the one with the uneven, floppy hair that he periodically shoves out of his eyes. He's thinking that he doesn't even know his name but he doesn't care in the slightest.

They haven't even kissed, but the walk to his apartment is enough for Maddox. He likes that he knows nothing about this guy. He likes that he just wants to fuck him. He hasn't done that in a long time. It makes him feel free, like it doesn't fucking matter if he knows the guy or not.

He can feel himself growing warmer as they walk, a thrum of something exciting coursing through his body, the cold no longer affecting him as he starts to picture what it'll be like once they get to his place. His eyes are on the guy's fingers, the pads rough with calluses from he doesn't know what. He doesn't need to know, and that's the best part.

He wants another cigarette as they reach his building and he opens the door and the guy brushes up against him as he passes through, lingering a second too long against Maddox, and Maddox swallows slowly. It's like some kind of electric charge passes through his body at the touch that isn't even a real touch, barely there, a slight pressure against his side.

Letting out a breath, he leads the way to the elevator, hyper aware of every movement they're making now. His fingers still itch for a cigarette, but he masters the impulse as he presses the button to the elevator and takes a small, sharp breath as the guy presses up against his back, mouth barely brushing against his ear.

"What floor?" the guy asks, voice low, and Maddox wants to lean into the warmth of his breath on his ear. It's doing things to him as they stand there, the guy's hands sliding to his hips as if waiting for his invitation.

Maddox hasn't done this in a long time but he still remembers how it goes, how it used to go before Joel told him he was too much of a slut, before they'd actually started dating. Maybe he used to sleep around too much but it hadn't stopped him from being faithful.

As the anger builds again Maddox forces it away with the ding of the elevator. This isn't about Joel. This is about him and what he wants.

"Seventh," he replies as he steps inside, the guy following step for step, fingers brushing against a sliver of bare skin as Maddox pushes the button and the doors slide shut.

He shouldn't be surprised, but he is when the guy shoves him up against the back of the elevator as it starts to rumble upwards. For a second he's disoriented at the assault of feelings that flood his mind—a flash of shock, followed by guilt, then finally overridden by a burning desire to just stop feeling anything.

The elevator is rising and the guy's mouth is on his neck, hot and demanding, echoing the push of his hands under Maddox's shirt, rough, calloused fingers sliding over his stomach, and Maddox sucks in a breath. Reaching down, his fingers wrap around the guy's and he pushes, shoving him back so he's the one in control. He's sick of not being in control. The guy doesn't protest one bit, eyes darting eagerly over his face, mouth half open and breath hot against Maddox's lips as he presses their mouths together.

It's not a finessed kiss in any way, rough and raw, teeth biting and tongues sucking whatever heat they can find. Maddox's hand is still wrapped around the guy's wrist, pressing it into the elevator wall as they're rushed upwards.

"What-what's your name?" the guy pants.

Maddox pulls his mouth away to take a gulp of air and the elevator jerks to a stop. "Maddox," he mutters, jerking the guy's wrist forward as the doors slide open and they stumble out.

He glances down the hall but it's empty. His neighbors aren't much of night owls anyway.

His apartment is down a few doors, and he feels the guy behind him, his free hand sliding to his hip and squeezing. A strange thrill runs down Maddox's spine and he pulls his keys from his pocket and fits them into the lock.

"I'm Rory," the guy says without prompting, breath hot against Maddox's ear.

Maddox shoves the door open, barely pulling the keys from the lock before it's slammed shut. The dim, front hall light flips on. He's got Rory boxed up against the door.

Rory's eyes are a beautiful hazel color and his lips are a light, rose-pink. There's a dark freckle under his left eye just above his cheek and his hair falls unevenly into his eyes. Maddox thinks vaguely that he probably doesn't look much more put together when the apartment behind him is strewn with takeout boxes, unclean shirts and mismatched shoes.

Maddox goes for Rory's mouth, wanting to feel it, feel the difference between him and Joel, even if he's not supposed to be thinking about Joel. There's a clear difference from the very beginning, as Rory doesn't hesitate to push at Maddox's clothes, pushing his jacket off and tearing off the dirty tee shirt underneath.

Rory's hands skim over Maddox's thin waist, the pale skin, brushing over the tattoo that rises up on his hip bone and swirls around his back, the cherry tree Joel used to laugh at. He knows Rory's fingers are tracing the petals even though he can't see, too busy biting at Rory's mouth, rough and hard, pressing him back against the door until he's close enough to feel the bulge in Rory's jeans.

Panting, he glances down, hating the squeeze of uncertainty that grips his heart for a moment, the thought that it can't be for him, but Rory chooses that moment to reach for Maddox's neck, steering it to the side so he can nip at his neck, teeth scraping down and a hot mouth closing over the skin and sucking until Maddox slips, pushing his hips into Rory's and groaning as a hot lick of friction darts through him.

"Mmm," Rory hums, mouth never leaving Maddox's neck as his hands go for the button on his jeans, jerking his hips forward unexpectedly. He gets the zipper down before Maddox even opens his eyes and his hand shoves underneath, cupping Maddox through his underwear.

Maddox's hands slip against where they're pressed against the door, boxing Rory in. One falls to Rory's hip, squeezing tightly and pulling him in flush even as Rory palms him, drawing out a low moan.

"Fuck," Rory mutters, and Maddox agrees, rutting into his hand.

He can feel the flush crawling up his skin, pink rushing up to his cheeks, the back of his neck, and, for the first time in months, he doesn't feel embarrassed about it.

Rory's mouth slides up quicker than Maddox expects, biting at his lower lip before sliding his tongue inside Maddox's mouth, exchanging hot air between them, a frantic motion that Maddox loses track of within seconds.

"I wanna suck you off," Rory pants a moment later, hand still wrapped around Maddox's cock, grip firm and hot, and Maddox would never argue. "Let me suck you off."

"Fuck yes," Maddox replies in one huffed breath, watching with a flicker of fascination as Rory drops to his knees without a second's hesitation, hands pulling Maddox's jeans down his thin hips to bunch around his ankles.

He almost feels exposed, standing in his living room, surrounded by last night's Chinese boxes, the couch that is currently buried in jackets and shirts, the stacks of unorganized DVDs strewn around the TV, but as soon as Rory licks a stripe up his cock he forgets everything.

His mind is cloudy and all he can feel is the hotness, the slick, wet slide of Rory's mouth on his cock. He bites down on his lip as he watches; watches Rory take him in, back and forth, sucking and licking. Rory's hand is wet when it wraps around the base of Maddox's cock, stroking and pulling, rubbing over the hard prick until Maddox can feel the heat rising all over his body.

"God, fuck," Maddox mumbles as Rory tongues the head of his cock, almost a teasing slide of his tongue. "Jesus Christ, your mouth, fucking fuck." He doesn't know what he's saying, reaching down to tangle his fingers in Rory's dark hair. It's soft to the touch, clean and shiny, and Maddox's fingers clench as he gasps sharply.

Rory's mouth is either extremely talented or Maddox has gone way too long without getting any, or it could be a little of both. Either way, Maddox clenches his teeth as he tries not to choke Rory, but a part of him, that little reckless part that even thought this was a good idea, doesn't care at all about this stranger.

Rory makes a noise, soft but insistent, and he pulls back before Maddox can protest, raising his eyes up and Maddox stares down. Rory's mouth is puffy and red, and Maddox just wants his cock back inside it, wants to fuck his throat until it's raw. Rory's staring up at him, though, hot breath puffing over his prick, and Maddox closes his eyes as blood thuds south.

"Fuck me," Rory pants, voice rough but firm.

Maddox opens his eyes, meeting Rory's eyes, and he hates that he hesitates, hates that he stops to think about it. He shouldn't be thinking about anything.

So he grabs Rory's upper arm and drags him off his knees, pushing him over to the couch. There's nowhere to sit on it, so Maddox steers him to the backside, pressing him against it. His hard cock rubs against Rory's ass slowly, torturously, and he wonders why Rory still has his pants on after all of this.

"Take off your pants," he orders him. "I'll be right back."

He won't admit to scrambling to the bathroom, glancing back only once to see Rory drop his pants unceremoniously and kick them away.

He fumbles through drawers, trying to find the right one, pushing aside combs and half-empty bottles of gel and toothpaste. In the furthest drawer from the door he finds the box that Joel left, probably as a hurtful reminder, but Maddox just rips it open and pulls out a condom. He snatches the lube out with it and hurries back to the living room.

Rory stands by the couch, completely naked, cock already hard and waiting as Maddox returns.

Pushing him back against the couch, Maddox gets the condom open and on before he flips open the lube. He fumbles when Rory presses back against him, ass rocking back against his cock. He needs to take control, he thinks, shoving Rory's hips back against the couch, tearing his eyes away from a freckle on Rory's hip. It's in the vague shape of Florida, he thinks, shaking himself and slicking his fingers with lube.

He doesn't go slow as he pushes in the first finger, watching Rory's back arch, hearing the moan he lets out, like he just can't get enough.

"Yeah, fuck, more," Rory says, pushing back against him. "Fuck yes, Madd, fuck yes."

Maddox pushes in a second finger despite the way Rory whines, like he just needs more. A shiver of something unfamiliar runs down Maddox's spine, dropping into his stomach as he watches Rory rock backwards. He shakes it away, though, pulling his fingers out and replacing them with his cock.

Rory is mumbling profanities as Maddox pushes in through the tight, throbbing muscles that clench around his already pulsing cock. He's hard as fuck, harder than he can remember ever being with Joel. He attributes it to this being the first time in months he's been inside anyone else, had anyone else gripping his thigh and begging him to move, to go faster, to fuck him as hard as he can.

Rory's not a quiet one, cursing every time Maddox moves, every time he slides in harder, rocks deeper inside him. He keeps up a stream of commentary on how fucking amazing Maddox's cock is, how good it feels, how much more he wants.

"Fuck, fuck, touch me, shit, please, holy shit," Rory mumbles, head bowed forward, and for the first time, Maddox notices a tattoo dropping below his hairline, hidden by his hair. He can't tell what it is exactly but it's all black, like a shadow etched onto his skin.

Rory rocks back onto Maddox's cock harder, forcing him to go faster, to fuck him deeply. The hot flush that spreads over Maddox's body is becoming nearly unbearable and he grits his teeth as he thrusts sharply into Rory. His hands are pressing long, red bruises into Rory's hips, but Rory isn't complaining. If anything, he seems to like the flare of pain, the reminder for later.

Maddox reaches for Rory's cock with barely any time to spare, gripping hard as Rory comes without warning, with only a hitch of breath, the hand clenched around the back of the couch going white as he grips the cushion.

"Fuck yes," Rory hisses, still pushing back onto Maddox's cock, and Maddox lets go then. He lets go of everything, anything he was holding back, pounding Rory against the couch, and Rory doesn't complain at all, groaning and panting down at the cushions.

"Shit!" Maddox bites out as his stomach clenches hotly and his fingers dig into Rory's hip, and he comes, hips jerking into Rory. It's a crashing wave of heat that washes over him, sweeping through his stomach and tingling in his fingertips as he finally releases Rory's hips. The red marks press into Rory's pale skin as Maddox steps away.

Rory is still cursing under his breath as he turns around, glancing at Maddox. "Shit, that was good," he says, a smile curling the corner of his mouth, and Maddox lets out a short breath.

Maddox wants a cigarette and he backtracks to where his jeans are bunched on the floor near the door. Digging in the pocket, he comes up with the dented pack and taps one out. When he glances back, Rory is just leaning against the couch, still completely naked, and he makes no effort to cover up but neither does Maddox.

"This place all yours?" Rory asks as Maddox lights the cigarette and takes a grateful inhale of nicotine.

Maddox's eyes are drawn to the messy room, the bedroom door ajar behind Rory, the coffee pot in the kitchen still half-full from that morning.

"I'm moving," he says instead because he realizes as he stands there that there's no way he wants to stay there.

Rory nods after a second and reaches for his shirt instead, pulling it on.

Maddox doesn't say anything as Rory dresses, buttoning his jeans and running a hand through his hair. It sticks up messily in places but Rory doesn't seem to care. Maddox takes another drag of his cigarette and watches Rory pick up his jacket and sling it over his shoulder.

Rory casts him a short glance before making a detour to the kitchen counter and scribbling something down on a piece of paper there.

He brings it over to Maddox and presses it into his free hand. Maddox arches a skeptical eyebrow, but Rory just smirks at him.

"Call me when you're in your new place," he says, stealing Maddox's cigarette for a second and taking a drag. Maddox stares for a second. "Seriously."

Rory saunters to the door and leaves with an interested quirk of his eyebrow before he disappears.

Maddox stares at his cigarette clutched between his fingers, and it takes him a second to grab his jeans and pull them on haphazardly. He flops down on the couch a minute later and reaches into the pile of newspapers that goes back the last three days, coming out with the classifieds.

Taking a drag of his cigarette, he flips it open to the apartments section and settles down, stuffing the crumpled note in his hand inside his pocket and he sinks into the darkness but it's not quite as dark as before.

From the Storm

Chapter 1
In the Tempest

"I'll see you on Monday."

Bailey glanced up from his desk, scattered with papers, case files stacked in every corner. He could never seem to keep it neat like the other defenders in the office. Shelley stood in the doorway to his cubicle.

"Yeah," he replied, momentarily distracted from his files "Have a good weekend."

"Don't work too hard," she said as she left. Bailey laughed, but deep down, he knew he was looking at a long night.

A clap of thunder brought his attention to the gathering storm clouds outside the office window. His eyes itched from the hours he had already spent that day reading the stacks of briefs on his desk. He swore he had gone through every one of them twice—it wasn't the first time he'd been assigned a case where the kid was almost eighteen and the judge wanted him tried as an adult. If he could figure out a deal, the kid might have a chance to start over.

It was after five already, but he wasn't leaving until he found something. Being a public defender wasn't the most glamorous job, and some cases he'd fought had tested his morals. Then there were cases like this; a kid arrested for breaking and entering after running away from foster care for the third time. The ecstasy he'd had on him hadn't helped either. Cases like these were why Bailey had decided to go the public defender route instead of joining a rich, well-established firm.

The air conditioner was on the fritz, had been all day, leaving the whole floor hot and humid. Bailey was sure he looked a mess, brown hair pushed back so many times it stuck up in odd angles. Appearance was usually the least of his worries, except when it came to the courtroom and looking professional—he was average looking, average height and build, dark brown eyes, and a scar over his eyebrow from the time he'd fallen out of a tree as a kid. His saving grace was that he looked damn good in a suit.

This time, this case, he had to help. If Adam was tried as an adult, he could go to jail for a long time. The felony possession could turn into something much worse. A mark like that on his record would ruin anything else he wanted to do in life.

Bailey's skin was sticky with humidity coming from the rain outside, heat pressing in all around him with no way to get rid of it. Thunder rumbled again behind him; he ignored it, but it was hard as the office got steadily darker and hotter. This case was the only thing on his mind at the moment, but he just couldn't figure it out. Judge Pearson was not one who tended to be lenient toward kids.

Rain battered the windows and his light flickered ominously. Glancing up, he frowned and tried to ignore his growing unease. Bailey had always lived in a large city, growing up in San Diego. He'd stayed there for undergrad, though those years hadn't always been kind. New York, though fundamentally different than San Diego, had its benefits. He'd moved to New York for grad school at SUNY Cortland, and he'd gotten hired at the public defender's office two years ago, after graduation. It was a change from the path he'd once expected to go: his dad had probably been insulted that he'd become a public defender instead of joining the family firm (not that Bailey knew for sure since he hadn't heard from him in years), but Bailey wouldn't have joined even if his dad miraculously apologized for everything. He hadn't become a lawyer just to please his parents or make money.

Rubbing his eyes, Bailey stretched in his uncomfortable chair. The storm shook the windows behind him, gathering strength. Bailey's tie choked him and he tugged it open. The tiny fan on his desk did little more than move the sticky air around. Despite all the things he liked about New York, summer storms were not included.

He dreaded the thought of getting home. There wouldn't be any cabs in the rain and the subway would be crowded and hot at this time of night—rush hour in New York City was always a bitch and lasted forever. It was barely six.

Another clap of thunder shook the office and Bailey jumped, surprised, knocking over the cup filled with pens. They rolled and dropped off the edge of the desk, clattering to the floor. He bent down to them scoop up, looking up sharply when he thought he heard a noise. The worst part of being alone in the building was the irrational fear, the prickle on the back of his neck every time he thought he heard something or someone. He didn't like the idea of the unknown creeping around in the darkness even though he was probably the only one in the office, aside from maybe a janitor. Everyone else had had the good sense to leave.

Bailey wasn't leaving, though, not until he figured out a way to help this kid. He'd been that kid before, the one who had no one to turn to in the darkest moments. He'd been lucky enough that when he had hit rock bottom, it hadn't landed him in jail or worse. Instead, he was simply drowning in student loans, but who wasn't?

"Get a grip," he told himself as he set the pens back in the cup. "You'll figure it out. Maybe we can talk the drug charges down to a misdemeanor."

"Talking to yourself is the first sign of madness."

Bailey jerked, startled as Ian stepped into the doorway. "Hey," he said, shaking away his momentary surprise. "What are you still doing here?"

Ian shrugged, a smirk on his face. His tie was tugged apart as well, the first few buttons of his shirt undone, a glisten of sweat on his forehead.

"Research on the Shale case. The glamorous life of an intern."

Bailey smiled. He remembered those days of endless research and meetings. Not that life had changed much except he got a real salary for his work these days—not all that much of a salary but enough to keep the creditors off his back. Ian wasn't much younger than him, a year or two, finishing up his graduate degree. He was cocky and confident, not to mention entirely too good-looking, with close-cut blond hair, a strong jaw, and a knowing smirk he always seemed to wear around Bailey.

Outside, rain pounded the window and Bailey could hear gusts of wind slamming into the pane.

"You almost done with yours?" Ian asked, rounding the desk and checking Bailey's computer.

Bailey laughed. "Not even close."

"I heard Judge Pearson's a hard ass. You plan on making a plea deal?"

"Depends if Adam's going to be tried as an adult or not." Bailey really hoped Adam wouldn't be—it was his first offense, after all, and he seemed like a good kid underneath the bravado.

Ian slid onto the desk as Bailey sat back in his chair. "What if he is tried as an adult? That'll be a longer sentence, right?"

Bailey sighed, tossing his pen on the desk and gazing at Ian. "Almost definitely a longer sentence if he's tried as an adult, and he'll go to prison rather than juvenile detention. Expunging his record will become nearly impossible, which means a much lower chance of being able to start over once he gets out. The only advantage to being tried as an adult is the right to a jury, which could work in his favor."

"You'll figure it out," Ian said confidently. "You can talk your way out of anything. After all, you talked me into going out with you."

"As I recall, you made a very inappropriate comment about sex at work to me," Bailey said, a smile growing. He left out the part where he had followed Ian into the lobby bathroom afterward and Ian had stuck his hands down Bailey's pants. It had been a damn good hand job and Bailey had jerked off to the memory for a week afterward. They'd been out a few times since, and Ian was becomingly increasingly distracting for Bailey. Not exactly a good thing when he had cases to work on. Luckily, their coworkers remained none the wiser, and Bailey wasn't too keen on finding out what the policies on inter-office romances were.

Ian grinned. "Subtlety is not my forte."

The flirting came easily to Ian; he was much less guarded than Bailey usually was. Even though they'd been out a few times, Bailey wasn't sure what he and Ian were exactly, but they were definitely something, possibly something very good if they could find time outside of work to figure it out.

"How long until you're done here? Does this mean our date is off?" Ian asked, tugging the neckline of his shirt open more in the heat. He grabbed the fan off Bailey's desk and pointed it at himself. With his shirt open, Bailey could see the tiny details in the orchid tattooed on his neck, half disappearing beneath the neckline of his shirt. He tried not to stare, but his mind immediately went to tracing the petals with his tongue.

Tonight was supposed to be his and Ian's third official date, though Bailey doubted there'd be anywhere to go even if he finished his work. Dating was kind of weird for Bailey: most of the time, he met guys on nights out and either didn't see them again, or else they ended up in fuckfest relationships that always ended badly. In undergrad, he'd been solely focused on getting through school without massive amounts of debt, and since his parents refused to pay for a "gay" education once he came out Sophomore year, most of his free time had gone toward doing whatever it took to pay the bills.

Even now, with a steady job and just enough money to afford somewhere to live—even though it was only a shitty studio apartment, not even big enough for a full-size fridge—guys were not a high priority. The last guy he'd dated had been back in grad school. Greg had refused to move to the city with him when he'd suggested it. He'd said it was career differences, but Bailey suspected it was whoever had owned the strange jacket he'd found in Greg's closet the day he moved out. Since then, there had been no one serious. Work came first anyway.

"You knew what you were getting into, dating a lawyer," Bailey said, shaking his head. Ian was still hogging his tiny fan, not that it did him any good anyway. Maybe he could just take the work home. His air-conditioner was a tiny box in his window, but at least it was cool.

"You really care about this kid, don't you?"

"I know what it feels like when people give up on you. Money shouldn't prevent people from having a good lawyer and protecting their basic rights."

Ian smiled. "I thought most lawyers were cutthroat and vicious, you know, the kind I want to be." He leaned in towards Bailey, eyes softening.

"But I think what you do is awesome, even if public defenders make shit money."

"I didn't become a lawyer to get rich off other people." Bailey wouldn't exactly say he'd always made the right choices—he had definitely made some terrible ones in the past—but becoming a public defender hadn't been a bad choice. Being a lawyer had always been in the cards, even after his parents had refused to help. "You've got to do what you think is right."

"I completely agree," Ian replied sincerely. He leaned forward, fingers brushing against Bailey's neck. "I think you're amazing, and also that it's way too hot in here."

Bailey agreed, and Ian touching him wasn't making him any less hot, but he still had work to do. Ian's fingers sliding down his collarbone was almost enough to give him pause. If they could get out of there, they could somehow get to Ian's apartment....

"I just have to finish—"

The lights flickered, and with a rumble of thunder, everything went dark.

The computer screen died and his fan spluttered to a stop as Bailey raised his eyes to the ceiling. Every light had gone out, and whatever remnants of air conditioning had been blowing through the office stopped.

"Shit," he breathed, pushing back from his desk. He turned to the window as a bolt of lightning lit up the floor.

"What do we do?" Ian asked.

"Check the stairs," Bailey said immediately, pushing himself up from the chair.

As Ian left to check, Bailey moved out of his cubicle, into the hall where things were pitch black. The only light was Ian's cell phone as he weaved through desks. Fumbling, Bailey pulled out his phone and turned on the flashlight app, glad for the small flood of light so he could at least see where he was walking.

"They're open," Ian said as he came back, his light shining in Bailey's face. "Think we should leave?"

After a moment, Bailey shook his head. "If the power's out, all the traffic lights will be too. The subway'll be chaos. We'll never get a cab. Looks like we're stuck."

Another roll of thunder made Bailey jump and rain battered the window. Bailey told himself that he shouldn't be worried. The power would come back on eventually. He just may never finish going through the files. He had a meeting with the judge in two days.

"Are you okay?" Ian asked.

"I'm fine," Bailey assured him. "I guess I'm not getting any more work done today."

Ian's hand wrapped around his wrist, warm and firm in the light of their cell phones. "How about we get a drink?"

"Doubt there's any good stuff in the kitchen," Bailey pointed out as he followed Ian's cell phone's beam of light toward the kitchenette.

"Guess we'll just have to settle," Ian said, pulling out a couple of bottles of water from the fridge.

"Rule number one of being a lawyer—if you can settle, do it." Leaning against the counter, Bailey set his phone on it so that the flashlight created a bubble of light between him and Ian. Ian set his down as well. With the two phones, it cast a white light over the countertop that dimmed as it climbed up to the ceiling.

"Not great life advice, though," Ian pointed out, taking a swig of his water. "Funny how those things don't translate." He paused, watching Bailey. "What did you mean when you said you know what it's like when you don't have anyone?"

Bailey took a drink, feeling the cold water sliding down his throat. He shrugged. "Let's just say my parents didn't take my coming out so well." Actually, they'd sent him to a counselor, then when it hadn't changed anything, cut him off and he'd been left to struggle to pay for the rest of his undergrad and grad school alone. He hadn't spoken to them in almost five years.

Ian's eyebrows went up. "Well, that's their loss. And apparently the downtrodden of New York's gain."

"They don't all appreciate it," Bailey pointed out. He'd had plenty of cases where his clients despised him. It was his job to help them despite that, no matter how hard it was.

"I'm sure Adam does, in his own surly, teenage way," Ian said simply. After a minute, he sighed and wiped sweat off his forehead. "Jesus Christ, it's boiling."

"I hope we're not stuck here all night."

"Don't worry," Ian said, sliding his hand up Bailey's arm. "We'll find something to do. It could be worse."

"We're stuck twelve stories up with no air conditioning and no lights and no one else in the building." Bailey laughed. "How could it be worse?"

"You could be alone."

"Maybe I'd get some work done," he pointed out, arching an eyebrow at Ian, unable to hide his smile; it was hard enough concentrating on casework when he didn't have hot grad students bending over the copy machine every time he went to print something.

"Do I distract you, *sir*?" Ian smirked and tugged at his tie. "It's too fucking hot in here. I'm getting out of these clothes."

Chapter 2
Cool Down

Bailey leaned against the counter, tilting his head to the side and enjoying the view when Ian untucked his shirt and unbuttoned it. He grinned as Ian pulled it off, leaving him in a thin under shirt, so thin that Bailey could see the dark outlines of his tattoos. A flush of excitement ran through him as he watched Ian strip. They hadn't quite gotten this far on any of their dates. Not that Bailey hadn't thought about it. He'd thought about it quite a bit in the last few weeks.

"You don't have to be cavalier," Ian said as Bailey stood there, too busy admiring Ian's body to consider joining him. Ian reached for the buttons on Bailey's shirt. A thrill ran through Bailey at the touch. Anytime they touched, whether by accident or design, Bailey got a thrill of expectation. Of course, everything about Ian gave that to him.

Ian was the first person since Greg to make him feel like something more than a one-night stand, which might have been why he hadn't jumped into bed after that first night out. It was different with Ian, even if Ian would leave for school in the fall. Rushing things had never worked out well for Bailey.

He definitely wasn't getting any work done, not that he could without lights or Internet. Bailey snapped out of his reverie a minute later as Ian got the buttons undone. Bailey tugged his tie open enough to yank it over his head and Ian pushed the shirt over his shoulders. He forced himself to stop staring and fantasizing about running his tongue over every inch of the tattoo and Ian's stomach. He planned on doing just that in a minute or two. Air breezed over his arms, and it was a momentary relief.

"Better?" Ian asked.

"Yeah." It was slightly better despite the thunder rumbling all around them, the darkness outside the dim light their phones provided. Ian's face was gilded in blue and white from the light and he smiled at Bailey.

"You look hot," Ian said finally, and Bailey wasn't sure which way he meant it. He didn't move as Ian went to the fridge and pulled open the freezer. Bailey didn't stop himself from staring at his ass. It was a very nice ass.

As Ian rummaged in the fridge, Bailey closed his eyes for a second, trying to remember what being cool felt like, but he couldn't. His mind still lingered on the briefs back in his office, but it became more difficult to concentrate when Ian grabbed a handful of ice and dropped it in a cup on the counter.

"I think we should both cool down," Ian said, coming back to Bailey.

"I don't think the boss would approve," Bailey said, smiling slightly and leaning against the counter.

"Well, I think it's hot in here and you've worked very hard today," Ian replied, cornering Bailey and smirking. Bailey almost groaned, but it was cut off by a gasp as something cold and wet slid along his collarbone, gliding up the bone, sliding up the length of his neck as he tilted his head back, swallowing slowly.

The refreshing coldness only lasted for a second, wherever Ian slid the ice cube, leaving a cold trail behind that seemed to dry within seconds. He felt the brush of Ian's fingers, calloused from his hours plucking at guitar strings. He tried not to shiver, focusing on the way they grazed against his skin.

He felt the ice melting as Ian let it slip down his throat and back to his chest. He breathed out slowly, stretching his neck back and closing his eyes.

It wasn't how Bailey had imagined it, but he'd imagined it in an air-conditioned bedroom, not the tiny office kitchenette where they drank stale coffee and listened to coworkers' gossip.

The ice melted completely, and only Ian's fingers were left, trailing the last bit of water along his collarbone, but when something warmer, softer, pressed against his skin, Bailey's eyes opened.

Bringing up a hand, he slid it into Ian's soft hair as Ian's lips brushed against him. All the blood seemed to be rushing to his cock as Ian's mouth continued its exploration of his collarbone.

"I don't think that's going to help cool us off," he managed to say, biting back a moan at Ian's soft touch. Any lingering worries about the case left him as Ian ran his tongue up his neck and nibbled at his jaw.

"Not supposed to," Ian replied, plucking another ice cube out of the mug and cupping Bailey's jaw. The ice slid against him, shivering cold, a sharp contrast to the heat pressing in around them, thick and muggy.

Bailey kissed Ian first, capturing his lips before he could speak again, licking inside and drawing out a shaky moan. Ian's hand clutched Bailey's neck, the ice cube melting rapidly, cold water sliding down his skin, dripping to the floor.

His cock twitched eagerly when Ian pulled back and grinned wolfishly through the eerie light of their phones. It was finally happening. Ian's hand swept across his stomach, his palm hot as it landed on his hip, fingers pressing into his skin. With his free hand, Ian slid another ice cube to the curve of his neck, cradled there by his hand. Water slithered down his shoulder and onto the floor.

"God," he breathed, breaking the kiss, hands pawing at Ian's undershirt, shoving underneath to get to the skin.

The ice melted and Ian's hand went to Bailey's thigh, sliding up the slick fabric of his dress pants. Fuck, he really needed to get out of those. As far as he was concerned, there was no need for clothes at this point.

Ian tugged at Bailey's shirt, ruffling his hair as he got it over his head. Bailey pulled at Ian's shirt as well, eager to finally get a good look at his body. He wasn't disappointed as the fabric lifted over his head. Bailey had been right—Ian did have more tattoos. From the orchid on his neck, a trail of different flowers formed the tail of an alligator across his chest. For a moment, he was caught up staring at the intricate details he'd be able to see better in more light. Something to look forward to. Three dates and this was the first time he'd seen Ian shirtless. That first hand job in the bathroom had been quick, but this was better. He only wished it could have happened somewhere else; somewhere where the lights worked, where it wasn't a thousand degrees.

For a long moment, Bailey's eyes devoured the tattoo, reaching out and skimming his fingers over the different lines spreading over the skin. Ian's suits covered them, hid them from the partners and everyone else. Bailey was one of the few who got to see them, and even better, touch them.

Reaching over, Ian grabbed another ice cube from the quickly melting pile and brushed it against Bailey's lips. Bailey flicked his tongue out to taste it, cold on his tongue, and Ian watched intently, gaze darkening as he slid it down Bailey's skin instead, brushing over his stomach. Bailey jumped at the coldness tracing his muscles, circling around his bellybutton and brushing to the waist of his pants as it melted.

Bailey moaned, hand tight around the back of Ian's neck, keeping him close as their lips collided, desperate, eager. He didn't want Ian to stop.

"Ian," he breathed, barely able to make his mouth work when Ian's cold, wet hand slid down to his chest, pressing what was left of the ice cube to his nipple. "Oh, shit... yeah."

Ian smiled against his mouth, and Bailey could feel it.

"Shit," Bailey breathed, squeezing his eyes shut for a minute. "Pants?" he asked vaguely, hopefully, reaching for Ian's slacks, but Ian moved faster, yanking Bailey forward by his belt, sliding halfway off the counter as Ian got the belt open, the zipper down, and slipped his hand underneath. His hand grazed down his stomach, wrapped around his cock, and tugged.

Bailey groaned against Ian's neck. Third dates were the best.

"Bailes," Ian said, using that warm, affectionate tone that made Bailey's stomach twist stupidly.

Dragging Ian's mouth to his, Bailey kissed him. This kiss was harder, pushing up against Ian like some horny teenager who couldn't get enough of his hands on his skin. Despite how hot he already felt, Ian's mouth just made him hotter.

Ian's hand tightened around Bailey's cock, stroking slowly, purposefully. Bailey's leg wrapped around Ian's thigh and he groaned into the kiss, mouths pressed together in a breathless exchange of moans, soft, sliding exhales and sharp, sudden gasps.

"Fuck," Bailey breathed when Ian pulled back for half a second, pausing and licking his lips. His head swam dizzily as Ian nuzzled his cheek, drawing him into a slow, burning kiss.

Everything was too warm, heat racing over his skin, panted breath against Ian's mouth as each kiss broke. A second to breathe before their mouths collided again. Over the distant rumble of thunder, Bailey heard Ian's panted breath as they moved together, bodies writhing up. He heard Ian's soft noise, almost a sigh against his lips. Bailey's hand twined into Ian's hair as his hips pushed into Ian's grip.

Ian's mouth collided with his, hot and biting, sucking his bottom lip as Bailey moaned against him, straining in his grip. It wasn't enough, and Bailey opened his mouth to say so, but Ian slid his hand up, jerking Bailey off torturously slowly.

Bailey broke from the kiss with a gasp, head falling back. A roll of thunder shook the room, but he could barely hear it over the rush of blood in his ears, the thudding of his heart against his ribcage.

"Oh, God, Bailey," Ian breathed as Bailey squirmed beneath him.

"Fuck," Bailey muttered. "Ian, fuck." He slipped completely off the counter, standing on his toes. Ian's free hand curled around the back of his thigh, but he didn't try to lift him back onto the counter.

Ian pulled back to look at him, breaking the kiss, leaving them both panting. "Not bad for a third date," he murmured, his hands abandoning their tasks and moving to tug at Bailey's pants.

Bailey could only nod in agreement. It wasn't the third date he'd pictured, but it was ending the way he'd hoped.

Ian slid down slowly, tongue grazing along Bailey's stomach, hands shimmying Bailey's pants over his hips, slipping to the floor. It was going to be a bitch to iron all that, but Bailey wasn't thinking about ironing, not when Ian was on his knees on the ugly linoleum floor. His cock jumped excitedly, expectantly, as Ian traced the lines of his hips.

Bailey said nothing as Ian's mouth enveloped his cock—too hot, too wet, too slick—and he gasped for breath. Anything he might have said would have been inadequate to express the pleasure that rippled through his body as Ian went down on him.

Stretching his neck back, Bailey tried hard not to push his cock into Ian's inviting mouth. Heat rushed to his skin, oppressive as he leaned against the counter, the sharp edge cutting into his back. He would never be able to look at this place the same again. His palms pressed against the counter, gripping tightly as Ian sucked, moving his mouth back and forth over his throbbing cock. He wished the air conditioning would come back on. His skin burned feverishly as he tried to focus, but his mind was fuzzy, and all he felt was hot, Ian's mouth, Ian's hands pushing his legs apart, fingers gliding up his thighs.

Ian moaned around his cock, and Bailey's hips pushed up, following the movement of Ian's mouth. Bailey spent a lot of time, time he should have spent working, fantasizing about things like this, like Ian's mouth on his body, teeth sinking into the skin the way he liked it but never told anyone about.

He let out an embarrassing whimper as Ian took him in deeper, swallowing around his cock. It was too much, too much for Bailey, and he groaned, pushing against Ian's shoulders, trying to warn him.

Ian didn't pull back, despite Bailey's insistence, the way he strained, letting out a choked whimper, body shaking as he came.

Bailey squeezed his eyes shut, gasping for breath as he came, Ian's mouth still around his cock, tongue sliding over the ridges. His hips jerked as the tightness released in his stomach, uncurled slowly as the wave of heat crashed over him and he couldn't hold back.

Sweat beaded on his forehead as he let out a shaky breath, blinking slowly. This was much better than any date could have been. Except, maybe, if they had done it somewhere cooler. Third dates had definitely risen in his estimation.

Ian pulled back, licking his lips and wiping at the corner of his mouth with his hand. He met Bailey's eyes, though, and smiled, pulling himself up by the counter and leaning into him.

"You're so hot," Bailey breathed, kissing Ian softly, reaching between them and pressing his hand into the bulge in Ian's slacks. Ian moaned in appreciation at the touch, shuffling closer to Bailey.

"Yeah, hot," he agreed eagerly, pushing into Bailey's hand.

With a little maneuvering, he got Ian's slacks undone and slid his hand underneath. Ian's cock hardened in his hand, and a ripple of satisfaction ran over him as Ian groaned and shifted into his grip, urging him faster.

"Shit," Ian cursed under his breath. "Bailes...."

Bailey kissed Ian hard, biting down on his lower lip and sucking as he jerked him off, listening to the subtle changes in Ian's breathing, the breathless moan against his skin as his hips jerked and Ian came.

For a long moment, neither of them moved. Bailey's hand was still wrapped around Ian's prick, but he pulled it away slowly, sliding out of his jeans. For a moment, he was sure that this was possibly the best date he'd ever been on, then a crash of thunder so loud it shook the whole building made Bailey jump, heart rising in his throat.

"Jesus," he cursed. He really didn't appreciate the loud, sudden noises.

"It's okay," Ian assured him, stroking a hand down his neck.

Bailey shook his head. "I'm really not that partial to storms."

Ian smiled, running a hand through Bailey's sweaty hair. "It'll be over soon."

Bailey nodded, stealing a kiss. "Then we can plan our next date."

Ian paused thoughtfully. "I was thinking the copy room."

Bailey laughed. "Or we could just go to my place, order pizza, fuck on my oh-so-glamorous futon bed."

"That sounds like an excellent idea, if we ever get out of here," Ian agreed, kissing Bailey soundly.

As if on cue, the lights flickered on above them. Ian looked up.

"Maybe that was the universe's way of agreeing with us."

"Or it was good luck," Bailey said, grabbing his undershirt off the floor and pulling it on. He buttoned his dress shirt, ignoring the wrinkles. "I need to get back to work. No more distractions."

Ian tugged on his shirt and turned back to Bailey. "How about we take the files back to your place and I'll help you?"

Bailey smiled slightly. The case was his, after all, but the one thing he'd learned over the years was to always accept help when it was offered, especially if it came in the form of a hot guy.

"Let's get out of here," he said, heading back to his office and gathering up the files. Ian helped him pack them in his briefcase, brushing his hand against Bailey's as they stepped away. Bailey met his eyes and smiled, heading for the stair door. He wasn't going to let Adam down, but that didn't mean he couldn't have a life as well.

Brush with Death

Chapter 1: Not-so-invisible Roommate

It's not as if Grant actually believes in ghosts anyway.

When he tells his brother about it, Keith laughs at him, vaguely amused, and yeah. Grant is never telling anyone else about the ghost that lives in his apartment.

When he moved into the building, Grant hadn't expected anything other than a few leaky pipes, maybe the walls would need to repainted, and maybe, if it was really bad, he'd find a dead mouse in a corner. He hadn't expected to wake up one morning with a strange feeling of being watched and find that he actually *was* being watched.

Joey is the kind of ghost that Grant always pictured as the kind he'd like to live with, if he had to live with one. Which, now, he does.

He can't really explain anything about Joey, doesn't really understand anything, except that he's always there, and maybe it had freaked Grant out a little when he'd woken up that day with Joey fucking *hovering* over the bed, but he's gotten used to it. Mostly.

"Ghosts are overrated," he says when Joey drifts after him into the kitchen where he pours coffee beans in the grinder.

Joey pouts at him because he can't have any coffee. Grant finds it slightly odd that ghosts can pout, but then he finds it odd that he can talk to Joey at all.

Joey laughs at that, crossing his arms, the same impish grin on his face as always.

"You only say that because I'm here. I bet before you met me, you denied they existed."

"Didn't you?" Grant asks, because, honestly, it's true, but he doesn't tell Joey that. Joey knows him too well by now anyway. He knows exactly what Grant is thinking after all this time.

Joey shrugs, picking at the sleeve of his ripped tee shirt. Grant has never asked how he died, though he's wanted to. All he knows is that Joey has a tear in his shirt down the front, and it never goes away no matter how much Joey tries to fix it.

"I believed in zombies and vampires. How could ghosts be much different?"

Grant has to give him that one since he's pretty much completely obsessed with vampires, too. He pours himself a cup of coffee and takes a sip, Joey watching him sadly. Grant has heard enough about Joey's love of coffee to know that he misses it, possibly more than he misses sex, but Grant tries not to think about Joey and sex.

Joey, despite being dead, is a very good-looking ghost with his shaggy brown hair, big hazel eyes, and the tongue stud that Grant is sure can't actually be there. Sometimes, Grant has dreams where Joey is corporeal, and they somehow get into situations he wouldn't mind acting out if only it were real. But it's stupid and pointless and crazy, so Grant does his best not to think of Joey like that.

Joey never seems to notice the way Grant stares at his mouth, the curve of his jaw as he thinks about drawing it in one of the notebooks he's tried to keep hidden under his bed. Joey just sighs at the coffee and sweeps his transparent hand through the countertop..

"Can you see other ghosts?" Grant asks as he leaves the kitchen for his studio.

He used to think it was weird, having gotten the apartment so he could live alone and work on his art, only to find Joey and, clearly, Joey wasn't going anywhere—Grant hasn't asked about that yet either. He's not sure if he's scared to know or if it really doesn't matter. Joey never says anything.

Joey drifts after him lazily, ruffling his hair, and Grant looks away, because, like everything else with Joey, he has nice hair too.

"I've never seen any others," Joey replies vaguely. "But I don't really leave the apartment."

Grant pauses as he gets out his paints, glancing at where Joey is hovering over a stool, legs folded beneath him. He's not touching the chair. Grant has long given up trying to figure out how it works. Instead, he selects a shade of green paint from his many jars.

"Can you?"

"Can I what?" Joey asks, unfolding his legs and drifting over to peer over Grant's shoulder.

"Leave the apartment," Grant adds, turning and accidentally running into Joey, or well, stepping through him might better describe what happens. If he couldn't see Joey, he wouldn't even notice, but it's surreal as he just stumbles back. Joey hardly looks perturbed. Grant thinks that if he was real, he might be able to touch him, feel his smooth skin. Instead, he feels awkward as he maneuvers around Joey.

"Never tried," Joey replies thoughtfully. "But why bother? I don't see why anyone needs to go outside. I've got everything I need here."

His grin is as bright as the fucking sun, and sometimes, Grant wishes he did live alone so he could paint canvas after canvas of it, and Joey would never know.

Joey hovers over the stool, head tilted to the side curiously, watching Grant dip his brush in the black paint. Grant tries not to wonder how he hovers. It makes his head hurt when he tries to figure it out, and sometimes, just thinking about his art gives him a headache. That might be due to the paint, though, and not that he can never get the blood spatter right on the canvas.

He stares at Joey, brush still in his hand until he remembers he's supposed to be painting, not lusting over a ghost. Right. He's totally normal.

"Can I see it?" Joey asks eagerly, and Grant hesitates.

The painting doesn't really look like Joey, not compared to the sketches he's got tucked away where Joey can't find them. Because Joey can't touch things, so he figures hiding them in a drawer would be safe enough.

"It's not..." Grant says, awkward. This is one reason he'd rather just keep his paintings to himself, especially ones where he gets to stare at a really hot guy all day.

"Let me see," Joey insists, gliding off the chair.

Grant takes a stumbling step backward, tripping over a can of paint that sends him sprawling backwards, arms flailing like a spider on its back. He hits the wall with a loud thud, stars blooming before his eyes.

"Holy shit!" Joey says, and he's there in the blink of an eye, hand hovering over Grant's face as if he wants to touch him, to make sure he's okay. "Grant? Grant?"

Grant blinks slowly; reaching back to rub his head, but there's no blood. Thank God. He might faint if there was. Joey's panicked eyes dart all over him, and Grant realizes just how close they are. Close enough to touch... if they could touch.

His cheeks flush in embarrassment and a little of something else as he tries to shift, pushing himself up.

"Do you have a concussion?" Joey demands, pressing his hands together since he can't do anything else. He reaches forward, and Grant watches his hand pass the side of his face, a ghost of a touch. He swears he can feel the breeze, but that's insane. Joey can't even sit down. He can't make air move.

Something aches deep inside Grant as he stares up at Joey. If only he were real, if only he could reach up and touch him. He shakes himself sharply, though. Joey is dead, has been for a while. Maybe he does spend too much time with his paints.

Joey doesn't stop hovering over him until he finally rises from the floor, rubbing the bump on the back of his head. He needs more coffee.

"I'm fine," he mutters, shoving his hair back and feeling like an idiot. Not that that's a new sensation. It just sucks when a ghost is worried about your safety.

If he could be any more of a loser, he would be, but Grant can't help it. He's an anti-social painter who'd rather spend his time drawing than going out in the real world. He doesn't see what's wrong with that, though he's sure Keith could make an entire list's worth of reasons.

"I'm not that fat, am I?" Joey asks, staring at the painting, eyes squinted to make out what is more or less his shape, twisted in red mist.

Grant blushes as Joey pulls up his ripped shirt to stare at his own abs. He's not fat.

Grant really does need to get out more.

"How's the ghost?" Keith is still sort of laughing at him, and Grant rues the day he ever brought it up, but it had been fucking weird the first time! He'd had to tell someone. Of course, when Keith had come over; Grant determined to prove he wasn't crazy, Keith hadn't been able to see Joey. Joey had spent all the time making fun of Keith's glasses.

Grumbling, Grant sips his coffee and tries to remind himself that it is a good thing to meet his brother at least once a week. It's mostly so Keith can be sure he hasn't died in an avalanche of canvases, and the poor neighbor won't have to find his body a week later.

"He's real," he insists, annoyed. Keith still doesn't believe him, and he might be beginning to think that Grant is losing it, shut up in his apartment with only paint fumes for company.

"Right," Keith mutters, clearly humoring him. Rolling his eyes, Grant sinks down into his chair instead. Keith pushes up his glasses, glancing at Grant. "So what time is the show next week?"

"Starts at seven," Grant mutters, thinking about the paintings stacked up in his studio, the ones that Joey actually agreed to pose for.

"And you're actually going to be there and talk to people, right?" Keith asks, arching an eyebrow behind his glasses. "Because it's your show, and sometimes people like to talk to the artist."

"Yeah, yeah," Grant mumbles. So what if he prefers to stay home? Home is nice. It's just, he needs the money. Otherwise, he'd never leave his home. Being a starving artist is all well and good until you starve to death.

Keith nods slowly. "Maybe you should bring a date."

"A date?" Grant stares. He hasn't been on a date in God knows how many months, can't remember the last time he did. He certainly hasn't been with anyone since he realized Joey could float through walls and locked doors. Things can be difficult when he just needs relief and ends up thinking about Joey. He doesn't want Joey to float in while he's got his hand shoved under his boxers. It's awkward enough to be thinking about a ghost, let alone one who could float in at any moment.

Luckily, Joey seems to understand the personal space thing pretty well, and has only surprised Grant a few times in the shower.

"Yeah, like a living, breathing person," Keith says, as if it's obvious. "You do remember what those are? Not a ghost."

Grant glares. "Yes, I know."

Keith only shrugs, reaching for the cinnamon on the table, turning it over in his hands instead of putting it in his coffee. "Just making sure you can still tell the difference."

Grant is never telling Keith anything about his life again.

Grant is always frazzled before gallery shows because people call, about framing and layout and color schemes, and he doesn't know what to tell any of them. He can't deal with people. Which is probably why he gets along with a ghost so well. Gallery shows are really more of a social anxiety fest than anything else.

His agent calls repeatedly, reminding him to actually show up, so much that he nearly throws his phone in a jar of paint, but Joey is there, whispering soothing things into his ear about how he should channel his frustration into painting, which he does, and it turns out pretty well considering it's an abstract piece about strangling a phone.

Grant doesn't like gallery shows for several reasons. Mostly, he doesn't like having to talk to people he doesn't know. He doesn't like the stress of gathering things together either, and of all things, he doesn't like being there when people critique his art. As Keith would remind him, though, and has a million times, if he wants to keep living in his ghost-filled apartment, he needs the money.

He drops a jar of red paint and cuts himself on a broken glass. He nearly faints once he figures out it's not all paint, and his hand is bleeding profusely.

"Are you okay?" Joey asks as Grant holds his hand under the sink, head turned away and eyes squeezed closed. If he doesn't look at it, it's not real, right?

"Uhh," he says, heart pounding. "Yeah. Just... Yeah."

Joey whispers soothing words as Grant tries to bandage it up. He's not good with blood or needles, or anything like that, which is weird considering how much blood he paints. It's only one bump in the road to the gallery show, though.

"You shouldn't freak out," Joey tells him as he hovers near the studio door, away from where Grant is flinging blue paint at the canvas. It's already in his hair and covering his fingertips. He frowns as he glances over at Joey.

"Easy for you to say," he mutters. "You're dead."

Joey quirks a smile. "Wasn't always. And I know it sucks, but think of afterwards."

"When I can come back here and pretend I didn't spend a day schmoozing people who don't give a fuck about art?" Grant asks, rubbing his forehead tiredly and smearing more paint over his face.

Joey drifts over, and Grant imagines that if he could actually touch things, he might be hugging him, but as it is, he just pauses next to Grant.

"After you make a ton of money on your awesome paintings and everybody wishes they were as awesome as you," he says warmly instead, and Grant catches his smile.

"Are you actually a muse spirit or something?" he asks, and Joey grins.

"Nope, just a regular, run-of-the-mill ghost, trying to make life a little easier."

Grant raises a skeptical eyebrow, but Joey's smile doesn't falter.

"You know," Joey says, "if you died, your paintings would be worth more."

Grant frowns, turning back to the canvas. "If I died, it wouldn't matter 'cause I'd be dead." He glances at Joey. He could ask Joey how he died, and Joey might answer, but Joey is behind him, frowning slightly, something sad in his gaze, and Grant can't bring himself to ask.. He sighs instead.

"Okay, so after everyone tells me I'm awesome, what do I do?"

Joey immediately grins, and Grant almost wishes he were dead so he wouldn't have a ridiculous crush on a ghost.

There are a lot of things Grant has never asked Joey, and granted he's only known Joey for about four months, but there are things he wants to know. He wants to know what it's like to die, if it really hurts, if there's some sort of catch to coming back as a ghost. He doesn't ask, though, because as much as he wants to know, Joey doesn't ever talk about his death, and whenever Grant hints at it, he usually changes the subject.

Sometimes, late at night when Grant can't sleep, Joey will lie on the bed, as though he can almost feel the warmth of the covers. Grant's not sure what he can feel and what he can't, or if he can feel *anything*. Sometimes, Joey will stay up with him—he's not sure if Joey sleeps either—and listen to him talk about all the strange things he thinks about, like vampires and zombies, his irrational fear of spiders. Like how when he was younger, he and Keith used to play hide and seek in his grandmother's basement, how he'd gotten stuck in an old box once filled with musty clothes and they didn't find him for hours. It probably doesn't make much sense since Grant knows that Joey *is* a ghost, and he can't do anything except listen and offer his opinion, but it makes him feel less alone, and he knows it's stupid, but sometimes, he really wishes he had met Joey when Joey was alive, because he's pretty sure it would have been awesome.

As it is, Joey is transparent and spends his time drifting around the apartment aimlessly, never leaving when Grant does, and always there when he gets back.

Joey talks back too, though, tells Grant stories of when he was alive, his friends. He tells Grant he should be more careful when he crosses the street as Grant tells him of the time he nearly got run over by a bike the week before. Grant ignores that since it doesn't matter. He's not going to die anytime soon, he's pretty sure, unless a plane crashes into the side of his house, or unless Joey really is right and that would sell more paintings.

The night of the gallery show, Joey watches Grant pull on a nice jacket and jeans, forgoing the uncomfortable shoes and just wearing his paint-splattered converse instead. It's his show; he should be comfortable.

"You look awesome," Joey says, and Grant thinks he hears a hint of longing in Joey's voice, but Joey just smiles at him in the mirror. Grant wants to ask about ghosts and mirrors, but he doesn't, turning around.

"Yeah?" he asks uncertainly, ruffling his messy blond hair, trying to remember the last time he got it cut, but he can't. His shoulders are too thin for the jacket, and it hangs on his frame, like a kid playing dress-up. He doesn't like dressing up. Hell, he doesn't like dressing at all, and he'd lounge around all day in his pajamas if he *actually* lived alone.

"Yeah," Joey echoes firmly. "You're gonna sell a million paintings."

"I'm only showing forty."

Joey rolls his eyes fondly. "Same difference."

Grant doesn't correct him and sweeps his hair back uselessly, but it falls back into his eyes a second later. "Okay," he says finally. "I think I'm ready."

"Go sell those pictures," Joey says as he turns from the mirror. "And look both ways before you cross the street."

Grant doesn't ask what that means as he stuffs his wallet in his back pocket and leaves, locking the door behind him.

"You didn't bring a date."

Grant wants to scowl, but Keith is arching a knowing eyebrow as if he expected it to happen, and really, he should have. Grant never said he would bring someone. He has no one to bring anyway, and the one person he would have liked to have brought is see-through and currently hovering over his couch.

"I brought myself," he replies instead. "That's enough."

Grant is counting the hours until he can go home to Joey and tell him that it was just as bad as he'd expected.

"There you are," a woman says from behind him, clamping a hand on his shoulder and turning him around. Grant sighs as he catches sight of the long, dark purple hair of his agent.

Lindsay already has a glass in hand and ignores the way Grant's face falls. "Good to see you out and about." She nods at Keith. "How'd you manage it?"

Keith shrugs, and Lindsay turns back to Grant.

"Have you seen Aaron's new stuff? It's gorgeous. You and he should think about doing a team exhibit one of these days, branch out from your red and black palette."

Grant hates gallery shows. He'd rather just let someone else do the selling while he paints more canvases. But he needs the money. There's no denying that. He wouldn't do it with Aaron, though, the guy who always seems to out-sell him no matter what the show is.

"Look, there's a buyer who wants to talk to you," Lindsay says seriously, and Grant closes his eyes and wishes for home. "Stay here and don't sneak off."

As she leaves, Grant groans, and Keith doesn't roll his eyes but nods through the crowd at a man with short brown hair, over by one of the paintings.

"Aaron brought a new guy," he only says. "Someone from work."

"A new toy?" Grant asks dully because Aaron always seems to have one.

"Just a friend, Troy," Keith replies. "Apparently."

The short, sinewy guy with lanky brown hair standing next to Aaron looks a little bored to be honest, and Grant doesn't blame him. Art isn't for everyone, especially when they're dragged to a show against their will. Although Grant would like to think that his paintings aren't as boring as some of those impressionist artists who stick a can on a pedestal and call it art.

"You should go talk to him," Keith says, and Grant knows it's a push. He doesn't need a push, okay? He's perfectly content with the way his life is going even if he barely sees anyone other than Joey and Keith.

"I don't want to talk to him," Grant says firmly, but when Keith just shrugs and his gaze strays across the room to his friend, Luke, on the other side, he knows it's only a matter of time before there's a plan to get him and Troy together. Luke can never resist a set-up, especially when Keith asks him.

Troy isn't a bad guy, and actually, Grant kind of thinks he's pretty hot, which might explain how they end up stumbling up the stairs to his apartment, Troy's hands pawing at his belt before they even get to his hallway.

Troy pushes him up against the wall, a little rougher than Grant is used to, a dark gleam in his eyes as he tugs at Grant's belt, the clink loud in the empty hall as he gets it apart.

"Troy," Grant gasps as Troy goes for his neck, biting down hard, so hard there'll definitely be a mark the next day. Grant tries to remember that they're still in the hallway, and he may not know his neighbors very well, but he's pretty sure they'd be upset if they walked out and found him having sex in the hallway.

Troy pulls away for only a second, hands moving to the zipper on Grant's jeans and pulling the button undone.

"Aaron said you weren't adventurous, but I think he was wrong."

Grant jumps at Troy's hand shoving into his jeans, and he gropes helplessly at the doorknob to his apartment.

"Yeah," he breathes, fumbling to pull the door open as Troy returns to his neck, sucking a dark bruise against the skin.

When they finally stumble in, Grant tugs Troy in after him, breaking him away from his neck as the door slams shut. Troy doesn't seem to care, lunging at Grant as they trip over the couch, falling backwards onto it, Troy on top as he kisses Grant hard, hand digging into his jeans until Grant gasps and arches up.

"Troy," he mutters against Troy's mouth, breaking away to pant for breath and look up as Troy grins darkly, hand wrapping around his cock and stroking once.

Mouth falling open, Grant lets his head fall back against the arm of the couch, eyes closing as Troy tugs his jeans down, jerking roughly until they slide down a few inches and his hand is back, pulling his cock from the confines of his pants.

"Fuck," Grant breathes, eyes fluttering open at Troy's mouth on his stomach, tongue swirling over the skin, biting his hip. Troy's fingers trail down his thighs quickly. Troy's an impatient man.

It isn't until Troy's mouth finally encloses around him that Grant sees *him.*

Joey is hovering in the doorway to the kitchen, arms crossed, eyes narrowed, and anger brimming on his face as he watches unblinkingly.

Grant's eyes widen, and he curses under his breath. "Shit."

Joey doesn't move, just stands there and watches.

Flushing with embarrassment, Grant struggles to sit up, pushing Troy off him.

"What?" Troy asks, wiping his mouth almost as an afterthought, and Grant feels a tight clench of in his gut, flushing in what might be embarrassment or shame. He's glad Troy can't see Joey because Grant is pretty sure if Joey could touch things, he'd be strangling Troy right now.

"I-I," Grant says, glancing back to where Joey's mouth is a thin line, but Joey doesn't say anything, glaring. "I can't do this."

Troy gives him a strange look. "What?"

Struggling up, Grant zips up his jeans and backs away from the couch. "Sorry, I-I just can't."

Troy still looks confused as fuck as he pushes himself up; glancing at the way Grant is obviously hard.

"I thought you were weird," he says after a minute, sweeping his lanky hair back, "but seriously? You don't want to fuck?"

Grant doesn't reply, licking his lips and feeling horribly awkward about the whole situation, especially considering Joey hasn't said a word and he looks about two seconds away from punching Troy. Or him.

When Grant doesn't say anything, Troy scoffs and rolls his eyes. "Call me if you ever get less weird," he says as he lets himself out, the door shutting behind him a little harder than it might normally.

Letting out a breath, Grant turns to Joey, but Joey has already vanished from the doorway. Grant doesn't see him the rest of the night, and he ends up taking a shower and jerking off because he *was* hard, no thanks to Troy.

He curses to himself as his hand skates over his aching cock, so hard, but it's not Troy he's thinking of as he bites back a whine, a hand propping against the wall to keep his balance. He can see Joey's thick brown hair, feel the way he might suck him off, tongue ring scraping along his cock. He shudders, bowing his head against the hot stream of water.

When he comes, Joey's face swimming in his vision, he gasps at the heat crashing over his body, the tremble in his legs as hot come coats his fingers. He lets the water wash away all evidence of his slip-up and redresses in silence, no sign of Joey anywhere.

When he crawls into bed, he can't help thinking about the look on Joey's face, tempered anger as if all he wanted to do was tear Troy's head from his body. Rolling over, he tries not to wonder what that means because, as he reminds himself for the millionth time since he moved in, Joey is dead and dead people don't make good boyfriends.

Chapter 2:
Some Things Aren't Transparent

The next morning, Grant makes coffee like normal, waiting for the smell, or the sound at least, to draw Joey out of wherever he's hiding. He dawdles in the kitchen, taking his time grinding the beans, measuring it out, listening to it percolate. He doesn't know why he's so worried. Maybe because Joey has never been mad at him before. He doesn't like it.

Eventually, Joey appears in the kitchen doorway, hovering lower to the ground than normal, a flat expression on his face as though he knows what Grant is doing, trying to lure him out with coffee he can't drink.

Grant never thought having a ghost in the house could be so much trouble.

"Hey," he greets him quietly when Joey doesn't speak, just hovers in the doorway sullenly. "Joey," he says after a minute, but Joey shakes his head.

"Sorry about last night," he says, although he doesn't really sound sorry, and he isn't looking at Grant. He rakes his hair back. Grant's pretty sure that if Joey slept, he wouldn't have last night. "Didn't mean to interrupt anything."

Grant isn't sure if Joey is still mad or if he's actually apologizing. Either way, he's not sure how to reply. "Uh," he says instead while Joey shifts his weight and finally glances at him.

"How was the show?"

"Fine," Grant replies, not knowing what else to say. What else do you say to a ghost who caught you with another guy? "I sold some stuff. I didn't die. All in all, not horrible."

Joey's expression seems to harden at his words instead of alleviating the tension as Grant had hoped.

"You're meeting Keith today?" he asks instead, and Grant pauses.

"Yeah. Lunch."

Joey nods slowly. "Watch out for busses."

Grant doesn't understand why Joey keeps giving him useless warnings, but he takes it as a good sign that Joey isn't yelling at him for the night before. He knows he shouldn't feel ashamed because it's not as if Joey is really there, not like they're in some sort of relationship. Although if Grant actually pauses to think about it, they probably kind of are.

"Sure," he mutters instead. Why everything feels like a marital spat, he can't explain.

Joey doesn't say anything more, just casts him one last glance before drifting the other way.

Lunch with Keith is the same as always except that when he asks about Troy, all Grant can do is shrug and mumble a vague answer.

"But he actually liked you," Keith says like he can't believe how much of a loser Grant is, and really, it should be no surprise. They did grow up together.

Grant can't tell Keith that it got interrupted by his ghost roommate because all he'll get is a skeptical look and a resigned sigh.

Instead, he shrugs into his coffee, frowning at the bottom of the mug. He hears Keith's sigh but tries to ignore it. It isn't as though he has a particularly exciting life, and one guy wasn't going to change that.

Well, one guy who's actually alive. A dead guy on the other hand…

Keith stares at him, shaking his head, and even Grant feels a little ashamed at himself.

"Lindsay says you did well," he said after a minute, changing the subject, but it hasn't been forgotten. Keith never lets go of anything. "Sold the decapitated girl painting."

Grant shrugs. He doesn't really care what he sold or what he didn't. He doesn't paint for other people. He paints so he can get out everything he can never say. Which is probably why he's got ten paintings of a transparent Joey shrouded in black mist.

After lunch, Keith gives Grant a bemused shake of his head. "You should really try to get out more," he says as they stand on the sidewalk and the light turns from red to green. "Maybe you'd have more friends than an imaginary ghost."

"He's not imaginary," Grant argues, but the woman next to him is giving him a strange look so he just scowls as Keith shrugs.

"Either way. You should go out more."

"Thanks," Grant mutters sarcastically. "Same time next week?"

Keith nods easily. "You should bring a date."

"Shut up," Grant just mumbles, turning to cross to the subway station on the other side of the street.

"Grant!" Keith calls sharply, eyes wide, a hand outstretched uselessly when Grant steps out.

Grant stops to look back, half a second's pause. The last thing he sees is a yellow taxi screeching towards him and then everything goes dark.

Grant's head feels as though somebody took a jackhammer to it, or like that time after the New Years' party in college when he'd woken up with a hangover to end all hangovers. This isn't like a hangover, though. This is ringing and hammering and pounding all combined and he wonders where the hell he can get some extra-extra strength Tylenol.

As he sits up, he realizes he's in his apartment on the couch. The least Keith could have done was take him to the hospital because he's obviously suffered some sort of head trauma, if the throbbing pain in his temples is anything to go by.

"Grant!" Joey's voice is entirely too loud, and Grant winces in pain. Joey immediately quiets. "Oh, right."

"Right what?" Grant grumbles, wondering why his head hurts so much. The rest of him feels fine except the hems of his pants are ripped, and his shoes are more scuffed than usual.

"Your head," Joey says as though he knows the pain now pounding in his temples. "Hurts, right?"

"Yeah," Grant grumbles. "Where is the aspirin?"

Joey only smiles, and Grant thinks it's a little mean to be laughing at his pain right now.

"You don't need aspirin," Joey tells him, drifting over to the couch and hovering in a sitting position next to him. He hesitates a second before reaching out.

Grant expects his hand to go right through him like it usually does when Joey accidentally moves through him instead of around him, but this time, he can feel the press of calloused fingers against his skin, a hand on his shoulder.

"How are you—" he asks, confused and amazed since he's never been able to feel Joey before. "How did you do that?"

Joey pauses before giving him a sad look. "Grant, I hate to be the one to tell you this but...you're dead."

Grant stares. "Dead?" he echoes dimly. "What do you mean 'dead'?"

Joey pauses. "I mean you're dead, gone, worm food, dust in the wind."

Grant still stares. "What are you talking about? I can't be dead."

"Sure you can," Joey replies, moving his hand down, and Grant can feel the touch on his skin, sort of glowingly warm, and he's pretty sure ghosts don't feel warm.

"No, I'm not dead," Grant replies firmly as panic rises in his stomach, as though Joey is crazy, as though the fact that he can feel Joey is just a weird coincidence to go along with the piercing headache.

Joey just sighs. "You are. You wanna know how I know?"

Grant doesn't believe him and he scoffs, trying to climb up from the couch, but his hands don't push off the cushions at all and his legs aren't quite moving the right way.

Joey watches him struggle. "There's a reason only you can see me, you know," he says finally, and Grant glances back at him, still trying to figure out why he can't move. "Only you can see me because only people who are about to die can see ghosts."

Grant's face transforms into a disbelieving frown. "You're crazy."

"No, you're dead," Joey replies simply, taking Grant's arm and pulling him up. Grant flails for a second, but when he looks down, he sees that his feet aren't touching the floor and that's when he starts to get really scared.

"What do you mean I'm dead?" he demands, ignoring Joey's sympathetic look.

"I mean you got hit by a taxi and you died," Joey says. "I warned you."

"You warned me about busses!" Grant cries semi-hysterically. He can't possibly be dead, and if he's dead, why is he still there? Why are his feet hovering inches over the floor and why are his legs transparent? He can see the wood floor through them now. This is just wrong.

He's surprised when Joey pulls him into a hug, and it's just like he imagined it would always be, sort of warm and all-encompassing, Joey pressed against him, arms squeezing tightly.

"I'm sorry," Joey murmurs into his shirt. "I didn't want you to die. I tried to help."

Grant is still confused as fuck and none of this makes sense. He tries to calm himself down, tries to figure out exactly what's going on, and why it feels so good with Joey wrapped around him.

Swallowing, he tries to calm down. "So if I'm... dead," he says finally, forcing the word out. "Why am I still here? Shouldn't I have moved on or something?"

Joey pulls back after a second, pausing as if considering his answer. "Some people don't move on," he replies after a minute. "Sometimes they stick around for other reasons."

"I don't have a reason," Grant argues. He doesn't have anything to stick around for except maybe to tell Keith goodbye. "Oh God, Keith," he says, suddenly stricken.

"He's okay," Joey assures him. "Well, not okay, but okay enough, you know?"

"No." Grant shakes his head. "Can I see him?"

Joey hesitates. "Can you move?"

Grant tries. He can move his arms finally but his legs are a different story. With nothing to push off from, he goes nowhere.

"What's wrong?" he asks, confused, and Joey sighs.

"It takes a while to figure out," he just says. "It's like relearning how to walk."

Grant wonders why he couldn't have just moved on like a normal ghost. Groaning, he lets his arms fall limply to his sides.

"I'm dead," he says finally. "I'm dead."

Joey gives him a sad look. "Yeah, but you're still here."

"Well, what does that mean?" Grant asks, frustrated.

Joey pauses, biting his lip, and Grant bets he could feel the tongue stud now. Shaking away that thought, he tells himself that this is the exact wrong time to be thinking about Joey's piercings.

"Grant," he says finally, slowly. "I know this is probably a bad time since you just died and all, but it's not like you have anywhere to go."

Grant frowns. Even if he is dead, he doesn't want to be reminded. He just keeps thinking about Keith and his parents and his art. What is he going to do with all his art?

"I kinda wanted to tell you for a while," Joey continues, "but it was stupid 'cause I couldn't even touch you, but now that you're a ghost… well, now, it's different."

"What is?" Grant asks, confused when Joey drifts closer, and Grant really wishes he could figure out how to move on his own.

"I can touch you now," Joey says, reaching out and grazing a hand down his arm. He pauses, licking his lips. "And ghosts can't feel real warmth, but we can feel the glow from other ghosts. I can feel you now." He glances up at Grant, who's still confused, but he can feel a tingle of nerves on his skin, and he wonders if ghosts can even feel things like that. Now is not the time to be contemplating the intricacies of ghosts, however, as Joey drifts even closer and he can't move. "And I've wanted to do this pretty much since I met you."

Grant doesn't ask what because Joey is leaning in and kissing him, and Grant thinks that maybe he should die more often if he actually gets to do this with Joey.

He kisses Joey back, noticing that Joey somehow hovers higher to get their heights right, one hand twined in his hair. Joey kisses him hard, like he's wanted to do this forever and never could, which, Grant thinks, is probably true.

"Shit," Grant mutters when Joey pulls back, breathing against his bottom lip, and somehow, Grant can *feel* it, although he's pretty sure he's not supposed to be able to. He takes a shaky breath when Joey moves back, fingers loosening in his hair. He smiles slightly, licking his lips again.

"Yeah."

Grant isn't sure what he's supposed to be feeling since he just found out that he's dead, but Joey is still there, and Joey just kissed him, and Joey is giving him that look that Troy gave him the other day except there's less predatory gleam and more genuine care.

"I wanted to do that, too," he admits after a second, and Joey's smile widens.

"I knew when you died I could finally tell you, but I still didn't want you to die," he replies quietly. "Nobody really deserves to die for nothing."

Grant frowns. "Death by taxi. What a great headline."

"I'm sure Keith will think of something better to put on your headstone," Joey assures him with a nod, and Grant feels that same sinking feeling in his stomach. He wishes he could sit down, but it doesn't seem to be working. He glances sadly at the couch.

"I can't believe I'm dead," he says again. "And you knew it was gonna happen the whole time?"

Joey looks apologetic. "Whenever someone sees me, it always means they're gonna die. I can't help it. I think it's just a force of supernatural nature or something."

Rubbing his hands through his hair, Grant sighs. "But what happens?" he asks. "Is this it?"

Joey shrugs. "It's different for everyone, I guess. I don't really know. I've only known two other people like you."

"What about when you died?" Grant thinks he's allowed to ask now that he's dead too.

Joey shrugs again. "I don't know. When I died, I was kind of like, 'this is it?' and that was it. My friends came to my apartment, here actually, and cleaned out my stuff, and I couldn't talk to them at all. It sucked, but there's nothing you can do. The best thing is to just accept it. The bright side is you don't have to worry about anything anymore."

Grant doesn't really see how that helps at all, but he sighs.

Joey gives him a small smile. "Hey, it's gonna be okay. You've still got me."

Grant laughs slightly, thinking that Joey's all he's had for a while now; he just didn't realize it until it was too late.

"So the other day with Troy," he says after a minute, and Joey frowns at the memory. "Were you jealous?"

Scoffing, Joey shakes his head. "No, Troy was disgusting."

"He was pretty hot," Grant points out, but Joey's expression darkens.

"Well, you aren't the only person who lives in this apartment," he points out moodily.

"You're dead!" Grant says with an obvious look.

"Well, so are you!" Joey replies.

"Not then, I wasn't!" Grant says indignantly. "Then I was a guy who hadn't had sex in, like, a year."

"Really?" Joey asks curiously, and Grant immediately flushes.

"Yeah," he muttered finally, "and now I'm dead, right? So I guess I'm never gonna do it again."

Joey pauses, a smile tugging at the corner of his mouth. "Weren't you listening before?"

"To the part about Troy being disgusting?"

Joey shakes his head, pulling Grant closer. Grant still feels unbalanced as he drifts forward into Joey. "To the part about ghosts and mutual senses of touch." His hand wraps around Grant's arm, and he somehow maneuvers Grant down so he's hovering over the couch in a sitting position. Grant will definitely have to ask him how to do it later.

As for now, Joey is straddling him, and it doesn't even feel like they're hovering. He can feel Joey's weight on top of him, and he doesn't really want to think about the physics of this because he was never good at science or math and this surely can't make any sense.

"We can do everything other people can, but only together. Make sense?"

"No," Grant replies honestly, because it doesn't, but he kind of doesn't care when Joey leans in, placing kisses to his throat, working his way down. He can feel the scrape of his tongue stud, and he wonders how that's possible, but it doesn't matter when Joey nips at his neck, tongue sliding over the dip in his collarbone.

Joey shifts on top of him, an impression of weight over Grant, and it doesn't matter that it's more an illusion than the real thing.

"I can touch you," Joey mutters, fingers sliding under Grant's transparent shirt, rough pads gliding over his skin, and Grant *really* wishes he had met Joey when they both were alive, but this was going to have to do. "I can kiss you." The kiss he presses to Grant's neck is wet and open-mouthed, tongue slicking up his skin as he licks up to his ear, biting the lobe while Grant shifts underneath him. He won't admit that he's thought about this pretty much since he woke up that first morning and fell out of bed at the sight of Joey. "I can feel you getting hard."

Joey grins deviously, reaching down and cupping Grant through his torn jeans, and Grant groans softly. None of this even really makes sense. He's never been a logical thinker, but this is just too weird even for him.

"How—" he tries to ask, but Joey shakes his head, using his free hand to tilt Grant's head back, licking his bottom lip slowly as he presses forward with his hips.

"Stop thinking about it," he murmurs, teeth scraping over his skin as he sucks on Grant's bottom lip. "You don't need to worry about anything anymore. Death is actually a lot better than most people think."

Grant doesn't question that, although he wants to, because Joey's hand is digging into his cock, rocking forward, and he can't help but push up into the touch, thinking that—dead or not—it has been a fucking long time.

"Joey," he mutters against his mouth, tongue flicking out to lick at Joey's lip. He pushes up, needing more, *more*.

"Yeah, fuck," Joey whispers back, untangling his hand from Grant's hair to undo the zipper and shove the jeans halfway down his thighs. When Grant glances up, Joey just shrugs. "Can't take things off all the way. Doesn't work like that."

"You've had experience?" Grant asks, and he wonders who the other two ghosts Joey had met were. It must show because Joey quirks an eyebrow.

"Just because I can't breathe or eat anymore doesn't mean I don't still want to have a steak," he says. "Doesn't mean watching you get dressed doesn't make me want to fuck you so hard you'd moan my name and your neighbors would think you were crazy."

Grant sort of stares, but Joey's hand is working its way under his underwear, warm fingers wrapping around his hard prick, and he laughs finally, cheeks flushing with embarrassment.

"They already do," he admits, and Joey smiles, stretching up for a kiss that starts out slow and quick, but turns hard and dirty as Grant drags him back when he tries to pull away.

"Thought so," Joey replies, shoving Grant's underwear down and starting to stroke.

Grant doesn't care if this is real or not; it feels good, and he can't remember the last time he had a guy as hot as Joey jerking him off.

"Here," he mutters as Joey licks a line down his palm and reaches back. Grant stutters as he reaches forward for Joey's pants, pulling the button undone and shoving his hand underneath. When Joey gasps, he takes it as a good sign and wonders just how long it's been for Joey, too.

"Fuck," Joey pants, thrusting into Grant's hand while trying to keep up the pace with his own hand. His mouth presses against Grant's neck, open and hot as he pushes forward with his hips and strokes down with his hand at the same time.

Grant tries to keep focused, but things are sort of spinning when Joey's grip tightens, and he bites back a moan instead, pushing up into Joey's grip and almost stalling out on Joey until Joey grunts and thrusts forward again.

"Sorry, sorry," Grant pants, but Joey cuts him off with a kiss, mouth dragging against his, biting his bottom lip and sucking hard. He just pushes forward, thrusting into Grant's lax grip as Grant tries to keep up when Joey squeezes around his dick and he feels the sharp tightening in his stomach.

"Just… shit," Joey mumbles, jerking Grant off as quickly as he can, and Grant feels everything going fuzzy as he pulls back from the kiss, gasping for air that he can't breathe and feeling the same illusion of release except that nothing happens. He feels the tightening and release, the strength and the fulfillment but nothing happens, and Joey doesn't pull away, biting at his jaw.

Shaking himself, Grant decides not to focus on it as he smoothes his thumb down Joey's length and Joey shudders against him, a low whine caught in the back of his throat as he reaches his high and comes down slowly. It's surreal, Grant thinks, when he pulls his hand back and it's completely clean. He supposes that's what Joey meant about mutual senses.

"Fuck," Joey mutters against Grant's cheek. "That's so much better than jerking off alone."

Grant doesn't know what to say to that, so he remains silent, feeling Joey's weight sinking against him still, warm and comforting, which is nice when he starts to think about his death again. He supposes that he really shouldn't think about it, but there are things he should have done, people he should have talked to; mostly Keith.

Joey must sense what he's thinking because he wraps himself around Grant somehow, and Grant is glad there's no post-coital stickiness to ruin the moment.

"Being dead isn't so bad," Joey murmurs. "And I kinda lied. I can leave the apartment. I just didn't want to."

Grant frowns slightly, but isn't really upset that Joey lied. Maybe he could go see Keith, if he could ever figure out how to use his legs.

"How did you die?" he asks finally because he thinks he deserves to know now.

Sighing, Joey's arms tighten. "Jersey mafia."

Grant is silent for a moment before he laughs, and Joey scowls.

"Shut up," he says. "It's true."

Grant tries to stop laughing, grinning at Joey now. "Seriously?"

Joey nods. "I was a waiter and I caught them doing a deal. I was a goner after that."

"Is that why you stuck around?" Grant asks finally because he can't really figure out why he's still around. He doesn't have any unfinished business.

Joey shrugs. "Who knows. The world works in mysterious ways."

"Do you think I have some other weird reason for still being here?" Grant asks after a moment, and Joey glances up at him.

"Are you a vampire or any other undead creature?"

"Not that I know of."

Joey pauses then shrugs. "Maybe it's just what's supposed to happen, being a ghost and all." He leans back against Grant, and Grant thinks that maybe this is why he's still here. Finally, he just sighs.

"Ghosts are overrated," he mutters, and Joey just laughs, holding tighter.

If you enjoyed this story, you can sign up for a free membership at ForbiddenFiction.com and discuss it with other readers and the author at the *Brush with Death* story page at http://forbiddenfiction.com/story/EEG-1.000073.

We do our best to proof all our work, but if you spot a text error we missed, please let us know via our website Contact Form at forbiddenfiction.com/contact.

Checking Out

Chapter 1
Louder Than Words

Dominic's fingers clenched over the paper in his hand, and it crinkled loudly before he forced himself to drop it on the otherwise spotless front desk. The reservation ledger sat open behind the computer, but he wasn't looking at it. Instead, he glared at Sean standing a few feet beyond the desk.

"So that's just it then?" he snapped, blue eyes narrowing, and Sean sighed, lips pressing together as if Dominic didn't have any right to be angry with him. But Dominic thought he had every right. He'd heard the phone call, seen the phone number scribbled down on the piece of paper on the bedside table.

"Look, I didn't say I would go," Sean replied finally, lifting his hands, but Dominic was already sneering, turning away.

He glanced out the sliding glass door of the lobby, the one that faced the lake and the mountain that rose beyond. Fir trees clustered up the path leading down to the docks, but the blue sky peeked through the tops. The lobby was lit up brightly from the sun shining in. The light fell across the desk, landing in a square over the carpet and the back of the couch facing the empty fireplace.

Sean's words did nothing to reassure him, and he turned back, eyes hard.

"If you want to go, then go," he said, and Sean shot him a look.

"Dom," he said, using that tone that always meant he thought Dominic was being unreasonable, but Dominic thought he had a damn good reason to be. "It was just an offer."

"One you should take," Dom said sharply, staring at Sean and his big brown eyes, the way his lips pressed together again, the way he pushed at his short, brown hair in an exasperated motion.

"Why are you so stubborn?" he asked, and Dominic looked away, glaring at a bird outside the window, twittering away without a care in the world.

Dominic merely shrugged, a jerk of the shoulders. "I'm just being realistic. Obviously you want to go."

"I didn't sa—" Sean threw up his hands. "You're impossible!"

"Um, excuse me?" Another, timid voice spoke from behind Sean, and Sean turned sharply. Dominic's eyes snapped to the couple peeking their heads through the front door, suitcases in hand. The guy cleared his throat, glancing between them. "Is this the Honey Creek Inn?"

Mastering himself with a small jerk of the head, Dominic put on a smile while Sean frowned and crossed his arms.

"Yep, come on in. You must be the Cavanaughs," he said, glancing at the reservation book.

The woman giggled slightly, grabbing the man's hand as they entered, dropping their luggage by the door. "Just married."

"Congratulations," Dominic replied, and Sean stared at him from behind their backs, but Dominic ignored him, turning to the computer.

Frustrated, Sean made threw up his hands before turning around and stomping out the front door. Dominic's eyes flashed to the door as it shut with a loud snap behind him, but he didn't falter otherwise, checking the couple in.

"Welcome to Honey Creek," he said, starting the spiel he'd memorized many years ago. "I'm Dominic, I'm the owner. If you need anything, just let me know. Um, we serve breakfast starting at seven, but the kitchen's usually open if you feel like a snack. Sean..." His gaze flickered to the door again. "Sean is the chef. He makes a delicious eggs Benedict. Rose!"

A clatter came from the stairway leading off behind the desk, and a young woman with short, strawberry-blonde hair appeared, a bright smile on her face as she caught sight of the couple.

"This is Rose," Dominic said. "She'll show you to your room. I hope you enjoy your stay." He handed over the key to the guy and watched them titter over the view out the window.

The view was picturesque, which was exactly why Dominic had chosen this location to open the bed and breakfast. In the summer, the sun shone down through the trees in a beautiful dappled pattern, greens and yellows scattered across the dirt paths down to the docks and the boats bumping softly against them in the water. In the winter, snow covered everything, weighing down the limbs of the fir trees, and, with a raging fire in the fireplace, it was the perfect scene.

As Rose grabbed the suitcases against the man's protestations, she glanced at Dominic.

"Don't forget about the meeting with Glen."

He shook his head, glancing down at the paper he'd crumpled laying on the desk. "No," he said, and she turned to the couple instead.

"Right this way!" she said, starting up the stairs. "Did you know that Honey Creek has the biggest number of apple orchards in the state ?" Her voice trailed off as they climbed higher, but Dominic didn't pay attention, stepping over to the window and gazing down the path to the lake.

Dark shadows fell across the ground from the tree branches hanging overhead, and he squinted to the end of the path and the dock that jutted out into the water, but he couldn't make out anything other than the lonely boat rocking in the water.

He turned away. He didn't want to think about Sean and what he may or may not be doing with all those phone calls and people inviting him to the city. He had a meeting to attend, and Sean wouldn't be leaving this very second. Probably.

Hunter picked his way along the shoreline, tossing broken branches out of the way and sweeping the fallen leaves off the path. There weren't many leaves, but the few scattered along the bank were an indication of autumn on its way.

A bird chirped in the tree over his head and a chipmunk scurried along the edge of the path before launching itself into the underbrush. He kicked away another rock and glanced up as the dock came into sight.

The water lapped at the dock quietly, the boat tied to the post bumping against the wood with the wind. The sun barely brushed the edges of the overhanging tree branches, threatening to dip below and take away the last bit of afternoon shade. In the distance, the mountain stood tall and proud, snow lacing the top point even in the late summer.

Someone sat in the low-slung chair, brushing back their hair, and Hunter could hear his sigh as he came up on him.

"Shouldn't you be making sure Dom doesn't burn down the bed and breakfast?"

Sean turned, eyes landing on Hunter, and he barely smiled.

"Shouldn't you be making sure people don't drown?"

Hunter shrugged, glancing at the boat bobbing against the dock. "No one out right now." He paused, taking in Sean's ruffled appearance, the frustration etched in his face. He looked much older than he was at the moment, considering he was barely twenty-seven.

Sean sighed, glancing across the water. The sunlight bounced off the top, making it look shiny grey instead of blue.

"So..." Hunter said slowly, and Sean grimaced. "What are you fighting about this time?"

That had to be the reason Sean was down there, and they both knew it. After all these years, Hunter knew when Sean and Dominic had been fighting. Sean always ended up down here staring at the water when

Dominic was being particularly stupid. It was usually just a matter of how stupid.

After three years of the ups and downs of the Sean and Dominic show, Hunter could recognize the signs, though for the most part it was usually Dominic's fault.

Shifting in the chair, Sean pushed at his hair and bit his lower lip. "I got a job offer in the city."

Hunter's eyebrows moved before anything else of him did, dipping down. "And?"

"And I don't know," Sean said, shrugging. "I don't want to leave the bed and breakfast, and you guys, and... Dom, but, I mean, what's keeping me here?"

Hunter frowned. "We are," he said obviously, staring at Sean. He almost couldn't believe what he was hearing, but a part of him wasn't surprised.

He'd known Dominic longer than Sean, all the way back from the first hotel he'd worked at with Dominic, where Dominic had spent his time enumerating the problems and talking about how, when he had his own inn, things would all go perfectly. He knew Dominic could be kind of a hard-ass at times.

Sean sighed. "I know, but I always wanted to be a chef in a big town where I'd get reviews in newspapers and people would rave about the dinner they ate the night before. I can't do that here. It's such a small town."

"What about Dominic?" Hunter watched him closely, and Sean winced guiltily, staring out at the water.

"I love him," he said, staring at the cracks in the dock, the shimmer of the water underneath. "But he's never gonna ask me to stay."

They both knew it was the truth, so Hunter didn't argue, and Sean frowned.

"Would you? If he did," Hunter said after a minute, and Sean smiled slightly.

"Yeah, but he won't. He's too proud. He won't even admit that he can't chop firewood. I always talk him into letting me do it, so he can save his pride." He smiled down at the dock and then shook his head. "You know him as well as I do."

"Well, maybe if you asked," Hunter suggested, and Sean shrugged. Hunter knew it would never work, but he had to at least suggest it.

"Look, I didn't say I'd take the job. Everybody's just blowing it out of proportion." He tossed Hunter a smile, but Hunter only raised a skeptical eyebrow, not convinced. "It'll be fine. I'll talk to Dom later."

The bird twittered loudly and the branch rustled as it took off, dipping low to the water before swinging back up. Hunter didn't say anything, leaning back in the chair and staring out over the lake.

Sean bit back another sigh and brushed a needle off his knee instead.

Dominic picked up the blueprint, inspecting it as Glen twirled a pen between his fingers, glancing around the small office. The desk in here was scattered with papers as opposed to the spic and span one in the lobby.

"What's the scheduled completion date?" Dominic asked, thinking of the backyard that was scattered with building tools already, a half-finished addition attached to the side and back of the bed and breakfast.

The construction crew had started in the spring, but the addition seemed to be very slow-going. Dominic could swear it hadn't taken this long to remodel the current property back when he'd opened the place. Back then, though, imagining adding on several more guest rooms had seemed like such a distant dream.

Now it was a reality, but it meant that he and his staff had been tripping over hammers and plywood for the past four months. He'd be glad when it was over, and he needed it to be over. He'd budgeted strictly for this project and he really couldn't afford it to go on much longer, not to mention that it was nearly autumn, time for the festivals and full houses, and he didn't need his guests waking up to hammering any more than was necessary.

"Should be done early October if nothing goes wrong." Glen laughed, but Dominic merely arched an eyebrow. Nothing could go wrong. He couldn't afford it. "This is, what?" Glen asked curiously, plucking a photo of Sean off the desk and glancing at it a moment before setting it down. Dominic watched him, eyes on the photo before looking away. "Your fifth year in business?"

Dominic nodded slowly. "Time for expansion."

"You guys are doing good, then?" Glen asked. "You and Sean?"

Glancing up, Dominic frowned slightly. The town was far too invested in their relationship for his tastes, but everyone liked Sean. Even the crotchety old woman who lived alone with too many cats always invited Sean in for tea when he passed by.

"Everything's fine," he muttered instead. "And by the way, can you tell your crew to put on shirts? It makes some of the guests uncomfortable."

"Sure, whatever you say," Glen replied, rolling the blueprints up and snapping a rubber band around them.

"I'll see you later then," Dominic said as Glen headed for the door. Glen merely nodded with a smile and showed himself out.

Dominic turned to the desk, catching sight of Sean's photograph. He stared at it for a long moment, unsure what he was feeling, caught between anger and sadness, but neither won out as he pushed the photo away and strode out of the room.

The dim hallway was lit only by the few small, square windows on the outside wall as Dominic went back to the lobby.

The television was on as he stepped into the lobby, shutting the door that concealed the hall behind him and rounded the desk.

Rose glanced over the back of the couch as the door clicked.

"Cavanaughs all settled in?" he asked, pausing to glance at the TV but it was nothing interesting that he could see.

"Yep," she agreed, reaching for the remote. "They're going on an orchard tour tomorrow."

Dominic made a slight noise, gaze straying to the sliding glass door and the porch outside. Rose glanced up at him carefully.

"Everything okay?" she asked, and Dominic tore his gaze from the window.

"Yeah," he said shortly. "I need to go look over the building inspection stuff again." He paused, ignoring Rose's gaze drilling into him, and he knew she'd overheard him and Sean arguing, not that it was hard in a place this small. "If you see Sean, tell him I need to talk to him."

She nodded simply, waiting for more, but Dominic had nothing else to say and turned on his heel, heading back to his tiny office instead,

Dominic's eyes opened as he felt the bed dip, the covers rustling as Sean pulled them back and slipped in. He didn't have to pretend to be sleeping since Sean would know. Dominic had always been a light sleeper and trying to sneak in around him was almost impossible.

Sean slipped in behind him then, edging into his back and sliding a hand over his bare shoulder as Dominic kept his eyes on the curtained window instead, moonlight pressing in through the cracks. Crickets chirped somewhere outside, but otherwise, all was silent.

"Dom," Sean said quietly, staring at the way Dominic's dirty blond hair curled around his ear, the slight rise and fall of his body as he breathed.

"Where were you?" Dominic asked finally, and Sean pressed a kiss to his shoulder.

"I went into town," he murmured. "Just to get a drink. You know Jessie added a new flavor of ice cream?"

Dominic didn't care about Jessie or the ice cream shop. Frowning, he didn't turn over but moved his neck out of the way of Sean's mouth.

Sean sighed softly. "Can we talk about this?"

"I don't see there's anything to talk about."

"Fine," Sean gave in a second later. "Then let's not talk."

He pressed his mouth to Dominic's neck, sliding his tongue up even as Dominic shifted under his hand.

"Sean," Dominic said sternly, rolling onto his back, but Sean moved in before he could say more, capturing his mouth in a kiss.

Dominic resisted slightly, his hands against Sean's stomach, two seconds from shoving him away, but Sean pressed closer instead, licking against his lips, wanting nothing more than for Dominic to just let him, to just forget about the whole day for a minute.

Dominic was stronger than him though, taller, more muscular, and he got his hands between them, pushing Sean away, turning his head from Sean's mouth.

"Dom," Sean said, eyes flicking over his face, brushing a piece of hair off his forehead even as his eyes followed the stern line of his mouth. "Can we just forget about the job? Just for a minute?"

Honestly, Dom didn't want to think about it all. He would rather that Sean had never said anything, but he couldn't forget about it now. Not when the only thought running through his mind was that Sean was going to leave.

Glancing at Sean, he paused. In the darkness, he could just make out the curve of his mouth, soft lips sliding up to his small nose, eyes staring down. He didn't want to talk about it anymore or listen to Sean's inevitable explanations that wouldn't make a difference. Dominic knew when Sean wanted something, and he could see it in his eyes.

He rolled Sean over instead then, onto his back, and kissed him hard and fast. He pressed his mouth to Sean's, tasting the last remnants of the drink he'd had in town, tart and tangy on his tongue, but Sean's mouth was hot, opening for him as easily as it always had, drawing him in with a soft moan.

Inhaling sharply, Sean hummed against Dominic's mouth, under the soft slide of their mouths together, the warm flush rising on his skin as his hand slid over Dominic's shoulder, tracing down the muscles of his back. Dominic had always been stronger than him, and when Dominic grabbed his hand, pulling it away and pinning his wrist to the bed, Sean didn't fight it.

Dominic could feel Sean's pulse beating against his thumb, faster than normal, excited the way he always got when they did this.

Sliding down, Dominic pressed kisses to Sean's stomach, nipping at the skin above the waist of his boxers, hearing Sean's quiet whimpers. He wasn't worried about being heard. The walls of the bed and breakfast were soundproofed as well as they could be. Besides, Sean usually kept quiet aside from the occasional whine or groan.

His hands slid away from Sean's wrists as he moved down further, tongue licking over Sean's hip, and Sean shivered, letting out a shaky breath, eyes closed against the darkness.

Sean bit his lip as Dominic's fingers pulled his waistband down, following its slide with his mouth, biting along the ridge of his hipbone. His cock was already hard, waiting for Dominic to do something other than tease around it, licking the inside of his thigh, sucking a dark red mark that would be easy to hide come morning.

"Dom," he gasped, keening up towards him when Dominic pulled back an inch, breathing heavily over Sean's skin.

Dominic didn't usually do this part, hand wrapping around Sean's cock and tongue flicking over the head as Sean moaned and stretched his arms out, fingers closing tightly around the sheets near his head. Normally, Dominic was the one stretched out, a hand tangled in Sean's hair instead, but nothing was the same anymore, and Dominic had only one way to show Sean what he wanted.

Leaning in, Dominic listened to Sean's high-pitched whine that he tried to muffle in the pillow; the breathy exhale that stuttered as Dominic sucked on his cock, hard and fast until Sean's fingers clenched around the sheets and he pushed his hips up.

Dominic let him, pushing his tongue against Sean's prick, sliding back to suck on the head as he listened to Sean's increasing pants for air. He merely sucked harder, sliding back and forth over the hardness, tracing the ridges with his tongue and making little noise as he sucked Sean off, hands sliding up the smooth skin of his thighs, pushing them apart.

Sean's back arched off the bed an inch, fingers clenching, and he bit his lip, sighing as Dominic's hand twisted around his cock and the heat on his skin flared, hot and tight.

"Dom," he said quickly, half a pant, scrambling to untwine his hand from the covers and reach down. "Dom."

Sean's hand pushed weakly at Dominic's shoulder as he cursed under his breath, biting his lip, and coming before he could get Dom away, but Dominic swallowed slowly, and Sean's breath caught, panting as the heat ebbed on his skin and he opened his eyes.

Unclenching his hand, he glanced down at Dominic, who pulled away from his spit-soaked cock, crawling back up and flopping onto the bed next to Sean.

Sean exhaled slowly, catching his breath as outside a cricket chirped loudly. Scooting over, he turned Dominic's chin, pressing a long, slow kiss to his lips, ignoring the fact that Dominic's hands remained at his sides instead of grazing over his neck like they might have normally.

"I love you," he murmured against his mouth, eyes flicking up, but Dominic didn't reply, sliding a hand around his waist instead, and Sean let his head fall to the pillow, eyes closing.

Chapter 2
Inn or Out

Dominic stepped into the lobby the next morning, lured by the delicious scent of pancakes. The early morning sun shone in from the east side window, illuminating just the top of the mountain on the other side. Clinking silverware came from the table near the sliding glass door, and Dominic found the Cavanaughs already there along with the lone man checked into room number three, the couple in four, and the two hiking guys in room number one. They were full up at the moment, and Dominic wished Glen and his crew would hurry up and finish the addition. More rooms meant more guests.

Sean emerged from the kitchen as Dominic paused to survey the scene, hands full of plates brimming with blueberry pancakes and more blueberries sat in bowls on the table, freshly picked by Rose a few days ago from one of the farms around town.

Sean met his eyes as he set down the plates, but he didn't say anything to him, instead smiling at Mrs. Cavanaugh.

"Here you go! Hope you enjoy!"

"Come and sit!" she insisted, and Sean hesitated.

"I've still got some things on the stove, but in a minute, I promise." He winked at her, and she grinned, snuggling into her husband's arm.

Dominic was never surprised by how quickly people took to Sean, as if he was their personal pet they wanted to spoil. He'd felt the same way at one point or another.

"Good morning, everyone," he greeted them as Sean breezed back into the kitchen.

The guy on the other side of the table nodded at him but said nothing else, and the couple both smiled, looking too deliriously happy for Dominic's tastes, but he smiled back anyway.

"How'd you sleep?" he asked instead, brushing back his hair as the front door opened and Rose entered, carrying another full bucket of blueberries.

"Hi, everyone!" she called as she brushed past without pausing, into the kitchen.

"Wonderfully," Mrs. Cavanaugh replied, smiling sweetly at her husband, who nodded along. "It's so beautiful here, just like a story book."

"Well, if you'd like," Dominic said, dishing a few pancakes onto his plate and reaching for the syrup, "we could get you two set up on a lake outing. Hunter, our dock hand, would be happy to outfit you with a boat and give you some ideas of where to go."

"That sounds wonderful," she replied earnestly, eyes big as she turned to her husband. "Doesn't it?"

"Yeah," he agreed, watching Dominic. "Great."

"Sean," Dominic said as Sean returned with sizzling plates of bacon and eggs, and Sean looked over carefully, setting down the plates. "Sit down. Join us."

The corner of Sean's mouth twitched into a smile and one hand was on the chair next to Dominic's, but his phone rang at that moment, and he pulled it out. The smile faded almost immediately. He hesitated, glancing at Dominic, who barely blinked, staring up at him.

"I just," he said slowly, glancing at the screen as it rang again. "I have to take this."

Rounding the table, he answered the phone and slipped out the sliding glass door to the porch. Dominic watched him head down the path to the docks and frowned, turning away.

"I brought fresh blueberries," Rose said as she popped in from the kitchen, taking the seat Sean had been about to fill and setting a bowlful of perfectly ripe berries on the table. "Dom, take some. Antioxidants are good for you."

Rose was always too peppy in the mornings as well, and she only smiled sweetly at him as she spooned a few berries onto his plate.

Rose strode down the path to the dock under the shaded trees, scaring away a bird nestled on one of the branches. It burst out, twittering madly as it flapped away. A few needles dropped to the ground as she walked, tucking her hair behind her ears as she came upon the lone figure slumped down in the chair facing the water.

"Get up, you lazy bum," she said, and the figure stretched luxuriously, like a cat coming out of a long nap, craning his head back to look at her.

"Why?" Hunter asked, waving a hand at the gently-lapping water. "It's a beautiful day, Rose. Relax for a second."

He planned on relaxing as long as he could before he had to actually do his work. The trails wouldn't keep themselves groomed, and he had to clear out the rest of the blackberries near the fire pit before winter came. It wasn't a job he was particularly looking forward to since he always came out of it with scratches everywhere.

Sighing, Rose rounded the table and sat down, but she didn't slide back. Instead, she sat perched on the edge, arms on her knees as she frowned at Hunter.

"They've been fighting more."

"You're not their mother," Hunter pointed out, ignoring the way her frown deepened.

"You're not worried at all?" she pressed, eying him and the way he shrugged slowly. "What if Sean actually leaves?"

"Then he leaves," Hunter replied, rustling his hair and shaking his head. "We can't stop him."

She glanced out at the water, watching a leaf floating on the surface as it ebbed and flowed. "Dominic could."

Hunter barked out a laugh, and Rose shot him a look. "Don't be so naïve."

"Like you aren't thinking the same thing. Dominic'll be a wreck if he goes."

"Then it's Dominic's problem," Hunter replied, jerking his shoulders as Rose sighed at his lack of response.

"I thought you'd care more," she said. "You know, since you've been with Dom since the beginning and Sean is your friend too. I just thought you'd be more interested is all."

Sitting up straighter, Hunter turned to face her head on, noting the accusation in her eyes, the disbelief.

"I do care," he said finally. "But I can't do anything, and if they want to fuck up their relationship, who am I to interfere?"

"Their friend?"

"You do it then."

Rose sat back slightly, making a doubtful face. "Dominic barely listens when I tell him to eat fruit."

"My point exactly," Hunter said simply, scrubbing at the scruff on his jaw, and Rose sighed, defeated. "You think he would listen to us about this?"

"No," she admitted with a huff. He was right; she knew it, grudgingly admitted it. She didn't like when Hunter was right. It somehow felt wrong.

"Besides, Sean might not even leave," Hunter said, but Rose could tell from the look on his face that he didn't really believe that. Neither did she.

Sitting at the table, Sean riffled through his box of recipes, plucking a blueberry from the bowl next to his elbow and popping it into his mouth. He pulled out a few cards, setting them on the table and looking through more.

He only looked up at the sound of the sliding glass door. Rose stepped in, pushing it shut.

"What'cha doin'?" she asked, sliding into an empty chair and picking up the recipes.

"Planning dinner for the Cavanaughs," he replied, pushing the bowl of berries over to her, and she took a few from the top. "They asked for a romantic, candle-lit affair down on the docks."

"They're sweet," she replied, setting down the cards, and Sean nodded vaguely. Glancing over, she fell silent for a moment, watching Sean.

Thumbing through the desserts, Sean paused at the silence and looked over.

"What?"

"Nothing," she said quickly, grabbing a few more berries and turning them over in her fingers.

Rose watched him still. She didn't want him to leave, but there was nothing she could do as Hunter had not-so-lightly put it. She didn't want the bed and breakfast to go up in flames, though, and Sean leaving would do just that.

As they sat there, a big husky stepped up to the sliding glass door and scratched it with her paw. Rose started to rise, but Sean looked up.

"If you let her in here, you're gonna have to clean up any muddy footprints."

"It's summertime," Rose reminded him, sliding open the door, and the dog bounded in, making a beeline for Sean, setting her panting head on his knee as he pushed his hand into her plush fur. "And she's your dog."

"Mine and Dominic's," he muttered as he patted Vanilla's head. Her tail thumped loudly against the floor as she tried to edge closer.

He sighed, closing the box and gazing down at the dog instead. She looked up at him through her mismatched eyes, one blue, one brown, tongue lolling out of her mouth.

"Have you talked to him?"

Rose sat back in her seat, arms resting on the tabletop as Sean looked up sharply.

"No," he said finally. "I mean, yeah, but." He shrugged. Talking hadn't seemed to do either one of them any good lately.

"If it makes any difference, I want you to stay," she said, and Sean smiled slightly.

"Thanks."

She frowned. "It doesn't, does it?"

"Yeah," Sean said quickly, but he couldn't help the sinking feeling in his chest as he watched her. Her short, straight hair hung around her heart-shaped face. "But it's a great opportunity, and I just don't know."

Vanilla licked his hand when he stopped petting her, whining loudly. This was the real reason she wasn't supposed to be inside. Dominic was a softy, though, and he let her in sometimes on the cold winter's nights.

Rose didn't reply, looking away, and Sean picked up his recipes instead.

"I know," he said finally, and Rose looked up hopefully. "Blueberry cheesecake. The perfect summertime dessert." Leaning over, he pecked a kiss on Rose's cheek before rising and taking the recipe box with him into the kitchen as Rose sighed and Vanilla whined and bounded after him.

The stars twinkled in the sky, the crescent moon reflecting in the shimmering surface of the lake. The flicker of candlelight from the table on the dock was just visible from where Dominic stood, leaned in the doorway out to the porch. The cool evening breeze blew his hair into his eyes and he shook it away.

Down on the dock, the Cavanaughs were nestled close together, talking and eating. Dominic could make out the clink of silverware, the chink of wine glasses knocking together.

He could remember a very similar situation not three months ago, a candle-lit dinner for a couple from the city celebrating their thirtieth anniversary. It had ended with Sean getting a job offer to move to Seattle and assume a head chef position. There was nothing Dominic could offer him that was as good, nothing he was willing to offer anyway.

A moth fluttered around the porch light above his head, but he didn't go inside.

He barely jumped as a hand slid around his waist and a warm body pressed into him from behind.

"Isn't it romantic?" Sean asked, hooking his chin over Dominic's shoulder but keeping a careful eye on him in case he decided to pull away.

Dominic merely grunted. "Looks familiar."

He felt Sean sigh, mouth pressed against his shoulder through his shirt. "Dom...."

"Don't," Dominic said, turning, and Sean was forced to drop his hand. "I know you don't want to be here anymore, so just go."

"That's not true," Sean said, shaking his head and frowning at Dominic, but Dominic didn't budge, a hardness to his blue eyes that Sean rarely saw. "I like it here."

"Don't lie to me, Sean," Dominic replied, stepping away from the door, and Sean followed, leaving it open for the moths to flutter in. "If you want to go and be a big-shot chef, then go do it. Don't fucking pretend like you want to stay here, out in the middle of the countryside where the biggest entertainment of the year is the apple festival."

"And don't tell me what I want," Sean said just as sharply. "I came here for a reason."

"Yeah, because I gave you a job," Dominic said harshly.

Sean could see him biting his tongue from saying more, and he knew it wasn't something he'd want to hear.

"I could have been cooking in France." Sean stared at Dominic, shaking his head. "I could have been anywhere, but I wasn't. I was here. With you."

"You weren't in France because you were afraid," Dominic replied, and Sean winced as though he'd been hit. Dominic felt a flicker of guilt. It was a low blow, he knew, but it was true. "And you're not now. Now, you can leave if you're not happy."

"I didn't say I wasn't!" Sean threw his hands into the air as Dominic didn't budge. "God, Dominic, are you even listening to me?"

Dominic looked away, a scowl on his face. Nothing he could say would change what was happening.

"I know you want to go," he said at length, eyes on the couch. "I know you're tired of being here, so do us both a favor and leave."

Sean stared at Dominic. "Dom," he said slowly, reaching out for him, but he stopped, fingers inches from him. Instead, he swallowed. "If you ask me to stay, I will."

Silence enveloped the room around them aside from the chirping crickets and a few frogs outside. Sean stared at Dominic, and Dominic stared back.

Dominic knew he could stop Sean from leaving and all it would take was a few words, but as he stared into Sean's deep brown eyes, he couldn't bring himself to do it, to open himself up like that.

Dominic stirred finally, jerking his chin slightly. "You should go," he said, and Sean gaze flickered.

Dominic turned away from the tears pricking in Sean's eyes, the way his hand trembled as he stood there, swallowing thickly and searching for words, but Dominic didn't let him speak, stepping away and leaving him exhaling a shaky breath into the silence.

Chapter 3
Burnt Pancakes

Dominic didn't show up when Sean tossed his suitcase in the back of the car along with a few books and movies he'd managed to scrounge up.

Glancing back at the bed and breakfast, he sighed, but he didn't have time to lament Dominic's actions as Rose grabbed him into a tight hug, and Hunter stood behind her, a slight frown on his face.

"Call us when you get there," she said, squeezing him again before she let go and backed away.

"Guys, it's only a few hours away," he said, but a few hours might as well have been a million.

"Here," Hunter said as Sean grabbed his second suitcase to toss it in. Sean let him hoist it into the car, shoving it back against the other. Hunter paused, glancing up at Sean. "I'll make sure Dominic doesn't try to chop any wood."

"Thanks," Sean replied, and Hunter patted him on the shoulder, a soft squeeze before the pressure was gone. Sean straightened up, glancing around the empty parking lot, the trees crowding in around it and the sun shining brightly above. "I guess this is it."

He looked at the porch again, but it was empty.

Rose sighed. "He'll come to his senses," she said, but Sean shook his head.

"It doesn't matter. I should get going."

Stepping around to the driver's side, he pulled out his keys, taking one last deep breath of the trees, the lake, the dirt under his feet. He hesitated as he stood there, and Hunter and Rose looked on.

Eventually, he huffed out a heavy breath before shaking himself and sliding into the car.

He waved to Hunter and Rose as he turned around in the lot and left, down the dusty gravel road, the bed and breakfast vanishing into the trees behind him.

Inside, Dominic turned from the window, letting the curtain fall back as the dust settled in the parking lot. He grabbed a few magazines off the floor near the couch as the front door opened and Rose and Hunter came in. Tapping them on the table, he glanced over, but Rose merely frowned disapprovingly and swept past to the kitchen without a word.

"What's wrong with her?" he asked, laying the magazines back out on the table.

Hunter shrugged. "Girl stuff." But they both knew perfectly well what it was. Neither said anything, though, and Dominic went to the desk instead, placing the pens back in the holder on the corner.

"So when are you gonna find someone new?"

Dominic's head snapped up sharply, eyebrows furrowing. "What?"

"For the kitchen," Hunter replied, frowning slightly. "Can't have a bed and breakfast without the breakfast."

"Oh," Dominic muttered, looking away and shaking himself. "I don't know. I'll put out an ad tomorrow. In the meantime...." He gave Hunter a significant glance even as Hunter balked at the idea.

"Wha—no! I can barely cook my own meals, and that's usually only 'cause I have a microwave. Can't you get Rose to do it?"

"Rose already does the housekeeping and reception and takes the guests out on town walks," Dominic pointed out, closing the reservation book and staring at the cover. It had been a gift from Sean a few years back, warm leather smooth under his hand. He turned away from it, though, fixing Hunter with a firm gaze. "You just hang around the lake all day. You'll just have to start getting up earlier."

"I fix stuff—" Hunter tried to say even as Dominic stepped out from behind the desk. He sighed, though, at Dominic's look, groaning softly. "Fuck, why did Sean have to leave?"

Dominic turned before Hunter could catch the sudden shift to his face, but it was gone in a second, and Dominic let Hunter leave through the sliding glass door. For a moment, he stood at a loss in the perfectly spotless lobby, listening to the birds chirping outside.

There was nothing to do, nothing that he wanted to do, so he headed for his bedroom instead, intending on changing his shirt and taking the dog for a walk, but when he reached the room, his eyes fell on the battered book sitting on the bedside table, bookmark still stuck somewhere in the middle as though someone had just been reading it.

Grabbing it, he sunk down onto the bed, turning it over in his hands and running his fingers over the cracks in the spine, the dog-eared pages that always drove Sean crazy. As he sat there, he felt a heaviness wash over him, dragging down his limbs and making him tired.

He couldn't deal with this right now, though. Right now, he needed to get a grip on himself. Sean was gone, and he wasn't coming back, and that had been his choice. Dominic wasn't going to force him to stay where he didn't want to.

He shoved the book in the drawer and pushed himself up, shaking himself firmly. Thinking about Sean wasn't going to change anything. There were things that needed to get done. The builder would be there on Monday, and he had plenty to do to get ready, plenty to keep his mind off Sean, but as he changed his shirt and headed outside, whistling for Vanilla, he couldn't help glancing in the kitchen window, expecting Sean to be there, but the window was empty, just like the parking lot.

The main street of town didn't stretch very far, down past the corner of the bakery and around a corner where it ran into Beech Street and continued on. Little shops lined the street, all familiar as Dominic walked past, keeping a tight grip on the leash as Vanilla attempted to run to the shop that sold dried meats and cheeses as gifts. The owner always had a strip of meat for her, and Dominic thought she seemed a little pudgy around the middle.

The street was full of little knick-knack type shops, geared mainly towards the tourists that overtook the town from April to November. The scent of apples wafted out of the soap and trinkets shop next to the little café which was adjoined to the ice cream shop on the other side. A few people sat in chairs outside the shop, and Dominic paused before hooking Vanilla's leash to the bike rack outside and heading in.

A bell announced his arrival, and Jessie, a middle aged woman with bleached blonde hair and a round face bustled out of the back, her face lighting up as she saw him.

"Dominic!" she greeted him, as though she hadn't seen him in months. "Glad to see you! We've got a new flavor this month!"

"Yeah, Sean..." Dominic paused, and he didn't miss the way Jessie tilted her head to the side in the universal sign for pity. "He told me."

She nodded, already grabbing a cone without Dominic having to order. "How's he doing? Have you heard from him?"

"He just left this morning," Dominic replied, glancing around the brightly-colored shop. It looked almost as though the Easter Bunny had thrown up in there. "I'm sure he's fine."

"I'm going to miss him." Jessie sighed, her head stuck in the freezer as she dug ice cream from the slot. "But I suppose he couldn't turn down a job like that, could he? A big fancy chef in the city."

Dominic frowned, beginning to regret his decision to come in, but she popped up a second later, handing over the cone. It was piled high with a green ice cream that Dominic cocked his head at.

"What is this?"

"Green apple!" she chirped with a smile. "Just in time for the season to start. You'll still have a booth this year, right? At the festival?"

"Of course," Dominic murmured, licking the ice cream tentatively, but it didn't taste nearly as bad as he'd expected. The taste was slightly tangy followed by a rush of sweetness on his tongue and he hummed softly. "But that's not for a while."

"Never too early to start planning!"

Dominic jerked his shoulders in response, licking the ice cream. He couldn't really think about the apple festival right now, not when so many other things seemed intent on taking up his mind. As his gaze fell on the wall behind the counter, he found the cork-board Jessie had up, tacked with photos of people in the town, all their friends. In the bottom left hand corner, hanging crooked, was a picture of him and Sean at last year's festival. They were grinning at each other, faces barely inches apart, and Dominic tore his gaze away.

He had half a mind to ask Jessie to take it down, but he couldn't bring himself to say it, so he merely turned away, gazing out the window to where two little girls were petting Vanilla, who wagged her tail furiously and tried to lick their faces.

"Speaking of planning," he said, turning back to Jessie, who had also been watching the girls with a smile on her face. "If you know any cooks looking for a job, we've got an opening."

She frowned slightly at his cool tone, but Dominic didn't let her reply, grabbing a napkin from the holder on the counter.

"I'll see you," he said, pulling open the door, and the girls scurried off to their mother down the street. "I know, I know," he murmured to Vanilla as he unclipped her leash and she tried to jump up. "Let's go home."

Down the street, he passed the local watering hole, but though the door was thrown wide, the inside was empty. It wasn't surprising considering it was barely noon, but he glanced in anyway. He caught sight of someone, though, a man talking to Bill, the bartender. He couldn't see much of the guy from the darkness of the bar. Instead of seeing who was drinking in the middle of the day, he turned Vanilla back towards the road that led to the bed and breakfast.

"Pancakes again?" Rose asked as she hovered in the doorway to the kitchen, and Hunter glanced her way before returning to the sizzling pan.

"Hey, it's the only thing I can cook," he replied. "If you want something else, make it yourself. I'm not a chef. And it is far too early in the morning to be arguing about this." He rubbed his eyes and groaned. "Shit, I gotta get these out."

Rose followed him as he grabbed the plate and headed to the dining room, trying to put on a smile as he set down the plate.

"Here you go," he said, glancing around at the odd assortment of guests. Dominic wasn't there yet, and Hunter didn't see where he got off sleeping in while he had to be up at the ass crack of dawn to cook breakfast when it wasn't anywhere near his job description.

"Wonderful, man!" said one of the guys wearing a tie-dye tee shirt and a bandana. The woman next to him nodded as well as they all dug in. There were too many of them in tie-dye for Hunter to tell apart, so he just nodded and returned to the kitchen. At least the rooms were full-up, though.

Rose followed, sighing slightly.

"What?"

"Have you talked to Dominic?"

"No," he replied, pouring more batter into the pan. "If he's gonna be an idiot about Sean, it's his problem."

"Not about Sean," she said, rolling her eyes and stepping closer. "About finding a cook. I'm sure the guests don't want to eat pancakes forever."

"I have an idea," Hunter replied, turning to her, spatula in hand. "How about you cook?"

"I have other things to do in the morning."

"Like folding and vacuuming."

"Do *you* want to fold and vacuum?" she asked obviously, and Hunter made a face. "I didn't think so."

Hunter turned back to the pan. "Yes, I told him he needs to get a cook unless he wants pancakes for the rest of his life, and mine are nowhere near as good as Sean's."

"I wish he'd just go talk to Sean, call him or something."

Hunter rolled his eyes. "That's not gonna happen."

Sighing, Rose crossed her arms. "So what are we supposed to do?"

"Nothing," Hunter replied, glancing at her. "Can't fix everything."

Rose frowned, but whatever she might have said next was interrupted by Dominic stepping into the kitchen.

"Pancakes again?"

Frustrated, Hunter threw up his hands, bits of batter splattering Rose's shirt, and she made a face, wiping it off.

"If you don't want pancakes, hire a real chef!"

"Calm down," Dominic said simply, picking a blueberry from the bowl next to the batter. "I'm seeing some people today. We'll have a chef in no time."

Rose and Hunter exchanged a look, and Dominic ignored them. He didn't want to talk about how the best chef they could have gotten was now far away and probably never coming back. He didn't want to think about it.

They all looked up at the sound of cursing coming in from out the window. The sounds of a saw stopped and Hunter rubbed his face. He was beginning to get sick of builders traipsing over the backyard and through all the plants he'd worked so hard to keep nice. Despite what Dominic said, Hunter didn't spend all his time messing around in the lake. He did all the landscaping work, not to mention maintenance, and now he was being forced to cook. He wasn't a cook.

Dominic frowned out the window, and Hunter turned away from it.

Hunter snorted, indignant. "If you'd just let me sit on my dock, I'd be perfectly content. We need Sean back."

"Don't talk about him," Dominic barked, sharp enough that Hunter blinked, and Rose frowned. Dominic sighed slightly, running a hand through his hair and grabbing another blueberry. "I've gotta go talk to Glen. Rose, the Meadowflower party wants some hiking trail advice, but I'd keep an eye on the leader. He looks the type to go streaking in the woods."

Rose didn't smile but nodded. "Sure."

Dominic nodded, leaving the kitchen, and she turned back to Hunter with a significant look, but he just shrugged.

"Nothing we can do."

She sighed instead, watching him flip over the pancakes, the backsides burned slightly.

"I'll make French toast tomorrow, okay?" she said at length, and Hunter glanced at her curiously before smiling.

"You're the best."

Rose merely shrugged and left the room as Hunter grinned to himself and popped a berry in his mouth.

Dominic battled his way into the smoke-filled kitchen, waving the smoke uselessly away from his face as he coughed.

"Is everything okay in here?" he called out just before the rush of a fire extinguisher sounded and he stumbled over to the window, throwing it open as the alarm went off.

Waving the smoke out, he searched out the woman standing over the stove, fire extinguisher pointed at the burner.

"Your stove is really sensitive," she said, spraying the smoking pan again.

"Yeah," Dominic muttered, frowning as the smoke began to clear slowly, wafting out the window and all he could smell was something burnt. "I think this is enough for today."

"Oh," she said, setting down the extinguisher with a clunk on the floor. Dominic turned off the stove for good measure, moving the pan off the burner. "I could make something else or...."

"No," Dominic interrupted with a tight smile. "That's alright. I'll be in touch."

"Okay," she said, flipping her hair over her shoulder and leaving the kitchen as Dominic sighed and turned on the stove fan.

Leaning against the counter, he shook his head at the linoleum. This would never have happened to Sean; Sean, who had gone to cooking school and worked as a sous-chef in a well-known, five star restaurant for two years before moving to Honey Creek.

But Sean was gone, he reminded himself with a pang, waving away some more of the smoke as it slowly dissipated. He had to find a new chef.

"What happened in here?" Rose asked, nose wrinkled as she poked her head in the door.

"Chef interviews," Dominic muttered, grabbing the now-ruined pan and dumping it in the sink.

"I hope you're not hiring that one."

"I won't be," he assured her, heading to the lobby and flopping down on the couch. Rose followed, standing behind it with her hands on the back cushion as she stared down at him. "What?"

"Nothing," she replied, looking out the window instead. "The Meadowflower party has been gone for a while."

"They're probably 'communing with nature'," Dominic replied, adding air quotes and kicking up his heels onto the coffee table. "At breakfast, one of them said that the planets were in perfect alignment for me to make a change in my life. That, and I looked like I needed a good aura cleanse."

Rose barely held back her laugh, and Dominic shot her a look.

"Aura not oral, though I wouldn't say no to that either."

Rose frowned but didn't say anything about it. "How many more interviews do you have?"

"One tomorrow, one on Tuesday. We'll see."

"You better hurry," she said, tucking her hair behind her ear. "Or the guests are going to get sick of pancakes. And you might end up with a suicidal dock hand."

"Hunter can handle himself," Dominic said dismissively. He wasn't worried about Hunter getting tired of cooking breakfast. It did him good to get up earlier and do more than laze around the dock all day. "Besides, no girl wants to date a guy who can't cook, right?" He looked up at her, and she frowned.

"Well, you can't cook," she pointed out. "And Sean still dated you."

Dominic turned away, jaw tightening, and he pushed himself up. "Can you go spray something in the kitchen to get rid of the smell?" he asked instead, pushing his hair back and rising from the couch.

He left Rose behind him, stepping out the sliding door and leaving it open, closing the screen instead.

Walking the familiar path down to the dock, he glanced up at the bright sunshine pushing through the trees. Tree needles scattered under his feet, and he stepped onto the dock, gazing out across the lake. The surface rippled in the slight wind coming from the south, bringing the hot air with it.

The chair Sean usually sat in stood behind him, and Dominic paused a second before sitting down. His cell phone was in his pocket, and he could talk to Sean in less than a minute if he wanted to, could hear the relaxing tone of Sean's voice in his ear.

Everyone liked Sean, and it wasn't any secret why. He'd won everyone over the minute he arrived with his bright smile and big, Disney-like eyes, not to mention his amazing apple tartlets. When they'd first started working together, everything had been an argument, from how many eggs Sean really needed to order every week to what time they should really start breakfast. Sean had a way of breaking him down, though, and he'd certainly done it well.

Dominic sighed loudly, rubbing his forehead as he watched a bird dive at the water. He knew what Rose and Hunter wanted him to do: go to Sean and beg him to come back, but he wouldn't do it. Sean wouldn't come anyway, and he wouldn't prostrate himself like that to someone who wanted to leave.

Everyone always left, though, and he shouldn't have been surprised that Sean had gotten tired of being there. Honey Creek wasn't exactly on-the-edge-of-your-seat exciting. The only movie theater in town showed movies three months late, and it was newsworthy when the ice cream shop got a new flavor.

The scenery was beautiful, though, and the town was quiet even if the gossip seemed to flow a bit too freely at times. Dominic had picked Honey Creek to build the bed and breakfast for exactly those reasons. He didn't want a big corporate hotel in a giant city. He wanted a small, intimate place where he could get to know the guests and their special quirks.

He jumped at a cold press against his hand, but it was just Vanilla, tail thumping against the dock as she leaned against his legs. He patted her slowly, sighing.

Things had been going fine up until now. He didn't know quite when Sean had gotten under his skin like this, to the point where he cared that he was gone, that he wasn't coming back, that the thought of it made his stomach clench painfully and the sound of Sean's name made his chest ache in a way he hated.

Messing up his hair, he sighed then raked it back. He had to move on from this, he told himself firmly, but he couldn't. It had barely been a week, but he couldn't stop thinking about Sean, glancing out the window every time a car pulled into the parking lot, hoping. He had to get a grip. There were other things to think about.

"Dom!"

Rose's voice interrupted his solitude, and he held back his sigh as she came hurrying up.

"What now?"

She let out a breath, the phone still clutched in her hand. "The Meadowflower party got arrested."

Dominic almost smiled, but he didn't, rubbing his face. Just one thing after another.

Chapter 4
Echoes of the Past

Three Years Previously.

There were plenty of things about Sean that bothered Dominic, from the way he insisted goat cheese was the only way to go in most dishes to the way he teased him about being a perfectionist. Unfortunately, those weren't the only things that bothered Dominic about Sean.

It also bothered him how good-looking Sean was, how confident he was both in the kitchen and out of it, how the townspeople had taken to him like a duck to water. It bothered him that Sean always smiled at him in the mornings when he arrived to make breakfast, like Sean didn't know what Dominic was thinking.

"What do you want for breakfast tomorrow?" Sean asked, plopping down at the table next to where Dominic was trying to figure out the reservations. Somehow they'd gotten all messed up, but he blamed the new computer system.

"Whatever," he muttered, grabbing the white-out.

Sean tilted his head to the side when Dominic didn't do much more than cast him a cursory glance. Dominic tried to ignore him, just like he'd been trying to ignore Sean for most of the time since he'd hired him, but two years had passed and he was finding it increasingly difficult.

He heard Sean sigh but didn't look up.

"You don't have any opinion? Nothing to say about goat cheese?"

Dominic rolled his eyes. "You're the cook."

"And you're the owner," Sean pointed out, arching an eyebrow. "Isn't there anything you want?"

There were plenty of things Dominic wanted when it came to Sean, but he wasn't going to be stupid enough to act on them. Mixing business and pleasure was always a bad idea.

He looked up in time to see Sean lick his lips, though, looking frustrated at Dominic's lack of response.

Dominic stared a second too long, a tug of longing in his gut, something he'd been denying since the first time Sean had smiled at him.

Sean must have caught it, though, because his mouth curled into a smile after a second and he scooted his chair closer to Dominic's.

"There's nothing you want?" he asked quietly, watching Dominic carefully, and Dominic turned away, taking a deep breath.

No matter how hot Sean was, sleeping with him would be a bad idea. He just knew it. Except that Sean was really all he thought about most nights when he was jerking off, alone in his room. Two years was a long time to go without being able to act on it.

"Dom?" Sean asked, and he was close enough that Dominic could kiss him if he wanted to.

He didn't like that Sean could charm even a rock with just a smile, and he didn't like that half the guests liked Sean better than him, but even he had to admit that he liked Sean more than he liked himself sometimes.

It was that thought, perhaps, that propelled Dominic forward, pressing his mouth to Sean's.

Sean seemed to have been expecting it, maybe even waiting for it as he opened his mouth under Dominic's and kissed him back.

It was better than Dominic had imagined, hot and rough, Sean reacting pliantly to whatever he did. He could feel Sean melting under his hands, moving easily when Dominic pulled him into his lap.

Sean's arms slid around his neck, pulling their bodies closer as they kissed, pausing only to take quick, rushed breaths before going in for more. Sean hummed against his mouth, sucking his bottom lip and gasping at Dominic's hands tightening on his thighs to keep him from slipping off his lap.

They should really move out of the lobby where any of the guests could walk in at any time and see them, but after all this time of waiting, Dominic didn't care who saw. All that he cared about was that he got Sean's bare skin under his hands, got him moaning and, finally, not so cocky.

"God, you don't know how long I wanted this," Sean murmured as Dominic pushed up against him, a rush of heat spreading between them.

Dominic's mouth moved, grazing down Sean's neck, sucking on the skin even as Sean whimpered softly and ground down against him, almost desperately.

"Come on," Dominic said finally, regaining his bearings at the sound of footsteps somewhere outside.

He pushed Sean off his lap, practically scrambling up, but he wouldn't be the one to admit he was in a hurry despite the tightness in his jeans or the dark glint in Sean's eyes as they rushed out of the lobby and back towards Dominic's room.

Sean had never been in Dominic's room before, but then most of the staff hadn't. He hardly spent any time in there as it was.

The moment they got inside, Sean stripped off his shirt without waiting for Dominic to say anything. He turned to Dominic, standing alone in the middle of the room, and smiled.

Dominic took a step forward; all of a sudden things slowed down. He pulled off his shirt too, dropping it on the ground and stepping up to Sean. For a second, he could swear Sean swallowed nervously. He'd never seen Sean nervous before, and his stomach did a strange little flip. He made Sean nervous.

"How long have you been waiting?" Dominic asked, reaching for Sean's belt and pulling it apart with a clink. He watched the way Sean's chest moved up and down with every breath.

Sean smiled indulgently as Dominic got the zipper down, sliding a hand inside and cupping his hard dick through his boxers.

"Probably as long as you," he replied, slightly breathless, licking his lips and looking up into Dominic's hazel eyes.

Dominic would never admit he'd been waiting for this, but he didn't have to. They both knew it. Instead, he smiled slightly, pushing his hand against Sean's cock and enjoying the shaky noise Sean made in response.

"Who says I was?"

Sean moaned softly, reaching for Dominic's waist, long fingers pressing into his skin. "Hunter," he replied after a second, breathing out quickly as his eyes closed and he gasped. "Rose. Everybody." He smiled, leaning into Dominic's neck and pressing his mouth to the skin. "I could just tell."

Dominic didn't reply, releasing Sean's prick and pushing him backwards onto the bed. Sean fell onto the covers with a flump, scooting back as Dominic crawled on top of him, taking a moment to smooth his hands over his skin, tracing the thin scar on his thigh.

He felt Sean watching him, eyes taking in his every movement as he slid up, wedging a knee in between Sean's and forcing his legs apart. Sean didn't fight him, though, encouraging whatever he did.

Sean pulled Dominic into another kiss when he got close enough, harder than the first one, biting teeth and breathless groans as their bodies arched together, cocks rubbing together. Dominic bit back his gasp at the friction, the heat racing over his body.

He'd been waiting for this a long time too, almost two years, and not just for sex. That wasn't what this was going to be and he already knew it. The thought scared him a little when Sean reached for his waist and pulled him in flush, pressing up against his mouth, tongue grazing against his.

Sean felt so right underneath him, his body pliant and easy, warm and soft against his touch. He broke away from the kiss for a second to take a breath, staring down at Sean, his messy hair and reddened mouth half-open as he panted for breath.

Then Sean smiled, reaching up to touch Dominic's jaw, and Dominic was fucked. Maybe he always had been, but now it was official.

"I want you to fuck me," Sean breathed, eyes never leaving Dominic's. "I want to feel you inside me." He pushed up his hips, his hard cock pressing against Dominic's. "Please*, fuck me*."

Dominic's mouth smashed into Sean's before he even finished talking, hands scrambling to push off Sean's jeans, to get them to the floor.

Sean's hands reached for Dominic's jeans, fumbling with the zipper as his mouth was distracted by Dominic kissing him hard, dragging their lips together, biting at his mouth. Dominic just couldn't get enough, not enough of Sean's mouth, of his smooth skin under his hands, the warmth of his thighs as he pushed them apart.

He had to pull back long enough to get his own clothes off, but he came back almost immediately, biting at Sean's neck as his hand groped blindly in the bedside table drawer for the package of condoms. His hand searched for too long before landing on the box.

Sean moaned as their cocks rubbed together, and Dominic could feel Sean's pounding heart against his chest, the way he swallowed as Dominic tore open the box and pulled out a condom.

Of all the things that Dominic thought bothered him about Sean, he couldn't remember any of them now, not when Sean's legs wrapped around his back, scooting their bodies together. He watched Sean bite his lower lip, tipping his chin back and taking a deep breath.

Sean was beautiful, Dominic thought, as he rolled on the condom and popped open the lube.

Sean moaned appreciatively as Dominic slid in the first finger, eyes flicking to Dominic's, and Dominic almost paused at the look in Sean's eyes, a mixture of unbridled desire and a flicker of uncertainty that could only be from the last two years.

For two years, Dominic had tried to ignore this, ignore the feeling in his chest whenever he looked at Sean, whenever they argued over cheese costs or even when Sean pouted at his answers. He couldn't ignore it anymore, though, and pulled out his fingers, lining up his cock and ignoring the uncertainty in Sean's gaze.

The first push was too hard, but Dominic couldn't stop himself, and Sean didn't protest. He only groaned appreciatively and reached for Dominic's upper arms when he leaned over him.

Dominic didn't slow down, not that he could anyway. Each noise that Sean made shot straight through him, skin tingling at the heat searing through him, the tight squeeze of Sean's ass around his cock. Everything was perfect, much better than fantasies late at night could provide.

"Dom," Sean gasped, heels slipping on his lower back as Dominic thrust in, the headboard knocking against the wall, and Dominic thanked God the bedroom butted up against the kitchen and not a guest room.

He didn't reply, pushing in harder, faster, until Sean whined, a half-choked noise as he cursed loudly.

"Fuck, yes," Sean breathed, fingers tightening over Dominic's arm, sure to leave indents, almost painful, but Dominic just leaned in, mouth brushing against Sean's.

The kiss was too light, too easy compared to the brutal rhythm of their bodies, but Sean pushed up against him, lips barely brushing, noses bumping with each breathless thrust.

Sean swallowed thickly, exhaling shakily against Dominic's mouth, eyes closed, and Dominic pressed a last kiss to his mouth, open and wet, messy as they moved together.

Dominic's hand reached for Sean, smearing pre-come over his cock, feeling Sean's gasp against his lips, hearing the way he groaned long and loud at the touch, the way Dominic jerked him off, rushed and too hot.

Sean came first, groaning and cursing, hands moving to Dominic's neck and keeping his head in place, centimeters from his mouth but not quite kissing, as his body arched upwards and he let out small, choked noises.

Hot come coated Dominic's stomach, and he stroked it out of him, swallowing the soft groan Sean let out as he melted underneath him.

Dominic wasn't going to last much longer, gripping on to Sean's hips and pushing in. The muscles clenched around his cock, and he came, cursing to himself and trying not to slip as he thrust in, losing what little control he had left.

"Fuck," he cursed a moment later as he slid down on top of Sean, not bothering to roll off. He could feel Sean's heart pounding in his chest, feel the rapid breaths he took.

"Jesus," Sean echoed, hands sliding over Dominic's shoulders and to his hair, combing through the locks. "If I'd known it would be that good, I wouldn't have waited for you to make a move."

"You were waiting for me?"

"Well, you are my boss." Sean smiled, pressing a kiss to Dominic's jaw. "You're not gonna fire me, are you?"

Dominic almost laughed, pulling back an inch so he could look in Sean's eyes. He paused. "No. You have your uses."

Sean laughed. "Thanks."

Dominic shut him up with another kiss, not caring at all if he was fucking up his business. Maybe Sean would be completely worth it.

-⊖-⊖-⊖-

"Why did I have to come with you?" Hunter asked, hitting a tree branch as they stepped into town, and Rose shot him a look.

"Because you have so many other things to do," she said, rolling her eyes. "You know the policemen, that's why."

"What did they get arrested for anyway?"

Rose sighed, passing by Main Street and heading to a smaller road that ran parallel. She'd never been to the police station, but most people hadn't. In a town like this, there was no need to unless you were a Girl Scout selling cookies.

"The officer said they were communing with nature... naked."

Hunter laughed and led the way down the street. The station stood a little ways down the road, the outside weather-beaten over the years, but cheery-looking despite its purpose.

"I bet that was a great sight for the sheriff," he said, pulling open the door and going in ahead of Rose, who frowned and caught the door before it closed.

Inside, the light filtered through small, square windows high on the wall down onto the dusty floor, the desk in the corner piled high with papers. A small, barred space took up the back part, and Rose was almost sure she'd just stepped into Mayberry.

"Tom, what's up?" Hunter greeted the guy lounging behind the desk, and the guy looked up from the magazine he appeared to be reading, nodded back at Hunter, but he dropped his feet quickly as he caught sight of Rose.

"Hey, Hunter," he said, eyes still on Rose, who shot him a smile. "Who's your friend?"

Hunter frowned. "Rose. Look, we're here about the Meadowflowers?"

"Yeah," Tom said slowly, watching Rose, and Hunter eyed him carefully.

"Yeah?"

Tom shook himself a second later. "Yeah, they were arrested for public indecency."

"Hey, man, the woods is no one's property!" one of the guys in tie-dye called through the bars.

Hunter smiled slightly. "Come on, Tom, they were just having fun. They didn't hurt anybody. How about I buy you a drink and we forget all about this?"

Tom hesitated, eyes flicking to the keys on the hook behind the desk. Then he looked at Rose, who smiled slightly. Tom was handsome, as far as policemen went, with his short blond hair and square jaw.

"How about you get a drink with me instead?" he said to Rose, and Rose blinked, surprised.

"Oh, uh," she said slowly, glancing at Hunter, who didn't look very amused, crossing his arms behind Tom's back. "Sure, I guess."

"Great," Tom replied, smiling and turning back to Hunter. "Let's get your friends out of jail."

Hunter didn't reply, turning with Tom as he grabbed the keys.

Dominic sat at the table, staring at the plate before him, laden with what he thought was supposed to be eggs Benedict. His fork sat unused beside him and he stared down at it, remembering how perfect Sean's eggs Benedict used to look, drizzled in sauce and with a sprig of parsley on the side.

He was glad that most of the guests were either sleeping in or had left early for town. Maybe there was still time to get Hunter in there, though he knew Hunter would hate him for it. He'd hired this cook on a whim, but he was beginning to severely regret it.

Hunter wouldn't cook forever, though, and he looked more and more frazzled each early morning that he dragged himself in. The scruff around his jaw had started to grow into a beard.

"Hey," he said as Rose came clattering down the stairs, arms full of sheets and towels. "Come taste this."

"Oh no," she said, juggling the ball of fabric in her hands and making a discerning face at the glob on his plate. "Not after that last cook. I'll never be able to eat hash browns again."

"It wasn't that bad," he muttered, looking back at his plate and nudging the eggs with his fork. The white broke and yellow yolk oozed out unappetizingly.

"It was pretty bad," she replied, watching him make a face at the plate. "You know what you could do...."

"Don't," Dominic interrupted sharply. He looked up, expression serious as Rose frowned, biting her lip. "He's gone, and that's that. We have a new cook."

Determined, he dug his fork into the mess on his plate and stuck it in his mouth. He knew immediately it had been a bad idea as the flavor hit his tongue and he almost gagged, spitting it out as Rose turned away from the sight.

"Just not this one," he said, shoving the plate away and wiping at his mouth, but the sharp aftertaste lingered.

Rising from the chair, he started for the kitchen, but he didn't get very far before there was a loud bang, and Rose jumped, a few crumpled sheets falling to the floor.

"Don't tell me that was the cook," she said, forlorn, but Dominic turned to the sliding glass door as Glen came puffing in.

"Everything's fine!" he said reassuringly. "Someone just dropped a nail gun."

As he left, Rose sighed. "How much longer is this going to go on for? I thought it was supposed to be done in July."

"Well, you know contractors," Dominic replied, turning towards the kitchen, and he wasn't surprised when she followed him, grabbing the sheets from the floor and tucking them in. "Things always take longer than you expect."

"What about the guests?"

"Rose," Dominic said firmly, grabbing a glass and filling it with water. The cook was nowhere to be seen, and Dominic had to find him soon and fire him before he cooked anything else. He glanced out the window to where the construction crew had spread out all their equipment and Glen was shouting instructions. "They've managed so far, and I know the noise is annoying but the additions need to be made."

"And what about the fact that all the fixtures are back-ordered?"

"It's just going to take longer than we thought," Dominic replied, frustrated. He knew what he was doing, for God's sake. He had been to business school, gotten a degree in hotel and restaurant management. He knew how to run a business. He turned to Rose, who had the decency to look slightly abashed. "Everything's going to be fine."

"Okay," she said finally, jerking her shoulders. "I should get these in the laundry."

Dominic sighed as she hurried out. He hadn't meant to snap, but he was getting awfully tired of people assuming he didn't know what was best for the bed and breakfast. He was the owner, for Christ's sake. Without him, there would be no bed and breakfast, and there would be no Sean.

What he needed was someone like Sean to walk in that door and apply for the job. He still remembered the first time they met, over five years ago. Dominic had been skeptical that someone with Sean's qualifications would want to work at a little bed and breakfast in the middle of the woods, and he didn't deny he'd suspected him to be lying, especially when he showed up and asked how Dominic felt about vegan cooking.

Luckily, he'd been kidding, and as they'd argued about the inclusion of thyme in an omelet, Dominic had hired him without so much as a formal handshake.

He needed someone like that to walk in that door, but there was only one Sean.

No, he told himself firmly, dumping the rest of the water in the sink and pulling himself together. There were plenty of other good cooks out there, and he was going to find one. Before his whole staff got food poisoning.

At the moment, though, he needed something a bit stronger than water to wash the taste of bad eggs from his mouth, so he put the glass in the dishwater and headed for the parking lot.

Outside, the late afternoon sun faded to a warm yellow, gilding the trees in an autumn-like glow as Dominic followed the road towards town. It wasn't a very long walk, about ten minutes until the small houses began to pop up alongside the road and cars became more frequent as he reached the first bit of sidewalk.

The local bar's door was thrown wide open on Main Street, and Dominic stepped into the cool darkness, the sounds of softly thudding glasses and the old radio in the corner meeting his ears.

He passed the people he knew with slight nods, not in the mood to really talk to anyone.

"Evening, Dom," the bartender said as he slid into a seat at the counter. "How's things?"

"Be a lot better if I could find a decent cook in this town," he muttered, glancing up as Bill set a bottle in front of him. He didn't even have to order. Everyone knew everyone in Honey Creek.

"Talent pool's a little small," Bill said obviously, grabbing a rag off the tap and wiping down the counter near Dominic. A classic bartender trick, Dominic knew, and he wouldn't rise to it, no matter how well Bill claimed to know everyone in town. "Maybe you should be casting a wider net."

Dominic shrugged, taking a sip of the beer. What Bill really meant was, 'Maybe you should go crawling back to Sean and admit how stupid you were.' He had no intention of doing anything of the sort.

"Actually," Bill said after a minute, and Dominic looked up at his tone. Bill looked thoughtful, though, almost as if he was hesitating to say more.

"What?"

"Well, my nephew, well, step-nephew? Anyway, he's been in town for about two weeks now, looking for a job. He's not a bad cook."

Doubtful, Dominic took another long drink, wishing it were stronger. "Yeah, and does your sister build things? I could probably use her on the addition."

"Don't scoff," Bill said, tossing the rag back over the tap and placing his fat hand on the counter. A simple gold wedding band encircled his left ring finger, and Dominic frowned at it. Bill had owned the bar for as long as Dominic had known him, and most people considered him a staple in the town, the sage old bartender who'd heard it all. He had salt and pepper hair, a round face and body, but he was friendly to everyone who walked into his bar. "You need a cook."

"And in the last two weeks, I've seen one who nearly burned down the kitchen, one who gave my staff food poisoning, and one that lasted all of two days before quitting. I'd rather not discuss how scarred I'll be for life."

"Look, I can vouch for the kid," Bill assured him. "I mean, I've only met him a few times since his father's my step-brother, but he makes a mean goat cheese omelet."

Dominic's stomach twisted at the mention of an omelet, but he didn't let it show, grabbing his beer instead.

"I guess," he said at length, sighing. "I guess I could give him a try. But if he poisons anyone or explodes my kitchen, I'm telling all my guests that you were shut down for rats."

"Fair enough," Bill said with an amused smile, but Dominic wasn't amused. This was getting to be a problem, and he had to hire someone soon or they'd start losing guests. "But you may be surprised."

Dominic doubted it, but he didn't bother arguing, draining what was left in the bottle.

"Speaking of surprises, how's the remodel going?"

"Lots of hammering," Dominic replied, not really in the mood to talk. That wasn't why he'd come down there, but he supposed he should have known better. Everyone always wanted to talk in this town. Sean had taken to it like a fish to water, but maybe that had been why everyone loved him so much.

Dominic shook himself firmly. He had to stop thinking about Sean, but everything always seemed to come back to him. Even the beer in his hands; it was Sean's favorite brand, and Dominic frowned, pushing it away. Bill merely set another in front of him a moment later.

"Must be expensive," Bill commented, taking away the empty and tossing it under the counter.

"I've budgeted."

Bill shrugged. "Unexpected things always crop up. When I redid this place, I had to spend an extra five thousand on the ceiling. Nearly collapsed the whole project."

"I'll be fine," Dominic said slowly, pushing his hair back and glancing away.

A few tourists sat at the tables in the bar, talking over the low hum of the radio in the background. Dominic could see the street from the bar, the few people wandering past in the fading daylight.

He turned back to the bar, fingers closing around the bottle, the condensation soaking his fingertips. Behind the bar, the shelves were lined with empty, multi-colored bottles of alcohol along with a few pictures of Bill and his wife and their daughter, but Dominic had never met the daughter. She lived somewhere overseas, he thought Bill had said once.

"How long you been married?" he asked after a minute, and Bill paused to think, glancing at the picture of his wife behind the bar.

"Oh, I'd say we'll be going on thirty five years this winter," he said at length, nodding after another second. "Pretty sure that's right. I'm sure she'd have my head if it wasn't."

"That's a long time," Dominic muttered, raising the bottle to his lips and pausing. He drank after a second, though, holding back a sigh.

"Doesn't feel like it," Bill replied with a shrug. "When you really love somebody, time just seems to stop."

Dominic frowned, setting the bottle down on the counter with a soft clunk. "And you never fight?"

"Oh, well, sure," Bill said. "Everybody does." He eyed Dominic as he said it, but Dominic reached for his bottle again. "But you work it out."

Dominic caught Bill's eyes for a second, and he frowned, not liking the hint in them. He had nothing to work out.

Pushing back from the bar, he got to his feet and grabbed his bottle. "I'm just gonna relax for a minute," he said, nodding to one of the empty tables, and Bill nodded.

"Call me if you need a refill."

As Dominic slid into the seat in the corner, he thought that bartenders were too nosy for their own good.

Chapter 5
Sous Chef

"Why are you going out with Tom?" Hunter asked as he dumped the last kayak onto the dock, alongside the other three. A bucket of soapy water sat on the dock, and he wondered how long he could put this off before Dominic forced him to do it. He'd avoided scrubbing them down most of the summer, but autumn was quickly approaching and they had to be cleaned before they were put away for winter.

Rose looked up from her book, glancing over as Hunter dropped to the dock and sat cross-legged before he dragged the first boat towards him.

Vanilla sniffed around the boat, wagging her tail when Hunter shoved her away.

"Why do you care?"

Hunter jerked his shoulders slightly, keeping his eyes on the boat as he scrubbed. "No reason. Tom's just, you know."

"What?" she asked, frowning but not closing her book just yet.

"Well, you don't know him very well, but Tom's kind of a loose cannon."

"Hunter," Rose said reproachfully, fitting her bookmark in the pages and closing the book.

"I'm serious!" he said, glancing up at her as he dunked the scrub brush back in the water. The soap spilled over the edge. "Like, during the festival last year, he was in the dunk tank, and he got so mad when this kid dunked him, nearly punched a hole in the tank."

Rose arched a skeptical eyebrow, clearly not believing him, but Hunter had witnesses. Most of them had just been too drunk to remember.

"I guess I'll find out for myself then," she said when Hunter just scrubbed the kayak. "You can't tell me who to date."

"I'm not," Hunter said obviously, scrubbing hard at a spot on the kayak even after the dirt came off. "If you want to date him, go right ahead."

"I will," she said slowly, frowning and shaking her head. Hunter didn't look up, dunking the brush again and water cascaded over the edge of the bucket.

Somewhere overhead, a bird chirped and the branches rustled in the wind coming off the water. A couple from the bed and breakfast were in a boat out on the lake, and Hunter watched them for a second before returning to scrubbing. The dog whined, crawling along the deck towards Hunter. He scratched her ears for a second.

"Has Dominic said anything about hiring a permanent cook?" he asked finally. "The last couple he hired have been stupider and stupider."

Rose sighed. "Maybe he doesn't want to hire someone."

"He *has* to."

"No, I mean, hiring someone will mean that Sean's really gone."

"He is," Hunter pointed out bluntly, and Rose huffed.

"Way to be optimistic."

Rolling his eyes, Hunter tossed the brush into the bucket and twisted to look up at Rose. "I've known Dominic for a long time," he said simply, "and if someone leaves him, then they're gone."

Frowning, Rose cocked her head to the side. "What do you mean?"

Hunter turned back to the kayak, scowling at the dirt. "He better hire someone good soon," was all he said as he turned the kayak over and scrubbed at the bottom instead.

Dominic had his doubts about Bill's step-nephew or whatever he was, but he'd agreed to at least interview him. Nothing said he had to hire him or taste the food he cooked if it looked like something dead. After the last few cooks, Dominic's hopes had lowered significantly. He just hoped for something edible.

Amidst the hammering and sawing going on outside, Dominic wasn't in the best mood as two o'clock on Friday afternoon rolled around. A guest had already canceled due to the construction, and they'd run out of eggs that morning since no one had made a note to get more.

If the guy didn't impress him within two minutes of walking through that door, he wasn't about to give him the benefit of the doubt.

Sitting behind the desk, he grudgingly took out the canceled guest's reservation. He needed all the occupancy he could get, especially since summer was waning, and after the apple festival ended, the tourists would drop off significantly until the spring. The addition was contingent on keeping up occupancy rates, and he couldn't afford to lose any.

The front door opening caught his attention, but he didn't look up yet, trying to calculate in his head the number of guests scheduled before the end of fall.

"Are you Dominic?" the guy standing before the desk asked, a messenger bag slung over his shoulder, jeans too tight on his legs, and black hair hanging in his eyes as he looked down at Dominic.

Dominic glanced up once quickly, but stopped as he caught sight of the guy's high cheekbones, the silver ring through his nose, and his tight, tight jeans.

"Yeah," he said after a minute, shaking himself firmly. He rose from the chair and paused, eyes scanning the guy slowly. "You must be Bill's nephew." The guy couldn't have been more than twenty-three years old from the looks of him, and Dominic liked the looks of him.

"Nathan," the guy said, licking his lips slowly as Dominic's eyes reached his face again.

"Uh, great," Dominic said, looking away sharply. He shouldn't be thinking what he was. "So, can you cook?"

Nathan shrugged nonchalantly. "Well, no one's ever complained about staying over yet." He smirked, and Dominic caught the interested slide to his gaze as he looked him up and down.

Dominic smiled slightly, pausing as he watched Nathan lick his lips again, in what was clearly an invitation.

"You want to cook me something then?" he asked, and Nathan smirked.

"It'd be my pleasure."

They didn't actually get around to cooking anything, since as soon as Nathan bent over to open the fridge, and Dominic caught sight of his ass in those jeans, he was fucked. It didn't help that Nathan seemed intent on giving him the best view he could no matter where he turned.

Dominic wasn't thinking about the job or even Sean as he shoved Nathan through the bedroom door, snapping it shut behind him and clicking the lock.

"You're so hot," Nathan murmured against his collarbone as he turned around, pushing his hands under Dominic's shirt and shoving it off. "Bill said you were, like, thirty, but you're really hot for thirty."

"Shut up," Dominic said, shoving Nathan back, and he fell onto the bed, bouncing slightly on the mattress. He wasn't in the mood to chat about how hot he was or not.

"Mm, bossy too," Nathan replied, a sly smile curling his mouth, but Dominic shut him up with a hard kiss.

Dominic herded Nathan up on the bed, ignoring the guilty clench to his stomach as Nathan went easily, as easily as Sean would have. He shook it away, though. This wasn't about Sean. This was three weeks without sex and a guy whose eyes never left his body.

Nathan's body was skinny but warm under his touch as he pushed up Nathan's shirt. Nathan's hands went for Dominic's jeans, tugging the button undone and shoving under his boxers. Dominic sucked in a sharp breath at Nathan's hand, the warmth soaking into his skin.

Nathan was too bony, he thought, but that didn't stop him from rolling Nathan over onto his stomach, not wasting time with the subtle touches, the careful drag of skin against skin. He just wanted to do this and he didn't want to think about why.

Nathan went easily, though, pliant in his hands as he let Dominic shift him onto his stomach and yank his jeans down. It took a moment, they were so tight, but Dominic was rewarded for his struggle at the sight of Nathan's tight, round ass.

He grabbed a condom out of the drawer of the bedside table, from the box that had barely been opened, and he pushed away the sudden onslaught of feelings as he remembered the last time he had.

Nathan was waiting, though, moaning into the covers like an obscene whore, pushing his ass up towards Dominic.

The preparation was quick, a few slick fingers pressing into Nathan's body, and Dominic's chest tightened at the noises Nathan made with each finger, slick with lube.

He shook away the tightness, though, and focused on the heat, the warmth that engulfed his cock the moment he pressed into Nathan.

He'd barely known this guy more than ten minutes, and here he was fucking him until Nathan was groaning his name over and over, clutching the pillow and grinding his teeth together, encouraging him to go faster, to fuck him raw. He barely knew him, didn't even know his last name or if he could cook an egg.

He didn't want to know any of those things, though. Knowing it only made things more complicated. He'd known everything about Sean, and look how well that had turned out. It was better this way, better as he slipped deep into Nathan, pressed in through the tight, hot muscles that made his hips twitch, his cock harden inexplicably.

Nathan was a good fuck, there was no denying it. He knew how to twist, to drive Dominic in deeper, harder. He moaned long and low, thrusting his hips back with Dominic, demanding more even as Dominic's stomach twisted with a burning heat, and he gasped, reaching forward to push against Nathan's shoulder.

His back was a pale expanse of skin aside from a bird tattooed on the back of his left hip, and Dominic thought of Sean as his eyes landed on the tattoo, the way Sean had point-blank refused to get a tattoo the year before when they'd gone to L.A. for a weekend. Though Dominic had teased him, he preferred Sean's skin unblemished, a perfect light olive color that seemed to contrast so well with his own skin.

"Shit," Dominic cursed as he came, fingers tightening over Nathan's shoulder, nails digging into the skin, and Nathan only groaned for more.

His body felt tight as he pushed into Nathan's ass, rocking in as he came down, the heat slowly ebbing from his skin and his breath coming in pants. He heard Nathan's groan, saw his hand moving fast over his cock, but he didn't bother to help.

Letting out a slow breath, he felt it when Nathan came, his body stiffening under his and the grunt as his hand stilled.

Pulling out, Dominic tossed the condom away, rolling over and flopping onto his back.

He stared at the wood-lined ceiling, like the inside of a cabin. Every room in the place had the same ceiling, half-circular logs to give the illusion of a real cabin. The light hung down from the ceiling, turned off as it was the middle of the afternoon and sunlight streamed in through the window.

Outside, a saw screeched to life, and he sighed.

"So do I get the job?" Nathan asked after a second, propping himself up on his elbow, a dark glint to his eyes, and Dominic hesitated, a frown tugging the corners of his mouth.

"You haven't cooked anything yet."

"Mm," Nathan hummed, sliding a hand up Dominic's bare stomach. Dominic lay still, unable to explain the tightness in his chest as Nathan leaned over him, head cocked to the side and a smirk gracing his mouth. "I'll go make us a snack then."

He didn't kiss Dominic, and Dominic felt a weight lift as he didn't, but slid off the bed instead, heading towards the door.

"Wait," Dominic said as Nathan reached it, a hand on the knob. He leaned over the side of the bed, grabbing Nathan's clothes that still lay there. "Get dressed. This isn't a brothel."

He threw the clothes to Nathan, and they hit him in the chest.

He didn't watch him dress, but lay back as the door clicked behind Nathan. Rubbing his forehead, he sighed, blinking at the ceiling. An uncomfortable feeling settled in the pit of his stomach, and he didn't like it, didn't like it at all. He shouldn't feel guilty about fucking someone else. Sean was gone. They had broken up. He shouldn't feel guilty. But somehow, he still felt something as he groaned in frustration and reached for his shirt.

"That's it!"

Dominic looked up from the morning newspaper, thankful that the only guests currently staying at the bed and breakfast had gone on an early-morning hike around the lake. The others had all checked out the night before, a day early, which he blamed on Glen's crew striding in at five in the morning and making a ruckus.

Hunter strode out of the kitchen, spatula in hand, and pointed it threateningly in Dominic's face.

"I am not a cook!" he said, violently brushing away the flour staining his clothes. "I fix boats and make sure people don't drown! For fuck's sake, Dom, suck it up and hire someone!"

He slammed the spatula down on the table and strode out the door before Dominic could do much more than stare after him.

"He's right."

Dominic turned sharply at Rose's voice coming from the stairs. She stepped out a second later, folding a towel slowly.

"I did hire someone," Dominic muttered, turning back to the newspaper. He couldn't read any of the articles, though, thoughts stuck on his cook-less bed and breakfast. "They all quit."

The crew had finally gotten around to working on the pipes for the addition, which meant shutting off the water for long periods of time, something the guests were quick to complain about.

"What about Bill's nephew?" she asked, placing the towel on the table and carefully picking up the spatula. She took it back into the kitchen. "Didn't you see him?"

"Yeah," he agreed reluctantly, frowning at the picture on the front page of the sports section, another article about the Seahawks losing again. "But I think if I did, he'd want to fuck again."

"*Again*?" Rose's head popped suddenly around the door, eyes wide as she stared at Dominic, who tactfully ignored her expression.

"He wasn't half-bad, though."

"Dominic!" she said, mouth falling open as well.

"At cooking," he clarified, rolling his eyes. He shook his head. "Jesus, Rose."

"Well, I'm sorry," she said, stepping out from the kitchen finally, but she looked concerned. "But what am I supposed to think? Do you like him?"

"No," Dominic said simply, folding the paper up and sighing. Gazing out the back door, he could see the scattered debris left behind from Glen's crew from the day before, hammers and planks of wood stacked up haphazardly.

"Then why did you sleep with him?"

Running a hand through his hair, Dominic didn't know what to say. He didn't really know the reason himself, except that Nathan had been hot and clearly wanted it. There hadn't been much thinking between the kitchen and the bedroom.

"Haven't you ever had a one-night stand?" he asked instead, and Rose shrugged.

"Well, once."

"Then that's why." He had no intention of sleeping with Nathan again, but they did need a cook before Hunter threw himself into the lake in desperation. "But he can at least cook."

His gaze fell on the fireplace, empty at the moment, but soon enough it would be winter and they'd have a fire every evening for the cozy couples who always came to ski and enjoy a winter wonderland. He wasn't looking forward to it nearly as much as he usually did.

"So you are going to hire him?" Rose still had a frown on her face, and Dominic didn't need to ask why.

It wasn't her relationship, or lack thereof, though, and Dominic had things handled just fine.

"Don't really have another choice," he said, rising from the table and tossing the paper onto the coffee table. Since there wasn't going to be breakfast that morning, he might as well go find Nathan and give him the good news. "Maybe you could find Hunter and let him know. Maybe Nathan will last more than a week."

He grabbed his jacket off the desk chair and stepped out onto the front porch, into the cool morning air. The sun was barely climbing up in the east, the porch and parking lot lost in cold shadows as he stepped down the stairs and started towards town.

The road stretched quietly before him as he walked, kicking the gravel, each step heavier and heavier as he thought about what he was about to do. He had to, though. They needed a cook, and Sean wasn't coming back. He'd had three weeks to change his mind, and Dominic hadn't heard a single word. He was pretty sure Rose had talked to Sean, though she kept silent on the subject, for which he was glad. He didn't want to hear how well Sean was doing.

In town, he stopped by the café on the corner and grabbed a coffee, carefully deflecting Annie's questions about Sean. Even the waitresses loved him. Sometimes, Dominic wished Sean had been less loveable. It would have made things a million times easier.

The town seemed fairly quiet as he walked through, bypassing the stores that weren't quite open yet and turning onto a more residential street filled with quiet houses under leafy trees with perfectly green yards. It looked like something out of a nineteen fifties television show.

He turned into the driveway of the house with two pink flamingos stuck in the yard and knocked on the door instead of ringing the bell. It was too early to wake up the whole house.

He wasn't surprised, though, when Bill answered the door, fully-dressed and with a coffee cup in his hand.

"Morning, Dom," he greeted him as if this was an everyday occurrence, but in this town, it was. "What can I do for you?"

"I need to talk to Nathan."

Bill nodded, not a hint of suspicion in his gaze, and Dominic gathered that Nathan hadn't said anything about the "interview."

"I'll get him," he said instead, leaving Dominic at the door and turning inside. Dominic didn't follow him, though he knew if Doris saw him standing out there, she'd invite him in.

A few moments later, Nathan came shuffling down the hall in only a pair of boxers, hair mussed and blinking in the sunlight. He looked barely awake, but he perked up at the sight of Dominic in the doorway.

"Well," he said, smiling slowly at him as he reached the door. "Finally came back, huh?"

Dominic paused, glancing in the house. Bill had apparently returned to the dining room, but that didn't stop Dominic from nodding Nathan out onto the porch. Nathan came, shutting the door behind him and shivering in the cool breeze.

"That's not why I'm here," he said seriously. "It's not gonna happen again."

Nathan sighed, leaning back against the house, sharp hip bones angled towards Dominic. "Then why'd you get me up at fuck all hours of the morning?"

"The job's yours if you want it," Dominic replied, ignoring the slight. He had bigger problems than Nathan's attitude. "Although if you take it, you'll be getting up earlier than this."

Nathan shifted, pushing off the house and raking back his hair. He contemplated Dominic for a moment. "Can't let your guests starve, I guess," he said at length. "And you might change your mind about me."

Dominic sincerely doubted it, but he said nothing, gaze cool.

"Good. You start Monday. Breakfast is at seven, so you'll need to be there by six-thirty at the latest. I'll see you then."

"Yeah, you will." Nathan smirked at him as Dominic stepped off the porch.

He didn't look back as he turned down the street, sipping his coffee and catching sight of the first golden leaf on a tree as he passed and headed for the bed and breakfast.

Chapter 6
Under Construction

The axe swung down through the air with a swift *schwhick!* of the air, landing in the piece of wood on the tree stump. Hunter picked it up and cracked the axe and log down, splitting it in two. The pieces toppled over the edge and Hunter grabbed one, setting it up on the log again.

"What are you doing?"

He looked up at Rose's voice from the back porch but swung the axe down anyway against the piece of wood, lodging the axe in the top.

"What does it look like?"

He slammed the piece down onto the log. It tumbled off the log and to the ground.

Rose picked her way over, avoiding the piles of wood left by the construction crew. Hugging her arms in the slight morning chill, she watched Hunter grab another piece of wood.

Winter was coming, and Hunter wasn't going to give Dominic the opportunity to cut himself all up trying to chop wood.

"How's Tom?" he asked after a minute passed. The axe swished down into the piece of wood, splitting it down the middle.

Rose sighed, crossed her arms over her stomach and frowned slightly. "Fine."

"And how was your date?"

"You were right," she admitted after a moment, shrugging. "He's kind of a jerk."

"Told you." Hunter didn't look at her. Instead, he grabbed the wood and began to toss it on the pile stacked up between two tall maple trees.

"Dominic hired a cook."

"Finally. Maybe this one will last." Hunter brushed his dirty hands on his jeans and glanced at the mess behind the bed and breakfast.

The back of the inn looked like a shell, with the foundation poured and the outline of the walls at least put up. There was a roof, but at the moment it was merely covered with a tarp and Hunter wondered if they were ever going to get around to finishing it. He swore even he could do it faster. The land around the addition just looked like a disaster area.

Rose paused. "He slept with him too."

Hunter didn't falter as he tossed more wood on the pile, adjusting a few pieces and watching a spider crawl out of one of the holes.

"Well?" Rose asked from behind him, an urgent tone to her voice.

"Well, what?" he asked, brushing the spider away and stacking more wood. They needed a good bit more if they were going to make it through the winter without Dominic trying to do it himself.

"I don't know!" she said, frustrated. "He slept with someone else!"

"So?" Hunter turned towards her, shrugging obviously. "He's a grown man, Rose. It's not our responsibility to stop him from doing stupid things."

"I can't believe you don't care!" she said, staring at him with her big blue eyes. "I mean, look at this place. It's practically falling apart."

"It's construction," Hunter explained calmly, setting the last piece of wood on the pile. He glanced around, but even he had to admit she had a point.

"Guests are canceling," she said seriously, crossing her arms again. "And Dominic hasn't done anything. We've been through three different cooks in a month."

"What do you want me to do about it?" Hunter asked, grabbing another log and setting it up on the stump. He raised the axe over his shoulder.

"Can't you talk to him?" she asked desperately. "You are his best friend."

"We've known each other a long time," Hunter corrected her, swing the axe down into the wood. "And he doesn't listen to me any more than he listens to anyone else."

"So we're just supposed to let everything fall apart?"

Hunter sighed, turning with the axe still in hand to face Rose. "We're supposed to let him live his life even if it means messing up the only good relationship he's ever had and running his bed and breakfast into the ground. If you try to say anything, he's going to resent it. And I know you mean well, and you're nice to a fault, Rose, but you can't help everyone, and some people don't want to be helped."

"Have you tried before?" she asked after a minute, eyes narrowed slightly.

Hunter turned back to the wood. "I came out here with him. That was help enough."

"Can you tell me why that's help enou—"

"No," he interrupted sharply, slicing the wood in one quick movement. "That's his past, not mine."

"Well, I'm not giving up," she said, frowning at Hunter's back. "I can be stubborn too, you know."

Hunter smiled to himself, turning away from her. "Sure," he agreed.

She glared at him, then headed back for the bed and breakfast as he grabbed another piece of wood to chop.

The day had started out badly, with the hot water shutting off somewhere in the middle of his shower, leaving Dominic shivering as he reached for a towel. It hadn't gotten any better once he'd made it out to the lobby to find the guests whispering together and shooting annoyed looks out the back door to the construction crew lounging around, half of them unattractive, shirtless men.

Breakfast, at the very least, was edible, but as Dominic pushed around his scrambled eggs, he remembered how Sean used to sprinkle Parmesan cheese on his eggs and bake his own fresh bread.

"How long is the construction going on for?" the man, Mr. Schauber, Dominic thought, asked, tapping his fork against his plate, eyes on Glen outside.

"A few more months," Dominic replied, pushing his eggs away. He didn't have much of an appetite, especially not when Nathan emerged from the kitchen wearing impossibly tight jeans and a tee shirt that would have been more at home at a death metal concert. "But we'll have two new private suites. You're welcome to take a look at the progress." He forced a smile at Mr. Schauber's unimpressed expression.

"Anyone for toast?" Nathan asked, setting down a plate, but no one took any. The man's wife frowned disapprovingly at Nathan's shirt.

Dominic sighed. He was certainly no Sean.

"Didn't you used to have another cook?" the man asked as Nathan shot Dominic a wink and sauntered back into the kitchen.

"Yeah," Dominic replied shortly.

"What happened to him?"

"He moved, got a job in Seattle." He forced another smile at the displeased look on the man's face.

"Too bad."

The day didn't seem to get any better after that. When he talked to Glen about the water, he said they'd have to turn it off for the rest of the day while they worked. To say the Schaubers were unhappy was an understatement. They'd practically had their bags already packed.

Dominic waved to them as they pulled out of the parking lot amidst a cloud of dust. He sighed. How much worse could the day get? It was barely eleven in the morning.

He supposed he shouldn't have asked that when, the moment his hand touched the doorknob to go back in, a voice called to him from down the road.

"Dom!"

Jessie was walking towards the bed and breakfast, waving her arm, a folder tucked under her other arm. Sighing, he forced himself to turn, suppressing the annoyance he already felt.

"Hey, Jessie," he said as she reached him, puffing slightly as though the walk had been long from town.

"I nearly got run over there!" she said, glancing down the road. "Who was that leaving?"

"Just some guests," he muttered, frowning and trying not to think of the lost income, especially with the season ending soon and the inevitable prolongment of the addition. He didn't see what was so hard about getting the walls up, but Glen insisted the plywood wasn't up to code.

"Oh," she said, gazing at the settling cloud of dust.

Rubbing the bridge of his nose, Dominic tried not to sigh. "Is there any particular reason you came to see me?"

Jessie smiled immediately, holding out the black folder in front of her. "I have been appointed the official apple festival booth manager! I need to talk to you about yours."

"Oh, right," Dominic muttered, turning from the road at last. "Come on in."

A jackhammer turned on as they stepped in the lobby, and Dominic groaned, marching over to the sliding glass door and shutting it tightly. The sound deadened only slightly.

He gestured for Jessie to take a seat on the couch.

"You want something to drink? We've got a cook again, so there's actually food in the house."

"You hired someone else?" she asked curiously, peering at the kitchen door as if she might be able to see whoever it was.

"Bill's nephew," Dominic replied, sitting next to her when she didn't respond about the drink. "He's decent."

"But no Sean, I'm sure," she said, opening her folder while Dominic frowned at her. Smiling, she pulled out a list and a chart filled with boxes. "So I've got a few good locations still available for the festival. You can either be next to my booth, or here, next to Natalie who's going to be selling her jewelry like usual. Or there's a spot next to Bill, and he'll have his hard apple cider again!"

"Best to avoid that, don't you think?" Dominic asked with a small smile, and Jessie giggled, pushing at his arm.

"But Sean won't be here to get us both drunk this time," she pointed out. "Do you think he might stop by?"

Dominic grabbed the map of the booths, frowning at the little boxes. "I doubt it."

Jessie sighed sadly, pressing her hands together and glancing up at the photos above the mantel. Dominic had taken down the ones of Sean, tucked them far back in the closet, unable to actually throw them away. Instead, only the pictures of him, Hunter, and Rose were left, along with a few of the regular guests they'd known for years.

"Put me down next to Natalie," Dominic said instead of commenting on the way Jessie frowned at the change in pictures. He set the map back on the table, and Jessie looked down slowly.

"Sure thing," she said, scribbling down Dominic's name in the box. "What are you going to do this year?"

"I'll have to talk to Nathan, but maybe some apple tarts and homemade applesauce."

"Ohh, Sean always made such good applesauce! What was his secret?"

Dominic shrugged, pushing away the clench in his stomach. "I don't know. He never told me."

"You should have found out before he left." Jessie said sadly. "But I'm sure this Nathan will be just fine too." She patted his arm reassuringly. "Anyway, the apple harvest should be starting next Friday, and the booths will open on the next Saturday after that, so be sure to tell all your guests!"

"Will do," he assured her as she rose from the couch, gathering her papers together.

She smiled at him as she reached the front door. "Don't worry about Sean. He loves you."

Dominic didn't know how to reply as she left, the door swinging behind her. He swallowed down the lump rising in his throat and shook himself.

A crash from outside shook the walls, and Dominic squeezed his eyes shut. This addition was going to be the death of him.

Two Years Previously.

Dominic stared at the puppies rolling all around his feet. There were too many of them to count, but Sean had stars in his eyes as he stared at them all, and Dominic knew there'd be no arguing. Not that he was going to argue, especially when one of the puppies ambled up to him and plopped down on top of his feet.

"Aren't they so adorable?" Sean asked, hardly able to contain his joy, and Dominic smiled at his enthusiasm.

They hadn't exactly been planning on getting a puppy, but Dominic had always liked dogs, and now that things at the inn had settled into a comfortable routine, and now that Sean had moved in for good, it seemed a good time to get a puppy.

"You're adorable," he said instead, ignoring Sean's pout. He reached down to stroke the puppy sitting on his foot.

"Do you like that one?" Sean asked, setting his chin on Dominic's shoulder and gazing down at the puppy.

"They're all cute." Dominic shrugged. Most of them looked the same to him, the same fluffy coats and pot-bellies as they rolled around and yipped at each other.

"Have you had dogs before?" the woman standing nearby asked, keeping an eye on the puppies as they ran around the yard.

"When I was a kid," Dominic replied, watching the puppy at his feet gambol after the others and bite another's tail.

The last dog he'd had had disappeared along with whichever step-mother that had been. He thought it was Helen, one of the ones he'd actually liked, but he'd learned quickly not to get attached, to the dog or the woman.

"You never told me that," Sean said, tilting his head to the side, and Dominic shrugged. There were still plenty of things he'd never told Sean, but most of it wasn't important.

"Which one do you like?" he asked instead, and Sean glanced around, bending over. One of the puppies, the one that had been sitting on Dominic's feet, he thought, came running over immediately, licking Sean's fingers.

"That's the girl," the woman said. "The only one left."

Sean picked her up, and she barely struggled in his arms, licking at his nose and biting it.

"I like her," he said, turning to Dominic.

"Then we'll take her," he said, smiling as Sean leaned in for a quick kiss.

Sean made cooing noises at the puppy as Dominic paid the woman and they took her to the car. Sean was still grinning as they slid inside, the puppy firmly on his lap. He glanced over at Dominic.

"You know, if you'd told me three years ago that we'd be getting a puppy together, I would have said you were crazy."

"No, you would have suggested we put some goat cheese on it."

"Shut up!" Sean laughed, hugging the puppy, and she licked his chin. Dominic only smiled as he put the car in drive and they headed for home.

Hunter wiped the sweat off his brow as he raked the leaves off the parking lot, piling them up on the sides even though he was probably supposed to throw them in bags, but it was hot, and he'd been at this for over an hour.

Raking leaves was one thing, a very long, arduous thing, but when Dominic had asked him to clean out the oven by hand, he had almost lost it.

"Isn't that why you hired a cook?" he'd demanded, gesturing at the kitchen where Nathan was wriggling his hips as he flipped over the bacon. Hunter's eyes narrowed.

"He just started. He doesn't know how," Dominic had replied simply, jerking his shoulders. "It's gotta be done."

"Can't you teach him?"

"Yeah, I'll get around to it," Dominic said vaguely. "But I've got to talk to Glen about the addition right now."

"Yeah, when are they gonna stop turning off the water?"

"Soon," he'd assured him.

"Hopefully before every guest cancels."

"It'll be fine," Dominic said firmly, and though Hunter didn't think even Dominic believed himself, he couldn't argue.

Hunter was there to fix things like blocked toilets and blinky lights, not clean out ovens and the other things Sean used to do. He had enough on his plate what with winterizing the inn, putting away the boats, cleaning out the shed before the snows set in.

He may have known Dominic the longest of anyone at the bed and breakfast, but that didn't mean sometimes he just didn't understand why he had to be so goddamn stubborn about everything.

Muttering to himself, he raked the leaves with a forceful push, scattering them over onto the grass. He'd probably have to rake those up later, but right now, he didn't care.

"No, Vanilla!" he shouted as the dog came barreling around the side of the house, leaping into the leaves and scattering them.

He sighed as she rolled around in them, tongue lolling out of her mouth. If only the rest of their lives were as simple as Vanilla's.

The trees above him had turned from green to a mixture of gold, yellow, and red, leaves crunchy underfoot when he stepped on one. Normally, it was his favorite time of year, but this year he was just dreading the onset of winter, when the tourists would drop off, and he'd be stuck with Dominic for the next six months.

By the time he finally finished raking, cleaning up Vanilla's mess, sweat was dripping down his face, and he wiped it away uselessly as he tromped into the lobby. A lone man sat on the couch, staring at the mantel. He had a notebook in his lap, but nothing was written down. Hunter knew the type, a "writer" looking for inspiration. They got a lot of those out here.

The other guests were probably in town trying to escape the constant roar of the saws and nail guns coming from out back. What the crew could possibly be doing since none of the toilets or sinks had come in yet, Hunter had no idea.

He bypassed the man without interrupting his staring contest with the mantelpiece, heading into the kitchen.

He glanced out the window as he filled a glass with water, pausing as he caught sight of Dominic talking with Glen. Perhaps "talking" was the wrong way of putting it when Dominic gestured wildly at the mess surrounding the back of the bed and breakfast, and Glen held up his hands in an explanatory way. Dominic certainly didn't look happy, though.

The sliding glass door slid open, and Hunter jumped even though he could plainly see Dominic still arguing with Glen out the window.

His glass overflowed, and he quickly turned off the faucet. Rose came up behind him, shaking her head as she glanced out the window.

"What are they arguing about now?"

She sighed. "Glen says they need to redo the wiring, but I don't think Dominic has the money."

"I thought he budgeted."

"He did, before Glen took an extra three months, before we lost Sean.... That's changed a lot."

Hunter took a long drink of his water, still wiping sweat from his brow as he turned from the scene in the backyard. Rose had her arms crossed again, fingers tapping against her forearm almost nervously. She glanced up at him after a second.

"I'm worried."

"It'll all work out," he said flippantly, taking another sip. "Glen's just a blowhard. Put some pressure on him and it'll get done on time."

"Not about that," she said, "about Dominic."

Hunter rolled his eyes. "Look, I told you there's nothing we can do."

"I know, but that doesn't mean I'm not worried. When Sean was here, he could always calm him down, talk him out of doing stupid things, like that one year he wanted to have a Christmas party down on the docks in the middle of the snow. Now, what are we going to do when Dominic gets frustrated?"

"Toss him off the end of the dock," Hunter replied, draining the last of his water. He shrugged. "Why don't you stop worrying about him for a minute?"

"If I don't, who will?" she demanded. "You never think of anyone else. If we're going to keep this place afloat, someone's got to think about it."

"I just know when to stop pushing," Hunter retorted, setting his glass in the sink and glancing out the window, but Dominic and Glen had disappeared. "Clearly not something you're skilled in."

"Being pushy gets things done," she replied, eyes narrowing. "At least I'm not a lazy deckhand who just sits around all day pushing people off into the lake."

"I do other things."

"Only because Sean is gone and you have to now."

"Why are you arguing about Sean?"

Dominic's voice cut through them, and they both jumped, turning quickly.

"Jesus, Dom," Hunter muttered, exhaling slowly.

Dominic merely arched an eyebrow, looking between the two. Rose fidgeted under his gaze like a guilty child, but Hunter held his ground.

"Rose, I want you to clean the carpets in rooms two and three today, and since you seem to have nothing better to do, Hunter, you can do room number four. Scrub out the bathrooms while you're at it."

Hunter glared at Rose, whose shoulders drooped.

"Good job making things easier," he muttered as they trooped up the stairs together. Rose glared instead.

"Shut up."

Chapter 7
Room Service

"Why do I have to make breakfast if there are no guests?" Nathan asked, setting down a plate in front of Dominic, who rustled the paper and didn't glance up.

"It's just a slow week. There will be guests soon. The harvest starts this weekend, and then there's a festival."

Nathan paused, looking down at Dominic, sliding a hand to the back of his chair as he leaned into his space.

"About those apple tarts, are you going to be my taste-tester?" He ran a hand along Dominic's arm even as Dominic jerked it away.

Looking up, the paper crumpled in his hands, Dominic arched an eyebrow at Nathan. Nathan's eyes were dark with intent, and the corner of his mouth curled into a smirk despite Dominic's unimpressed gaze.

"I'll have Rose do it," he said firmly, shaking the paper back up, but it didn't deter Nathan.

Nathan slid into the neighboring chair, scooting it closer to Dominic's.

"But you have a much more refined palate. I mean, you hired me."

"Nathan," he said tiredly, nudging him away as he leaned in. "Go do the dishes."

Rolling his eyes, Nathan scoffed and leaned back. "You were more fun when you wanted to fuck."

Dominic ignored him, turning the page in the paper as Nathan left him alone. He just wanted to read the paper in peace and not think about Nathan or Glen or the addition or all the money he was currently losing.

He froze as his eyes fell on the front page of the living section, the small picture in the corner accompanied by the headline, "New Chef Cooks Up More Than Delicious Calamari."

Dominic's eyes moved too fast as he tried to read, to absorb it all in the same moment, but he forced himself to slow down, catching snatches of paragraphs.

Newly appointed head chef at Fever, one of Seattle's premier restaurants, Sean Nichols has certainly proven to the rest of us that fine cuisine can come at any price! In less than a month, Fever's menu has been transformed from stuffy haute cuisine to delicious new dishes most people might never think to try, like his spicy calamari dipped in a cool cucumber sauce.

Nichols is quite modest about the transformation to the restaurant, where lines often exceed an hour to get a seat on the weekends.

"I'm really just here to cook good food," he says with a charming smile as he puts on his chef's hat for the day.

Good food isn't all he's cooking up, though! With Nichols' vigor in the kitchen, his enthusiasm has spread to the rest of the restaurant, and patrons are more than willing to wait the extra time to get a seat.

One guest, Rebecca Sanchez, said she'd sell her firstborn to eat at Fever every night if Nichols was cooking.

Dominic didn't read the rest, which was surely going to be nothing but praise. Instead, his stomach felt hollow, as if it had completely fallen out of his body. The paper crumpled in his hands, and he dropped it on the table.

Most of the time, he tried to pretend Sean was off in some distant country where they didn't have news or TV or internet, and that's why he never called, and why Dominic never went to visit him. It would have been better if he was because things like this made Dominic's stomach twist painfully, an unpleasant feeling welling up inside him.

Of course everyone would love Sean in his new job. They probably revered him as some sort of a god.

Dominic stared unseeingly at the paper in front of him, thoughts unbroken even by the rush of a saw outside, the shout of a construction worker in the back. Sean really had gone, and he shouldn't have been surprised. Hadn't he told him to? Well, it didn't matter now.

"There are no dishes to do," Nathan said, appearing in the doorway and looking bored, arms crossed over his chest. His hair fell into his eyes, but he didn't shake it away, arching an eyebrow at Dominic.

Turning the paper over, Sean's face disappeared, and Dominic drew himself together, a wave of something closer to anger washing over him. Sean could go be a big shot in the city for all he cared. Everything was fine here. They didn't need Sean. Dominic didn't need Sean.

He glanced up sharply at Nathan, and Nathan eyed him carefully.

"Come with me," he said suddenly, rising from the chair, and Nathan didn't question him, a smile gracing his features as he followed Dominic towards the back hallway.

Rose came in the front door as they passed the desk, and Dominic opened the door that led to the hallway, his office, and the bedroom.

"Where are you going?" she asked, but Dominic grabbed Nathan's shirt and pulled him in after.

Shocked, Rose stood there as the door shut behind them. For a moment, she didn't move, but then she took halted steps towards the table, picking up the newspaper to get the plate underneath. As she turned it over, she caught sight of Sean's picture and her heart fell. Glancing at the closed door, she sighed and refolded the paper instead.

One Year Previously.

"Oh, Jesus," Sean cursed, fingers curling around the sheets of the unfamiliar bed, face pressed into the pillow as he bit his lip and pushed back against Dominic's tongue curling against his entrance.

Dominic's hands grabbed Sean's hips, pulling him back flush as he licked inside him, already slick with spit. He didn't stop at Sean's choked noises, the whimper as he pushed his tongue in deeper. Dominic knew Sean always liked this, liked the dirtiness of Dominic's mouth pressed against his ass, licking deep inside him until he could come just from that, without any other touches.

Dominic didn't touch Sean then, aside from smoothing over his ass cheeks, pulling them apart as he delved in deeper, listening to Sean's shaky breathing in the hotel room.

They should have been outside in the warm spring sunshine, eating at a fancy restaurant in town or taking a walk around the park, but Dominic wouldn't choose to be anywhere but here as Sean gasped loudly, biting down on the pillow to muffle the sound.

Dominic didn't slow down, licking around his entrance, pushing his tongue through the tight muscles until Sean was whining, high-pitched and desperate as his hips ground down against the mattress. He was close, Dominic could tell; from the way Sean's thighs trembled, the way his fingers clenched around the sheets and pulled.

"Dom," he managed to gasp a second before he came, hips stuttering forward against the bed, gasping for breath.

Pulling back slowly, Dominic took a second to regain his breath, sliding his hands up Sean's sides as Sean slid down, carefully avoiding the mess beneath him.

Sean hummed contentedly as Dominic moved up his back, pressing a kiss to his shoulder blade, mouth grazing up to his neck, and he squirmed, smiling as he turned to Dominic. He looked ruffled and sated as Dominic lay down beside him.

"Happy anniversary," he murmured, reaching out and grazing his fingers over Dominic's forearm. Stretching, he scooted in towards Dominic, who pulled him closer with a sigh.

Dominic could hardly believe it had been two years already, two years since they'd gotten together. Sometimes he kicked himself for waiting so long.

Dominic didn't reply, leaning forward to kiss Sean. He wasn't surprised when Sean pulled him in closer, humming against his mouth and pulling Dominic on top of him.

"We should go do something," Dominic tried to say a minute later, but Sean shook his head, dragging him back and smiling against his mouth.

"We are doing something," he replied, licking Dominic's lower lip slowly, gaze crawling up to Dominic.

"I meant something outside."

Sean made a face, pushing aside Dominic's hair and brushing his nose against Dominic's. "Outside is overrated. Outside bad, inside good."

"It's not much of a trip," Dominic said as Sean kissed him again, "if you don't go outside." His words were lost to Sean's mouth, though, and he groaned into the kiss. Technically they didn't need to go outside, he supposed.

"It's our anniversary," Sean replied, and Dominic ignored the jolt in his stomach that happened every time Sean said it. It shouldn't have been so shocking, but considering how long most of Dominic's other relationships had lasted, two years was a miracle. "We can do whatever we want."

Sean reached down to where Dominic was still hard, hand curling around his cock and stroking once.

"Shit," Dominic breathed at Sean's touch, knowing he was losing this round.

"Mmm," Sean agreed, pushing his tongue into Dominic's mouth. His hand moved slowly, fingers dragging against the skin, rough and hot.

Dominic tried not to give in, but Sean always knew just where to touch to get him going, not that it ever took much when it came to Sean.

Sean sucked on Dominic's bottom lip as his hand tightened for a second, then relaxed, sliding down.

"I love you," Sean breathed against his mouth, and Dominic's heart skipped a beat, chest tightening, but he tried not to panic, not responding as he ducked his chin instead, focusing on Sean's hand around his prick.

He couldn't remember the last time anyone had said that to him, and if he was honest with himself, he was surprised Sean hadn't said it sooner considering how open he was. That didn't mean he was prepared for it, though, and he could force himself to say it back, and he knew Sean would want him to. That was why people said it, wasn't it?

Sean's hand moved faster, though, and Dominic concentrated on the rough slide of his hand against his cock instead.

His eyes fluttered shut as the heat spread, flushing up his collarbone and cheeks as he bit back a groan and came, heart pounding furiously in his ears.

Sean pulled his hand away slowly as Dominic didn't move, licking his lips and taking a steadying breath.

Dominic cursed to himself as Sean was silent.

"Dom," Sean said a second later, and Dominic glanced up finally, pushing back his hair and pushing down the anxiety rising in his chest.

For a second, Dominic was sure Sean was going to say it again, to ask if he'd heard, but he didn't, pulling him up and kissing him softly. Dominic took over the kiss a second later, knowing he couldn't say it, couldn't do anything about the pain Sean was probably feeling right now. He just couldn't do it.

Sean didn't mention it, though, as Dominic pulled away and rolled to the side, grabbing the hand towel they'd thrown there earlier and cleaning up a little.

"Do you still want to go out?" Sean asked a minute later, glancing at the clock on the nightstand. It was nearly dinnertime.

Dominic paused a second, staring up at the ceiling. It wasn't like his ceiling at home, and nowadays he found it odd staying at other hotels. He was always noticing things they did differently.

"If you're hungry," Dominic replied, glancing over at Sean, who shrugged.

Sean smiled, though, after a second, softly. "It's not much of a trip if you don't go outside, right?"

"Fuck it," Dom said, rolling over and kissing Sean again, ignoring the guilt, the confusion jumbling his stomach. "Let's order in."

Sean hummed in agreement, and Dominic broke away to reach for the telephone on the table. As he dialed room service, he tried not to think about Sean's words and if he could ever say them back.

"Get some champagne," Sean said, sitting up and sliding his hands over Dominic's shoulders. He pressed a kiss to Dominic's neck, and Dominic only nodded.

Sean was ignoring it for now, but they couldn't ignore it forever.

"Glen!" Dominic said as he clattered down the stairs of the back porch to where Glen stood under the large maple tree.

"Ah, just the man I wanted to see," Glen replied simply as Dominic strode towards him.

"This is getting ridiculous," Dominic said, gesturing to the shell of the rooms, exposed wiring visible and garbled spray painted Xs in places. "I'm not paying you to break everything!"

Glen held up his hands. "You know how these things go. Accidents happen, and we're on our way to fixing it." He waved away some of the guys working nearby. They grabbed their tools and trotted off, probably to break something else. "We got the walls up."

Dominic frowned. "Two months late," he pointed out sharply. "I don't care what it takes, but you get the roof done by next week or I'm finding a new contractor. And don't tell me things are back-ordered. Get them here or we're done."

"Gotta tear things down to rebuild it right," Glen said, puffing up his chest slightly.

Dominic glared. He was getting tired of listening to Glen's excuses, the extra time and money this was all taking, how many of his guests had complained about the noise or the shirtless men puffing around in the backyard. Even Hunter had complained about them trampling his perfectly manicured plants.

Frustrated, Dominic shook his head. This had to get done and soon. He knew Hunter was frustrated with him, and Rose was too nice to actually say anything, but even she seemed strained the last time he'd seen her.

"You just stop wrecking everything in sight, and fix the pipes!" he said angrily, poking Glen hard in his pudgy stomach.

Turning on his heel, he strode back into the lobby only to be met by Rose.

"Oh, there you are," she said, and he sighed. "We're almost out of soap. Should I order another batch? And last time, the guy asked about changing the logo."

Dominic didn't have time to worry about soap, not when Nathan emerged from the kitchen, immediately coming over and placing his hands on his shoulders.

"Hey," Nathan breathed in his ear, and Dominic gritted his jaw. He really wasn't in the mood, and Nathan wasn't someone he wanted to see right now. The other day had been a mistake, clearly. "Want to take a relaxing nap?"

Rose frowned disapprovingly, and Dominic couldn't say he disagreed. Stepping out of Nathan's grip, he turned to him, a tight smile on his face.

"What I want is for you to get back in that kitchen and make apple tarts until you never want to eat apples again." He turned to Rose. "Don't order any soap. It's not like we're going to need it."

He left them both in the lobby and strode to his office, locking the door behind him. He just needed to be alone to figure this all out. He could figure it out, and he didn't need anyone's help.

Rose frowned at Nathan as he emerged from the back hall, the door snapping shut behind him, but Nathan merely shrugged and wandered off. Annoyed, she decided not to go after him and give him a lecture on proper work etiquette, which didn't include sleeping with the boss.

Instead, she strode out the back door, past Glen and his crew, and down the path to the docks. It was strewn with leaves now, but the boat was still tied up in its usual spot as she reached the end.

"Hunter?" she called, looking around. She spotted him a few feet down the path that led around the lake.

Hunter was bent over a spot in the grass but rose, a little duckling in his hands. Turning to the lake, he let it go, watching it swim away, quacking loudly.

"What?" he asked as Rose reached him, cleaning his hands in the lake. The water was chilly now, and he shook it off as he rose.

She paused, watching him a minute. "Look, I know you think I'm being nosy, and that I should just butt out, but I can't. I can't watch the bed and breakfast fall apart all because of Dominic's stubbornness. We're running out of basic things and can't afford to buy more. You and I are both working too much as it is, and don't get me started on Nathan."

Hunter didn't interrupt, watching her with an arched eyebrow. A golden leaf fluttered to the ground at his feet, and a cool breeze swept up from the water.

"We have to do something before he self-destructs, and if you don't want to help me, then fine, but I'm not waiting anymore."

Hunter was silent for a moment, gazing across the water. The mountain in the distance was already covered in snow almost to the tree line. It wouldn't be long before the snow was everywhere. Finally, he turned to her.

"What did you have in mind?"

Rose stared, surprised, but she smiled after a second and was glad to see Hunter return it.

Chapter 8
Sleepless in Honey Creek

"Half an hour just to get in?" Hunter said, pulling at his jacket. The sleeves felt too tight. He didn't like dressing up, and he didn't see why they had to just to talk to Sean.

"Well, we don't know where he lives, so this is the only option," Rose reminded him under her breath as they sat at their table, surrounded by happy, laughing groups of people. "Besides, you'll finally get a decently-cooked meal."

"Yeah, haven't had one of those in a while," he muttered, shoving back his hair and glancing around.

The restaurant was one of those too-hip-for-its-own-good places with different colored lighting over every table, reds and blues bathing the place like a night club. The pictures on the walls were in black and white, artsy photographs of old jazz clubs, and Hunter wished he was back in his little shack of a house he rented on the edge of town.

"Do you think we should just go talk to him?"

"How? Sneak in the back?"

Rose shrugged. "Maybe. Maybe we can ask to talk to him."

Hunter tilted his head to the side doubtfully. "He's a big shot chef now. He doesn't have time to talk to everyone who asks."

"Then I'll think of something," she shot back, gesturing at a server that passed by. The man stepped up eagerly.

"Yes?"

"Hi, I was wondering if we could talk to the chef. We're old friends."

The server hesitated. "Well, he's busy right now."

Hunter shot Rose an obvious look.

"If we could just get a minute? I'm his sister, Rose."

Hunter's eyebrows went up, but she shot him a look not to say anything. The waiter hesitated again.

"I'll go check."

As he scurried away, Hunter leaned over the table. "His sister? You two sure look a lot alike."

"Be quiet," she said, frowning. "He went to ask at least."

Hunter rolled his eyes. "And Sean's gonna get that? He doesn't have any siblings."

"At least I'm coming up with something instead of dumping on every idea. If it doesn't work, at least I tri—"

"Rose!"

Sean's voice behind them caught them both off-guard, and they turned. Rose was already halfway out of her seat as Sean grabbed her in a hug.

"And Hunter!" he said as he caught sight of Hunter over her shoulder. He let go of her finally and pulled Hunter into a hug as well. "What are you guys doing here?"

"Just came by to sample the local cuisine," Hunter replied when Sean let him go.

Sean grinned, eyes sparkling as he looked between them. Something else flickered there for a minute as he took in the table, only two glasses. It was gone in a blink, though, and he shook his head.

"I can't believe you're here," he said, smiling and hugging Rose again. "God, it feels like it's been forever."

"I missed you," Rose said, squeezing him tightly. "It's just not the same without you."

"I'm sure you're managing," Sean replied, ducking his head slightly and glancing at Hunter, but Hunter frowned slightly. "Are you staying in town for the night? I really should get back to the kitchen, but I'd love to talk."

"Yeah, we need to talk," Hunter replied slowly, and Rose shot him a glare.

She smiled at Sean, though. "Yeah, we can stay. What time do you get off?"

"You're lucky. I get off at a decent time tonight. I should be done by eleven. There's a great coffee place just around the corner from here. Could you meet me there?"

"We'll be there." Rose nodded.

Sean grinned. "Great. Oh, I'm so glad you guys are here."

As he left for the kitchen, Rose turned to Hunter.

"Could you try to be a little more subtle?"

"Sorry," he said, shrugging obviously. "I just thought that's what we were here for."

"Not to scare him."

Hunter sat back down in his seat, reaching for his drink. "I don't see how it won't."

Rose sighed as she sunk into her seat and frowned across the restaurant to where Sean had disappeared.

The coffee was good, Hunter thought as they picked a table out of the way of the main thoroughfare.

"Seattle's great," Sean said as they sat down, grouped around the small table. "The people are nice, and they seem to like the food."

"I'm sure they do," Rose said, patting his arm and smiling softly at him.

Sean looked between them, though. "So, what's been going on? It's the apple festival this weekend, right? How's the B&B?"

Rose and Hunter exchanged a glance, and Sean's expression grew concerned.

"We need you back," Hunter said bluntly, and Rose didn't even bother reprimanding him.

"What?" Sean's eyebrows furrowed as he glanced between them.

Rose sighed, her hand closing around his arm. "It's true. Everything's falling apart without you. *Dominic's* falling apart without you. The bed and breakfast is in chaos, but he just ignores it, and he won't listen to either of us."

"So you want me to come back?" he asked slowly, and she nodded.

"We need you."

Sean paused, looking at Hunter, who shrugged and gripped his coffee. "It's getting pretty bad."

Sean took a sip of his coffee after a minute, brushing his hair back. "Dominic doesn't know you're here, does he?"

Rose's face was covered in guilt as she grimaced. "Well, no, but you know him. He's not going to admit he failed until he's living in a box on the street."

Sean sighed, shaking his head. "I know you guys probably mean well, but I can't help Dom."

"You're the only one who can," Rose said seriously, staring at him with pleading eyes. He shook his head again.

"I'm not coming back, guys. I like it here. My job is great. I have a nice apartment. I've made friends. And if Dom doesn't want to come ask for himself, I'm not going to put myself through it again." He sighed, swirling the coffee in his cup as Rose and Hunter watched. "I'm sorry about the B&B, really. I love that place as much as you guys do, you know that. But there's nothing I can do to help. I'm sorry."

"Don't be sorry," Rose said, sliding an arm around his shoulders and giving him a squeeze. "We just want you back is all."

Sean nodded. "I know."

Hunter sat back in his seat, staring at his coffee. He didn't say anything the rest of the evening until Rose excused herself to the bathroom, leaving them alone.

"Are you mad at me?" Sean asked as she disappeared, and Hunter set down his empty cup.

"I won't say cleaning ovens is fun," he said, "but I get why you're not coming back."

"I would if Dominic...." Sean trailed off, shaking his head uselessly. "It doesn't matter."

Hunter leaned forward, elbows on his knees, and looked at Sean seriously for a moment. "I've known Dominic for a long time now, and he's the most stubborn person I've ever met, but there's a reason he pushed you away."

"He didn't want me to stay. He never even said he loved me," Sean muttered into his coffee.

Hunter shrugged. "Maybe he didn't, but a lot of people in his life have just left, and when people leave you, you stop hoping that they'll stay. You start waiting for them to leave instead, and when they do, you're not disappointed."

Sean frowned. "What are you talking about?"

"You ever wonder why Dom's parents never come to visit?"

"They're divorced, aren't they?"

"Yeah. When he was eight or something. And his dad's been married four more times since then. I think it'll be number five next spring."

Sean didn't say anything, rubbing his forehead and twirling his cup in his hands.

"So are we ready to get out of here?" Rose asked as she came back, smiling sadly at Sean, who shook himself.

"I wish you didn't have to go," he said, rising from his chair and drawing her into a hug.

"We've got a bed and breakfast to save," she replied quietly, giving him an extra squeeze before she pulled back. "And don't be afraid to come visit, even for the day. You're still our cook."

"We'll see you," Hunter said, giving Sean a quick hug. "I hope Seattle is everything you've ever wanted."

Sean bit his lip as Hunter moved away, a hand guiding Rose towards the exit.

"Bye," he said as they reached the door, and they both turned one last time before they were gone.

The sun shone brightly overhead, but Dominic wasn't in a very sunshine-y mood as he sat behind his booth next to Nathan, an array of decent-tasting tarts in front of them. They weren't nearly as good as Sean's might have been, but they were edible, and that was what mattered.

"You know, if you get bored," Nathan said, sliding a hand over to Dominic's knee. "We could ditch this booth and have some fun behind the fun house."

"There is no fun house," Dominic replied shortly, pushing his hand away with a stern look. "And no one's ditching anything. Try to be charming for a few hours at least."

Nathan rolled his eyes and looked away, down the main street where the rest of the booths were set-up. Plenty of tourists and locals milled around the leaf-strewn street, making impressed noises at the different booths.

They'd sold a few tarts so far and given away a few more business cards, but it just wasn't the same. All Dominic could think of was his half-demolished bed and breakfast and the scattered remains Glen's crew had left behind last Tuesday when Dominic had finally had enough. He'd fired Glen, but all that had left him with was a half-finished addition and winter looming on the horizon. If he didn't get it finished now, he'd have to wait until spring to start again which would mean another entire season ruined by hammers and saws, not to mention he was quickly running out of money for the project. He'd cut as many corners as he could in the B&B, but without getting another loan or winning the lottery, he was practically screwed.

He had to get it done, though, and that meant finding a new contractor, one who wasn't going to make excuses about timing and supplies. He'd find the money somewhere. He didn't want to think about all the money that had already been wasted on the addition so far, or all of Glen's excuses.

The only bright side was they'd managed to fix the pipes. Dominic wasn't sure if he would have been able to explain to guests in the dead of winter that they had no hot water.

"Honey Creek Inn?" a man asked as he stepped up to the booth, glancing at the array of tarts and jars of applesauce.

Forcing himself to focus and ignore the sultry look Nathan was shooting at him, Dominic put on a smile.

"We are Honey Creek's premier bed and breakfast, right on the lake and with access to hiking trails and skiing in the winter, boating in the summer."

"I heard you were having a little trouble," the man said thoughtfully, and Dominic didn't frown, but took a longer second to look at the man.

He wore a suit jacket over a tee-shirt and a pair of black slacks. He had to be in his late thirties with jet black hair and a chiseled chin. He looked friendly enough, though, as he turned over a jar of apple butter in his hands.

"I've seen the place," he said when he caught Dominic watching him. "Walked down the other day just to take a look. It's a beautiful property."

"Thank you," Dominic replied slowly, still cautious. "Mind me asking what you were looking for?"

"Oh," the man said, digging into his jacket pocket and coming out with a business card. "Name's Derek. I work for a hotel chain and we're always looking for charming properties. Yours is beautiful."

"It's not for sale," Dominic said, barely glancing at the card.

"Sure," Derek replied distractedly, as if he couldn't care less about the property and only the apple tarts interested him at the moment. "But if you do, I'd be prepared to make you a generous offer. A good businessman never turns down an opportunity."

Dominic didn't reply, folding the card in two instead.

Derek set down the jar, twisting it so the label faced forward. "This is from last year's harvest?"

"Yeah." Dominic nodded. "The stuff keeps forever, and last year's was a particularly good year. This year's is a bit sour."

Derek nodded, digging a few dollars out of his wallet, which he handed to Dominic. "Don't lose that card," he said as he turned away. "I'm serious about your bed and breakfast. It's just what we look for."

Dominic's smile lasted just until the man had turned away before it fell into a scowl and he shoved the card into his pocket. He wouldn't be calling Derek.

"Bored yet?" Nathan asked, arching an eyebrow. "There's a spot behind Jessie's boo—"

"Shut up," Dominic interrupted tiredly.

Speaking of Jessie, she came up a moment later, bubbly as always.

"Good morning!" she greeted them. Dominic returned the smile, but Nathan looked away, bored. "Have you gotten many visitors?"

"A few," Dominic replied, straightening the jars on the table.

Jessie glanced at the apple butter. "Is this Sean's?" she asked, turning it over like Derek had.

"Yeah," he muttered.

"Well then, I have to get some," she said, digging out her wallet. "How are things otherwise?"

Dominic didn't sigh, although he wanted to. "You know, slowing down now that summer's over."

She hummed as though she knew. "But it won't be long until the skiers and romantic couples stop by. Maybe we'll even get a wedding this year."

Dominic doubted it, but he didn't want to crush her hopes, so he nodded along, taking the money she handed him.

"Did you go with Rose and Hunter the other day?" she asked, eyeing the tarts interestedly.

"Go where?"

"To see Sean!" she said, smiling curiously at him. "Rose said they went up the other day."

"Did she?" he asked, frowning as annoyance bubbled deep inside him.

"Yes, she said he was doing really well up there. It's just too bad." She sighed sadly. "I guess I was still hoping he might come back, but summer's over. Time to let winter come."

Dominic merely frowned. He couldn't believe Rose had done that. He couldn't believe *Hunter* had done that.

"You know, I shouldn't, but I think I'll have a tart too," Jessie said, pulling a few more dollars out of her wallet.

"What's wrong with you?" Nathan asked after Jessie had left and Dominic hadn't moved for a good two minutes, staring blankly at the booth across the street.

"Take over for a minute," he said suddenly, sliding off his stool and ducking out of the booth. "Don't do anything stupid."

He didn't heed Nathan's rolled eyes as he stepped into the blend of tourists and residents meandering down the street. He moved intently, checking every booth he passed, but he didn't find what he was looking for, not until he came upon Bill's booth.

"No, Hunter," Rose protested as Hunter tried to push a glass of hard apple cider into her hands. "Don't you remember last year?"

"That was Dom, not you. Come on, give it a try."

Bill grinned. "It'll put some hair on your chest!"

Rose looked even less likely to take it now.

"Dominic!" Bill called as he caught sight of him. "Can I tempt you?"

"No, thanks," he replied shortly, turning to Hunter and Rose. "You went to Seattle?"

Rose's eyes widened, and Hunter tossed back the entire cup. Without waiting for her response, Dominic grabbed both their arms, dragging them to the end of the street and a little ways into the park. There were still people here, but not everyone could see them as he moved behind a clump of trees and waited.

"Well?" he asked expectantly. "Is that where you were on Monday? In Seattle talking to Sean?"

"Yeah," Hunter said finally when Rose just mouthed uselessly. "We went to see Sean. We went to ask him to come back."

"Did I ask you to?" Dominic demanded. Anger welled up inside him, and his hands curled into fists. How could they go behind his back like this? Sean was none of their business.

"No," Hunter said simply, shrugging, and not looking the least bit apologetic.

Dominic glared, drawing himself up to his full height, which was a good few inches above Hunter. "Sean is my business, and you went behind my back to ask him to come back, which I don't want him to. He's gone and that's that, and you should have listened to me the first time. This isn't your problem."

"Yes, it is," Hunter replied angrily. "It's our jobs, the bed and breakfast, our livelihoods, and you're going to let it all go to hell because you can't suck up your pride and go tell Sean how you really feel. Instead, we have to suffer through mediocre cooking, no hot water, overworking, incessant construction, and the constant threat that the bed and breakfast isn't gonna make it without Sean! Just face it, Dom! You need him! And not just to keep the B&B alive. You need him for yourself, for your sanity! You can't possibly like Nathan, that hipster wannabe slut. So get your head out of your ass and fix this!"

Dominic stared, and Rose had her hands pressed to her mouth as she stared at Hunter as well.

Dominic stirred finally, eyes narrowing and shoulders bristling. "This is *my* bed and breakfast, Hunter," he said slowly, deceptively quiet. "And if I want to let it fall into ruin, I can damn well do it. And I don't need you telling me how to run things. If you don't like it, go somewhere else."

Hunter scoffed, rolling his eyes. "Nice try," he shot back. "But I know you better than anyone, and there's no way in hell you're getting rid of me, no matter how stupid you are. I tried to help you out of this mess, but now I'm done."

He threw up his hands as he turned away, stomping back towards Main Street. Rose and Dominic stared after him, but Rose scooted after him quickly enough.

"I should go… talk to him," she said quickly before practically vanishing down the road.

Exhaling slowly, Dominic pushed out the pressure in his chest, the deep clawing in his stomach as Hunter's words took hold. He felt suddenly weak, and he leaned back against a tree trunk, taking deep breaths and watching a butterfly flutter past.

He was screwed. Hunter was right, though it killed him to admit it. The bed and breakfast was falling into disrepair. He had to do something fast if he was going to fix it. He couldn't go to Sean, though. Sean wouldn't want to see him.

He could still fix this, he told himself firmly. There was still the rest of the festival, and he was booked pretty solidly through that, but not enough to get him up to what he needed to continue the addition. It was looking more and more foolish by the day. How could he have been so headstrong? Without Sean, the bed and breakfast was a shell of its former self.

His hand closed around the folded business card in his pocket, but he forced himself to release it. He wouldn't call Derek. He wouldn't sell the bed and breakfast.

The B&B was the only thing he had that was all his, something he could cling to when things went wrong. He'd spent years looking for the right spot, saving up the money for the down payments, to build it in the first place. He could take out another loan, but the amount he'd be in debt made his head swim.

He'd find some way, he told himself. He wasn't ready to give up yet, and he wasn't ready to admit he needed Sean either. He could do it on his own. He'd gotten this far.

Shaking himself, Dominic took a breath and sighed slowly. There was still the festival to get through, and he'd have to be on his toes if he was going to deal with Nathan for the rest of it. He sincerely regretted ever sleeping with him as he trudged back through the park towards the booths. Maybe he would have been better off just leaving Hunter as the cook and living on pancakes forever.

Chapter 9
Last Resorts

Hunter tossed the pieces of wood over into one big pile, occasionally dragging the two-by-fours over and stacking them up. Later, he'd cover them with a tarp to prevent decay over the winter. If they ever got going on the addition again, rotted wood wouldn't be the best way to start. Nails and screws were scattered all over the ground, and he picked up each one, painstakingly making his way through the cover of leaves.

He didn't look up at the sound of footsteps coming down the stairs, recognizing Rose's light steps. He grabbed a few more nails and tucked them in his pocket.

"Have you talked to him?" she asked after the pause lengthened.

A cold breeze shuddered the leaves on the tree overhead. A few more leaves dropped to the ground, one landing on Hunter's shoulder, but he brushed it away.

"Nope," he replied, keeping an eye out for more nails. It wasn't his problem if Dominic wanted to run his bed and breakfast into the ground.

"Maybe he'll fire Nathan."

"Maybe he'll just sell the inn."

Rose frowned, tucking back her hair and wrapping her arms around herself in the chilly autumn air. "Why would you say something like that?"

Hunter shrugged, pushing aside a few leaves with his foot. "Look around, Rose. We've got one guest, winter is coming, and if I have to show Nathan how to turn on the gas burner one more time...." He growled under his breath, grabbing another nail he spotted. "It's time to face the facts. Without Sean, we're all screwed, and Dom's never gonna admit that he needs him. Might as well start looking for work."

Rose stared. "How can you be so pessimistic?"

Straightening up, Hunter sighed. "I know Dom's a good businessman. He was before he met Sean, and he will be afterward, but things are just not working out this time. Might as well start fresh while you're still young enough to do it."

"We could still make it."

"It's nice you believe that," he said, tossing the nails into a bucket. They clanged as they hit the sides. "But it's time to face the music."

She frowned, eyebrows furrowed. "I still have faith that things will be okay."

Hunter shrugged. "Your choice. I choose to be realistic."

Rose crossed her arms instead of answering, and Hunter returned to his search for nails.

At the sliding glass door, Dominic stepped back into the lobby. He crossed the empty room quickly, shutting himself in his office and sinking into the desk chair.

The desk was strewn with papers, most of which made his head hurt from all the money he didn't have. The message machine blinked with a message, but he knew what it said. It was Derek, calling to ask if he'd reconsidered his offer to sell. He should delete it, but for some reason, he hesitated every time he went to press the button.

Was it really coming to this? Had everything really fallen into such disrepair that he'd have to sell?

Back when he'd first built the bed and breakfast, everything had seemed to work out so perfectly. There'd been almost no construction glitches, and he'd found Rose almost immediately after opening. Hunter had come with him, of course. He had never been able to shake him, but at this point, it was useless to try.

Then he'd hired Sean, and things had taken off. Guests loved coming to see Sean, to talk to him. He was almost an attraction, but he was much more than that.

"Knock, knock."

The door opened before Dominic had even looked up, and Nathan stepped into the frame, propping a shoulder against it and taking up most of the space.

"Since the place is dead," Nathan said, inspecting his nails as though painfully bored, though his eyes slid slyly to Dominic after a second. "How about you and I check out your ceiling."

Rising slowly, Dominic placed his hands on the desk, looking Nathan in the eye.

Everything about Nathan annoyed him, from his ridiculously tight jeans to the ring in his nose, and especially the way he eyed him like he was a piece of meat, only good for one thing.

"You're fired."

"What?" Nathan asked, almost laughing, staring at Dominic.

"You're fired," Dominic repeated firmly even as Nathan's face contorted slightly.

"Did you find another cook?" he asked, a slight sneer to his mouth. "Or did your boyfriend come back?"

Dominic blinked, surprised. He'd never talked to Nathan about Sean.

"I know all about the ex," Nathan drawled, shoulders stiff. "Everyone in town talks about it, how dumb you were to let him go, but you're obviously still in love with him."

Dominic stared. "That's none of your business."

"It's why your bed and breakfast is going broke," Nathan replied sharply. "It's why you're gonna have to sell to that hotel guy. It's why you're a jackass to all your staff."

"Well, you don't have to worry about that anymore, because you're not one of the staff," Dominic shot back. "So go get your stuff and get out of here."

Rolling his eyes darkly, Nathan pushed off the doorframe. "Good luck keeping this place alive without a cook."

He left finally, the door snapping shut behind him, and Dominic sunk back into his chair with a long sigh. What little elation he'd felt from firing Nathan was gone, replaced with a sinking feeling of dread. Even Nathan was right. He had to do something if he was going to save the bed and breakfast.

There was really only one option, and he'd known it all along. He just couldn't bring himself to admit it. Everyone else had said it, over and over again, but he always pushed them away because admitting it would mean admitting a lot of things he tried never to think about.

But did he really have a choice? Was he really going to let his own pride be the determining force between success and failure? And did he really have the strength to suck it up and do what he needed to in order to survive?

Dominic didn't know any of the answers, and he dropped his head down on the desk. Things were never meant to be this complicated.

The message machine beeped at him, and he groaned, slapping the 'ignore' button and sighing into the desk.

Everything was falling apart. Dominic couldn't stand it. Frustrated, he left the office and headed for his bedroom.

Dominic sunk down onto the bed, staring out the small window. He could just see the treetops, golden and red, blowing in the wind. Somewhere in the distance, Vanilla barked. He was surprised Sean hadn't even bothered to try to take Vanilla with him. They'd gotten her together, picked her out of a roly-poly litter of puppies nearly three years ago. She'd always liked Sean better, but then, so did everyone else.

He sighed, yanking open the drawer in the bedside table. The box of condoms there was still half-full, and he pushed them aside, hand falling on a book.

Pulling it out slowly, he sighed at the cracked cover of *Jane Eyre*. He slipped it open to the bookmark, glancing down the page, eyes falling on a section of text someone had marked with a pen. It certainly hadn't been him. Dominic hated when people wrote in books. It must have been Sean.

I am strangely glad to get back again to you: and wherever you are is my home—my only home.

He stared at the passage for a long moment. He'd read that book plenty of times, but he never remembered that passage. Sean must have, though. Sean always did remember things like that.

Closing the book, he set it on the table, sitting in the silence of the room. There was only one option left, he just didn't know if he could take it.

Dominic didn't know what he was doing as he stood outside in the shivering cold, a slight mist persisting as he debated with himself, unable to go through the doors.

He moved out of the way as two women bustled out the door.

"Did you hear what the chef did last week?" one asked, as she opened her umbrella and peered up towards the rain. "He came out for some couple's tenth wedding anniversary and personally congratulated them. He even made a special mini-cake! I wish I'd seen it."

"He's so sweet," said the other one, pulling on her jacket.

"And hot," the girl said. "I wonder if he's single."

They stepped away down the street, and Dominic frowned. Could he really do this?

He could, he told himself firmly. He had to. It was his only chance for saving the bed and breakfast, and he had to get Sean to come back. He… he needed Sean.

It pained him to admit it, to admit that he'd been wrong this whole time, and he wasn't sure if he'd actually be able to say it once he got in there. The sheer terror of actually admitting it to Sean made his stomach twist up in knots. He'd never so much as admitted to caring about anyone he'd dated, let alone told them that he needed them.

His breath fogged before him as he let out a slow breath, fortifying himself. He could do this.

Inside the restaurant, Dominic saw immediately why Sean would love it. Despite the largeness of it, it was also small and intimate in spaces, not too high-brow or a slum. The atmosphere was pleasantly noisy, no cello bands in the corner or candles on the table.

It was already late, probably near closing time, but Dominic wasn't there to eat, so he ignored the host telling him they couldn't seat him, and headed for the kitchen.

It probably wasn't proper protocol, but he didn't care. He didn't want to waste time anymore, not when he was so close to fixing everything.

The door to the kitchens was shut, but Dominic could see in through the two small windows in the top. A few people bustled by, but all in all, everyone seemed to be moving slowly, more relaxed now that the night was nearly over.

As a server came out, Dominic caught a snatch of laughter, Sean's laughter, and his heart clenched. Moving over carefully, he glanced in the window, finding Sean standing over a dessert, drizzling chocolate artistically over the top. He grinned at something someone said, eyes lighting up as he finished the dessert with a chocolate disk on top.

He said something as he straightened up, gesturing at the creation, and the few people present gave a cheer.

He looks so happy, Dominic thought, a cold clench of dread squeezing his stomach. It had been a long time since Dominic had seen that smile, and he wanted more than anything for Sean to always look like that. Even if it was here and not with him.

He took a step backwards, turning away. He couldn't do it.

"Dom?"

A voice stopped him ten feet from the kitchen door, and he paused. He could see the front door, the host turning around the open/closed sign.

"Dom?" the voice spoke again, and he turned around slowly to face Sean.

"Hi."

Sean stared at him in disbelief. In his hand, he clutched his chef's apron, but his eyes darted over Dominic's face as if to make sure he was real.

"What... what are you doing here?" Sean asked finally, ignoring the people who called goodbyes to him as they passed.

Dominic didn't know what to say, now that he was faced with Sean. "Nothing," he said as the pause lengthened between them. "I have to...." He started to turn, but Sean took a few quick steps forward.

"Wait," he said, reaching for Dominic's arm. "Why'd you come?"

Dominic shrugged. "I was just in town," he lied, "but I should get back."

Sean paused, eyes meeting Dom's, and Dominic resisted the urge to look away. This had been a stupid idea in the first place. He'd actually been ready to ruin everything that Sean had always worked for? For what? His little bed and breakfast? His own, stupid, selfish reasons.

Sean tilted his head to the side in a way that made Dominic want to take back everything he was feeling.

"Do you have to leave right now?"

Dominic glanced at him slowly, hating the ache in his stomach as he took him in. The months hadn't changed him much except his hair, which was slightly longer. He looked as lean and healthy as ever.

"I guess not this very second," he said, and Sean smiled, fingers tightening over his arm.

Chapter 10
No Vacancy

They didn't get coffee or anything so mundane, and by the time they made it back to Sean's apartment, Dominic was having trouble remembering why he'd wanted to leave.

The door slammed shut behind them, and Dominic shoved Sean up against it. The keys dropped to the ground near their feet, but Sean was already dragging Dominic into a hard kiss, groaning against his mouth.

Sean's skin was warm to the touch despite the chill from outside. Dominic felt him exhale softly, a half moan against his mouth as Dominic's hands shoved his jacket off and slid under his shirt. His fingers were cold, and Sean jerked slightly.

Dominic didn't even take in the room as Sean pushed back against him, forcing them from the door. He tripped over something on the floor, a shoe or something, but his focus was on Sean, Sean's mouth, his hands against his stomach, pushing insistently at his shirt.

"God," Sean breathed when he pulled away long enough to get Dominic's shirt over his head, and Dominic worked intently on Sean's belt. "I missed you."

Dominic's eyes flicked up, half a second's pause as something heavy settled in the pit of his stomach, but luckily, Sean didn't seem to expect him to respond.

Sean kissed him before he could say anything, and his back hit the couch. It was rushed and not finessed as he got Sean's jeans apart, dragging the zipper down and shoving his hand inside.

Sean broke away with a gasp, biting his lower lip and reaching for Dominic's hips. He leaned into Dominic's neck, licking up his throat and sucking the soft skin under his jaw.

It had been far too long, Dominic thought dimly, eyes shutting at the feeling of Sean's mouth on his skin, biting and licking, sucking until a red patch blossomed under his lips. Sean still knew all the right places to touch him, to get exactly what he wanted.

Sean's cock was hard and heavy in his hand, a perfect fit as he stroked him slowly, building him up, feeling the tension in his body, the push of his hips grinding with him.

"Dom," Sean breathed, a sigh in his words, hands sliding up Dominic's bare stomach, tracing every inch of his skin.

Dominic squeezed Sean's cock once before shoving him away roughly. Sean stumbled back, but no trace of surprise crossed his face, only half a smile as he came back, enveloping Dominic in a warm hug as he pressed their foreheads together.

"You came to see me, didn't you?" he whispered, nose brushing against Dominic's. His breath ghosted over Dominic's lips, but Dominic didn't reply.

Instead, Dominic kissed Sean, fast and hard as they stumbled back, dropping to the roughly carpeted floor.

Sean didn't complain about the scratch of the carpet against his back, only dragged Dominic's mouth to his, unwilling to let him go very far.

Dominic couldn't believe how much he'd missed this, the easy slide of Sean's body in his hands, the way he knew the right way to move underneath him, not trapped but not trying to escape.

They were both panting when they broke apart, but Dominic wasted no time, shoving Sean's jeans off and going for his chest, licking and sucking his way down as Sean whined above him.

"Where's your stuff?" he asked, tongue circling a nipple as Sean groaned and stretched his neck back.

"B-bathroom," Sean panted, gasping at Dominic's teeth nipping at his skin, hands skating down his hips and pressing into his thighs.

Dominic made a soft noise, pushing himself up after a second. He didn't glance back but heard Sean's loud exhale as he searched for the bathroom. It wasn't hard to find in such a small apartment, and he pulled open the drawers, looking for the condoms.

As he pulled out the box – brand new, he noted – his eyes fell on a picture taped to the mirror. It was the same one Jessie'd had in her shop, the edges wrinkled and faded. He paused a second, staring at Sean's face. Then his eyes flicked to the other photos, pictures of people he didn't know, at a bar, in a restaurant, at Fever.

Shaking himself, he grabbed the lube and turned from the mirror, stepping back into the living room.

Sean still lay on the floor, staring up at the ceiling, but he looked back as Dominic paused. He smiled after a second.

"What?"

For a second, nothing had changed. They were just on vacation somewhere, somewhere far from the bed and breakfast, and there were no problems between them. Dominic knew it wasn't true, but he didn't want to listen to the ache in his heart as he dropped to his knees beside Sean and crawled back over him, shoving off his jeans and tearing open the condom.

He rolled it on and flipped open the lube, ignoring the way Sean gazed up at him. There was no uncertainty this time, not like the first time, only a calm, cool demeanor, a thrum of excitement in the air.

Pushing Sean's knees up, he scooted in, ignoring the way he hesitated a second. He'd never hesitated before. Sean didn't seem to notice, though, eyes watching him intently as he pushed his fingers in.

He didn't want to take too long, dragging his fingers against the inside of Sean's body, listening to the sharp intake of breath as he stretched him. He looked away as he pulled his fingers out and shifted forward until their hips were flush, the head of his cock against Sean's entrance.

Sean cursed almost immediately, letting out a breathy exhale as Dominic slid inside. He tilted his head back, stretching out his neck, and Dominic leaned in without thinking, licking a stripe up his skin, listening for Sean's whine that always followed.

The heat coursing through Dominic's body only seemed to increase with each movement he made, each slide and thrust as he pushed into Sean. He couldn't help admiring the strain in Sean's body, the pull of the muscles in his stomach, the pressure of his legs wrapped around him, heels digging into his lower back.

Sean's fingers wrapped around his hips, pulling him in sharply, searching for the right angle that made his toes curl, for them both to lose the control Dominic always tried so desperately to hold on to.

The carpet was rough against the palm of his hand as Dominic pressed against it to keep his balance as his hips thrust into Sean, harder and faster now, a desperation in both their movements. Dominic *needed* this, more than he'd ever needed Nathan.

"Dom, *Dom*," Sean gasped, breath catching with each sharp push of Dominic's hips, each little jolt as their bodies met and melded together.

Groaning, Dominic leaned down, meeting Sean for a kiss that was anything but finessed, a mess of teeth and tongues sliding together, Sean's teeth sinking into his bottom lip, panted breath between them.

His skin felt hot, sweat beading along his collarbone, on the back of his neck as he pushed in, rocking with Sean's hips, needing to get off. He reached for Sean's cock as he felt the tightening in his stomach, the quick clench.

As he listened to Sean groan, cock hot in his hand, he cursed under his breath, chest seizing up as he thrust in again and everything exploded.

He groaned loudly, head bowed down, hand still tight over Sean's prick but barely moving as he came, hips pushing in erratically, unable to stop.

"Shit," Sean said a minute later, mouth falling open.

Dominic felt the hot come cover his fingers a second after that, wet and slick as he pulled his hand away.

Letting out a shaky breath, Dominic pulled out slowly, wiping his hands on Sean's jeans a few feet away. Sean didn't protest, breathing hard as he lay on the floor, gazing up at Dom. Dominic settled on the floor a second later, staring up at the ceiling.

That wasn't why he'd come, not that it had been bad. His stomach ached as he lay there, thinking about what he was supposed to say, why he'd come there at all.

"So are you gonna tell me?" Sean asked once the silence had lengthened.

"What?"

"Why you're really here?" Sean rolled over, propping himself up on his elbow and gazing down at Dominic.

Dominic frowned, looking away. "Told you. I was in town."

"You never come to Seattle," Sean pointed out. "You came to see me, didn't you?"

"It doesn't matter," Dominic replied simply, eyes on the back of the couch. He wondered where Sean had gotten it, if it had come with the apartment.

"Yes, it does," Sean insisted, cocking his head to the side, eyes widening. "Dom, tell me."

"No, it really doesn't," Dominic said finally, looking back at Sean, gaze firm. "You're happy here. You have friends. Your customers love you, and why wouldn't they?" He sighed. "This is your France."

Sean stared. "I-what? What are you saying?"

Dominic sighed, pushing himself up and looking around for his shirt. "I'm saying this was a mistake." He spotted it by the opposite end of the couch and grabbed it, pulling it on. "I shouldn't have come."

Sean still looked confused, shaking his head as Dominic grabbed his pants next. He stopped him with a hand on his wrist, turning Dominic to face him.

"Do you want me to come back?" he asked, eyes darting over his face as if searching for the truth.

An irrepressible wave of something like guilt and pain washed over Dominic as he stared at Sean, knowing that if he said yes, Sean would be packed and ready to go that night. He couldn't do it, though. This was what Sean had been waiting for all these years, his chance to make something more of his life than a cook for a tiny bed and breakfast out in the country. He hadn't gone to France when he'd had the chance, too scared to leave home, but now was his chance.

"No," he said finally, swallowing the lump in his throat.

Sean's face fell slightly.

"You have to stay here."

"Why?" Sean demanded. "Because you can't admit how you feel about me? After all this time, you still just can't say it. It's three fucking words."

Dominic stared at Sean, the pressure tightening in his chest, the words welling up before he could stop them.

"I do, Sean," he said, each word wrenched from his mouth. "I... I love you, but you have to stay here."

Sean's mouth moved wordlessly, unsure what to do or say, panic appearing in his eyes as Dominic rose to his feet, pulling on his jeans. Sean scrambled to stand up.

"What are you doing? I don't understand."

Dominic paused, forcing down the painful swelling in his chest. "I'm going home."

"Dom!" Sean said, following him doggedly to the door.

Dominic turned, one hand on the knob, taking a last look at Sean. He hadn't even known his heart could break like this, the painful severing of something deep inside as he tried to wrench himself away. He could barely stand to look at Sean, the confusion, the accusation in his eyes.

He kissed Sean, then, one last time, closing his eyes and trying to savor the moment, not to think about how he was going to keep the bed and breakfast alive, or how he was going to manage without Sean in general, but he had to do this. This was what Sean needed, and it wasn't about what Dominic wanted anymore.

Pulling away slowly, he sighed, before he twisted the knob and opened the door.

He didn't say goodbye as he left, the taste of Sean still on his tongue as he shut the door and left down the hallway.

"You did what?" Hunter demanded, and Rose looked just as flummoxed as they both stared at Dom behind the desk.

Dominic sighed, shuffling papers together. "It's for the best."

"He would have come back," Hunter said, but Dominic shook his head.

"I wouldn't let him. Seattle is something he's always wanted, and I'm not going to take it away from him for stupid, selfish reasons."

"The bed and breakfast isn't stupid or selfish," Hunter argued, but he knew it was a lost cause when Dominic shook his head again.

"There will be other inns and other cooks, but for most people, there's only one chance to live their dream."

Hunter and Rose exchanged a glance.

"Are you sure we couldn't get him to come back?"

"No," Dominic said firmly, looking up at both of them. He wasn't going to ask Sean to come back. It was over, and he had to deal with this on his own.

He didn't want to think about Sean anymore, not when doing so made his heart ache in a way it never had before. He couldn't remember feeling this way about anyone before. Ever since his parents had divorced, he'd never bothered getting close to anyone. It all seemed like such a waste, when his dad went through women as though they were razors.

"You're gonna sell, aren't you?"

Dominic frowned down at the desk, eyes falling on the message machine, blinking red with one message from Derek. It had already been a week since he'd gone to see Sean, but he hadn't called yet. He supposed there was no point in putting it off since he was probably about to go under as it was.

"We'll see."

Hunter didn't look convinced, and Rose frowned.

"I don't know why you had to get all noble all of a sudden," Hunter muttered, reaching for the door.

"I'm sure things will work out," Rose said, almost desperately, but she followed Hunter out the door, closing it behind her.

Dominic didn't sigh this time, pushing more papers together. He was going to have to organize this if he was going to sell it. The thought wasn't appealing, but he didn't have much of a choice. It was either that or let his credit go down the drain. He could get a different job, save up again, start a new bed and breakfast eventually in a different town, one that didn't know about Sean. It would be a clean start.

Things would start working out as soon as he called Derek.

Pressing the button, he sat back to listen to the message for the fourth time since he'd been back.

"Hey, Dominic, it's Derek Handsfeld again. I hope you've given some thought to selling that charming bed and breakfast of yours. I'm prepared to make a generous offer, and I'll even keep on the staff if you'd like. Give me a call. I'd like to get going on this as soon as possible."

The machine beeped, and Dominic rubbed his forehead. He reached for his phone, though, despite his reservations.

"You're not seriously thinking of selling?"

A hard voice surprised Dominic and he fumbled the phone, dropping it with a clunk onto the desk as he looked up to see Sean standing in the doorway.

"Sean?" he said, standing up, frowning. "What are you doing here?"

Sean paused, glancing around the messy office. "I thought about what you said, and I decided that you picked a hell of a time to become selfless."

Dominic blinked.

"You're losing the bed and breakfast," Sean pointed out, staring at Dominic, reproach in his eyes. "You have no cook. The addition looks almost the same as when I left. What did you expect to do?"

Dominic frowned. "How did you...."

Sean shrugged, and Dominic sighed.

"Rose."

"It doesn't matter," Sean said seriously. "*You* should have told me."

"So you'd feel guilty and come bail me out?" Dominic asked, a sharp bite to his words. "That's exactly how I wanted you to come back."

"And instead, you told me not to come at all?"

Dominic shook his head tiredly. "Seattle is good for you, Sean. It's everything you've ever wanted in your career. I'm not going to be the one who takes that away from you. It doesn't matter how I feel or how badly the bed and breakfast is doing."

"It matters to *me*," Sean insisted, staring at Dominic. "Look, I care about my career, and Seattle was a good opportunity, but opportunities come and go, and you have to know which ones to take."

"And you took the right one."

"No!" Sean shook his head. "*You* were the one I wanted to take, but you didn't let me."

"Then why are you back here?"

Sean sighed, stepping around the desk finally, moving until he and Dominic were toe to toe in the small space.

"Because you let me go."

Dominic frowned.

"Because you let me go, and when you did, you chose me over the B&B, and I know how much you love this place. And I can't let you lose it... or me."

"Sean," Dominic started to say, but Sean cut him off with a kiss, soft and sweet, the kind of kiss that stirred in his chest like nesting butterflies.

"I've got enough money to finish the addition," Sean said when he pulled away. "And then I was thinking, maybe we could expand to a restaurant, breakfast and dinner to start. You know people will come."

"If you're the cook," Dominic admitted. "But I can't let you—"

"Yes, you can," Sean interrupted firmly. "It's about time you started listening to someone else for a change. Might as well be me."

Dominic sighed, but his hands slid to Sean's waist. "If I'd listened to you, none of this would have happened."

"Exactly." Sean grinned, pulling him into another, longer kiss.

Dominic wrapped his arms around him, tugging him in closer. He didn't care that Sean was right or that he was wrong. He only cared that something had finally gone right.

"Should we tell Hunter and Rose?" Sean asked a moment later, lips brushing against Dom's mouth.

"I suppose," he said. "I don't think I can stand another pancake breakfast."

"I'll make eggs Benedict tomorrow."

Dominic smiled. "God, I missed you."

Sean smiled too, brushing back Dominic's hair. "I missed you too. Now, erase that message."

Dominic didn't hesitate a second to delete the message on the machine. A weight seemed to lift from his chest as he looked back at Sean.

"Better?"

"Much." Sean grinned, sighing contentedly. "Now, did I miss all the festival or are there still some apples left to pick?"

"There are always apples around here," Dominic assured him, and Sean laughed.

"I'm glad you came to Seattle."

Dominic sighed, arms tightening around him. "I'm glad you came back."

"All you had to do was ask."

If you enjoyed this story, you can sign up for a free membership at ForbiddenFiction..com and discuss it with other readers and the author at the *Checking Out* story page at http://forbiddenfiction.com/story/EEG-1.000090.

We do our best to proof all our work, but if you spot a text error we missed, please let us know via our website Contact Form at k forbiddenfiction.com/contact.

By the Hour

Chapter 1
The Bar on Broadway

"Dude, we've got to celebrate this," Logan said, clapping Seth on the back as they stepped out of the gleaming office building into the afternoon sun. "You went from a twenty-four-year-old college grad to, what is it now? Executive assistant for the boss in less than a year. How'd you manage it?"

Seth shrugged, glancing down at the cracks in the pavement, a small smile curving the corner of his mouth. "I know how to please my men."

Logan laughed loudly, attracting the attention of a few pedestrians they passed. He shook his head. "You're hilarious, dude. So how about it? We can hit that bar down on Broadway."

Seth hesitated at the suggestion, loosening his tie. "I don't know. We could go to that new place on Fifth Street."

"Why do you never want to go to Broadway?" Logan asked plainly, arching an eyebrow as he swung around to face Seth, who jerked his shoulders, rubbing at his lower lip and the shiny silver lip ring. He didn't have an explanation that wouldn't make him sound like a douche or worse. "Is it because of all the hustlers? Afraid they'll hit on you?" He nudged Seth, who laughed shortly.

"No," he replied, passing it off with a smile. "Besides, you're more their type."

"Screw you," Logan said, laughing. "Then there's no excuse. We're going to Broadway tonight."

"If you want to be boring." Seth shrugged, forcing himself to smile, and he stuffed his tie in his pocket.

"Yeah, right, I'm the boring one," Logan snorted, waiting at a street corner for the light to change. "In the entire time I've known you, you never go out, you don't date anyone, and I've hardly seen you drink. It doesn't really match your..." He gestured at Seth, from his green converse under his slacks to his lip ring and the tattoo behind his ear. "...persona."

Seth sighed, pushing back his short, dark hair. "I was a wayward youth. Come on, I didn't finish college until I was twenty-four. What does that tell you?"

"That you're stupid?" Logan joked, and Seth elbowed him in the side. "Ow. I don't know."

"Let's just say I got a late start," Seth replied, glancing in a window of a shop they passed. It was filled with grandmother-type trinkets, and he looked away.

"Yeah, well, tonight, eight o'clock," Logan said as they reached another corner, the one where Logan turned right and Seth turned left. "Bring your game face. I'm gonna get you drunk!"

Seth laughed. "You can try," he shot back smoothly, knowing there was no way he was getting drunk down on Broadway, no matter what Logan did.

"Count on it," Logan promised, though, hitting his arm before loping in the opposite direction. Seth stared after him for a minute and then turned away. He had to get ready for tonight.

The bar was new, or at least new since the last time Seth had been down in that part of town. He remembered the place being a crappy drug store with cheap cigarettes and a dirty bathroom floor. He stared up at the door, hands shoved in his pockets, and for a moment he felt like a seventeen year old kid again, before he'd learned anything about life.

"You made it!" Logan appeared by his side, and Seth shook himself. Nothing like that was going to happen tonight.

Instead, he turned to Logan. "You're late."

Logan rolled his eyes. "What is it with you and punctuality? You're like a Swiss clock, man."

"Time is money," Seth replied automatically, wondering how many times he'd said that in the past seven years.

"Not when you're drinking, it's not!" Logan said, grabbing his shoulder and steering him inside. Reluctantly, Seth let him, turning over his lip ring slowly as Logan guided him through the cluttered tables to the counter on the other side. "What are you having?"

"Look, I don't really—"

"Come on!" Logan interrupted. "You just got promoted at work. Cut loose for a minute! You're not a goddamn monk."

"I'll just have a Coke," Seth replied finally, and Logan rolled his eyes but didn't push it, gesturing at the bartender as Seth looked away, over the heads of the people taking up space at the tables, talking and laughing loudly over the music coming out of the ceiling.

A quick scan of the place told him there was no one he recognized there, no one who could recognize him. He relaxed, then, taking the drink Logan passed to him.

"See anybody you like?" Logan asked as Seth twirled the cold glass in his hands. He barely looked up and turned around, leaning back against the bar.

"No," he replied, ignoring Logan's exasperated stare.

"When was the last time you got laid?"

Seth shrugged, scratching behind his ear idly, at the little black four leaf clover tattooed there. "I don't know," he said instead of actually answering. "Does it really matter?"

"Um, yeah," Logan said, eyebrow disappearing into his hairline. "If you can't remember then obviously it's been too long." He turned to the room and spread his arms wide. "Look around. There's got to be someone in here you want to bang. That girl over there? That guy with the weird-looking arms?"

Seth didn't bother looking, rolling his eyes and grabbing his glass and taking a sip. "I'm just not interested right now."

"Yeah, something is wrong with you," Logan drawled, turning back around and knocking Seth's glass with his bottle.

Seth didn't reply, smoothing down a hand over his tight jeans. He toyed with his lip ring slowly, contemplating the bottles lining the wall. The dim light shined off the different colored glasses, reflecting along the back wall, a myriad of browns and greens.

"I'll buy the next round," he said instead, and Logan's eyes lit up.

"Now you're talking! Why are you never this guy at work? What do you do when you're not there anyway? You're like this little secretive animal who disappears once you go home. How come you never hang out with the guys?"

Seth signaled to the bartender as Logan talked. "I prefer being alone," he said simply, shooting a smile at the bartender.

The guy set another bottle in front of Logan, and Seth ignored the way the guy's eyes lingered on him for a moment. He turned away. Not interested.

"Tragic childhood?" Logan asked.

"Something like that," Seth replied easily, not bothering to elaborate. He preferred to keep his private life private, though everyone at the office seemed intent on finding out all his secrets.

Logan was busy staring at a pretty girl across the room, and Seth checked the time on his phone while he was distracted. To be honest, he would rather be home alone right now, but he couldn't escape quite yet. He would just have to suffer through another couple hours.

Seth watched Logan finish off his fourth beer and laugh loudly at whatever the girl next to him had said, though Seth was sure it was nothing quote-worthy. He was still on his first drink, but as it was just Coke, it barely mattered. Logan hadn't seemed to notice once Seth had gestured over one of the girls crowding random tables.

"I'm gonna get some air," he said, and Logan barely noticed. Sliding off his chair, he left his glass on the counter and weaved through the tables to the doors.

Outside, things seemed even busier than when they'd arrived, but it didn't surprise Seth. He'd been down that street enough to know what went on once night fell and the barflies appeared.

Standing outside the bar, his fingers itched for a cigarette and but he unwillingly mastered the urge. He wished that drugstore was still there, but he shook himself sharply. No smoking, he told himself firmly. He'd given it up a few years back, when he gave up everything else, every bad habit.

That didn't stop the itch in his fingertips, though, as he gazed down the street.

"Hey, cutie," came a voice from his right, "you look a little lonely. Interested in a nightcap?"

Seth almost smiled at the familiarity of the come-on, the way it went down smoothly, no hint of hesitation in the offer. He turned, though, and the smile froze on his lips.

The guy standing behind him had dark eyes under his mess of blond hair, a silver hook through his left eyebrow, and a devious slant to his mouth. Seth knew that slant, although he hadn't seen it in years.

"Caleb," he said instead of answering the question, and the guy frowned, eyeing Seth more carefully now, guards coming up. It took him a minute, eyes searching Seth's body, sliding up to his face, before he took a step back.

"Well, well," he drawled slowly. "Look what the cat dragged in. Seth." He pursed his lips slightly in disapproval as he took in the clean clothes, the expensive phone in his hand. "So that's where you disappeared to, huh? Took the straight and narrow?"

Seth shrugged, eyes scraping down Caleb's body. He hadn't changed much in the past few years. He still looked young, but so did everyone on the street. He still had a defiant edge as he stood there, a hip cocked to the side, chin raised even if he was taller than Seth by a few inches.

"If you want to call it that," he replied, and Caleb scoffed, tossing him a scathing look.

"That's the nicest way I can put it if that's what you mean."

Seth paused, and for the second time that evening, he felt younger than he was; he felt like the first time he'd seen Caleb. It had been on this very street, seven years ago, and Caleb had bitched him out over stealing his clients. Seth could only remember thinking how hot Caleb was, though, and that, at least, hadn't changed.

"How've you been?" he asked instead, and Caleb laughed, a sharp, unamused sound.

"Dandy." He eyed him again, eyes falling to the purple Converse he was wearing. "And yourself? Got yourself a sugar daddy?"

"Actually, a job," Seth replied, ignoring Caleb's scoff. "I went to college."

Caleb's eyebrows rose in what was clearly surprise, but he passed it off a moment later, digging in his pocket and coming up with a cigarette. "Guess there's hope for even the dumbest kid on the street," he mumbled around the cigarette as he lit it. Taking a long drag, he exhaled slowly, and Seth ached for one, but he stopped himself from saying anything. Caleb would never give him one anyway, even if he did ask. Caleb paused. "Then what the hell are you doing back here?"

"My friend just wanted to come to this bar," he said, waving vaguely towards the door. Caleb didn't even glance at it.

"Great," he muttered, unimpressed. "Well, you've wasted enough of my time." Turning, he started to walk away, but Seth frowned.

"Wait a minute," he said, and Caleb paused, turning back and tilting his head to the side.

He smirked. "Seth, you couldn't have me then so what's the point in trying now?"

A ripple of annoyance passed through him as Seth stared. Caleb was just as cocky as always.

"You still think you're better than me," he said, shaking his head.

Caleb shrugged, sucking the end of his cigarette.,though it was clear he agreed.

"Ain't it the truth?" He sighed, flicking the ash off his cigarette. "You could never best me and you could never have me. And it just ate you up, didn't it?" He smirked. "Well, looks like nothing has changed even with your fancy clothes and regular job. I still win."

He started to turn, but Seth's next sentence pulled him back.

"That's not true."

Seth watched Caleb pause, and for a second he wondered what he was doing. He'd vowed never to get involved in this again, not after all the pain it had caused him, all the struggle it had taken to finally get out of it. But seeing Caleb, still so absolutely sure of himself, so confident that he had Seth right where he wanted him, made him want to do something reckless and possibly stupid.

"I've got money now," Seth said slowly, and Caleb arched an eyebrow. "And we both know that whoever has the money has the power."

"Are you saying what I think you're saying?" Caleb drawled skeptically, and Seth jerked his shoulders in response, eyes on Caleb.

"If you're scared, you don't have to."

Caleb scoffed. "What the fuck do I have to be scared of?"

"That you'll finally prove me right," Seth replied, eyes meeting Caleb's and not wavering. Caleb stared right back, eyes narrowed. "That you might enjoy it, that I'm better than you."

"Honey, it's a fact that I am and always will be better than you, and no amount of fucking is going to change that. Isn't it about time you got over that little crush? You're never gonna get me."

"Five hundred dollars begs to differ," Seth replied coolly, and Caleb frowned, a flicker of something other than disdain in his eyes.

"You're gonna pay me five hundred—"

"Seth!" Logan's loud voice cut through them, and Seth took a startled step back as Logan came bursting out of the doors and stumbled down the stairs to the street. "What the fuck are you doing out here? Who's he?" he asked, noticing Caleb.

Seth glanced at Caleb slowly as Logan grabbed his shoulder and grinned at him, beer on his breath. "He's no one," he said finally. "We should get you home."

"Were you gonna get laid, buddy?" Logan asked as Seth grabbed his arm and steered him in the other direction, leaving Caleb with a dark expression on his face. "That would be, like, groundbreaking!"

Seth didn't reply, helping him up the street, though his thoughts were back on Caleb and wondering how far he might have pushed it if given the chance.

Seth's head hit the cool pillow, and he stared up at the dark ceiling of his bedroom. The only light came from a peek of streetlight slipping in through the crack in the curtains. He didn't bother climbing under the covers, blinking in the darkness and listening to the sounds of creaks in the hallway, the vague mutter of a TV from next door.

He couldn't stop replaying the night over and over in his head, running into Caleb, his self-assured words that even though Caleb was the one still hustling, he was still somehow better.

For years, Seth had kept an eye on Caleb, first trying to learn and then trying to beat him. He never quite could, though, and Caleb had barely given him a second glance in all the time they'd worked together. It used to bother him, wanting something he so obviously couldn't have, but in the past few years, he'd learned that he could have everything he wanted if he just went that extra step.

Caleb, though, Caleb would be harder to crack than most problems. At the moment, though, all Seth could think of was how Caleb had smirked at him, the devious pull to his perfectly pink lips.

Closing his eyes, Seth slid his hand down, pressed against his chest as he pictured how Caleb would look on his knees, at his mercy. He'd look so hot with Seth's hand tangled in his hair, cheeks red and flushed, panting against his skin. Seth would make him want it, like he'd wanted it all those years.

Stretching back, Seth inhaled slowly, hand wrapping around his cock and stroking slowly. He didn't know how long it had been since he'd had sex. Ever since he'd stopped hustling, he'd found he didn't remember how to pick up guys without offering them blowjobs in the backs of clubs. That wasn't really what he wanted, not now, but he always seemed unable to stop the words coming out.

He moaned softly as he jerked himself off, imagining Caleb's hand, soft and smooth, probably a little rough. He would probably go too fast, probably twist too hard and make Seth's stomach jerk excitedly, make him come all over his hand without warning, without any precursor, and Seth wouldn't stop himself.

"Shit," he breathed out loud, huffing out a small breath as he pushed his hips up, squeezing his prick and feeling the heat building.

It didn't take long for him to come, Caleb's face clear in his mind, thoughts on his devilish mouth, and he gasped as warm, wet come covered his fingers. Cock still twitching, he sighed and drew his hand away.

Opening his eyes to the ceiling, he stared at the blackness. Shaking his head, he told himself to forget about Caleb, but it was never that easy, and he slid over finally, padding to the bathroom and washing his hands. When he got back to bed, he rolled over on his side and stared at the window instead. Even as he tried to forget about him, he couldn't deny that tonight had been the first time in a while that he'd felt something other than ambivalence towards someone, and he knew exactly why.

Chapter 2
An Offer on the Table

"Why are you not hung over?" Logan asked as he bent over his desk, head in his hands, and Seth barely glanced up, typing away at his computer.

Around him, people bustled by in the large, open office space. Light streamed in through the tall windows on the far side of the building, bathing the desks in bright white. Logan cringed away from it when he chanced a glance up.

"Because I wasn't drunk."

"But that was the plan," Logan replied, dropping his hands finally and staring across at Seth. "You were supposed to get drunk and pick up some floozy for a one-night stand!"

"I don't do that," Seth muttered, digging through the papers on his desk.

"Everybody does that," Logan scoffed, rubbing at his forehead. "I mean, seriously, dude, are you celibate or something?"

"Why is it so important?" Seth asked, the paper sagging in his hand as he looked up. Personally, he didn't see that it was anyone's business about his sex life, and talking about it always made him uncomfortable, as if everyone was moments away from finding out about his life before he went to college.

"I don't know." Logan shrugged. "It's just, you don't really talk to anybody aside from the boss and me, and you never go out. You've been working here for, what, eight months now? I barely know your last name."

Seth frowned, setting the paper aside. "It's my life," he said finally, and Logan nodded.

"I know, I'm just saying people are curious. Are you gay, straight, bi, asexual? Give us a hint."

Seth took a moment, staring at Logan as he tried to organize his thoughts. He had little desire to become friends with anyone at work beyond what was necessary for good relationships, and he didn't need everyone to know the intimate details of his life. He didn't need idle gossip circulating about him, because as he knew, gossip turned to rumors which turned into secrets escaping, and *that* he did not want.

Looking at Logan, with his perfectly coiffed blond hair, soft waves gelled back, and his strong, square jaw, he reeled in the feelings of annoyance that he generally tried to suppress and smiled instead.

"I'm not celibate," he said finally, turning back to his computer and trying to ignore Logan's sigh.

"Fine," he conceded finally. "You're not celibate, but you do go out, right? 'Cause you never come out with us. You have other friends, right?"

Seth tossed him a smile. "Of course," he said, and it was a credit to his lying ability that Logan accepted it without question.

"You should bring one of them with you sometime, you know, prove to the rest of the office that you're normal." Logan grinned, and Seth nodded, looking away.

"Yeah, sure," he muttered, thinking there was about as much chance of that happening as it snowing in July. He'd just bring along one of his invisible friends. No one would think he was weird then. Yeah.

"'Cause, you know, most people in the office think you're an anti-social loner or something, which is crazy, right? You're totally normal except that no drinking thing. Hey, where are you from anyway?"

Seth wished Logan would stop talking as he stared at his computer screen.

"I grew up in Hartford," he muttered finally.

"Upper middle class, huh?" Logan asked. "Me too. My parents own their own architect firm and they think that makes them important." He shrugged, and Seth didn't reply.

His own parents hadn't spoken to him in almost eight years, but he assumed they were doing just fine in their historic manor home up on the hill. He doubted they even cared where he was or if he was alive. And he didn't care to tell them.

"Hey, if you tell me what you're into, I could probably set you up with someone," Logan said unexpectedly. "I know this really hot, kind of slutty girl. She'd be into you with all the tattoos and piercings."

Seth sighed loudly, turning to Logan dead-on, and not bothering to disguise the annoyance on his face. "Look, I don't need to be set-up," he said firmly. "So just leave it alone."

"Okay," Logan said, holding up his hands in defeat. "Just trying to help you."

"I don't need help," Seth replied sharply, rubbing his face and trying to get his emotions back in control. "My life is fine."

"Yeah... you just don't have sex," Logan muttered, finally turning to his computer, and Seth stared, mouth slightly agape, but Logan didn't speak again, and he figured that was as close to a win as he was going to get.

A warm breeze swept past, pushing against his back as he stepped onto the sidewalk and peered down the blackened street, pools of orange streetlamp lights wobbling on the ground, edges blurred and fading.

Seth walked purposefully, ignoring the people around him, the hustlers on the street corner waiting for him to glance at them and make some kind of nonverbal invitation. He passed them without a glance, heading for the spot where he knew exactly what he would find.

The street was down a little ways, past the corner with the club, thudding music pulsating beneath his feet whenever the door swung open. He turned the corner, and the lights seemed to dim, darkness thickening as he walked. A few guys stood lounged back against the brick buildings, talking to each other and sucking on cigarettes.

"Where you going, beautiful?" one called to Seth as he passed, checking their faces, but he only looked away and moved on.

Near the end of the block, he recognized the guy standing under the streetlamp immediately, the way he stood straight unlike the rest of the kids on the street, shoulders back and a self-satisfied tilt to his chin as he took a drag of his cigarette and flicked the ashes into the stream of orange light from above.

At Seth's approach, he didn't look over, though Seth knew he heard him, heard him slowing down. He fingered the end of his cigarette instead and smiled knowingly.

"Job not work out?" he drawled, and Seth crossed his arms, stopping a few feet from Caleb. His eyes stole up his body, from the dusty jeans up to his strong arms, small muscles visible even in the dim light.

"I'll pay you five hundred bucks."

Caleb flicked his cigarette away, scratching the back of his head and turning to Seth. His deep brown eyes scraped up his torso, a skeptical tilt to his eyebrow. "For what?"

"I think you know for what," Seth replied simply, and Caleb sneered, shoving his hair out of his eyes.

"For you to feel like a man, like you're finally better than me, like you've done so much more with your life." He rolled his eyes, ignoring when Seth stepped closer.

"Are you really in the position to turn down five hundred bucks?"

"Are you really that desperate?"

Seth laughed, biting his lip ring and shaking his head. "Have you forgotten, Caleb, that I was the one who went home with the Mercedes every night?"

"That guy was a complete asshole," Caleb drawled back, but Seth saw the flicker of annoyance in his eyes, and his hands reached for another cigarette.

"An asshole who helped pay my college tuition," Seth replied. "You really think you can't learn anything from me?"

"Considering you stole all of my moves," Caleb shot back, "no, I don't."

"Then you have nothing to worry about, do you?" Seth pulled out a wad of cash from his hand and held it up for Caleb to see. He knew he wouldn't be able to resist it, no matter how much he may have disliked him. Money was life to hustlers. He remembered how it was. "Five hundred and you're mine for the night."

Caleb bristled, clearly not used to Seth being so dominant, but then, when they'd known each other, Seth had been just barely finding his feet, and by the time he'd found them, Caleb wouldn't even glance his way except to sneer at him.

"I have other clients, you know," he snarled, and Seth shrugged.

"I don't care. Take it or leave it." He paused, though, pulling the money back as Caleb thought about it and then reached for it. "You do whatever I say."

Caleb shot him a patronizing smile. "Them's the rules."

Seth handed over the money, and Caleb counted it quickly. "Let's go then."

Caleb shot him a fake smile that only lasted a second and pulled out another cigarette as they headed down the road.

They didn't speak and Seth led the way, following a path he had never quite taken before. None of the hustlers spoke to him as he passed with Caleb this time. Caleb licked the tip of his fingers, pulling the cigarette from his mouth.

A part of Seth wasn't sure why he was doing this, but he was sick of everyone around him assuming he didn't have a life, that all he did was hide away in his apartment with nothing but the TV for company. Of course, it was true, but he also didn't feel the need to explain himself. Explaining would cause far more trouble than it was worth.

"We'll go to my place," he said as they reached the end of the street, and Caleb merely arched an eyebrow. Seth turned away, wondering how much trouble he was going to be. He wouldn't let him push him around, though. Gone were the days when Seth had been a scared kid with no clue about the world.

He didn't have a car, so he led the way to the metro stop, and Caleb waited impatiently beside him, sucking on the end of his cigarette and watching him.

"Your fancy college education couldn't afford a car?" he drawled finally, and Seth met his eyes coolly.

"Remember how you're supposed to do what I say?"

"You didn't say I couldn't talk," Caleb replied dully, shaking back his hair. "Unless you're into domination."

"You wouldn't know, would you?" Seth replied. "You were always too busy hitting on any guy that glanced your way."

"Pays the bills." Caleb dropped the cigarette on the ground as the car pulled up, brakes squeaking to a stop, and a few people stepped off. He went on first, not bothering to sit in any of the empty seats, but leaning against the back of one coolly, arms crossed. Seth grabbed the pole in the middle and took the time to admire Caleb's body. It had always been nice, tall and lean, but now there was a hint of definition in his arms, a strong line to his back. His sharp hips angled out as he leaned back and the car jerked forward.

Seth looked away when Caleb glanced over, tongue in his cheek as his eyes narrowed.

"I'm not doing this because I like you."

"No, really?" Seth shot back. "I thought you were secretly in love with me."

"No, that was you," Caleb pointed out, turning to stare at the black window as they rushed down the tunnel. The rest of the car was filled with an odd assortment of people, from an old lady with her shopping to what looked like a very flamboyant gay couple in the corner whispering and giggling together.

Seth didn't reply, knowing it would only dredge up old feelings, feelings he'd worked very hard to get rid of. He didn't even know why he was doing this. He'd never wanted to get involved with hustlers again. It felt like he might get pulled back in at any moment, and that was something he didn't want. He'd already worked so hard to kick his bad habits and he wasn't going to start again now.

His stop came about twenty minutes later, and he stepped off, Caleb following grudgingly. Walking the few blocks to his apartment, they didn't speak again, and Caleb shoved his hands in his pockets, eyes taking in the shiny cars all around, the plants hanging over the balconies above.

"Suburbia," he muttered as they reached Seth's apartment building, identical to those around it. Ignoring him, Seth unlocked the door and led the way up to his apartment.

Caleb trudged behind him, hand clasped around the cash in his pocket as they climbed the stairs and finally stopped on the fourth floor. He waited as Seth unlocked the door and entered, tossing his keys on the kitchen counter.

Seth turned as soon as the door shut behind Caleb, eyes landing on him intently. He felt like a tiger on the prowl as he kicked off his shoes.

"Take off your clothes," he said, and he couldn't think how many times he'd heard that before. He'd almost never been the one saying it, though.

Caleb sighed, shedding his shirt in a half a second and reaching for his jeans, but Seth interrupted.

"Slower."

Visibly annoyed at receiving orders from Seth, Caleb slowed his movements, unbuttoning his jeans and sliding his thumbs under the waistband. His eyes met Seth's and he licked his lips slowly. "Better?"

Seth shrugged, watching his hand inch lower, pushing his jeans past his hips. "If you didn't talk so much."

Caleb rolled his eyes, kicking his jeans away and waiting.

Seth took a step closer, eyes raking down his body, the pale skin, spending too much time on the smooth, softly defined muscles on his torso, sharp hipbones. His hands hovered over them for a second, mind flashing back to the hundreds of times someone else had done this to him, how nervous he used to be, and then how bored he used to be.

Leaning in, he didn't expect Caleb to jerk back out of his reach. "No," he said shortly, ignoring Seth's perplexed look. "No kissing. I don't care how much you pay me."

Rolling his eyes, Seth leaned back. Caleb crossed his arms defiantly, though, and he knew arguing the point was useless, but that wasn't what this was about.

"Fine," he said, grabbing Caleb's arm instead and jerking him forward. "Then get on your knees."

Fire in his eyes, Caleb slid slowly down, glaring up at Seth, but Seth didn't react, merely arching an eyebrow and waiting. He was going to get what he paid for.

The tables were turned for the first time in years. He had Caleb all to himself, under his control. He liked the feeling, the surge of power in his veins as Caleb unbuttoned his jeans without any prompting. Then again, Caleb was a professional despite his caustic remarks and cocky personality.

He paused, though, when he had the pants pushed down Seth's hips, cock visible but he hadn't touched it yet. Seth saw him lick his lips slowly, as if contemplating what he was going to do.

"You just want me to sit here?" he asked finally, and Seth didn't bother to bite down his annoyance like he would if he were at work.

"What the hell do you think I want you to do?"

"Paint you a picture," Caleb sneered, defiant even in defeat, but Seth reached down, pushing a hand into his soft hair and pulling his head forward.

"You know what to do," he said simply, not releasing his head, and he felt Caleb's hot and heavy sigh against his skin.

Caleb's hand was warm as he pulled Seth's cock out from the confines of his jeans, smoothing his hand over the length and taking a second to trace the ridges. He licked his lips before leaning in, pressing the prick up against Seth's stomach and licking up the underside. His tongue teased as the base, flicking up until he reached the head and sucked lightly.

Seth couldn't remember the last time he'd done this, and the last time had definitely not been this good. It might have been some stranger in a bar last year but it wasn't important, not now, not when he had Caleb on his knees, sucking his cock like it was the most important thing in the world. He knew he was just pretending but that didn't mean it didn't feel fucking amazing.

Tightening his grip on Caleb's smooth hair, he groaned softly, eyes closing as he stood in the middle of his living room and let himself get lost in the feel of Caleb's soft mouth, tongue hot and wet sliding over his prick. He exhaled slowly as Caleb reached for his hips, holding him steady, stopping him from pushing too hard into his mouth, but Seth merely pushed Caleb's head forward despite his muffled noise of protest.

"Thought you were a pro," Seth said sharply, eyebrow raised, when Caleb slid back and looked up with a glare. He felt a sudden ripple of anger that he couldn't explain, anger at Caleb and his fucking mouth, shiny and red, lips pressed together as he glared, but he moved back in a second later. He wanted Caleb to feel the way he'd felt, all those years ago, unwanted and invisible.

He cursed, though, when Caleb nearly swallowed his cock, relaxing his jaw in a way that Seth had never been able to master. Now he knew why Caleb made the big bucks, and a part of him wasn't surprised.

It felt good, the heat spreading over his skin, curling in his stomach and licking up his spine. Caleb's mouth closed around his cock, a hot, wet covering that made Seth's eyes roll back.

"Shit," he breathed, eyes closing, hand still twined in Caleb's hair, and Caleb made a vague noise, of derision or pleasure, Seth wasn't sure, but he'd be willing to guess the former.

The window on the far wall, the one facing the street, was smothered in darkness aside from a dim orange glow from the city beyond. There were no curtains in here, but he wasn't worried about anyone looking in. He barely knew his neighbors anyway. Mostly he kept to himself and they kept to themselves, except for the nosy girl down on the second floor who always wanted to chat when he picked up his mail. She was probably hitting on him, he thought belatedly, gasping as Caleb flicked his tongue over the head of his cock.

He didn't have time for naive girls, though. Biting his lip ring, he glanced down, watching the way Caleb moved back and forth, prick disappearing into his perfectly plump lips that were made for sucking cock. He knew exactly what to do too, from every lick and twist.

Seth's breath caught in his throat as his stomach tightened warningly, harder and hotter than before, than he could remember in the past few years. Cursing to himself, he barely pulled Caleb's mouth away before he came, come streaking the side of his mouth and down his chin. He saw Caleb wince as it hit his skin, a bit on the edge of his lips.

"A little warning might be nice," he grumbled, sitting back on his knees and grabbing his discarded shirt to wipe it away.

Breathing hard, Seth stared down at him, an unexplainable feeling of shame and anger washing over him. Why had he done this? He didn't feel any better about anything.

Caleb tossed away the shirt and glanced up at Seth. He was naked still, cock not hard at all, and Seth paused, staring down at him.

"What next?" Caleb asked, bored, and Seth looked away after a moment.

"Get out."

Caleb furrowed an eyebrow, leaning back on his haunches. "What?"

"Get out," Seth repeated, harder this time. He scooped up Caleb's clothes from the ground and shoved them into his arms as he rose slowly.

"Seriously?" Caleb said, skeptical, and the shirt drooped in his hand. "Five hundred bucks for a blowjob?"

Seth walked over to the kitchen, grabbing his keys off the counter and hanging them up on the little hook on the wall instead. He didn't look back, unsure why he was doing any of this. It didn't make sense, after everything he'd gone through to get out of that world. He was dragging himself back into it.

"Just go," he said, and he heard Caleb pull on his clothes quickly.

"You're fucked up," Caleb said as he pulled open the door and disappeared.

Sighing, Seth turned to the empty apartment. His clothes lay in a scattered pile across the floor, and he didn't bother to pick them up as he headed for his bedroom.

The dim light lit up his bed, corners tucked in messily, and the banged-up dresser he'd bought off some college kid a few years back. Sinking down on the bed, he stared at the blank wall opposite him.

A feeling of anger lay heavy on his shoulders, anger at himself, at Caleb, at everyone at work. It was hard enough, hiding his past from everyone, but even with Caleb, someone who should understand, it was too much. Caleb just brought back too many memories.

The sex, though, it had been good, as far as they'd gotten. Flopping down on his back, he rubbed his forehead slowly. Fuck, Caleb had been good, as good as he'd ever imagined. And of course Caleb knew he was good. He hadn't done a good job of proving his point, he thought, thinking of Caleb's words as he'd left. He didn't see how he would ever talk to him again without it being like it always had been.

Not that he wanted to talk to him, Seth told himself firmly. This had been a one-time thing, not to be repeated, a single slip-up in several years of going clean.

Fuck, he really wanted a cigarette right now. He could still smell it from Caleb's clothes. His fingers probably tasted like them. Seth groaned at the thought, rolling over and pressing his face into the sheets. Why was it so hard for him to get Caleb out of his head? He just wanted to move on with his life.

Some good job he'd been doing so far, though. He had no friends, no boyfriend, and everyone at work thought he was an anti-social celibate loser. A part of him didn't feel the need to prove them wrong, but the other part, the part that had listened to his parents say, "How you act is important. People will always judge you," wanted desperately to prove that he was just as normal as them even though he could never come close.

Sighing, he pushed himself up and blinked in the dim light. It didn't matter. He could do anything he wanted now, now that he was out, and he wasn't going to get sucked in. And he wasn't going to let Caleb get the best of him either.

At length, Seth rose and went to the bathroom, checking his reflection in the mirror. His hazel eyes looked tired under his short, dark brown hair. Scrubbing at his hair, he sighed and turned on the shower. He had work tomorrow after all.

Chapter 3
Like Old Times

Seth didn't go back to the street, didn't go looking for Caleb. For a week, he did nothing but work and go home, spending his evenings watching reruns on television and thinking he should get a dog just so he might have someone to talk to.

He would get a big dog even if his apartment could barely fit him some days.

He mentioned the idea to Logan one day over lunch as they sat in the sandwich shop down the road from the office, Logan picking onions out of his sandwich and dropping them on the paper wrapping.

"What do you want a dog for?" Logan asked, taking a bite of his sandwich and a few pieces of lettuce dropped onto the table.

Seth shrugged, glancing out the window. For late summer, the sky was unusually grey, making the street and the people walking past look unusually dull as well.

"I don't know. Why not?"

"Because you have to walk them and feed them and they're loud."

Seth arched an eyebrow as Logan took another large bite of his sandwich. Logan paused, though, and gestured at Seth with his sandwich.

"Where do you live anyway? I've never even been to your place."

"It's not too far from here," Seth replied, gazing out the window again. A guy with messy blond hair strolled past, and Seth did a double take, heart rising, but he shook himself a moment later. It wasn't Caleb. That was the second time in a week he thought he'd seen Caleb. He had to stop doing that.

There was absolutely no reason Caleb would even be in this part of town.

Logan didn't even notice, too busy devouring his sandwich. Seth's own sat half-eaten on its paper.

"Hey, you're coming to Jacob's bachelor party next week, right?" Logan asked a minute later, reaching for his soda and shaking the ice inside.

Seth made a face as he turned away from the window. "I don't know," he replied slowly. "I don't even really talk to him."

Logan rolled his eyes. "Here we go again. Look, he invited you, didn't he?"

"He invited everyone below thirty in the office," Seth pointed out, but Logan waved him away, mustard on his fingertips.

"What's your excuse not to go? There's gonna be beer and strippers and blackmail for life!"

Any of those three would have been grounds enough for Seth to stay home, but he couldn't explain that to Logan.

"Besides, if you don't go, everyone's just gonna think you don't like them."

It wasn't too far from the truth, but Seth frowned anyway. Maybe he needed to make more effort at work. The thought wasn't appealing, but if it was what he had to do to fit in, he would do it. Seth had never been good at fitting in, from high school as the nerdy guy with the best grades to college coming in with piercings and three years too late.

Logan looked at him as the pause lengthened. "*Do* you hate them all?"

"What? No," Seth replied quickly. "I just, you know, people aren't my... thing."

Logan arched a skeptical eyebrow, sipping his drink through the straw. "Isn't that what serial killers say?"

Sighing, Seth knew he had to give in. He wasn't going to win this one, not if he wanted people to think he was normal, or as normal as possible.

"When is the party?" he asked, defeated, and Logan grinned.

"Next Friday. We start at the strip club downtown and then go bar hopping. It's gonna be awesome. I mean, how can you say no to hot girls in underwear?"

Seth didn't reply, thinking he'd much rather have Caleb in a... No. He stopped himself sharply. He wasn't going to spend his time thinking about Caleb. There were plenty of other hot guys out there who weren't hustlers and didn't make him feel like a naïve kid all over again.

"Yeah," he replied vaguely when Logan waited for his response.

Logan didn't seem to care what Seth said, though, as he leaned back in his seat, hands behind his head as he grinned.

"It's gonna be an awesome night," he said again, and by the time they left for the office, Seth had already come up with six different excuses he could use the night of to get out of it.

Despite his best efforts to come up with a logical reason he couldn't come to Jacob's bachelor party, the next Friday found Seth stepping out of the strip club after an entire hour of ribbing about why he didn't want a lap dance from Shanda, the pretty brunette who had called him sailor and rustled his hair as she passed.

"She's just not my type," he said for the fifth time as Logan elbowed him in the side, and the rest of the guys burst out behind him, laughing loudly. They'd already been through several rounds of shots inside and they were off to do a few more in whatever bar they could find. Seth had stuck to coke, ignoring Logan's suggestion of a shot of rum. As much as he thought alcohol would help this evening, he wasn't going to cloud his judgments and say something stupid.

"Enjoying yourself, Seth?" Jacob asked loudly, coming up behind him and clapping a hand on his shoulder heavily. "You should have banged that chick!"

"I don't think she wanted me."

"She's a fucking stripper!" Jacob said, still too loud, and a few people passing looked over. Seth shot him a smile despite the clench to his stomach. "That's what they do! Man, I have never seen you just cut loose. That's what tonight is!"

"Yeah, it's your last night until you're shackled to one woman for the rest of your life," Logan piped up, and Jacob finally released Seth's shoulder to latch on to Logan instead.

"Man, only one woman," he slurred as they kept walking. "What am I gonna do?"

Logan shrugged. "One-night stand?"

Jacob laughed but shook his head. "Kristy would kill me, roast me on a platter and then display my head on a spike for the whole building to see."

"Then we'll just have to get you drunk!"

"Yeah, drunk!" Jacob repeated, and the guys behind cheered in response.

Sighing to himself, Seth didn't respond. He would much rather go home, but he knew there was no way Logan was going to let him leave until they were all too drunk to walk. He was stuck.

The bar they chose wasn't one he'd been to, but he didn't see how it mattered either way. It was just going to be another bunch of straight guys, and they'd probably try to force him on some poor girl he had absolutely no interest in.

"Let's go!" Logan said excitedly, grabbing Seth's shoulder and pushing him inside.

Seth stuck to his coke even as Logan ordered a round of shots from the bartender and the group took over a table near the middle of the room.

"It's my buddy's last night as a single man!" Logan shouted to the room. "Are you all with me getting him good and smashed?"

The rest of the bar seemed to swell up at the idea and cheered as Seth sunk onto his stool and checked the time. He wondered just how long this was going to go on for.

Then again, it wasn't as if he had anything else to do. His apartment was empty and aside from a little cleaning, he had no project to work on. He would probably be better off just staying with the guys and seeing how many shots it took to turn Jacob completely around. He bet it wouldn't be long now from the way Jacob grinned and swayed in his seat.

Passing by the shots as they were handed round, Seth sat back in his chair and watched the rest of the guys toss them back and slam them on the table.

He didn't necessarily have anything against the guys in the office, not even their ugly tee shirts or the way they had absolutely no tact when it came to addressing people who weren't their boss. He could deal with all that.

He just, he felt uncomfortable around them even if they were nice for the most part. A constant dread hung over him whenever he opened his mouth, whenever they asked prying questions into why he wasn't interested in the hot stripper or why he didn't drink.

"Who you staring at?" Logan asked suddenly, and Seth blinked, frowning.

"No one," he said, shrugging. He was pretty sure he'd just been staring at a spot on the opposite wall.

"Another round!" someone called before Logan had a chance to probe him further, and Seth sighed in relief, actually welcoming when the server came around, and he thanked God that she was pretty and most of the guys practically fell over themselves to impress her, leaving him to his own devices.

He preferred to be alone anyway.

Three rounds of shots later, Logan, or maybe one of the other guys—Seth wasn't paying attention, too busy replaying last night's episode of *American Idol* over in his head—suggested rather loudly that they start some karaoke.

The rest of the bar seemed in total agreement as they talked the bartender into turning on the mic and turning on the lights over the little makeshift stage in the back.

Seth took the opportunity while the guys were arguing over which song to make Jacob sing, which would be the most embarrassing, to slip away to the bar. He had no real reason for doing so except that he just couldn't stand there and listen to them argue over *Endless Love* or *This Kiss* for the tenth time.

At the bar, he set his head in his hands and sighed. He could feel the beginnings of a headache in his temples.

"Can I buy you a drink?" someone asked beside him, and he opened his eyes.

"No, I—" he started to say as he glanced up then stopped suddenly as he realized it was a man who'd spoken. His heart jumped into his throat as a sudden panic seized him. Did he know the man? Was he an old client he'd forgotten? "What?"

He must have looked petrified because the guy laughed, rubbing the back of his neck awkwardly. "You just look like you could use one."

Unsure, Seth forced himself to close his mouth, and he turned back to the bar. "Yeah, well, my friends are really drunk."

"And you're not."

The guy smiled as Seth looked at him again. He paused, examining his face, but he was fairly sure they'd never met. The guy seemed to grow nervous under his gaze, shifting on his feet and raising his glass to his mouth instead of speaking again.

Shaking himself, Seth turned around to face the bar instead. He didn't know the guy. He should really get a grip. Not everyone he ran into had paid him once.

"I don't drink," he said finally, eyes falling on Logan and the rest of the guys. They were fiddling with the microphone along with a server, although they seemed more interested in hitting on her than actually getting it to work. "Right now, though, I wish I did."

The guy laughed around his beer. "I know what you mean."

Seth glanced over, catching the look in the guy's eyes, the question. Smiling for a second, he stretched back against the bar.

It would be so easy, he thought, to give that guy one look and have him following him out of there like a puppy dog. It was written all over his face. He paused as he contemplated the notion. He could; just meet his eyes and smile, and it would be all over.

There would be no question. What was stopping him? The last few hookups he'd had had been... well, one he'd paid for and the other had been so long ago he barely remembered what the guy looked like.

There was no harm in giving in to his carnal desires, he told himself as he watched the guys finally shove Jacob up on the stage. He stumbled drunkenly, laughing in the mic.

No one would even notice he was gone, and if they did, he was quite an accomplished liar. It came with the territory after all.

After a long pause in which the guy next to him had started to grow visibly uncomfortable, as if sure he'd hit on entirely the wrong person, Seth glanced at him. Then he smiled, and the guy's shoulders relaxed. Seth knew the feeling, and he was glad to be on the other end of it this time.

Tilting his head towards the door, he left his drink on the counter and slipped unnoticed between the tables and outside. The guy followed him, trying to be just as unnoticeable.

Outside, Seth didn't glance back, walking purposefully around the bar to the back alley. Alleys had rarely failed him in the past. He didn't stop until he'd passed the tall trashcans near the back door.

Turning around to face the guy still following, he smiled. "Well?"

The guy returned the smile after a second, stepping up to him and reaching for his jeans.

"You always hit on guys in straight bars?" Seth asked curiously as he leaned back against the wall of the building, and the guy tugged his jeans down past his hips.

"Just the really hot ones," the guy mumbled as he got down on his knees and pulled out Seth's cock.

Leaning back, Seth closed his eyes. Despite being in an alley, feet from a door that someone might open at any moment, he felt relaxed. He let his hand fall to the guy's short, brown hair, gliding through the strands and not guiding him anywhere as he started to suck him off.

It was nice, Seth thought as he stood there, eyes closed against the darkness of the street. A cool breeze swept past and he shivered slightly.

Licking his piercing, he breathed out slowly, feeling the guy moving back and forth in a slow rhythm. It was nice. Nice, but not amazing.

As he stood there, he opened his eyes as a sudden feeling pressed over him, a strange sensation as he thought that it felt like... like back when he was a hustler. Back when so many guys had fucked him that he didn't even care anymore, that he felt nothing when they reached for his cock.

Not that he felt nothing when the guy sucked him off, but it wasn't anything special. He hadn't felt like anything special since... Oh fuck no.

His head fell back with a thud against the wall as the thought hit him. Cursing to himself, he couldn't concentrate anymore, not even as the guy took him in deeper.

"Fuck," he cursed loudly, pushing the guy away. Ignoring the guy's confused expression, he pulled up his jeans and pulled down his shirt.

"Hey, what are you—" the guy tried to say, but Seth was already striding away. He couldn't believe this, after all this time and all the guys he could be with, the only one he wanted, the only one who did anything for him was the one he didn't want to get involved with. He couldn't get involved with that stuff again. His mind was on something else entirely as he strode away, not returning to the bar but heading home because whatever he was thinking, he had to stop it. There was no way he was going back to Caleb. No way.

"Where'd you disappear to Friday night?"

Seth looked up from the computer to find Logan leaning against his desk, an expensive cup of coffee in his hands.

"What?"

"Friday," he repeated, setting his coffee down and shrugging off his jacket. He hung it on the back of his chair and shot Seth an expectant look. "You disappeared after the first bar. What happened?"

Seth frowned at the computer. He had known this would happen, but he'd hoped to avoid it at least for a few days. He'd spent most of the weekend avoiding any thought of Friday night.

"Uh," he said quickly when the silence stretched too long. "Yeah, I just wasn't feeling well, had to get out of there."

Logan plunked down in his chair, spinning around on the opposite side of Seth's desk. "Don't tell me you actually got drunk?" he asked, a curious lilt to his voice, but Seth shook his head.

"No, just needed some air," Seth muttered, looking away and staring at his computer, but the screen held no answers to his problems.

He'd tried not to think about Caleb, but he couldn't deny what he wanted, and he wanted to fuck him. He wanted to hear Caleb come, to know he was the one that did it, to watch him as he screamed out and submitted to him.

He didn't know if he could make that happen, but he still wanted to try. The only problem, aside from Caleb's grating personality, was his own willingness. He'd already spent so much time trying to escape that lifestyle and the people in it. He didn't want to get sucked back in.

On the other hand, though, Caleb was different than the other hustlers. He wasn't just a random prostitute on the street. And it would be nice to hang out with someone he understood, who he didn't have to hide from.

"Well, you missed the best part," Logan said, turning on his computer. "Jacob got completely wasted and called up his fiancée, and he told her that even if she was a guy, he would still marry her."

Seth frowned but hummed softly. "That's... nice."

"It was hilarious," Logan said, leaning back in his chair with his hands behind his head. "Can you imagine Jacob marrying a guy? Dude, can you imagine anyone? It's, like, so weird."

Seth didn't reply, frowning at his computer still.

"I can't even see Jacob kissing a guy. That'd be so weird." He laughed. "If you could marry anyone, who would it be? I would pick Charlize Theron. She's hot."

"Uh," Seth said again, trying to suppress the surge of annoyance at Logan's words. He tried to remind himself that Logan didn't even know that he was gay, didn't know that the reason he'd disappeared on Friday was to have his dick sucked in an abandoned alley by someone he didn't even know.

"Ooh, or that crazy chick from Black Swan. She was psycho, but that was still kinda hot."

"I have to get these copied for the boss," Seth said instead, rising from his seat and grabbing a random stack of papers before he knew what he was doing.

Logan shrugged, turning to his computer. "Oh, hey," he said as Seth stepped out from behind his desk. "The guys were thinking of hitting up a casino next weekend, maybe up in Jersey. You down?"

"I don't know," Seth said quickly. "I might be busy."

"Think about it!" Logan called as Seth left for the copier. "A weekend away might do you some good!"

Sighing, Seth hurried out of sight. He just needed to be alone. Or rather, he needed some release and he could only think of one place to get it.

Chapter 4
The Dark Side

It had taken over a week to talk himself out of his reservations, but given the choices of never being satisfied or sucking it up and going to Caleb, he'd choose Caleb. Besides, no one needed to know about this. It wasn't as if he had a lot of friends to tell.

So the next Saturday night found him stepping onto the long, dim street filled with underage kids shouting out to the cars that slid past and slowed down. He knew exactly where to find Caleb this time, down at the end under his lone streetlight, a cigarette in his fingers and hair falling in his face.

He glanced over at the scuff of Seth's shoes on the pavement and stopped, eyes flicking up to him before he smiled, a derisive curl to his mouth.

"What the hell do you want?"

Seth paused a second, breathing in the scent of Caleb's cigarette, a powerful itch of longing coursing through him. Tearing his eyes from the cigarette, even as Caleb lifted it to his mouth, he focused on Caleb. He hadn't changed in the past couple weeks, but Seth hadn't expected him to. Caleb was nothing if not resilient.

"I want you to come with me."

Caleb eyed him skeptically. "So you can act like a freak again? I don't think so."

"I'll pay you."

Caleb scoffed, exhaling a stream of smoke into the darkness. "You'll pay me for a blowjob and then kick me out."

"Isn't that what you do?" Seth replied sharply, not in the mood to bargain, although he knew getting Caleb a second time wouldn't be so easy.

Caleb barely reacted, but Seth didn't expect him to. Instead, Caleb took another drag of his cigarette.

"I don't waste my time on head cases," he drawled, glancing away.

Seth didn't roll his eyes. He'd known it would be difficult the second time around. "From what I can see, you don't have a reason to say no."

"Don't have a reason to say yes either." Caleb flicked the ash off the end of his cigarette and crossed his arms over his stomach, looking unimpressed.

"I can give you about five hundred reasons."

"Aren't you just made of money?" he replied, raising the cigarette to his mouth. "And here you want to spend it on one fuck. Are you really that pathetic that you can't get it anywhere else?"

Seth didn't reply that he didn't want anyone else, or that anyone else wouldn't do anything for him. It had to be Caleb, as much as he wished it didn't.

"It's not the money," he said finally, and Caleb shot him an unimpressed look.

"It's so you can feel good about yourself," he sneered. "That you're so much better than the rest of the people on this street. Well, I've got news; you're not. Once a hustler, always a hustler. What is your job anyway?"

Seth paused, thinking about how he ran errands and booked planes for his boss, did whatever he wanted him to do without questioning why. Like he'd said to Logan once, he knew how to please his men. An unpleasant shiver crawled up his spine at the thought but he shook it away, focusing on Caleb instead.

"Are you gonna come with me or not? I'm sure any of these guys would love five hundred bucks."

Caleb flicked his cigarette away, the red cherry vanishing into the darkness. "Then get one of them."

Fuck, Seth cursed to himself. Caleb had always been smart, and the way he arched an eyebrow told Seth that he fucking knew Seth didn't want any of those other guys. He had the upper hand here, even if he couldn't afford to pass up five hundred bucks.

"Seven hundred," he said grudgingly, and Caleb contemplated his fingernails, picking a piece of dirt out from under one.

He looked up finally, a smirk at the corner of his mouth. "Well, I guess if you insist."

Rolling his eyes, Seth reminded himself of how good it was going to feel, and how much it was going to be worth it to have Caleb underneath him. Still, though, he smiled to himself as he turned and Caleb fell into step next to him. It was going to be good.

Seth paused, allowing himself time to appreciate the view in front of him.

Caleb lay facedown on the bed, arms under his head and a slightly bored expression on his face. His pale body stood out against the deep blue of Seth's comforter, sunk comfortably into it. Seth's eyes traveled over his sharp shoulder blades and down the contours of his back, the soft rise up to his ass and back down to his thighs.

He could see the way Caleb bit back whatever he wanted to say, to hurry him up somehow, but Seth had made it clear early on that he wasn't allowed to do that, and he doubted Caleb would try again so soon.

Shifting up, he straddled Caleb's legs, stretching over him to yank open the bedside table where a box of condoms and lube rattled to the back with the force of it opening. He pulled them out, tossing the lube on the bed and rolling a condom on as he watched Caleb shift beneath him, licking his lips and turning his head so his forehead rested on his hands and he faced the bed.

Seth's cock twitched in anticipation as he slid his hands up Caleb's thighs, to his hips where he smoothed over his hipbones and drew him up, almost to his knees. He didn't bother with any extra preparation, just a squeeze of lube to make things easier. Caleb would only sneer and call him sentimental if he bothered with anything more than fucking, but Seth didn't really care what Caleb would say. It wasn't about him.

It was about the hot, tight slide as he sunk down inside him, the heat licking through his body as he pushed in, past the muscles squeezing around his cock. His hips snapped before he could stop them, sliding into Caleb until he was all the way in, deep inside him, and the blood throbbed in his cock as he paused a second.

Caleb barely reacted, sucking in the smallest breath when Seth slid in completely. He kept his face turned towards the bed, breaths even and slow, like he was trying specifically not to show any emotion.

Seth didn't care, though; didn't care that Caleb resisted all feelings because he felt amazing. It was nothing like the guy outside the bar, nothing like any of the guys before. It felt good and hot and he just wanted more as he started to move, started to build up a rhythm inside Caleb as Caleb licked his lips and breathed out again, a little sharper this time.

"Fuck," Seth breathed as he moved faster, hands gripping Caleb's hips to help find the right angle, cock gliding through the tight muscles as heat spread through his body, sweat pricking at his forehead as he thrust in and pulled almost all the way back out before slamming back in. He watched with a ripple of satisfaction as Caleb's back arched away from him and he bit his lip instead of speaking.

It hadn't been like this in a very long time, long enough that Seth groaned aloud and grasped Caleb's hips tighter. He didn't care that he was paying for it or that Caleb had no interest in him. For years, all he'd wanted was for Caleb to look at him, and now he had the power to do whatever he wanted. He could make Caleb come, whining his name, if he wanted. He could make anything happen.

Right now, though, he just wanted to feel Caleb. He wanted to feel the rough slide of his body, the smooth softness of his skin under his hands, the shiver in his spine as he rocked deep inside him. He could see the heat rising on Caleb's skin, feel it under his fingers as he slid a hand up his stomach as he moved, rocking harder, working towards the curling in his stomach, the hot coil of tension in his body.

Caleb's hips slipped in his grip as he lurched forward, gasping sharply as the feeling overwhelmed him, a sharp twist in his gut as he tried to hold on, to make it last, but as he caught sight of Caleb's face, eyes squeezed shut, his fingers curled into the comforter to hold on as his body was rocked back and forth with Seth, he lost it.

He came, cursing and gasping, pulling Caleb's hips back to his. Waves of heat crashed over him and he sighed as his hand slipped again, falling to the bed to keep him upright as it ended.

"Shit," he muttered as he pushed himself up and took a second to smooth his hands up Caleb's waist before Caleb could say anything or wriggle away.

Caleb didn't move, though, letting his hips slide down to the bed as Seth pulled out.

He turned over after a minute, though, glancing around for his clothes. His shirt hung crookedly off the bedpost, and he grabbed it as Seth lay down on his back, watching him for a moment.

"Are we done?" Caleb asked once he had his shirt on and began to hunt for his jeans. He found them in a pile on the floor and started to pull them on.

"I guess," Seth replied slowly, watching his ass as he turned away to zip up the jeans.

"Great," Caleb muttered sarcastically, already searching for a cigarette. He pulled it up to his mouth, but Seth stopped him.

"Don't," he said, and Caleb paused, arching an eyebrow.

"Why? Do you want one?" he drawled, though Seth was sure he didn't mean it.

God, he did, he wanted one, but he shook his head instead. "No, I don't smoke anymore."

Caleb laughed, somewhat derisively, but he shoved it back in his pocket for the moment. "And next you'll tell me you don't do body shots either."

"I don't."

Caleb frowned for half a second and then shrugged. "Guess you really have gone to the dark side. So tell me something then," he said, leaning over the bed, a curious eyebrow raised. "Why the fuck are you here right now with a hooker when there are probably plenty of shiny parties to go to?"

Seth didn't answer for a moment. He smiled after a second, pushing back his hair. "People are assholes. I don't need to waste my time with them."

Caleb's lip curled slightly, not enough to be a smile. Seth wasn't sure he'd ever seen him smile for real.

"Instead, you stalk me so you can get your rocks off. You really are fucked up."

Sliding off the bed, Caleb rooted around for his shoes while Seth frowned at his back, eyes narrowing slightly.

"You did say yes," he pointed out, and Caleb scoffed.

"Yes to money, not yes to you," he replied simply, tugging on his shoe and glancing back at Seth. "Sorry to burst your bubble, but you're not my type, sweetie."

Seth rolled his eyes darkly. "We both know your type is old and rich, preferably on their deathbed and naïve enough to believe what you say."

Caleb barely laughed. "Their loss is my gain." He ran a hand through his hair and glanced in the mirror as he passed the bathroom door. He paused at the doorway to the bedroom, shooting Seth a dark smile, quirking an eyebrow. "You have a lovely evening."

Seth didn't go after him as he heard the front door open and close. Instead, he slumped down on the bed and raised a hand to his forehead, feeling the last remnants of warmth fading from his skin as he sighed.

As he lay there, his phone went off on the side table, and he rolled over, wondering who could be possibly be calling him this late. He eyed Logan's name on the screen and waited another ring before answering.

"Hey."

"Seth!" Logan's voice blasted through the other end, and Seth held the receiver away from his ear.

"Logan? Where are you?"

"Jersey!" Logan shouted, the syllables slurring slightly. "Dude, it's awesome here! Why didn't you come? The girls are so easy in the casinos! We could get you laid in two seconds! You should totally come up! Catch a flight, man!"

"I can't tonight," Seth replied, but he wasn't sure Logan could even hear him over the loud casino noises in the background.

"Dude," Logan slurred again, trying to be serious, but he laughed a second later. "You know what Jacob said about you? He said, he said that you probably have some, like, super secret life that nobody knows about. But that's crazy, right? You just hate people!"

"I..." Seth didn't know how to respond to that, throat seizing up as the words came out of Logan's mouth.

"Oh!" Logan interrupted. "Shit, Jacob, where—"

The line went dead, and Seth lowered the phone, staring at it for a second before dropping it on the comforter.

The panic that had surfaced at Logan's suggestion that he had a secret life receded slowly, and he blinked at the ceiling, shaking his head and telling himself to calm the fuck down. Jacob didn't know anything. Nobody did.

Nobody needed to know.

He thought of Caleb, and after a second, a small smile crept onto his face. Logan would never need to know about Caleb. He would just make sure his secret stayed that way.

Chapter 5
Ghosts

Seth walked slowly in the cool morning air, glancing up at the tall, gray buildings he passed and watching the clouds float over the space of sky above. He was in no hurry to get to work.

A smile crept onto his face as he walked, crossing in front of the flower stand on the corner and pausing to wait for the light. He shook himself slightly. He couldn't go to work like this. Logan would immediately know something was up. Besides, it wasn't as if he had anything to really smile about.

He put on a more solemn face, then, as he crossed the street and entered the tall building across from him. No one noticed him as he took the elevator up to the fourth floor and stepped out into the maze of cubicles.

His desk was on the far side, outside his boss' office. He was surprised to see Logan already at his computer, though it looked as if he'd barely sat down as his coffee was still steaming next to him.

"Hey," Seth greeted him as he sat down and turned on his computer.

"Hey," Logan replied brightly, reaching for his coffee.

"How was Jersey?"

"I'm going to move there someday," Logan said, and Seth sincerely hoped he was kidding. "You can get laid so easy. Hell, we could have even got you laid!"

Seth frowned and didn't reply.

"What did you do this weekend anyway?" Logan asked, glancing over at him. "You said you were busy?"

"Oh." Seth frowned at his desk for a moment. He hadn't thought of what he was going to say before the words, "I can't, I'm busy" had come out of his mouth on Friday morning. "Uh, I had to, a friend came into town so, you know."

Logan nodded after a second, sipping his coffee and wincing as it burned his tongue. "You should have invited them along!"

"Maybe next time," Seth muttered instead, though he doubted very much if there would be a next time. At some point, they would stop inviting him, right? He could only hope. Logan seemed very determined to get him out of the office.

Logan was the closest thing Seth had to an actual friend in the city, an odd enough thing considering how long he'd lived there now. Logan was only his friend because their desks sat across from each other, and Logan seemed to consider it his duty to befriend everyone in the office, more so if they didn't want to be befriended.

Early on, Seth had tried to shake him, but Logan had clung on, and at this point, he figured he'd just wait until he gave up trying. It had to happen sometime.

"You always say that," Logan said, sounding distracted as he turned to his computer, but Seth knew he wasn't. Logan's sharpness was often clouded by distraction, but he was sharp nonetheless. It was a worrying combination. "But next time never seems to happen."

Logan looked at Seth over his computer, and Seth shot him a smile instead of responding with that would most likely be an inadequate response.

Truthfully, he found it trying to spend too much time around guys from the office. They all had their own trifling problems, and he just couldn't stand to listen to trust fund kids whining about rent prices or not being able to buy the newest car model. He also didn't appreciate the probing questions he always got about his own life, his family, growing up.

"I'm just busy," Seth said after a moment, thinking back to Saturday night. He'd prefer to be busy like that every weekend if he had his way.

Caleb was really the only person who probably understood him, he thought as he turned a pen over in his hands idly, even if Caleb seemed to dislike him so much. They were more alike than they pretended sometimes.

"Someday I'm not gonna take no for an answer," Logan replied, sipping his coffee.

Seth glanced up, catching the glint in Logan's eye. He tried not to swallow nervously, hoping that would never come to pass. Instead, he didn't acknowledge Logan's words and turned back to his computer. He'd be in trouble when that day came, but for now he'd do his best to avoid it.

Seth pulled out the stack of letters in the little box labeled with his apartment number. Sifting through, he pulled out the junk and tossed it in the trash. The rest were mostly bills, and he grimaced as he stuck them in his pocket.

"Anything good?"

He turned to see the pretty redhead from two-oh-seven standing next to him. A wave a dread passed through his stomach at the sight of her winning smile.

"Not really," he replied, already turning away, but she stepped in front of him, tilting her head to the side, and her hair fell over his shoulder in a rippling wave. Sammie was her name, but Seth usually tried to avoid talking to her if at all possible.

"I haven't seen you for a few days," she said, eyes flicking to his, and he pushed his hair back with a rough hand, glancing to the staircase to his right. If only he could get around to it. "Have you been busy?"

"Yeah, work, you know," he said, edging towards the stairs, but she moved with him, a hand playing with her hair.

She was pretty, Seth thought, if you were into that kind of thing, but as it was, he wasn't. She'd hinted many times at the idea of them going out, but Seth merely deflected the offer each time. He only wondered how long it would take for her to realize that the reason he wasn't interested had more to do with the fact that she was a woman than that they didn't "mesh."

"I know a great place to relax," she said, eyes bright as she watched for his reaction, but he flashed her a short smile.

"I can't," he said, but she wasn't discouraged. She never was.

"It's a little café not too far from here. We could get coffee and talk. You could tell me about yourself."

"Nothing to tell," Seth said, stepping around her for the stairs, but he didn't get far as she moved quickly.

"I saw a guy the other day," she said suddenly, and Seth froze, one foot on the stairs.

"What?"

Telling himself to calm down, he forced his hand to relax over the railing. She didn't know anything.

"A guy," Sammie repeated. "He came out of your apartment."

"Oh, he's just a friend... from home," Seth lied quickly. "He's thinking about moving here."

Sammie eyed him, and Seth forced himself to smile at her, calm and reassuring. He saw her body relax, if only slightly, and she sighed.

"If you ever want to hang out," she said, and Seth nodded.

"Yeah, sure," he replied vaguely. "I'll see you."

Sammie watched him go before sighing and turning away.

Trudging up the stairs, Seth shook his head. Someday, someday he wouldn't have to lie to everyone in his life. He didn't know when that would be, but he hoped it would hurry up and get there.

Back in his apartment, he flopped down in front of the TV, loosening his tie, tossing the mail next to him. The channels flickered by as he blindly passed through. Nothing good was on. Instead, he reached for the mail, riffling through more carefully.

After the rectangular shaped letters containing bills, he came on a smaller, square envelope, a yellow daisy sticker clasping it shut in the back.

Curious, he wedged it open with his finger and slid out a smaller envelope addressed with only his name. Inside this, he pulled out what looked like an announcement, the paper wrapped in purple and gold.

His stomach slowly dropped as he read.

Requesting the honor of your presence
at the marriage of
Madison Cranston
&
Trevor Smith

The third, November, two-thousand and twelve
New Haven, CT
Reception to follow

Madison. God, he hadn't talked to his sister in almost five years. The last time he had, his mother had found out and banned Madison from calling him again. Since then, he'd lost touch. He didn't dare call his parent's house, and he didn't know if she'd even ended up going to college or where she lived. He wondered how she'd found his address.

He stared at the card. A wedding announcement. His little sister was getting married.

For a second, he imagined showing up to the wedding. His parents would flip out, he was sure. He was fairly sure he never wanted to see them again anyway. Madison, though...

Shaking his head, his eyes fell on a phone number at the bottom of the card.

Sudden panic seized him as the thought of calling it entered his mind. He shook it away quickly, though. He shouldn't contact her. If he did, she'd know he'd received the letter. It was his fault in the first place that five years had passed without talking. He couldn't get her in trouble again.

Making a decision, he shoved the letter back into the envelope and rose from the couch. He stuffed the envelope deep into one of the drawers he never used, the one filled with empty pens and expired coupons. He didn't know what she'd been thinking even sending it to him. It was stupid of her, of both of them.

Pushing it out of his mind, he went to the stack of DVDs near the TV and dug out one of the old movies he hadn't seen in a while, an old action movie he knew every word to. He slipped it in the player and sat back on the couch, forcing his hands to stop fiddling with his shirt and allowing himself to get lost in the mindlessness of the movie instead.

Chapter 6
Routine Routine

"So is this going to become a regular thing?" Caleb drawled, arms crossed over his chest, unimpressed as Seth pulled off his shirt and reached for the shower, turning on the cold stream of water and waiting for it to warm up.

Seth rolled his eyes at Caleb's tone as he tugged open a drawer and rummaged in the back.

"Take off your clothes," he said instead, and Caleb, too, rolled his eyes but shed his shirt anyway, dropping it on the floor and leaning back against the countertop.

The sounds of Saturday night filtered in through the tiny, rectangular window, opened a crack, on the wall. Cars rushed past on the busy street and the lights always seemed brighter than the weekdays. The day didn't matter to Seth, though, except that he bet there was at least one message on his phone from Logan asking why the hell he wasn't at the bar with the rest of the guys.

Seth didn't bother checking the water temperature as he nodded to Caleb to get in. Caleb eyed him as he brushed past, stark naked as he stepped into the shower, leaving the curtain open behind him.

Seth didn't hesitate to follow, pushing down his jeans and stepping out of them. He twitched the curtain closed as he stepped under the hot spray of water. Caleb already waited, arms crossed, but Seth turned him around instead, taking the time to relax under the water, sliding his hands over Caleb's chest as the water drenched them.

Tipping his head back, Seth closed his eyes and let the water soak his hair, running down the tip of his nose and dripping off as he sighed.

Caleb remained silent, standing with his back to Seth, head bowed forward slightly as the water soaked his hair, flattening out the slight curl to the ends and plastering it to his head, around his ears.

Seth had found him under the exact same streetlamp as before, a cigarette dangling between his fingers. The evenings had begun to turn cold, a chill shivering the air as they'd walked to his apartment in silence. Summer was waning and autumn would grace the city soon enough.

Seth pulled Caleb in against him, taking a moment to enjoy the warmth of his body, the smoothness of his skin as he grazed his hands over his shoulders and pressed his mouth to the side of his neck. He felt Caleb exhale slowly, but he didn't move otherwise.

It felt different, nicer somehow, standing here with Caleb, like all his worries could melt away in the hot water pelting down.

Caleb shifted, though, as Seth's mouth grazed down his neck, ducking down to trace a droplet of water up from his shoulder blade to the back of his neck.

"So who am I?" Caleb asked, and Seth paused, confused.

"You're Caleb," he replied, tracing his fingers down Caleb's hips slowly, pressing his palms into the soft flesh. His nose grazed up the back of Caleb's neck as his tongue flicked over ridges in his spine.

"And who are you pretending I am?" Caleb replied, a slight drawl to his voice. "The loving boyfriend greeting you after a *hard* day's labor? The paperboy you fuck on occasion? An old boyfriend?"

Seth paused a second, annoyance surfacing. He pushed a rough hand into Caleb's hair, catching him off-guard as he pushed him up against the tiled wall. Caleb's hand slapped against it with a loud smack to catch himself, and Seth tugged his head back, licking up his neck painfully slowly until he reached his ear.

"You're my whore," he growled in Caleb's ear, and he heard Caleb's laugh that was sharp and caught in a gasp. He saw the way Caleb's mouth curled derisively, the way his tongue darted out to wet his lips. Seth paused. Caleb liked this. He liked provoking him into action, into roughness.

"Like I didn't know that," Caleb shot back, but Seth had seen the smirk. "And all you want is to prove how much better you are than me."

"I am," Seth replied, biting at Caleb's neck while Caleb made a disjointed noise in the back of his throat but didn't struggle against Seth's fingers curled in his hair, tilting his neck to the side and holding him there as he bit a trail from his neck to his shoulder, tongue licking over the teeth marks.

"Yeah, right," Caleb scoffed under his breath, but he shut up a second later as Seth pressed in behind him, hands anchoring his hips down, spreading his legs, their bodies aligning, his hard cock pressing in against Caleb's ass. He didn't hear anything from Caleb, but he saw his jaw working, tongue wetting his lips under the flecks of water bouncing off his skin.

Caleb's body was long and lean, thin, sinewy muscles flexing under his hand as Seth reached for his ass, curving over the outline, dipping down to his thigh before skating back up. He felt the stretch in Caleb's back and pressed his mouth to his sharp shoulder blade, tongue circling the bone and sucking hard.

He was going to make Caleb come this time, instead of the vague indifference from before. He just had to find that spot that made Caleb get hot all over, made him putty in his hands. Everyone had one. Hustlers just hid theirs better.

He didn't push in just yet, but he thrust against his entrance, rough and hot, hands slippery on Caleb's hips from the stream of water. The bathroom had started to fog up around them, the air growing heavy with every breath he took.

He felt a shudder run through Caleb as he pushed against him. Seth pressed his mouth to the base of Caleb's neck, his lips falling open in a silent gasp as a ripple of heat stole through his body, cock growing harder at the pound of blood flooding downward. The heat of the water caused a red flush along the back of Caleb's shoulders, and Seth couldn't help sliding his hands up to dig into the skin, feeling the muscles flex under his hands.

"What are you waiting for?" Caleb growled after a second, and Seth knew he'd never do this with a regular client. "Winter to come?"

"It's my money," Seth replied, voice low, teeth scraping against the skin under Caleb's ear, feeling the shiver he repressed. "We do what I want, isn't that right, *sweetie*?"

Seth couldn't count the number of times he'd called someone sweetie or honey, guys he never learned the names of, had never seen again after one night. Saying it to Caleb, though, felt powerful, like he could control at least this situation in his life.

Caleb didn't snap back the reply Seth could tell he wanted to say, sucking in a sharp breath instead as Seth's mouth closed around the patch of skin under his ear, sucking as Caleb shoulders went slack in his hands for a second, and he heard the breathy exhale that followed, barely audible over the slap of water against the tile floor.

He sucked until the skin was red and hot under his tongue, and Caleb held back his angry curse, as Seth nipped the sensitive patch and felt Caleb's body shiver beneath him. Caleb probably hated him right now, especially the way he only slid his mouth down, tracing the droplets of water clinging to his pale skin, drizzling over his shoulder blade and down his back.

Seth wasn't going to tease forever, though, not when he'd been thinking about this, about fucking him again, for the past few days, since Logan had mentioned that he knew a girl he could set Seth up with. He'd managed to deflect it somehow, though he wasn't quite sure now, and it didn't matter anyway.

Leaning back, he groped outside the shower curtain, grabbing the condom he'd set on the counter. Caleb barely lifted his head when he returned, keeping him boxed in against the wall. He pressed a hand to the cold tile as his other hand worked the condom on, closing his eyes for a second against the pressure in his cock.

Sliding his hand away from the wall, he touched Caleb's stomach, and Caleb jumped, gasping at the coldness of his hand.

"Shit!" he cursed. "That's cold."

Seth merely hummed against the back of his neck, warming his hand under the water instead, and Caleb didn't jump when he slid it back, gliding down to grasp his cock.

Caleb kept stubbornly silent as Seth pressed in behind him, hand wrapping around his cock. Seth felt the stirring interest and smirked to himself. Caleb couldn't hide from him.

"I'm gonna make you come," he whispered into the back of Caleb's neck as he stroked him slowly, dragging his thumb over the head as Caleb hissed slightly, though at his words or his hands, he wasn't sure.

"Fuck you," Caleb ground out, but Seth bit the top of his spine instead, hearing his sharp breath, his cock hardening in his grip.

"No, I think it'll be the other way around," Seth murmured as he reached down, knee knocking Caleb's legs apart, a hand guiding his cock to his entrance.

The water beat down on them too hot still, reddening their skin, and if he had pressed a thumb to Caleb's shoulder, it would have left a white spot behind. His hands were busy, though, one jerking off Caleb despite Caleb's best attempts to ignore him, the other finding the right spot and sliding inside his ass.

Caleb's neck stretched back, jaw clenched as Seth pushed in, hard and fast. He was still tight despite how long he'd been doing this. His muscles clenched around Seth's cock, and Seth had to take a second to catch his breath. He pressed his face against the back of Caleb's neck and breathed slowly, panted against his skin. He felt Caleb shift beneath him, but he didn't pull away.

His fingers ran over Caleb's prick, squeezing the hot, heaviness in his hand, feeling the thud of his pulse despite Caleb's best efforts. He could make him come, he knew it.

His teeth scraped down Caleb's spine as he drew his hips almost completely back before slamming back in.

Caleb's hand hit the wall with another loud smack that almost covered up his curse as Seth moved again, faster this time. Caleb was ready this time, letting his hips move with Seth's, pushing back and rocking in with him. Seth recognized the technique, the one that got it over with faster, but he wasn't going to let that happen.

Instead, he pinned Caleb's hips to the wall, his cock pressed against the cool tile, and Caleb let out a shaky breath, unintentional as the feeling of relief flooded through his body, the shock of the cold, but Seth's hand was still wrapped around him, hot and too tight to relieve him much.

"Uh uh," Seth reprimanded him softly, biting his ear while Caleb squeezed his eyes shut instead. "No cheating."

He pushed his hips in harder, faster until Caleb was panting for breath, cheek pressed to the tile as the hot water filled the bathroom with steam around them. He could feel Caleb's body tightening, the throb in his cock as he squeezed and pulled his hips back to allow some room to move.

"Fuck," Seth muttered as he pushed in, riding the heat spreading through him, the tight clench in his stomach, the feel of Caleb's body pressed against his, sort of like it fit there, though he didn't quite admit that. Instead, he pressed his mouth to the spot under Caleb's ear again, pleased when Caleb opened his mouth and barely huffed out a breath as he seemed to melt for a second before dragging himself back together and jerking away from Seth's mouth.

That was the spot.

Seth didn't go back to it, though. Caleb wouldn't let him anymore. Caleb was as hard as a rock now, though, and Seth didn't try to suppress the feeling of satisfaction filling his body. He was about to prove himself right.

"Jesus, I just wanna fuck you until neither of us can feel anything," he mumbled into Caleb's skin as his hips moved faster, snapping forward against Caleb's hips. "Until you can't even remember your own name."

Caleb didn't respond aside from a grunt as he pressed his forehead against the cool tile and swallowed.

Seth let him, grabbing on to his hip as he came, hips pushing roughly inside Caleb, the heat snapping through his body as the curl of his stomach unraveled and he cursed loudly, still gripping Caleb's cock, too tight from the way Caleb gasped for breath.

The water slapped the ground as Seth finally let out a long breath and muttered, "fuck" against Caleb's back, still inside him as the throb slowly disappeared from his cock. He flicked out his tongue over the bite mark on his shoulder and moved his other hand slowly.

"Come on," he whispered in Caleb's ear despite the way Caleb jerked away from him. "You know you want to. It's okay. I won't tell anyone."

"Who do you have to tell?" Caleb ground out angrily, but he gasped and cursed at the twist of Seth's wrist.

"Come on, Caleb," Seth said instead, dragging his hand against his cock, feeling the hot throb under his fingers. "Come for me."

"I fucking hate you," Caleb managed to force out before he came, head bowed as he panted for breath, half-leaning against the shower wall, groaning softly as the pressure dissipated.

"You don't," Seth replied a minute later, pulling out and stepping back under the shower to wash away the evidence.

Caleb glared but stepped under too after a minute, scrubbing the come off his stomach. Seth watched a drop of water slide down to the end of his nose and drop off. Caleb's brown eyes rested darkly on him, and Seth had a sudden urge to kiss him, but he pushed it away. Caleb wouldn't let it happen, and it was a stupid idea anyway, just an unexplained moment that passed in a flash as Caleb looked away.

Caleb stepped out of the shower a moment later, and Seth paused before turning off the water and yanking open the curtain. Caleb already had his shirt on, sticking to the water on his back. Seth didn't step out of the shower yet but crossed his arms and leaned against the wall.

"Not even going to say goodbye?" he asked as Caleb reached for the door, his shoes in his hands.

Caleb paused, looking back at Seth standing stark naked in the shower, not caring what he looked like. "Yeah," he replied with a sarcastic smile and the door clicked behind him a second later.

Smiling to himself, Seth sunk back against the cool tile. That was exactly how he would have been a few years ago, so he really couldn't blame Caleb. He'd see him again anyway. That much he was sure of.

"No wild parties this weekend?" Seth asked, though he knew he shouldn't. If he asked and there was one, he'd be expected to go, but it was already Friday afternoon and Logan hadn't said a word all week about going out.

"Nah," Logan replied. "Unless you want to go to the boss' charity thing. I think he's still got seats to fill, so you might want to avoid him. As for me, I'm going home."

"Home like home?" Seth asked curiously, and Logan shrugged.

"Better than a charity ball. Besides, it's my brother's birthday, and my mom's already mad that I skipped Christmas last year to go skiing, so I don't really have much of a choice." He grinned at Seth. "It won't be that bad, though. After the family dinner thing, I'm gonna hit up a few bars with some old friends."

"Sounds nice," Seth muttered. For a second, his mind flitted to the wedding announcement shoved deep in his kitchen drawer, but he pushed it away forcefully as Logan shrugged.

"Could be worse."

Seth didn't agree, though he knew it could be.

"Seth!"

Both he and Logan looked up as Maryanne, the woman from accounting, stopped at his desk, an overly sweet smile on her face.

"What are you doing this weekend?" she asked, and Seth hesitated just long enough that her smile widened. "Perfect because we need one more to round out the table at the event tomorrow."

Logan didn't bother to hide his cackle, and Seth glared at him. He didn't want to go to some boring charity event that he didn't care about.

"I—I'm—" he tried to say, but Maryanne interrupted him swiftly.

"We'll see you there at eight," she said, slapping down a ticket on his desk. "It's black tie. There's going to be a silent auction!"

She left before he could argue. Logan still laughed across the desk, and Seth sighed at the ticket.

"God," he muttered to himself, and Logan stopped laughing long enough to shake his head.

"Could be worse," he said, and Seth restrained himself from flicking him in the nose with a pen. Instead, he sunk into his chair and thought ruefully that he wouldn't be seeing Caleb this weekend. No, instead, he'd be wearing a suit and tie and bidding on things he couldn't afford.

Chapter 7
Backfire

It was times like these when Seth really wished he still drank, and he meant, drank so much he wouldn't remember the evening. He would even take waking up on some sidewalk on the opposite side of town to another minute of this mind numbingly boring evening.

He didn't know half the people there, and Maryanne, among others, kept insisting on shoving a glass of champagne into his hands despite how he always set it down and abandoned it on a table seconds later. His name was on the bottom of a lengthening list for a trip to Hawaii, and only because his boss had been watching him hover near the tables and he had to put something down. Someone else would outbid him, though.

Staring down at the most recent glass of champagne, Seth contemplated the bubbles, the golden sheen as he tipped the glass slightly. He could just have one or two, he thought, staring down. He could handle that. As he glanced up, though, he caught sight of Maryanne veering toward him again, and he knew two wouldn't be enough, so he clenched the stem in his hand and vowed to set it down when she turned away again.

"There you are," she said as if he'd been lurking behind the potted trees in the corner. He'd merely been keeping out of everyone's way and wondering if he could somehow sneak out the back. There were other, far more entertaining things he could be doing right now instead of pretending to be interested in bidding on a dinner with two Nobel laureates. He would have absolutely nothing to say to them.

He put on a smile, though, as Maryanne grabbed his arm and dragged him through the fancily dressed crowd, women in silk gowns and men in uptight suits.

"Have you met Brianna?" Maryanne asked as she stopped in front of a small group of similarly dressed people, and Seth pushed back the sigh that wanted to fall from his lips.

He smiled instead, turning to the young woman Maryanne indicated. Her blonde hair fell over her thin shoulders and the straps of her red, satin dress, and she looked just as pained to be there, her smile strained as she looked at him.

"No," he said smoothly. "I don't believe I've had the pleasure."

"I think you two would get along splendidly," Maryanne said, the lines around her eyes crinkling as she smiled. "You're both little loners in the office, aren't you?"

Seth could see the way Brianna's smile tightened more, but Maryanne didn't notice at all. Seth couldn't say he disagreed.

"Loner is a bit harsh," he said instead, putting on his most winning smile, and Maryanne giggled despite herself.

"You're more charming than I thought, Seth. You should come out more often!"

Seth just smiled and forced himself to stay that way as Maryanne tittered some more. Brianna didn't look half as convincing, crossing her arms and grabbing a glass of champagne as the waiter passed.

"You two should bid on that Hawaii trip!" Maryanne said a moment later, and Seth cast around for something, anything, to distract her.

"Maryanne, I think Mr. Blackstone is waving at you."

"Is he?" she asked, stretching up onto her toes to look across the room. "I'll be right back, then! Don't run off without me!"

Seth let his smile fall as Maryanne disappeared into the crowd.

"Thank you," Brianna muttered under her breath, tossing back half the glass in her hand.

Seth nodded in return. He had no desire to be set up with anyone, especially someone from work. He glanced at her, though. He didn't remember ever seeing her before.

"You work for Mr. Blackstone?"

"I'm in accounting," she replied, glancing around the room. "With Maryanne."

"I'm sorry," Seth said, and she smiled over the rim of her glass.

"Apparently I'm not her only hopeless case. It kind of makes me feel better."

"What makes you think I'm a hopeless case?" Seth asked, frowning slightly. He could get a date if he wanted. He just didn't want to.

"She tried to set you up with me," Brianna pointed out, finishing the glass and searching for the waiter again. She paused, though, eyeing him. "Why don't you have a date? You're good-looking."

Seth barely smiled, not flushing at the compliment. He'd heard it enough times in his life in many varied forms.

"I was roped into coming at the last minute," he said, which was true, although not the reason he didn't have a date. "They needed to fill seats."

"And you didn't have better plans?"

"Not that I could think of with Maryanne hovering over me," he replied, eyeing her. "And why are you dateless?"

Brianna sighed, grabbing another glass of champagne from the passing tray. Seth followed it with his eyes, wishing he could have ten of them, but that wouldn't help anything.

"I have a boyfriend," she said after taking a long sip. "But he lives in Rhode Island, so Maryanne thinks I made him up."

"No one listens to anybody."

She nodded, staring at her glass and not Seth. Seth didn't care. He checked the entrance to the room again, thinking that if he could just sneak past Maryanne, he could get out of there with his sanity intact. Maybe he could even salvage the evening, but glancing at his watch told him it was far too late. Caleb would be long gone by now, in the back of some rich guy's car sucking him off.

He caught Brianna watching him as he turned back with a disappointed sigh. There was no salvaging the evening now.

She hesitated, draining what was left in her glass. "I'll cover you if you want to make break," she murmured, and Seth's eyebrow went up, but she looked serious. "Go now while they're busy. I'll just say you went out for air. And in about ten minutes, I'll go look for you. It's a win-win."

Seth hesitated, but she shot him a look.

"Go!"

This may have been his only chance, so Seth took it, slipping through the crowd and ducking behind a plant as Maryanne wandered past, looking a little tipsy as she waved at someone. Carefully, Seth stepped out from the corner and slipped out the door.

Glancing back, he caught sight of Brianna being accosted by Maryanne, but she merely nodded at something and replied easily, eyes meeting Seth's over the crowd.

Mouthing, "Thank you!" he clattered down the stairs and stepped out into the cool evening air. It looked as though he'd finally made a friend at work. Too bad he'd probably never see her again.

Turning away, he felt as though a weight had been lifted off his shoulders, and he turned on his heel and strolled away, glad the night was finally over.

"Heard you made a friend this weekend."

Seth rummaged in his bottom drawer, searching for the folder with all of Mr. Blackstone's flight information for next week. He heard Logan's chair squeak as he peered over the desk, clearly gauging his reaction.

"Word around the water cooler is that you left the charity thing with Brianna from accounting."

"They must be putting something in that water cooler," Seth muttered instead, pulling out the file and straightening up. He would bet anything that Maryanne had spread that rumor the minute he left.

He had, in fact, spent the rest of the night after escaping the event watching movies and contemplating going to find Caleb, but it had only gotten later and later, so he'd just crashed instead.

"Why is it so hard for you to just admit you like someone?" Logan asked, and Seth arched a skeptical brow.

"What?"

"I've seen Brianna around," Logan said loftily. "She's not bad-looking, man. You could definitely do worse."

"I'm not doing anything," Seth said slowly, frowning and looking away. He didn't need to justify himself to Logan.

"And that is your problem." Logan nodded his head as if that was the answer to everything. "Seriously, man, what do you do when you go home? Spend all your time playing video games and jerking off to porn?"

Seth glanced around, hoping no higher-ups were listening in. It didn't seem the most appropriate topic for work. He didn't like the unpleasant feeling that settled in his stomach at Logan's words.

Luckily, Logan didn't wait for his answer, sitting back in his squeaking chair and shaking his head.

"The way you act, you should be lucky someone like her wants to go out with you."

"What is that supposed to mean?" Seth asked, slightly annoyed as he watched Logan shrug nonchalantly.

"You're not very sociable, dude," he said with a laugh. "For all I know, you're a mass murderer who spends his time talking to the severed heads in his fridge."

Seth stared, mouth falling slightly open, indignant. He jerked back after a second, slamming the drawer shut with a snap, anger coursing through him. "Well, maybe I don't want to advertise my personal life to the entire office like you feel the need to." He stood up sharply, ignoring Logan's surprise. "Maybe I have a little more tact about who I sleep with." He shot Logan a dark glare as he grabbed a random stack of paper. "I have to go copy these."

He strode away, working desperately to get himself under control. Work wasn't the place to lose his temper no matter how wrong everyone was. Forcing down his anger, he stepped into the copy room and paused, head bowed as he took a deep breath, standing over the copier. He wasn't sure why he'd gotten so angry, but he could still feel it, pulsing through his veins.

The only bright side was that Logan was a guy and therefore wouldn't bother coming after him to check if he was okay, so Seth pushed back his hair as he suppressed the curl of anger in his stomach and composed himself.

He didn't need copies of the papers in his hands, but he turned on the machine anyway, just so he'd have something to do.

"Oh, Jesus," he cursed, neck stretching back as he came, fingers pressing long bruises into Caleb's hips, and he heard Caleb's shallow breaths, felt the shudder in his legs as Seth thrust into him sharply, riding out the climax that covered him in a wave of crashing heat.

He stared down at Caleb's back, the smooth skin under his hands, the dimples just at his hips, the perfect fit for his thumbs. He watched Caleb bury his face in the sheets, muffled cursing coming back to him as Seth groaned and slumped down.

Caleb pushed him away first this time, but Seth merely rolled over onto his back and took deep breaths. He didn't hear Caleb getting up, and he was glad he didn't feel the need to rush out every time.

"What do you do," Seth said after a minute, settling his hands over his stomach, "when you're not picking up tricks?"

"Sleep," Caleb grunted, slipping his hands behind his head, and Seth glanced over at his abs, rolling his lip ring into his mouth thoughtfully. Caleb caught him looking and arched a skeptical eyebrow. "What?"

Seth shrugged. "You must do something."

"I could use a cigarette," Caleb replied instead, glancing at his crumpled pants on the floor, but he didn't bother getting dressed quite yet.

Seth sighed, glancing away. He couldn't help thinking of what Logan had said, that he sat around playing video games and watching porn. It wasn't true, but wasn't it? The most he did on a Friday night was pop in a movie and quote all the lines back.

In school, he'd studied business even though he'd thought it might be fun to take a few language classes or a history class, but he hadn't had the time or the money. He'd wanted to get out of being a hustler as quickly as possible which meant no extra classes, no hanging out with people after class, no relaxing. It had worked, at least, helping him finish his degree in only a few years. It had gotten him what he wanted.

Caleb shifted next to him, frowning as he watched Seth. "You're not gonna become one of those talking guys, are you?"

"What?"

"Shit," Caleb cursed, pushing himself up. "I am not interested in being the one you dump all your problems on."

"What?" Seth repeated, more incredulous this time. "I didn't say anything. Just lie the fuck down."

Caleb's eyes narrowed, unconvinced. He shoved his hair back. "You were two seconds away from telling me how lonely you are."

"I am not lonely," Seth argued, scowling, and he pushed himself up as well.

Caleb scoffed, giving him a once-over. "Yeah, it's Saturday night and you're spending it with a hustler. Don't you have anything better to do?"

Seth glared. "Just because I'm not out doesn't mean I couldn't be."

Caleb rolled his eyes. "Sure. But this is the third Saturday you've picked me up. I could afford cable at the rate you're going."

"Don't you ever want to be anything other than a hustler?" Seth asked suddenly, and Caleb shrugged as if he didn't care.

"Like what? A businessman? You fuck people just the same."

"You can't be a hustler forever, though."

Caleb arched an eyebrow as he climbed off the bed and grabbed his pants. "Says who? I'll just become a professional escort to all your fancy business parties."

Seth rolled his eyes, watching Caleb pull on his shirt, ruffling his already messy hair.

"But you could do anything."

Caleb scoffed, putting on his shoes and turning to Seth. "Is that something your mommy used to whisper in your ear late at night? Not all of us were so lucky, honey. Don't you worry about me. I can take care of myself. You, on the other hand, might want to find a hobby."

"I do things," Seth said before he could stop himself, but he could tell immediately that Caleb didn't believe him. He almost didn't believe himself.

"Fucking one guy isn't a thing. At least fuck around. *That's* a thing."

"So you have plenty of hobbies," Seth shot back, and Caleb shrugged, eyes glowing.

"You could say that. You're just one of the many."

Annoyed, Seth didn't reply, grabbing his shirt off the floor and pulling it on. He didn't know why he and Caleb couldn't seem to get through a conversation without biting each others' heads off.

Caleb was almost to the bedroom door when Seth caught him, a hand on the knob to stop him from leaving. Caleb shot him a look as Seth crowded into his space.

"And how many of them make you come like the whore you really are?" he asked pointedly, arching an eyebrow slowly as Caleb's expression darkened and he reached for the knob despite Seth's hand in the way.

"You of all people should know it's an act."

"Bullshit," Seth replied, shaking his head, not releasing the knob. "You only get hard for me, don't you?"

He wasn't sure why he was trying to provoke Caleb since it could probably only turn out badly. He saw Caleb's mouth twitch, eyes fixed on the door. He wanted the satisfaction of Caleb admitting he was right.

"I have people waiting for me," Caleb only said, wrenching the door open with a painful twist on Seth's hand.

Seth followed him doggedly, though, through the living room to the front door.

"Why can't you just admit you like when I come around?"

"Why can't you just admit that you're lonely and I'm all you've got?" Caleb shot back, opening the door and letting it slam behind him.

The silence fell deafeningly as Caleb left and the door stopped reverberating on its hinges. Seth stood near the couch, Caleb's words ringing in his ears, but he turned away at length. Caleb had no idea what he was talking about. He was perfectly fine being alone. Perfectly fine.

Chapter 8
A Different Kind of Favor

"Hey," Logan greeted him as he sat down in his chair, and Seth glanced up slowly.

Logan hadn't been there the day before. He'd wheedled it out of Maryanne that he'd called in sick. He'd never known Logan to call in sick the entire time he'd worked there, but one look at Logan's reddened nose and slightly puffy face erased all doubt that he'd just been avoiding Seth.

Seth shook himself stupidly. It was stupid of him to think that he was important enough that Logan would bother avoiding him after Friday. No. Logan had merely been sick, and was still if the way he coughed as he sat down and scrunched up his face was any indication.

"I feel like shit," Logan muttered into his usual coffee cup. He sniffed and coughed into his arm again.

"Why are you here then?"

"Can't leave you guys without me," he replied simply, scrubbing at his eyes and sighing. "Besides, how else would I flaunt my sexual exploits?"

Seth felt heat flood his cheeks, and he frowned at his desk.

Maybe Logan had noticed.

He'd never really been good at apologies, though, so he didn't say anything, and Logan arched an eyebrow as the silence lengthened. In the end, Logan coughed again and turned to his computer.

Cursing himself, Seth rued the day Logan had ever come up and introduced himself. If that had never happened, they wouldn't be sitting here in a stubborn silence as Seth wondered if he should really apologize. A part of him didn't see why he should. He had been right, after all. He didn't need to advertise his personal life to everyone he met. But another part of him knew Logan was only trying to be friendly. If there was one thing Seth didn't have a lot of, it was friends. Perhaps he should save the few he'd managed to accrue.

The moment had gone on far too long now, though, so Seth turned back to his computer, defeated by his own pride.

Seth sat in the hard, plastic chair, watching his laundry swish around and around in the washing machine, a mess of dark tee shirts and jeans plastered to the little window, mixed with suds. He could have been upstairs watching a movie or reading a book, but he chose instead to sit down there in silence with only the company of other machines.

The old, dismal clock tacked up on the cement wall ticked loudly as the hour hand passed the eleven. His laundry spun, an occasional clunk breaking up the whoosh of sound.

Sliding down in the hard seat, he didn't care what he looked like. There was no one here to judge him. He was wearing a thin tee shirt, the one with holes near the hem, and jeans a size too small. The rest of his clothes were a soapy mess at the moment.

The light above him flickered and hummed, stark against the dirty linoleum. A few abandoned magazines sat a few chairs down but Seth didn't pick one up.

He could have been doing anything right now, going out to a club or taking in a show downtown, but instead, he sat listlessly in front of the washer and tried not to think about the state of his life.

The sound of the laundry room door brought him out of his staring contest with the machine in front of him, and he straightened up slightly. He didn't want to look like a complete slob to his neighbors, even if he barely knew them.

"Seth!"

Seth's heart sank as he turned to find Sammie with a laundry basket under her arm, hair pulled over her shoulder and falling onto the baggy sweatshirt she wore. Underneath, she only had on a pair of shorts. She fidgeted, slightly embarrassed, and smiled at him.

"Oh, hey," he said slowly, praying she wouldn't want to chat.

"Hi," she said. "What are you doing here?"

"Laundry," he muttered, gesturing at the machine.

"Oh, no," she said, shaking her head and laughing slightly. Seth wasn't affected. "I mean, it's a Saturday night. Shouldn't you be out with friends somewhere?"

God, even she had to notice.

"I'm... going out later," he lied, glancing at the clock. Much later.

"Oh," she said again, sounding pleased as she looked at his clothes still in the washer. "Well, while you're waiting for your clothes, do you want to get a drink?"

Seth frowned down at his clothes. "I'm not exactly dressed for going out."

A blush colored Sammie's cheeks, and she tugged down the hem of her baggy sweatshirt. "Yeah, me neither."

Seth smiled tightly, looking away and hoping she would just put in her clothes and leave. She didn't, though. Opening a machine, she started to fill it while Seth remained stubbornly silent.

"So what happened to your friend?" she asked lightly after a minute.

"What friend?"

"The one that was staying with you a few weeks ago."

"Oh." Seth paused, trying to think up an answer. "He's... still looking for a place."

Sammie straightened up, pushing in her quarters, and Seth glanced at the time on his machine. He still had five minutes before he could move them to the dryer.

"You said you knew him from home? Where is that?"

Resigned to making up lies for the next five minutes, Seth scrubbed a hand through his hair and bit his lip ring.

"Connecticut," he said shortly, and Sammie took the seat next to him. He carefully ignored the way she crossed her legs, the shorts sliding up her thighs.

"What made you move to the city?" she asked, inclining towards him, and Seth looked away.

"Just thought it seemed a good place to go."

He still remembered the panic of those first few days, the realization that he had no one he could count on anymore, stumbling down the street and running almost smack dab into Caleb, who'd shot him a look as if he were the dirt under his fingernails.

He'd come to the city because it had seemed the best alternative to bumming around town, to becoming the kid everyone knew whose parents had kicked him out, the pariah. He'd left all his friends, though he hadn't had very many anyway, and took the first bus he could find.

Sammie hummed thoughtfully, and Seth didn't care about her opinion. She'd never know the truth anyway.

"And you're an assistant, right?"

"Executive assistant," Seth corrected her. He made more money than half the people in his office, booking flights and setting up meetings.

"You know, I do some modeling," she said, and Seth didn't know or care.

Luckily, his machine beeped at that moment, and he rose quickly, yanking the door open. Sammie watched him as he transferred his clothes to the dryer.

"I should go get ready for... tonight," he said as he shoved in the quarters.

"Oh," she said, a slight sigh to her words. "Okay. Maybe next time, when we're better dressed, we could get that drink."

"Yeah," Seth muttered. "I'll see you."

"Bye!" she called after him, and Seth clattered up the stairs, glad to be rid of her. He wished she would just take the hint and stop bothering him. Maybe, though, maybe if he had something to do on the weekends this wouldn't happen, he thought. It wasn't very encouraging, and he sighed as he made it to his apartment, in for an evening of reading and TV watching... just like every night.

Growing up, Seth had never been a social butterfly, but he'd always been able to manipulate what he wanted. He wasn't sure when that had turned into staying home every night and in bed by eleven. Probably around the time he left home and stopped caring what people whispered about him behind his back.

The only problem was that he still cared, especially now that he had a real job, and he worried every minute about his past creeping up on him, that moment when someone might recognize him from the street. It hadn't happened yet, but he didn't doubt that it would sooner or later.

It was that fear, perhaps, that compelled him to look up from his computer Thursday afternoon and contemplate Logan at the other desk. Logan wasn't paying him a bit of attention, but he'd seemed to be giving Seth the cold shoulder for a few weeks, or at least not pestering him about going out, which was as cold as Logan seemed to get.

"So," Seth said suddenly, and Logan looked up. "Anything going on this weekend?"

Logan's eyes widened for a moment, and he blinked slowly at Seth. "Did—did you just say that?"

Seth shrugged, feeling like a bright light was shining on him for the whole office to see. He rubbed at the tattoo behind his ear and bit his lip ring slowly.

"You always seem to know what's going on," he replied at length, forcing himself to drop his hand from the nervous gesture. He didn't know why inviting himself somewhere was so nerve-wracking, but it was, as Logan laughed, clearly surprised.

"Yeah, but you never want to come."

"Well, I do this time."

Logan stared for another second before smiling and shaking his head. "Okay then. You're in luck 'cause Saturday just happens to be Sasha's birthday! There's gonna be a little party thing down at the bar on Broadway. Everyone under twenty-five is gonna be there."

Seth smiled slightly. "Then I'll see you there."

"Yeah, you know," Logan said, tapping the desk with his finger. "You should totally bring one of your friends."

"One of my—what?"

Seth's stomach sunk like a rock as Logan's words sunk in.

"A friend," Logan repeated. "You know, like you said you had." He smiled, and Seth tried to hide the panic in his face.

"Yeah, of course, I was just trying to think who I could ask. They all work a lot."

"I'm sure you'll find someone." Logan grinned. "I really want to see who you call a friend considering you don't hang out with any of us."

"Right," Seth muttered.

"Saturday, eight o'clock, wow, this is gonna be awesome. The guys are never gonna believe you actually agreed to come out."

"Yeah." Seth sighed quietly as Logan went on disbelievingly at the situation.

Where the hell was he going to find a "friend" in two days?

Seth couldn't believe he was doing this. It was insane. It was crazy. It would never work. He'd be better off just grabbing a random guy from a bar and giving him a blowjob in exchange for this. Instead, he found himself trudging down the nearly empty alley except for the clump of underage kids calling out as he passed.

He ignored them, making for the streetlamp at the end where a dark figure leaned against the post, smoke wafting from the end of the cigarette in his hand.

"It's not Saturday," Caleb drawled as Seth approached. He took a long drag of his cigarette and glanced over. "And you missed last week."

"Did you miss me?"

Caleb scoffed, tapping the ashes off the cigarette. "Yeah, right," he said, rolling his eyes.

Seth paused, shifting from foot to foot and trying to convince himself this was an entirely horrible idea. He already knew it, but that hadn't stopped him from searching out Caleb.

"The hell is wrong with you?" Caleb asked after a minute, raising the cigarette to his lips again.

Steeling himself, Seth stood up straighter. "I need a favor."

Caleb laughed sharply, a puff of smoke dissipating into the air. "I don't do favors."

Seth sighed. He'd known that would happen. "I'll pay you."

Caleb glanced at him slowly, eyeing him up and down. "What kind of favor?"

"I need you to come to this work thing with me."

Caleb's eyebrows went up and he flicked the cigarette away, the red tip vanishing outside the circle of light. "Why?"

Licking his lips, Seth hated himself. Why didn't he have any actual friends that he could ask? The only one was maybe Sammie, but she would take it entirely the wrong way, and he had no intention of getting her hopes up.

"Because I'm supposed to bring a friend," he admitted finally, glaring as Caleb started laughing, not even bothering to hold back.

"Holy shit," Caleb said as he laughed. "You don't have any friends."

"If you don't want the money, then fine," Seth said when Caleb snickered. Shaking his head, he turned away. He didn't know why he tortured himself, doing things he *knew* would turn out badly, but he always did anyway.

"No, no, wait," Caleb said after Seth had already taken a few steps away. "Wait, wait. This could be entertaining."

Turning, Seth frowned at Caleb's obvious amusement. He shouldn't even bother, he thought, but the idea of turning up alone tomorrow after he'd already agreed didn't sit right.

"This isn't a game," he said seriously. "If you come, you won't say a thing about how we actually know each other. And this time, you won't be getting paid until the end of the night. If you don't keep up your end, you won't get anything. This is my life, and I don't need anyone messing it up."

"Relax," Caleb replied, holding up his hands, but he dug for a cigarette a second later. "No mention of prostitution, got it."

"And nothing about the drinking or the drugs," Seth went on, and Caleb shrugged, shoulders hunched as he cupped the cigarette and lit it. He hummed in agreement.

"No wonder you don't have friends," Caleb said, shoving the lighter in his pocket. "You don't do anything fun anymore."

Seth ignored him. Being clean wasn't about fun; it was about not dying at age twenty, about actually making something of himself instead of fucking strangers for the rest of his life.

"Meet me at my apartment tomorrow at eight. Wear something... clean."

"I'll wash my undies," Caleb drawled, tonguing the cigarette and scrubbing his hair, making it look artfully mussed.

Suppressing the urge to invite Caleb back to his apartment right then, Seth nodded instead.

"And try to keep the sarcasm to a minimum."

"Whatever you say, honey."

Seth didn't reply, turning away and hoping to God that he hadn't just made a colossal mistake.

Chapter 9
Masquerade

Seth grabbed Caleb's arm as he reached for the door to the bar, ignoring the look Caleb shot at him as he pulled him down a step. Twenty minutes late, Seth still didn't want to go in, but he'd rather have been late than early, and honestly, he'd rather not have been there at all.

"You remember the deal," he said seriously, hand tightening around Caleb's wrist as Caleb tried to pull away.

"Yeah, yeah," Caleb sneered. "We met at college. Mum's the word on the double life."

Seth rolled his eyes at Caleb's flippant tone. He needed this to go well, although if he'd wanted that, he probably shouldn't have asked Caleb to come along. There was no one else, though, and he couldn't come alone, not this time.

Caleb shook off his hand as Seth frowned.

"You know, if you want me to pretend we're friends, you might want to act a little friendlier."

Running a hand through his hair, Seth tried to get his emotions under control. He could only feel a mixture of panic, fear, and completely unwillingness to go through that door.

He rubbed at the tattoo behind his ear but forced his hand to stop the nervous gesture after a second. Everything would be fine as long as Caleb kept his mouth shut and they got out of there quickly without too many questions.

Their story was flimsy, at best, and Seth knew it. Anyone with any brains could poke holes in it and watch the water gush out.

"Fine," he said after a minute, bracing himself as he pulled the door open and stepped inside.

The crowded bar seemed loud as he pushed in past the knot near the door, Caleb following, hands stuffed in his pockets and a bored expression on his face. Caleb was wearing a simple pair of jeans and a tee shirt that

Seth had eyed doubtfully at the way it barely reached the waist of his jeans, revealing slices of skin if he raised his arms above his chest.

Seth spotted Logan and a few other people from work in a back corner, already passing around a tray of shots.

"Come on," he muttered to Caleb, sliding through the tables and pasting on a smile as he reached Logan.

"Hey!" Logan greeted him, and a few others smiled at him as he stepped up. "You came!"

"Said I would," Seth replied easily, biting down on his lip ring and glancing around. He knew most of the guys there and a few of the girls. He recognized Sasha at the very least, the girl with long, thick black hair.

"And you brought a friend!" Logan said, sounding surprised, and he grinned at Caleb beside Seth.

Caleb glanced his way, eyes looking him over interestedly, and Seth groaned to himself. That was the last thing he needed. If he could just get through the night unscathed, he swore he would never pick Caleb up again.

"Friend?" Caleb said as Seth didn't introduce him, too busy thinking up an escape plan and hastily turning down the shot someone offered him. "I think it's been long enough we can say boyfriend, isn't that right?"

Logan's mouth dropped open, and Seth's head jerked back to Caleb, eyes widening as he stared at Caleb and the devious glint in his eyes. It had to be payback, he thought, his heart sinking like a rock in his stomach.

A few people around him also turned to stare, the pause lengthening around them. Seth opened his mouth but nothing came out, and Caleb slid an arm around his waist, giving it a light squeeze.

"Boyfriend?" Logan repeated when the pause became almost painful, and Seth grimaced. Jesus Christ, he was screwed.

"Um..." he said, casting around for any kind of explanation, but Caleb seemed to be ready.

"You didn't tell anyone?" he asked, faux innocence written all over his face as he looked at Seth, and all Seth wanted to do was punch that pretty little face of his. "Are you embarrassed by me? He's so secretive, you know. It's impossible to get him to talk. But I have my ways."

Caleb arched his eyebrows at Logan, who still gaped like a fish out of water.

"Close your mouth, dear," Sasha said, leaning over and knocking Logan's shoulder.

"Seriously?" Logan asked a second later. He looked as if he was trying not to laugh now, and Seth glared at Caleb, who seemed highly pleased with himself. "Dude, wow, this explains a lot."

"Look, it's not what it looks like..." Seth tried to say, but he didn't know where he was going with it, and when Caleb leaned over and pressed a quick kiss to his cheek, he was so shocked he completely forgot what he'd been saying.

"See? He never tells anybody about me." Caleb brushed a piece of hair out of Seth's eyes as Seth shot him a look to stop it. *Stop. It.* Caleb ignored him, though, a sparkle to his eyes. "But I like him anyway."

Seth would have given anything just to sink into the floor or possibly shove Caleb through a wall, but he couldn't, not with everyone standing around him.

Someone pressed a shot into his hand before he could protest, and Caleb had already downed the one he'd accepted.

He shoved it at Caleb instead, who didn't question him at all, downing it as well. Logan looked sufficiently impressed, and Seth wished he could have drunk it.

"Why the hell didn't you say anything?" Logan demanded a second later as Caleb set the second glass down on the table and met Seth's glare with a devious tilt to his mouth. He knew Seth couldn't refute him now, not with everyone around him. "I mean, maybe I wouldn't have tried to get you laid so much, with girls."

Rubbing the back of his neck, Seth wished he'd never thought to invite himself to this. It was turning into one big disaster.

For one, he didn't need anyone to know that he liked guys, and for two, he definitely didn't need them to think that Caleb, of all people, was his boyfriend. This was just some devious ploy for Caleb's own perverse amusement, to watch him sweat after he'd specifically told him this was important.

"You never told me about that, did you?" Caleb said curiously, quirking his eyebrows as Seth glanced at him, exasperated. This wasn't funny.

"Didn't think it was important," he replied, teeth gritted as Caleb smiled too sweetly at him. He could just see how much Caleb was enjoying this.

"You guys are so cute," Sasha said, clinging to Logan's shoulder, clearly drunk already. "You should totally bring him to the Christmas party."

"That's a long ways away," Seth muttered, thinking that if he still had to pretend this at Christmas, something was really wrong with his life.

"What was your name?" Logan asked as Seth shook his head to himself.

"Caleb," Caleb replied, grabbing another shot as they were passed around. Seth sighed, rubbing his forehead as they both turned away, clinking the glasses together. "And you must be..."

"Logan," Logan supplied, downing the shot with a grimace.

"Right," Caleb said, sounding completely believable, and if Seth didn't know better, he'd almost think Caleb actually was dating him. "Seth's mentioned you before. He didn't say you were this cute."

Logan laughed, slightly awkward, and Seth stopped himself from clapping a hand to his forehead. Instead, he grabbed Caleb's arm as he reached for another shot.

"Can I talk to you for a minute, *honey*?" he said, less of a question than a demand, and Caleb shrugged, allowing Seth to practically drag him away from the group, out of earshot.

Turning to Caleb, he fixed him with a hard look.

"What the hell are you doing?" he hissed, and Caleb shrugged again, loosing his arm from Seth's grasp.

"Being friendly," he replied, meeting Seth's eyes coolly. "Your friends are totally buying every minute of this."

"I don't want them to think we're dating," he replied sharply, and Caleb put on a hurt look that Seth didn't believe for a second.

"I'm not boyfriend material?"

"We both know what you are," Seth said with an obvious look, and Caleb scoffed.

"And you're so much better than me," he replied, glancing obviously at the group laughing and passing around more shots. "You don't even like them."

Seth frowned. He couldn't exactly argue, but that wasn't the point.

"Well, I didn't ask you to come so you could lie."

Caleb's eyebrows went up and an incredulous smile curled his lips. "Oh really?" he asked facetiously, and Seth sighed, knowing what was coming, but something else caught his eye. Sasha had detached from the group and was winding her wobbly way over to them. A sense of panic rose in his throat as he watched her near. "You didn't ask me here to lie but you said, if I remember correctly, that you'd have my balls if I said anything about the pa —"

Caleb didn't finish his sentence as Seth leaned in and kissed him, catching him off-guard as he stumbled back a step, but Seth didn't pull away, mouth pressed against his in a half-open kiss.

Seth tasted the cigarettes on Caleb's tongue and a pang of longing shot through him. It had been so long since his last cigarette, but he mastered the urge to lick into Caleb's mouth and pulled away slowly.

"What the hell was that?" Caleb demanded the second Seth moved back an inch, glancing over, but Sasha was gone, turned towards the bathroom.

"I didn't want them to think we were fighting," he hissed, and Caleb glared, crossing his arms.

"So you thought making out would be better?"

"Wasn't it?" Seth asked, his turn to shoot Caleb a triumphant look in return for Caleb's sour expression. "You got us into this mess."

"That doesn't mean you can kiss me whenever you feel like it," he shot back. "That's not part of the deal."

"Well, the deal was to be friends, but that didn't work out, did it now?" Seth replied, feeling that at least he was getting back at Caleb somehow for his little stunt that he would never live down now. "So you get to deal with the consequences."

"And those include your tongue in my mouth?"

"If it keeps up the charade, then yes," Seth said sharply. He didn't feel as if he needed to make any excuses for his actions. Caleb was the one who'd started it all. If they'd stuck with his plan, they probably could have left by now instead of arguing in a corner.

As he said it, Sasha came stumbling back from the bathroom, and Seth didn't think as he grabbed Caleb again, despite the way Caleb pushed at his arms, and pressed their mouths together.

Caleb tasted of stale cigarettes, and Seth tried not to think about it, but he couldn't ignore the softness of Caleb's lips against his, and he pushed a little further as he heard Sasha stumble to a stop just feet away from them.

Hands cradled Caleb's jaw, and Caleb had stopped struggling now, standing still in Seth's grip, Seth licked against his lips slowly, coaxing him into opening his mouth, and Caleb bit his lip ring in return, too hard, but Seth took advantage of his distraction to push his tongue past his lips, dipping inside Caleb's mouth, tasting the cigarettes on his tongue, catching his lip as he pulled back. He only moved back an inch, feeling's Caleb's slow exhale against his chin, catching the way he licked his lips.

"Ohhh," came Sasha's squeal from behind them. "You guys are so adorable," she said, and Seth turned to her. Caleb stood behind him, shaking his head as though trying to rid himself of an annoying fly. "You should definitely come out more often."

Seth didn't reply as she stumbled back to the table, leaving them alone. Glancing back at Caleb, he didn't intend to apologize, and as he caught sight of a dark gleam in his eye, he thought that maybe he didn't have to.

Seth barely got the door shut behind him before Caleb had turned, shoving him back against it roughly, mouth covering his in a hard, biting kiss that Seth felt all the way down to toes.

Caleb's hands pushed him back against the door, the handle pressing uncomfortably into his lower back, but he didn't complain, twining his hand in Caleb's hair and biting at his mouth. He didn't care why this was happening, what made Caleb groan and yank him forward, hands scrabbling at his belt and pulling it apart with a loud clink.

"Is this extra?" Seth panted, pulling away, lips puffy and reddened.

Caleb seemed to pause for a second, but he let out a breath a second later and pressed his mouth to Seth's again, hungry and hot, biting at his mouth as Seth tried to keep up, pushing back, hand tight in his hair as Caleb's tongue slid against his and he finally got his jeans open.

"Fuck it, I don't care," Caleb breathed, shoving his hand in Seth's jeans and pressing against his cock.

Seth groaned loudly, but Caleb shut him up a second later by shoving him back against the door with a thud, cutting off the sound as he let out a breath of surprise.

Pushing back, Seth dragged Caleb in closer, sucking on his bottom lip, licking into his mouth slowly, tantalizingly, and he felt more than heard Caleb sigh. Stumbling back, he tried to get away from the doorknob denting his back.

Caleb's hands curled around his jacket as they moved, mouths breaking apart just for a second as he tripped over a chair, but neither cared, and when Caleb's back hit the wall, Seth went in for another heated kiss. He just wanted to feel Caleb, feel his lips, his tongue, the finessed way he managed to trace every inch of his mouth.

His hand slid from Caleb's hair, leaving it mussed and wild when he pulled away to take him in. Caleb's lips were red and swollen as he slid his tongue out to wet them, staring at Seth with dark, purposeful eyes. The corner of his mouth curled into a dark smile as the pause lengthened, but Seth didn't care what he was thinking.

Caleb tipped his chin up a second later, swallowing, mouth open as he breathed, panting slightly. "What the fuck are you waiting for?" he asked challengingly, eyes glowing, pleased, when Seth snapped to life, grabbing his waist and shoving him through the door to the bedroom.

Seth yanked Caleb's shirt over his head, catching on his ears, but he dislodged it after a second. The moment it was off, Caleb's mouth was back on his, hard and demanding, teeth closing around his lip ring and sucking like that was all he wanted to do.

Caleb's hands shoved up the waist of Seth's shirt, rucking it half up his stomach. His hands were cool as they pressed against Seth's skin, and Seth jumped slightly at the touch, moaning against Caleb's mouth, losing his control for a moment, and he knew Caleb felt it.

Caleb moved roughly, shoving him down on the bed and pouncing before Seth could do much more than roll onto his back.

He didn't complain, though, stretching back with a breathless groan as Caleb's fingers dug into the waist of his jeans and pulled, tearing them over his hips and off onto the floor. He didn't wait for Caleb to go down on him, though, dragging him up by his neck, wanting to taste him again.

Caleb's mouth was soft but hard at the same time, never allowing him to quite get the control back, going in and back out, tonguing his lip ring, and biting at his lips until Seth groaned, trapped beneath him, but he didn't fucking care that he no longer had the control. This was what he'd been waiting for, all those weeks of decent sex, but this was what he wanted, what he needed.

Caleb bit Seth's bottom lip once more before tearing away, not wasting any more time as he yanked down Seth's boxers, revealing his hard erection, and Seth sucked in a breath.

"Fuck," he panted, licking his swollen lips and staring down at Caleb, who looked like a lion on the prowl, taking no time to tear off his own jeans, his erection obvious as Seth watched, a thrill rushing through him at the sight. "Come on."

Caleb's glance flashed up for a second, but he leaned into Seth's stomach instead, teeth sinking into the soft flesh, and Seth couldn't help the whine that escaped from his throat, the flash of heat rising on his skin as Caleb slid his mouth down teasingly, nipping and sucking at the skin. There'd be marks the next day, but he didn't give a fuck right now. He wanted them, and Caleb wanted him to have them.

He expected to feel Caleb's mouth around his cock any second, but he was surprised as Caleb hauled himself up, hands grabbing his hips and forcing him to roll over onto his stomach. Caleb's mouth brushed behind his ear, over the tattoo, tongue darting out as Seth moaned. He could feel Caleb's hard cock pressed against his ass, not enough pressure for the blood thudding in his cock. He wanted to push back, but he bit his lip instead and hissed as Caleb bit his neck. He never knew Caleb had a biting thing.

"I'm gonna fuck you so hard," Caleb breathed in his ear, and Seth groaned, grinding his ass back. It felt so good, pressed against Caleb, every inch of their skin touching, Caleb's mouth trailing along his ear, down to his neck, and he wanted to kiss him again. He wanted to kiss him until he couldn't breathe, but Caleb moved too quickly, stretching out a hand to rummage in Seth's bedside cabinet.

His hand grazed down Seth's arm as he pulled out the condom and lube, tossing them on the bed.

Seth didn't strain back to look, letting himself relax as Caleb's nimble hands skated over his back, to his hips and pulled him up onto his knees.

He could only feel the heat racing over his skin as Caleb pushed in, too rough, too hard, too fast. It had been a while, though he couldn't remember how long, since he'd been the bottom. He bit his lip instead of protesting, burying his burning face in the covers.

"Fuck, you're tight," Caleb panted, words breathless as he pushed his hips flush against Seth's round ass, fingers tight around his hips. "Thought that after all this time, you'd be an easy fuck."

Seth merely groaned, fingers digging into the comforter when a shiver of pain shot through him as Caleb moved again, the unfamiliar stretch in his ass around Caleb's prick pushing deep inside.

Caleb didn't speak again, though, thrusting in hard and fast until Seth gasped for breath, panting against the bed, eyes squeezed shut against the mixture of pain and heat racing through him. His stomach clenched, curling like vines over itself as the friction of Caleb inside him shot straight to his cock.

"Shit," he cursed loudly as the bed started to squeak beneath them, and Caleb only moved faster.

His hands were tight around his hips, dragging him back with every thrust. He slammed in as Seth moaned.

It had been a while, Seth thought as Caleb pulled almost completely out before sliding back in, but it had never been like this, this carnal desire for Caleb to keep going no matter if it hurt or how fast it might be over.

He heard Caleb's sharp breaths from behind him, the increase in speed, the panting as he pushed in deeply, scraping against the muscles as Seth groaned.

He wasn't going to beg, but Seth almost couldn't stand the pressure building up inside him, about to burst as he reached for his own cock, jerking himself off swiftly to match Caleb's erratic thrusts. His toes curled and he bit his lip hard, muffling his groan in the comforter as he came, a flush of heat rushing over his skin, up into his shoulders and cheeks as come coated his fingers.

He heard Caleb's sharp breath and then a low groan, hips stuttering against him, speeding up and then slowing down, finally dropping to a stop.

Seth winced as Caleb pulled out, tossing away the condom and flopping down on the bed with a long sigh.

Sliding down, Seth opened his eyes finally, turning his head to face Caleb. Caleb had his eyes closed, hands lying at his sides. He was still breathing fast, and Seth watched his chest move up and down for a moment before sliding over.

He didn't know what made him do it, but he leaned down and kissed Caleb once, then twice as Caleb opened his mouth for him.

It only lasted a second, though, before Caleb's eyes shot open and he pushed Seth away roughly. "No, no, what are you doing?"

Seth arched an eyebrow as Caleb pushed himself up, shoving him back again, but he didn't go far.

"Really?" he asked instead. They'd just had sex, for free, and Caleb was hung up on the kissing? Of all the things he could say no to, this didn't make any sense to Seth.

"I said no kissing before," Caleb replied. "I don't do that."

"We just did," Seth pointed out, eyes flicking over Caleb's face for a clue, but there were none, and he frowned. "And I know you liked it."

Caleb scowled. "That's not the point."

"Then what is?"

Caleb shook his head, rolling off the bed and grabbing his jeans. Seth sat back, shoulders falling as he watched Caleb dress, his back to him.

"Wait," Seth said as Caleb pulled on his shirt and took a step towards the door. He jumped off the bed, grabbing Caleb before he could twist away, and pulling him into a hard kiss that made him want to fuck Caleb all over again. He could feel Caleb giving too, the way his mouth opened under his to his tongue, but Caleb shoved Seth away a second later.

"Stop," he said, panting for breath and wiping his mouth as he stared at Seth. He swallowed and licked his lips. "I'm leaving."

Seth didn't follow him out this time, frowning to himself as he sank back on the bed. He had no idea what that was about. Another thought returned to him, though, as he sat there, thinking back on the night. Monday morning was going to be hell, no thanks to Caleb, and it was that thought that pushed any questions he might have had about Caleb's weaknesses out of his mind.

Chapter 10
The B Word

Seth dreaded every step he took to work, thinking about the marks that littered his body. He'd spent half the morning tracing each one in the mirror—the bite on his shoulder, the bruises on his hips, the red mark behind his ear that didn't go away when he rubbed it. He hated to think what Logan was going to say, Logan who always pried into his life and who had spent most of Saturday night plying Caleb with shots and commenting on how much more fun he was than Seth.

The ride on the elevator seemed over all too soon, and Seth knew he was late. Not that it mattered. Mr. Blackstone was always at least thirty minutes late, on a good day. It also meant that Logan would already be there, though, and there'd be no avoiding him.

He was right, unfortunately, as he reached his desk and Logan was already typing away at his computer, a steaming cup of coffee next to him.

He stopped typing, though, as Seth approached, setting down his bag under his desk and pulling out the chair. Seth tried to ignore the grin on Logan's face, but it was difficult when Logan leaned over the desks towards him.

"How was the rest of your weekend?"

Seth paused, thinking about the way he and Caleb had left the party, in a rush with hardly a goodbye. He didn't remember much of the ride home, but the rest was crystal clear.

"Fine," he muttered instead, turning away and switching on the computer.

Logan still grinned at him when he glanced back a minute later.

"So what the hell, man?" he said finally, and Seth frowned, confused. "Why didn't you just tell me? Were you afraid we'd not like you or something?"

Seth didn't know quite what to say. He was in it now. He bet the whole office knew about Caleb already.

"I just," he said finally, shaking his head as he tried to come up with something. "I just don't like to share my personal life."

It was true, at least. He never planned on telling them about his first few years in the city, and he never planned on bringing Caleb anywhere again. Clearly, it had been a horrible idea in the first place.

"We're not all republicans!" Logan laughed. "Besides, your boyfriend seemed nice, a much better drinker than you. You should have brought him out before last weekend. Where did you meet him?"

"Oh, uh, in college," Seth muttered, fiddling with a pen and hoping Logan would go back to his work soon.

"Wait, so you've been dating him for over a year and never told anyone?"

"What? No." Seth shook his head quickly. "The dating thing was... unexpected." To say the least.

Logan nodded understandingly. "Snuck up on you, huh? Totally happened to me before. Turned out I was dating this girl for three months before I actually realized."

"No," Seth said slowly, frowning, but Logan wasn't listening.

"I didn't think sex meant dating, but I guess somehow it happened anyway, you know?"

Seth didn't reply, frowning at his computer. He and Caleb were definitely not dating even if he hadn't paid for the sex last weekend. No, that had just been a fluke.

"Anyway," Logan went on a moment later, grabbing his coffee and wincing as he burned his tongue. "Caleb seems cool, and you know, you don't have to hide shit like that from us. I expect to see him next time you come out."

"Yeah," Seth muttered, the same way he did whenever Sammie asked him out. He'd never be taking Caleb anywhere else if it was up to him. Who knew what shit he might make up next time?

"You left kinda early, though," Logan went on, "Sasha got completely wasted, ended up in the bathroom for almost half an hour. It was classic."

"Sounds great," he muttered unenthusiastically. He didn't feel any better with this fake boyfriend story going around. Just what he didn't need was another lie, but at least people seemed to accept this one, much better than his parents had. He supposed instead of deflating it, he might as well just let it go. He could always say they broke up if it got too bad.

Yes, that was what he'd do, he decided, watching Logan talk about the rest of the party. No one needed to know who Caleb really was or who he really was.

Seth stopped under the flickering streetlamp, frowning as he glanced around, but Caleb was nowhere to be found. Far beyond at the entrance to the street, a car turned, rolling slowly past the group of boys who called out.

"Hey," he said as a dark-skinned guy passed him, heading towards the car. "Have you seen Caleb?"

The guy shrugged, eyeing Seth interestedly. "If you want something better, I'm available."

Seth barely smiled, turning away. "No thanks."

"Caleb's old news," the kid went on scornfully. "You want someone young, someone with stamina."

Seth shook his head, glancing down the street, but it was empty except for another car turning down.

"Whatever," the guy muttered when Seth didn't respond, and he walked in the opposite direction towards the car idling down the street.

Seth checked the time on his phone, debating between just going home or waiting to see if Caleb would come back. He wasn't even sure Caleb would agree to come with him this time, not after last week.

He was surprised when the second car rolled to a stop a few feet away from him, and he frowned. This was definitely not what he was here for, but then the door opened and Caleb stepped out, still wiping his mouth and zipping up his jacket against the chill in the air.

He glanced up at Seth as he passed him, hands already pulling out a cigarette as the car left, and said nothing, lighting it with a flick.

"How was he?" Seth asked, glancing after the car, and Caleb shrugged.

"Old."

Licking his lips, Seth turned towards him, eyes flicking to the bruise on his wrist as he lifted the cigarette to his lips and his jacket slid down an inch. Caleb merely sniffed and let the smoke stream out before him.

"You want to come back to my place?" Seth asked instead, and Caleb licked his lips slowly, staring across the darkened street to the brick building on the other side.

"How much are you gonna pay me this time?"

Seth shrugged. "Same as usual." He eyed Caleb, but he couldn't tell that anything was wrong, and Caleb merely flicked the ash off the end of his cigarette.

"And you're not gonna get mushy?"

"I did not get mushy," Seth protested, crossing his arms, annoyed. "You're the one who freaked out."

Caleb didn't respond to that, sucking on his cigarette intently. He glanced at Seth finally, as if gauging his answer.

"Fine," he said finally, turning to Seth. "But no more kissing."

"What is the big deal with that?" Seth asked as he turned, and Caleb fell into step beside him, still fingering his cigarette, and Seth could smell the sweet nicotine. "I mean, you have a nice mouth."

Caleb merely scoffed, tonguing the cigarette. "And here I thought you'd be totally pissed about me outing you to your friends, but all you want to talk about is my mouth."

Scowling, Seth kicked the pavement as they walked, past the other hustler who'd approached him earlier. The guy gave him a dirty look as he walked past with Caleb. Caleb merely ignored them.

"Yeah, thanks for that," he shot back, momentarily forgetting about the kissing thing. "Now they want you to come to every party."

"Just tell them we broke up. Tell them I was too much for you to handle."

"I'll tell them you had a mental disorder," Seth muttered back, and he was too busy checking the street for cars that he missed Caleb's amused smile beside him as he lifted the cigarette back to his mouth and looked away.

"Oh, God," Caleb breathed as he flopped down on the bed, wiping sweat from his forehead, and Seth groaned, head bowed as the heat washed over him and he shuddered, arms shaking at the effort of keeping himself up above Caleb.

Caleb's heels slipped from his back, landing on the bed, his knees still up, and Seth took a breath, pulling out as Caleb closed his eyes for a moment, mouth half-open.

"You're getting better," Caleb commented as Seth rolled over onto his back, trying to catch his breath. He frowned, though.

"Better?"

Caleb hummed in agreement. "Not so jerky as before, but practice makes perfect, they say."

Seth rolled his eyes. "When are you going to admit that I'm just as good as you?"

"Is that something you'd be proud of?" Caleb drawled. "To be on the same level as a hustler? Is that why you keep coming back? Trying to prove something to yourself?"

"No," Seth said, frowning and shaking his head. "I let go of that when I stopped."

Caleb rolled his eyes. "Yeah, and that's why you pay me every week, because you let it go."

Seth sighed. "I don't expect you would understand," he muttered. "You're gonna be a hustler forever. You don't want to do anything else with your life."

"What's there to do?" Caleb asked pointedly. "Become a respectable member of society? I don't need anyone's approval."

"And you think I do?"

Caleb barely smiled, shaking his head. "I think you wouldn't have asked me to that party if you didn't."

Seth moved then, rolling over on top of Caleb, pinning his wrists to the bed, but Caleb didn't struggle, merely arching an eyebrow as if to say, "really?"

"Maybe I asked you because I wanted to."

Caleb scoffed. "Please. You could barely get it out."

Frowning, Seth pressed his wrists hard to the bed, pinning him in place as he stared at Caleb, the cool indifference in his eyes. He didn't care what Caleb had said earlier as he leaned in and kissed him.

Caleb reacted immediately this time, struggling in his grasp and turning his head away a second later.

"Stop," he said sharply, glaring up at Seth. "Don't you listen?"

Licking his lips, Seth sighed, gazing down at Caleb. "Maybe I don't care." He met Caleb's glare. "Maybe I want to kiss you. Is that so bad?"

He saw Caleb swallow, the darkness of his eyes as he looked up. "Yes," he said finally, stubborn to the very last, and Seth huffed.

"Why?" he asked. "Why is it so horrible? What are you afraid of?"

"I'm not afraid of anything," Caleb shot back, tugging at his wrists, but he couldn't move them or the rest of his body, pinned under Seth's warm weight.

"Have you ever been in love?"

Caleb groaned instead. "Oh, God. Fine, just kiss me then."

"You're not gonna answer me?" Seth asked, ignoring the way Caleb sighed loudly, clearly exasperated.

"No," he replied shortly, and Seth frowned, so he groaned. "Fine, once, maybe I thought, but it was a long time ago, and it doesn't matter now. So fucking do something already."

Seth leaned in closer, close enough he could feel Caleb's breath against his chin, and Caleb didn't struggle this time, merely let his body go slack under Caleb's. This wasn't how Seth wanted it, though, Caleb giving up. Caleb wasn't allowed to give up, so he slowly let go of his wrists and moved away, sitting back on the bed and running a hand through his hair.

Caleb looked over carefully as Seth moved away, eyes narrowed suspiciously.

"What are you doing?" he demanded, and Seth rummaged in the bottom drawer for the money he'd taken out earlier.

He handed it over to Caleb instead of replying, shaking his head. If he wanted any old hustler, he could get one, but he didn't. He only wanted Caleb, no matter how many other guys Caleb fucked on a daily basis or how many lies he told or how infuriatingly stubborn he could be.

"You're so fucking confusing," Caleb muttered as he counted the money and looked up at Seth.

Seth merely shrugged. He'd been called worse.

Caleb huffed a moment later, though, as though annoyed with Seth, and Seth was caught-off guard as Caleb moved over swiftly, tossing the money aside, and grabbed the back of his neck, dragging him into a hard kiss.

Seth's hand went to Caleb's thigh as he kissed him back, meeting his tongue and ignoring the warm flicker in his stomach as Caleb pressed his tongue against his, slowly and almost teasingly.

"What are you doing?" he managed to ask when Caleb pulled back to take a breath. Caleb paused, but his mouth was back against Seth's a second later, slowly edging him back against the bed.

"Giving you what you paid for," he replied, words muffled against Seth's mouth, and Seth didn't complain, sliding a hand into Caleb's hair and humming softly as he relaxed and kissed him back.

Seth couldn't explain it, but his life seemed to improve slightly over the next few weeks, even at work where he could stand talking to his coworkers for more than five minutes. This worked both to his advantage and disadvantage as he had to make up more lies about his past, and keeping them straight was starting to become difficult.

He usually bowed out before too many questions could come up, and he often found himself alone in the break room, staring at the pot of day-old coffee.

Leaning against the counter, having just escaped Jacob ribbing him about Caleb, he sighed. He should just tell everyone they broke up already, but then he knew he'd get even more questions, and he couldn't bear the thought of more lies at the moment.

"Hey." A new voice broke into his thoughts as he stood there.

Glancing up, he found Brianna entering, tossing her hair over her shoulder and reaching for the pot of coffee.

"Hey," he replied simply. He hadn't talked to her since the charity thing.

"So I hear you're cheating on me," she said, lifting the mug to her lips. "With a guy. It's a little insulting."

Frowning, Seth glanced over, but she didn't look upset. She shot him a small smile.

"Oh, yeah," he said finally. "Sorry about that."

She shrugged, taking a sip and making a face. Turning to the counter, she reached for the sugar. "It's okay. My boyfriend will be happy to hear it."

Seth smiled slightly as she emptied three packets of sugar into her cup and stirred it with a spoon, the edges clinking against the porcelain.

Brianna glanced up after a second. "You didn't mention him at the party."

"Oh," Seth said quickly. "Yeah, it was recent."

"Mmm," she hummed softly, and Seth's stomach turned over in apprehension. Did she know? "I hear he's cute," she said a minute later, though. "Sasha seemed to want to eat him up."

Pushing away the gnawing doubt in his stomach, Seth smiled. "Yeah, he's pretty good-looking." His mind drifted to Caleb's body for a moment, and he caught himself thinking over the last weekend and the way Caleb had gone down on him in a back alley before they even made it to his apartment, the intensity of the moment, how he'd come two more times after that once they'd made it to his place.

Jerking himself out of the memory, he cleared his throat and glanced around the room instead, away from Brianna's curious gaze.

"I'm glad you have someone," she said after a minute. "You seemed pretty lonely at that charity thing."

"People just aren't my thing," he said instead, and she smiled.

"I know what you mean. I'm also sad I can't use you as a beard. Maryanne won't let this one go."

"Sorry." Seth shrugged, and she did too.

"It is what it is." She sighed. "Sometimes you've got to tell a little white lie to save your sanity, you know?"

Seth knew. He knew that more than anything. He just wasn't sure what he was saving anymore.

Chapter 11
Losing What Never Was

"Do you like coming here?" Seth asked, eyes on the ceiling as Caleb licked at his neck, hips grinding down against his as he sat on the couch, legs splayed out before him.

"You pay good," Caleb replied, nipping at the skin, and Seth sighed, long and low, sliding a hand over Caleb's smooth lower back, over the waist of his jeans that he still had on, that they both had on, a hard friction against his cock whenever Caleb twisted his hips down. "And you're not as annoying as I remember."

"You are," Seth replied, but Caleb ignored him, tipping his head down as he bit at his mouth, letting out a low noise as he kissed him, a sound that scraped against Seth's skin and sent a shiver down his spine. All he wanted to do was kiss Caleb all night, as stupid as that sounded, and he knew if he said it out loud, Caleb would be out of there in a second.

It wasn't that he was falling for Caleb or anything ridiculous like that, but he liked the comfort he got from knowing that every Saturday night, he could find Caleb in the same spot, and it wasn't a fight to get him to come with him anymore. He thought Caleb might even like coming with him.

"It's part of my hustler charm," Caleb breathed a moment later, pulling away, but Seth followed, gasping against his mouth as Caleb ground down, a lick of heat flashing through his cock as it pressed almost painfully against his zipper.

"'Cause you're so charming," Seth muttered, half-laughing, and Caleb pushed his hips down purposefully, cutting off his laugh.

"More than you," he replied, and Seth shrugged. He didn't really care.

Instead, he brushed his hand through Caleb's hair and pressed a kiss to his chin, a little too intimate, and he could feel Caleb's discomfort as he tried not to pull away.

"I'm gonna start the shower," he said instead, sliding his hand away and pushing at Caleb's thighs, hauling him off his lap. "Come find me in a few minutes."

Caleb remained on the couch as Seth rose, heading for the bathroom and adjusting his jeans as he walked. Inside, he turned on the shower and went to the bedroom to rummage for the condoms and lube in the bedside table.

"Who's Madison?"

Seth's head jerked up as Caleb spoke, standing in the doorway and turning over a square piece of purple and gold paper.

"Where did you get that?" he asked sharply, and Caleb shrugged.

"In a drawer. I was looking for a pen."

"Why—what—no," Seth said sharply, striding over and pulling the invitation from Caleb's hands despite Caleb's confused frown.

"What's wrong?" he asked. "It's just a wedding."

It wasn't just a wedding, Seth wanted to snap. It was his little sister's wedding, his sister whom he hadn't seen in seven years, who his parents would die before they let him go near her, and she had sent him an invitation as if it would be okay if he just showed up.

"Well, I'm not going, and you shouldn't be snooping in my drawers," he said instead, shoving the invitation in the drawer by his bed instead.

Caleb scoffed. "I wasn't snooping. Like you have anything hidden that I care about."

Seth didn't know what to say as anger welled up inside him, though he wasn't sure at what exactly, but at the moment, it was Caleb, who stood there, an eyebrow arched as if he was being stupid to get so mad over one thing.

"No, you don't care," he said harshly. "You don't care about anyone but yourself, do you? As long as Caleb is happy, what does anyone else matter?"

Caleb stared at him for a second before scowling. "At least I'm not ashamed of my life and the people I hang out with. Whose wedding it is? Your sister's? You have the same last name. Are you too afraid to go?"

Seth glared, hands curling into fists at his side.

"I don't need you, of all people, to tell me what I'm ashamed of."

"Oh, right," Caleb sneered. "'Cause you have so many other friends. And how many of those people at work really know you? Know what you are? What you've done? What would they think if they knew? So tell me why then, why did you stop hustling and drinking and smoking? Who are you trying to please? Your family? When I first met you, all you said was that they kicked you out for being gay. That hasn't changed, now, has it? And putting yourself in a nice suit and getting a job in an office doesn't change who you are."

Annoyed, Seth pushed past Caleb into the living room, shaking his head as his words sank in. Near the door, he whipped around to face Caleb, who'd followed him.

"You don't know who I am," he growled. "And just because we've fucked a few times doesn't mean you can judge my life. My family is none of your goddamn business, and I don't see where you get off telling me who I am."

"Please!" Caleb scoffed. "I know who you are. You're just like every other guy on the street. And you think you've gotten away from it, but you haven't. Every time you come looking for me, you're right back in it, and it will always follow you around no matter how hard you try to shake it. So you ask why I don't want to do anything else? It's because you can't. It'll always be there no matter what you're doing, in the back of your mind, knowing you're just a little bit less than everyone else, but fuck it! Seth, if you don't accept it, you can't move on."

Seth glared, anger bubbling in his stomach, shoulders bristling.

"I accepted what I've done, but I don't want it to define my life, so fuck you if you think you can just waltz in here and tell me what to do. You're just a hustler, just a whore who gets paid to lie, and you'll never get out of it, but I have and I'm not going back, and I'm not going to see my family who wants nothing to do with me. So you can just fuck off for all I care."

Caleb's eyes narrowed, and he shook his head, grabbing his shirt off the back of the couch and striding past Seth.

"Well, fuck you too," he spat as he wrenched the door open and nearly ran into Sammie, whose eyes widened immediately as she stumbled back from the door. "He's all yours, sweetie," he said caustically, stomping past her, his shirt curled in his fist.

Seth felt like he couldn't breathe as he stared at Sammie, heart thudding wildly in his chest, growing lightheaded.

"Get out!" he yelled, and she jumped, scurrying from the door as Seth strode over and slammed it closed, turning the lock and collapsing against it.

Closing his eyes, he sucked in a breath, rubbing his face. Fuck Caleb and whatever he thought he knew about him. How could he know anything when even Seth didn't? Just, fuck him, he thought, sliding down to the floor and pressing his face to his knees.

Seth felt like he had a raging hangover, which was odd considering he hadn't had a drink in years, and he sat at his desk, staring blankly at the computer screen.

His mind had felt fuzzy all week, from the moment he'd woken up on Sunday morning to when he'd passed Sammie in the hall Tuesday morning to now as he tried to focus on his work but all he could think about was Caleb, how angry he was when he thought back on Saturday night.

Caleb had no right to go looking through his things or asking about his personal life. Seth never asked about his. Of all the hustler-client rules, even the unspoken ones, it was one he'd always obeyed. He and Caleb weren't just a hustler and a client, though, and Seth knew it. He'd known it from the first time he'd picked him up.

If he hadn't run into him that night outside the bar, none of this would have happened. He wouldn't be in this mess. He wouldn't feel like he'd been run over by an elephant right now.

"So guess what this weekend is," Logan said as he returned from the printer, and Seth barely stirred, blinking at the screen and trying to shake away the fog in his brain. "Jacob's birthday. We're gonna get him so wasted." He grinned at Seth. "You're coming, right? And you gotta bring Caleb. We've haven't seen him for weeks."

"No," Seth said sharply, sitting up, and Logan frowned.

"No?"

"I can't bring Caleb. I can't—I don't want to go. Out."

"Are you okay?" Logan asked slowly, eyeing him as if he were a strange alien.

Huffing, Seth pushed his chair back and turned to face Logan. "I don't want to go out," he said firmly. "I don't want to hang out with anyone in this office. I don't want to talk to anyone. I don't want to date anyone, and I don't want to talk about Caleb."

Rising from his chair, he grabbed his jacket and took off for the elevator, but when it took too long to get there, he took the stairs.

Jogging down, he told himself he just needed some fresh air, some time away from Logan and all his questions. He couldn't stand it, all the lying. Was he ever going to be happy with his life? The last time he remembered being happy was in elementary school before he'd known anything about liking boys or what sex was.

Outside, the cool autumn air slapped him in the face, and he took a deep breath. He didn't care that he was supposed to be working or that he might get in trouble for leaving unannounced. Instead, he fumbled for the pack of cigarettes in his pocket, the ones he'd bought three days ago but had been trying not to open them, but he didn't fucking care anymore. He'd denied himself so long, and what the fuck difference did it make?

Pulling one out, he grabbed the lighter from his other pocket and lifted it to the end. As it lit, he took a deep breath, sucking in the sweet, relaxing nicotine that flowed through his body, like a giant weight coming off his shoulders.

"What the fuck are you doing?"

Seth nearly dropped the cigarette at Logan's voice behind him.

"Jesus!" he cursed, scowling and shoving the lighter back in his pocket. He turned to Logan. "What does it look like?" He'd been trying to get away, but apparently that wasn't going to happen.

"I've never seen you smoke, or get that mad before."

Seth shot him a sneer, not in the mood to be polite or ignore all the things he usually wanted to say but never did.

"There's a lot of things I've never done around you, doesn't mean I haven't done it before."

"Seriously, dude," Logan said, stepping up to him, looking confused as he spread his hands. "What is up with you? Did you and Caleb have a fight?"

Seth scoffed, a stream of smoke disappearing into the cold, gray air. "Me and Caleb? Me and Caleb aren't dating, okay?" He shrugged, over-exaggeratingly. "It was all a lie, just like everything else in my life. We weren't dating. I didn't meet him at college. Hell, he has probably never been on a college campus in his life."

He shook his head, taking another long drag of the cigarette. God, he'd missed cigarettes. If he could make love to every stick in that pack, he would do it.

Logan stared, speechless for probably the first time ever, Seth thought. He should have felt satisfied, but instead, he only felt angry.

It took a moment, but Logan shook his head, as if trying to figure it all out, which question to ask first. "Wait, so how do you know him and why did you lie?"

"*He* lied," Seth pointed out sharply. "Because he's a sadistic fuck who likes to torture me, like he always has. God, I knew it was a bad idea, talking to him again, fucking him." He sighed, crushing the cigarette between his fingers as the hot wave of anger welled up in his stomach. "I should have seen this coming."

He cursed himself as he tossed the cigarette onto the ground, glaring at the glowing cherry until he put it out with his shoe, leaving a black scuff on the cement.

"You slept with him?" Logan asked, still trying to figure it out. "But you're not dating? Dude, I am so confused."

Seth glanced up. "Yeah, I did," he said, the words welling up inside him before he could stop them. He didn't care what he said at this point. He didn't give a fuck what anyone thought about him. They could gossip all they wanted and he knew they would, but why should he care? He didn't care about a single person in that office. He only cared about keeping his job, and at this point, what did that even matter? Caleb had said it; once a hustler, always a hustler. "And he did it because I paid him. He's a hustler, and that's how I know him, because I used to do it too. I used to fuck guys for money, and now you can go tell everyone in the office about my secret life and why I never want to hang out with anyone, and why I never talk about my family or my life. Now you know, and you can stop fucking asking me questions, and just leave me alone!"

He didn't care what Logan was going to say as Logan opened his mouth, shock plastered all over his face. Instead, he turned on his heel and strode away. He would call in sick when he got home. Hell, he didn't even want to go back. He could only imagine what things people were going to whisper now. He didn't think he could take it, but he couldn't stop it. He was sick of lying and hiding his past. It was so much work, so much effort, so much energy he expended every day making sure he covered his tracks. He didn't fucking care anymore.

Logan didn't follow him, to his relief, and Seth dug out another cigarette as he rounded the corner and headed for his apartment.

Chapter 12
What Goes Around

Seth called in sick the next day as well, lying on his bed and listening to the rain hit the windowpane. Tomorrow was the weekend so it didn't matter if he got up, if he did anything. He had no plans to ever do anything again.

Once upon a time, back in high school, he'd expected to go to a good college and graduate in four years with a degree in business or medicine or some other high-paying field that his parents would approve of. But everything fell apart when one of the cheerleaders, Valerie Morgan, had seen him kissing Brody, a guy on the swim team, in the parking lot one day. Rumors had spread in the small, exclusive prep school, and before long, his parents had packed him a suitcase and shut the door in his face.

A little part of him had died that day, as all his hopes had gone swirling down the drain along with his future.

It had taken him a long time to claw his way out of his new life in the city, the friends he'd made, the ones who told him the drugs were fun and wouldn't hurt him, that alcohol was good for taking the edge off before a job, that smoking staved off the hunger.

Now, his fingers itched for a cigarette, and he rolled over to the pack sitting on the bedside table. He pulled one out, looking for the lighter, but it wasn't there. Looking around, he couldn't remember where he'd put it. He searched the covers, but it was nowhere to be found. Yanking open the drawer, he slid his hand in, searching, but he stopped as his fingers hit a stiff piece of paper.

Pulling it out, he found himself staring at the wedding invitation. Only three weeks remained until the wedding, and he'd missed the RSVP date by a long shot. That wasn't important, though.

Dropping the cigarette, he sat up, grabbing his cell phone instead and dialing the number at the bottom of the page.

He swung his legs off the bed as it rang and his heart rose, stomach coiling into a tight ball of nerves, fingers trembling between the nervousness and the anger flooding his body. How could Madison have even thought? Shaking his head, he tried to take a breath as the phone rang and rang.

"Hello?"

A voice, a woman, something familiar in it but it wasn't the same, answered, and for a moment, Seth just sat there, frozen.

"Hello?" came the voice again, unsure.

"Madison," he said, forcing himself to speak, and there was a pause.

"Yeah, who's this?"

Seth pushed away the nervous fluttering in his stomach. He shouldn't feel this way with his own family, but he did. "It's me, Seth."

"Seth?" she asked, sounding as though she couldn't quite believe it. "Oh my God. How are you? You-you got my invitation? I wasn't sure I'd even sent it to the right place."

"Yeah, I got it," he replied slowly, reaching for the cigarette and turning it over in his hands. "Why'd you send it?"

He had to know. How could she have thought he could just show up to her wedding like nothing had changed? Their parents would have him kicked out in a minute, and that would be the end of that. She couldn't possibly be that naïve, could she?

"What do you mean?" she asked quietly. "I sent it because I want you to come. I haven't seen you in forever. I miss you."

Something tugged in his stomach at her words, but he shoved it away. That wasn't why he'd called. "And you really think Mom and Dad are gonna let me just show up?" he demanded, tone too harsh, but he couldn't help it. Seven years of anger at his parents wasn't going to go away just because his little sister invited him somewhere.

"I..." she said slowly, and Seth could just see her, twining a piece of her long, dark hair around her finger like she always did when she was nervous. "I don't know, but who cares? It's not their wedding. Seth, I want to see you. I want to talk to you. I-I want you to meet Trevor. I want to know what you've been doing, you know, d-do you have a boyfriend? How's the city? I want to know about you, and I can't do that if you never talk to me."

"I'm not the one who stopped talking to you," Seth spat despite how her words affected him.

"I know," she said, her voice dropping, sounding guilty. "But I couldn't with them watching me all the time, and when I got to college, I tried to call you, but the number was disconnected, and I didn't know how to find you. I'm sorry. I'm so sorry."

Seth could hear the tremble in her voice, and he knew she was crying. His chest tightened painfully and he forced himself to put the cigarette down.

"Seth, please," she said, voice nearly a whisper now. "Please, I want you to come. I don't care about Mom and Dad. If they say anything, then I don't want them there. I want you there. I want my big brother."

A lump rose in Seth's throat, and he forced himself to breathe. He couldn't go. It would be a disaster, he knew it, worse than taking Caleb to meet the guys at work. He'd spent all this time avoiding home, trying to make sure that if he ever went back, he could prove to his parents, *someone*, that they'd been wrong about him, that he could make it.

"Madison," he said slowly, but she interrupted him.

"Please," she begged again, voice cracking. "It took me five years to find you. Please, don't disappear again."

Seth swallowed thickly, not knowing what to say. "Madison," he said again, slower. "You don't know what's happened in the last seven years. I'm not the same. I've done things that I... shouldn't have done. Mom and Dad would never forgive you."

There was a pause on the other end, and Seth took a tight breath. He couldn't let her throw away her relationship with their parents just for him. He wasn't that important.

"I don't care what they think," she said finally, firmly. "You're my brother, and I love you no matter what, and even if you murdered someone, I wouldn't care. Please, Seth, please come. I need you to be there. And Trevor said you could be a groomsman if you wanted. I'm only going to get married once."

"I..." he said, torn. He wanted to see her, of course he did. It had been years. He wanted to see how she'd grown up, hear about her life, if she'd gone to school, what she was doing now. But he couldn't see his parents. They hated him, and he hated them, hated them for what they'd done, how they'd treated him. All the work he'd done to finally go to school, it had all been for them, even if they would never know. He didn't know why he had this desire to please the people who hated him, but he always did it. Not anymore, though. He wasn't a lost kid anymore, scared of the future. He was an adult who'd made it completely on his own without anyone's help.

He could hear Madison waiting with bated breath on the end, not daring to interrupt his thought process. She'd always been the patient one, waiting for just the right moment to get what she wanted. She was almost more manipulative than he was in that respect, but she had a better heart.

He sighed. "Okay," he said finally, and he heard her squeak on the other end. "Okay, I'll come." He was probably signing his own death certificate by parental glare, but Madison had gotten to him, and really, he'd never stood a chance of refusing her.

"Oh my God!" she squeaked excitedly. "I'm so happy! I'm so excited to see you! I'll put you down for the chicken. Oh, are you gonna bring someone? You should bring a date."

"I don't think that's a good idea," he said quickly, but she brushed past him like she always used to, and he couldn't help smiling at the way she did it, just like old times.

"You have to. I insist! And I'm the bride. You have to do what I say!" He could hear the grin in her voice, the utter excitement coursing through every word she spoke. "And don't worry about Mom and Dad, I will deal with them. You won't have to do anything. I promise." She paused, and Seth thought maybe she was crying again when she spoke next. "I'm just so happy. I can't wait to see you."

Seth smiled slightly. "I missed you, Mad."

"Yeah, me too," she choked slightly, sniffing into the receiver. "God, I can't cry like this every time I talk to you or I'm gonna be a mess on my wedding day!" She laughed. "So I'll see you there?"

"Yeah," Seth agreed despite the nervous flutter in his stomach, but the rush of relief that followed from her laugh pushed it away.

"Good," she said softly. "And you *can* bring a date. Anyone you want."

"Thanks," he replied, staring at the cigarette on the table. "Look, I gotta go, but... thanks for inviting me."

"Like I wouldn't invite you," she replied easily. "Just call me soon, okay?"

"I will," he agreed, and it wasn't like his replies to Sammie. It was genuine, and he knew she smiled when he said it. "Bye, Mad."

"Bye," she said, and he lowered the phone.

Sighing, he set the phone down and paused as his eyes fell on the cigarette. After a moment, he picked it up and shoved it back in the pack, crumpling the whole thing and dumping it in the trashcan. It was about time he put that behind him for good and just accepted who he was. His parents weren't ever going to, and no one else would if he never let them.

He rose from the bed finally, the first time in hours, and turned on the shower. If he was going to be a reformed hustler, he was going to have to face the music on Monday morning, and he'd have to face Logan, who was, in all honesty, the closest thing he had to a real friend in this place.

Seth stepped out of the elevator, glancing around carefully, but no one seemed to notice him except to toss him a smile as he passed. Uneasy, he frowned and continued on to his desk, glancing behind him, but no one whispered to their neighbor or shot him a weird look.

Unnerved, he set down his bag and looked around, sure someone was about to step up to him and confront him, and he braced himself as Sasha came up, looking concerned. This was it.

"Are you okay?" she asked, and Seth frowned, confused.

"What?"

"Logan said you were out sick," she said, eyes widened with concern. "I hope it wasn't too bad. You missed a great party on Friday. Caleb would have enjoyed it."

"Uh..." he said, thoroughly confused about what was going on, but she merely smiled.

"I'm glad you're feeling better," she said instead, patting his shoulder and leaving him frozen by his desk.

What the fuck was going on? he thought as he sunk into his chair, ears on alert for any whispered mention of his name, but he heard nothing, which only made him more paranoid. Everyone had to know by now. He'd given them an entire four days to gossip about him.

He nearly jumped out of his skin as Logan appeared, his usual coffee in his hand that he sipped as he plunked into his seat.

"Hey," Logan greeted him simply, and Seth's eyes narrowed.

"What's going on?" he asked, lowering his voice although there was no one nearby.

Logan arched an eyebrow at him. "What are you talking about?"

Seth stared, but Logan just took a sip of his coffee. "I think you know what I'm talking about," he hissed. "Why is no one else talking about it?"

Logan stared at him for another moment before sitting back in his chair and shrugging lightly. "It's not my personal life to advertise. And despite what you seem to think, I'm not a gossip. I keep my friend's secrets."

Seth didn't know what to say as he sat there. "Friend?" he asked after a long minute, and Logan nodded.

"I thought so, but I mean, you do keep an awful lot of secrets. And it kinda sucks that you don't feel like you can tell me that stuff." He traced the lid of his coffee with his finger slowly. "But that doesn't mean I think you're repugnant or something."

Seth let out a breath as he realized that Logan was telling the truth. He hadn't told anyone in the office. He was safe. A hot drop of guilt melted into his stomach as he looked away.

"Look," he said slowly, shifting uncomfortably in his chair. "I didn't mean to... blow up on you like that. It was just a really bad week, and I'm sorry I'm such a dick to you sometimes."

"All the time," Logan corrected him, but he was smiling when Seth glanced over and sighed.

"Yeah, okay, all the time," he admitted. "It's just hard to keep everything a secret from everyone all the time. It's really stressful."

"I bet," Logan said, taking a sip. "That's why you never came out with us, right? That and you hate everyone?"

"I don't hate everyone..." Seth said slowly. "I just, people aren't my thing."

"I thought hustlers had to be all about customer service?" Logan asked, and Seth shot him a panicked glare, glancing all around, but no one was near enough to hear, and Logan winced. "Oh, sorry, won't say anything else about that, promise." He made the motion of zipping his lips, and Seth sighed.

"I used to have friends," he said after a minute. "Back in high school, but when your parents kick you out, it's not easy to keep them. So I just didn't bother, really, after that."

"Your parents—" Logan's eyes widened, but he shut his mouth quickly. "That sucks. Though, I kind of get it now." He paused, leaning over the desk. "We should hang out, just the two of us, like watch a movie or something. I really want know more about your life. It's so crazy. Here I was, thinking you just were really anti-social, and wow, I had no idea."

Seth shrugged. "Yeah, I'm messed up."

"It's not that bad," he said. "You've still got Caleb, right? I mean, I don't know what's up with you guys, but he seemed to like you at the party."

"He was being paid to pretend," Seth muttered, feeling like he could breathe again. Logan wouldn't tell anyone, and he could finally talk to someone about something other than beer and girls. It was a huge relief.

Logan shrugged. "I don't know. The way he looked at you sometimes. I could have sworn it was real."

"You did think it was real," Seth pointed out, but Logan made a disbelieving noise.

"I'm just saying. He's either a fantastic actor or he really does like you."

It didn't matter now anyway, Seth thought as he sat back in his chair, and Logan reached for his coffee. He'd ruined any chance of actually being with Caleb, normally or paid. Besides, Caleb was right. He needed to move on. He just didn't want to.

It was a suicide mission, Seth knew it, knew it as his hand curled around the wedding invitation rolled in his pocket, something to hold on to as he stepped over a puddle and hopped onto the sidewalk, bypassing the cluster of boys at the entrance to the street.

Darkness pressed in around him, a chilly breeze lifting the hair on the back of his neck as he slowed his speed, chewing on his lip ring as he spotted the dark figure under the streetlamp, the mussed hair and the cigarette smoke trailing from between his fingers.

He almost stopped then, turned around, but his fingers clenched around the hard paper in his pocket and he moved forward.

Caleb glanced at him this time as he approached, gaze dark, a hint of anger there as he raised the cigarette to his lips and didn't speak.

"Hey," Seth said finally, and Caleb merely raised his chin, stuffing his free hand into his pocket.

"How much this time?" he asked sharply. "Five hundred? A thousand?" He glanced over, eyes narrowed. "I don't want your fucking money, and I don't want to see you."

Seth sighed, ducking his head. He didn't really know why he was there when he knew what Caleb's answer would be.

"You were right," he said finally, and Caleb didn't react, glaring at him and turning away. "I was just kidding myself, trying to pretend this part of my life never happened, but the truth is that if it hadn't, I never would have met you, and even though you were a jackass to me for most of the time I've known you, you were at least always honest."

"Well, that's nice," Caleb sneered. "But this isn't an after-school special, so get to the point."

Seth didn't roll his eyes though he wanted to. "The point is you know me better than anyone here, and maybe I could get another guy, probably whoever I wanted, but I want you."

Caleb frowned, tapping his cigarette instead of replying.

"And I know you're not going stop doing this, but I was hoping, maybe, maybe you would come with me to my sister's wedding."

"How much?" Caleb asked after a minute, and Seth shifted.

"Nothing. I want you to be my date, my real date."

Caleb scoffed. "And why should I?"

Seth shrugged. "That's something you have to figure out for yourself, but I want you to."

Frowning, Caleb sucked in the last bit of his cigarette before dropping it to the ground. It landed in a puddle and fizzled out with a small hiss.

Seth waited, hating how nervous he felt. He hadn't felt nervous around Caleb since the first year he'd known him, before he'd realized they were on a level playing field. Now, Caleb had all the power, just as he had back then, and he hoped he wouldn't lord it over him like he used to.

"If I said yes," Caleb said finally, slowly, licking his lips. "You do realize you'd be dating a hustler?"

"No," Seth replied, shaking his head. "I'd be dating you."

Caleb paused again, pushing his other hand into his pocket and hunching his back against the wind that whipped down the street, ruffling his hair.

"What about work?"

"Fuck'em," Seth said simply. "I don't care what they think. Besides, they really like you. I think they like you more than me."

"Not hard to," Caleb muttered, and Seth ignored him, sending him a look. Caleb pulled out another cigarette instead, the silence stretching between them.

It was a long shot, Seth knew that, and probably one of the stupidest things he'd ever done, asking out a hustler, but maybe if he'd had the courage to do this seven years ago, they wouldn't be in this situation right now. But they were, and Seth was at Caleb's mercy. He didn't know if Caleb even liked him, but he hoped that maybe he did.

Puffing on the cigarette, Caleb exhaled slowly, glancing at Seth, eyes scraping up him as he sighed. Seth shoved his hands in his pockets, waiting nervously, chewing on his lip ring.

At length, Caleb flicked away the half-smoked cigarette and jerked his shoulders. "Fine, I'll go."

"Really?" Seth asked, head rising, and Caleb shrugged, sighing as though put-upon, but Seth knew he wouldn't have agreed if he didn't want to. Caleb never did anything he didn't want to. He smiled, taking a step closer. "Will you get mad if I kiss you?"

Caleb shot him a look. "I guess you can, just this once," he said tiredly, but Seth caught the slightest hint of a smile as he leaned in and their lips met.

A light mist began to fall around them as Seth wrapped his arms around Caleb's shoulders, pulling him in closer, and for once, he didn't care who saw him. He only cared about the guy in his arms and the invitation in his pocket. Things were going to be just fine, or at least, better than before, he thought as he smiled against Caleb's mouth and kissed him again.

If you enjoyed this story, you can sign up for a free membership at ForbiddenFiction.com and discuss it with other readers and the author at the *By the Hour* story page at http://forbiddenfiction.com/story/EEG-1.000072.

We do our best to proof all our work, but if you spot a text error we missed, please let us know via our website Contact Form at forbiddenfiction.com/contact.

Stage Dreams

Chapter 1
Voluntary Submission

"Any big plans for tonight?" Laurel asked as she set beer bottles under the counter with a clink.

Jamie jerked his shoulders, swiping the bleached rag across the countertop of the bar. It was just after midnight. He and Laurel were the only two people left, cleaning up sticky alcohol stains and setting chairs upside down on tables before they left.

"Probably just head home."

"Make sure Drew isn't passed out on the couch?" Laurel asked, shooting Jamie a knowing look from down the bar.

Jamie knew full well what he would find at home, but he still felt the need to defend Drew. "He doesn't always—"

"Just the last couple months. Something is wrong with that boy." Laurel finished putting away the bottles and tossed him the keys. They nearly hit Jamie in the face before he managed to catch them.

There was nothing wrong with Drew. True, he hadn't been himself lately, but he was just tired. They worked all the time, after all, and what time wasn't spent working was spent editing the show. If they ever wanted to find a producer, a completed book was necessary.

"Lock up, will you?" she said, moving around the counter and grabbing her coat from the back room. "I've got a date."

"Not another blind date?"

"Unfortunately, yes." Laurel pulled on her jacket, flipping her straight black hair out from under the collar. The sleeves barely concealed the tattoos on her wrist. She started towards the door and paused. "Tell Drew he only has so many sick days left."

Jamie nodded, looking away as she left. Jamie wasn't fooling anyone with Drew's "sick" excuse and he knew it. Laurel was far from stupid and Drew would be out of a job if he didn't pull himself together.

He finished wiping down the counters and made sure the tills were locked before grabbing his own coat and locking up. When empty, the bar was a comforting place. Only a few dim lights in the back cast a soft yellow glow over empty tables, chair legs in the air, taps and fancy bottles of vodka and whiskey on the counter behind the bar. The piano tucked into the corner sat with its top closed, stool empty before it.

Flipping up his jacket collar, he shut the door behind him and stepped down the icy stairs to the street. A sharp wind blew past him, cutting through his coat, and he shivered, hurrying down the block.

His and Drew's apartment wasn't too far, just around the corner, and it took him less than five minutes to reach the steps of the tall, brick building.

Inside, he trudged up the stairs (there was no elevator to speak of, only a dangerously empty shaft at the end of the hall), shoving his hands in his pockets and praying that Drew had turned on the radiator.

Down the dim, grey hallway, he reached apartment four-oh-five and shoved the rusty key in the lock. With a loud click, it unlocked, and he pushed the door open.

"Drew?" he called as he stepped inside, shutting out the cold air. It was barely warmer in here, and he checked the radiator first. It hadn't been switched on at all. With a twinge of annoyance, he turned it up and shrugged off his jacket, tossing it on the pile of clothes that covered the back of the scraggly brown chair he'd gotten from the upstairs neighbor.

Old coffee sat in the pot as Jamie passed the dingy kitchen. There weren't many places Drew could be if he was home, not in the apartment that barely had room for two bedrooms. An open bottle of whiskey sat on the counter. Jamie screwed the top on, glancing around.

Bent over the couch, his face pressed to the coffee table, Drew slept. He hadn't stirred when Jamie shut the door or called his name.

Sighing, Jamie stepped over, reaching for his shoulder.

"Drew. Drew, wake up."

"Huh?" Drew blinked, eyebrows drooping. He lifted his head slightly. A napkin stuck to his cheek and he brushed it away. "What?"

Jamie's eyes fell on the empty glass beside him. He picked it up and gave it a sniff.

"Seriously? It's only Tuesday."

Drew rubbed his face, clearly not listening to Jamie. He ran a hand through his short, blond hair and tossed Jamie a look, the one that said that Jamie needed to stop worrying so much.

"I was thinking about the best friend character," he said, ignoring the way Jamie grabbed the napkins and shuffled them together, squinting at the scribbled writing, the few lines of music. "He's kind of an asshole."

"Yeah, well, he kind of is," Jamie replied, eyeing Drew with a frown. "You need to get to bed. You have the early shift tomorrow, and if you call out again, Laurel's gonna have your job."

"She can have it." Drew waved him away as Jamie tried to grab his arm and haul him up. He jerked it away. "Like I give a shit about that stupid bar."

"It's so we can pay rent on our shitty apartment, remember?" Jamie grabbed him again, around the chest this time, and pulled him up. Drew was a good few inches taller than Jamie and much thicker around his chest, but he managed to get him to his feet. When he let go, Drew wobbled, but Drew protested as Jamie steadied him.

"I'm fine."

"You're drunk."

"Barely. It helps me think."

"No one's ever gonna produce our show if you're drunk all the time."

Drew patted Jamie's cheek as Jamie dragged him towards one of the tiny bedrooms in the back. "No one's gonna produce it until you finish the script."

"And you actually write down the songs." Jamie wasn't in the mood to play this game. He kicked open the door to Drew's messy bedroom. Clothes lay strewn over the floor, the banged-up dresser, and hanging off the end of the mussed bed. Otherwise, the bedroom was painfully bare with not a single sentimental item in the whole place.

Jamie dumped Drew on the bed, letting him fall face-down into the pillow.

"Mmph," was Drew's only response. "Did Kristin call?"

Swallowing down the pang in his chest, Jamie checked Drew's phone on the bedside table. "No. Did you drunk text her again?"

"I'unno," Drew mumbled into the pillow and Jamie sighed. It seemed like they went through this routine every other week. There were times when Drew was a model employee, showing up to work on time, flirting with the customers for higher tips, even last month when he'd dropped a fully finished song in Jamie's lap and told him to put it in the book. And then there was today.

"Sleep and go to work tomorrow," Jamie said, shoving aside a clean path to the door. "We need the money."

"Yeah, yeah, Mom."

Back in the living room, Jamie pressed the heels of his hands into his eyes for a long minute until the darkness closed in and all he could see were spots dancing in front of him.

Shaking himself, he pushed back his hair as it fell in his eyes. He needed to get it cut, but with all the shifts he worked at the bar, he didn't have time. Instead, it was just a brown mop on his head, constantly getting in his eyes and garnering him comments from Laurel about workplace etiquette, not that she could talk considering her whole arms were covered in sleeves of tattoos. As the owner, though, she had the final say.

He certainly wasn't as attractive as Drew was, he thought, grabbing the pile of clothes from the chair and separating them into two piles—clean and unknown. Drew had blond hair and dark eyebrows, deep brown eyes and a jaw line that Jamie often had to stop himself from touching. They may have known each other since high school, but even that would have been crossing some sort of line.

Judging by how many women hit on Drew down at the bar and how few guys hit on Jamie, Drew was certainly the more attractive of the two of them.

Jamie wasn't exactly ugly, but he could probably do with a few more muscles, and his pale skin looked as if he'd never seen the sun despite growing up in Florida. Compared to Drew, he was short, but he was five-ten, not exactly tiny. Perfectly average, just the like the rest of him. David, his last boyfriend, had said that he could do with working out a bit more and losing the doe-eyed thing. Jamie couldn't say he missed David at all.

Jamie dumped the questionable clothes in a laundry basket by the couch and hung up his jacket by the door on the coat rack he'd found out by the dumpster. Their apartment wasn't exactly high class, but it was comfortable enough. They didn't really have a lot of money to spend, and whatever money Jamie managed to save, he used to go to Broadway shows. He said it was for research, but most of the time, he spent the hours in the theaters daydreaming about the day his and Drew's show would be performed in front of large crowds and garner standing ovations.

That day seemed a long way off, though, Jamie thought as he gathered Drew's napkins from the coffee table. Each had only a few sentences, fragments of thoughts that he never seemed to put down in the composing notebook Jamie had gotten him all those years ago for some birthday or other.

"It's all up here," Drew would say when Jamie asked, tapping his head. "Stop worrying."

Jamie couldn't help but worry, though. The whole point of moving to New York hadn't been to spend the rest of his life working at some crappy Brooklyn bar. He wanted to write shows, and Drew was supposed to be his partner. Three years later, he had a messy draft, only halfway edited, and only half songs to go with it. They needed so much more if they were ever going to shop it around.

Flopping down on the couch, he didn't feel like writing tonight—he'd been stuck on the ending for months, and no matter what he did, he couldn't figure out what was wrong. Even thinking about it made him groan in frustration. For a moment, he considered taking a leaf out of Drew's book and pouring himself a glass of something strong, but that wouldn't help ease his stress at all. Instead, he stretched back, closing his eyes against the red light blaring in through the frosted window, and hoped Drew would at least show up to work tomorrow.

"Enjoy your sick day?" Laurel asked as Drew passed behind her at the register. Jamie tensed, listening closely.

"Sure," Drew replied shortly.

Jamie wished Drew would at least be civil enough to keep his job.

"You're lucky you've got such an obliging coworker," Laurel said, shutting the register with a *ching!* "Jamie picks up a lot of your missed shifts. You should worship the ground he walks on."

Drew grabbed a bottle of tequila and began pouring a line of shots for the table in the corner.

"Jamie is quite obliging, yes," he muttered.

Jamie frowned, handing the woman at the table near the window her drink and the man across from her didn't even glance at him. He was invisible to them.

"Maybe you'd like to make up some of those hours," Laurel said as Jamie returned to the bar and slid his tray across the counter. Drew took it off and put it away without him asking. Drew didn't ask what Laurel meant, and Jamie knew he was biting his tongue to stop from saying something that would definitely get him fired.

"What's up?" Jamie asked instead.

Laurel put her hands on her hips, multiple gold bracelets jangling at her wrist. She wore an old, ripped tee-shirt over her usual jeans, hardly a professional look, but considering she let Jamie get away with his uncut hair and the rather large tattoo of a lily flower on his neck, he didn't think he had room to judge. He'd gotten the tattoo done after a night out in which he had drunk too much and decided he wanted to be anything other than what he was. Drew had been the one to remind him the next day and practically force him into the parlor. He wasn't sure it had changed anything.

"I need *volunteers* to bartend a private party on Friday."

"What kind of party?"

Drew turned his back on both of them, rearranging glasses on the shelf despite Laurel's pointed look.

"Some new Broadway show's opening night thing. Plenty of snotty actors and play people. Drew should fit right in."

"I'll do it," Jamie said quickly before Drew could respond to Laurel.

"I knew you would." She patted his shoulder. "Drew, I expect you to be there too."

As she left, Drew shoved back his hair. "Nice job. Are you going to volunteer us for karaoke next time?"

"You like karaoke," Jamie pointed out, but Drew shrugged.

"Not anymore."

Jamie didn't know when that had changed. Drew used to make every excuse to be around music. "Well, we need the—"

"Money, yeah, yeah." Drew turned away again and Jamie took a seat at the bar. It was pretty dead right then aside from the couple tables that now had their drinks.

For a moment, the only noises came from the clinking glasses and the low murmur of conversation from the tables. Jamie tapped his fingers on the bar, head in his hand as he glanced around. For nearly six months, he'd been working there. It was the same thing everyday, and a lot of the same people everyday.

He hadn't been naïve enough to think that they would move to New York and hit it big right away. He'd spent months planning everything out, finding an apartment within their budget, figuring out how they would get by in the months between. Drew never thought about any of that stuff. He was a get up and go kind of guy. If he wanted to do it, he did it. No thought, no planning, just an idea.

"I hate private parties," Drew said a minute later, a pained expression on his face. "They're always full of dickheads ordering you around."

"It is for a show," Jamie pointed out. "Maybe it'll be good for networking."

Drew merely grunted. "This whole town is full of fuckboy actors and directors."

"Would you rather be back in Florida working at the Crab Shack?" Jamie asked, an eyebrow arched. He couldn't imagine anyone would rather be in Florida, wading through swamps and watching the Weather Channel for hurricane warnings. The next time he went back to Florida, someone better have died.

New York was so much bigger, so much more exciting, filled with possibilities, and far away from the people back in high school who had shoved him into lockers for wearing his jeans just a bit too tight to pass as straight. He certainly didn't miss that.

"Maybe," Drew muttered, putting glasses away.

"But New York is great," Jamie insisted. Drew was just saying it to piss him off. Who would trade New York for Florida? Seriously. "You just need to do more things."

"I do plenty. I hooked up with that red-head on Saturday."

Jamie remembered the girl, although Drew probably remembered less even though he was the one to go home with her. "The one that looked like Kristin?"

"She did *not* look like Kristin," Drew snapped but his shoulders dropped and he sighed a second later. "Fine. We'll work the party. I'm sure it won't be that bad." He seemed to be talking to himself more than Jamie, but he offered Jamie a brief smile. "And like you said, we need the money."

Drew moved away and Jamie watched him go. He hadn't meant to bring up Kristin; it had just slipped out, but the girl had resembled her quite a bit. A lot of the girls looked like Kristin, now that he thought about it. He didn't want to think about why that was. Drew was just enjoying being single for once. Of course, that meant Jamie had to deal with all the girls he brought to their apartment where there was no escape.

What worried him more, however, was that fact that Drew had only written two songs since they'd arrived. At this rate, they'd have the book done in ten years, and Jamie wasn't willing to wait that long.

Chapter 2
One-Liners

"Jesus, I can't stand it in here," Drew said, not even bothering to lower his voice as he grabbed yet another bottle of wine from under the cabinet of their make-shift bar in the corner of the darkened room. It was someone's loft apartment; the living room alone was twice the size of their whole apartment. "It's like if perfume and sushi teamed up to commit evil on the city."

Jamie flashed a smile at the woman taking the glass of champagne from his hands despite her frown as she glanced at Drew. When she'd left, he turned to Drew.

"Why don't you go take a break? Have a smoke. I'll handle it."

"You're a saint." Drew said sincerely, squeezing his shoulder and tearing off the ugly black vest Laurel had forced them to wear for the night. Usually there was no uniform but private parties always meant uniforms so people could tell them from the guests.

Honestly, Jamie was just glad to have a moment of quiet as Drew left. He hadn't had much time to focus on the party since they'd arrived. Even though he was the bartender, that didn't mean he couldn't try to make some new contacts. The party was filled with Broadway professionals. If he could just meet one, it might be the break he needed.

"Come on, Merryn," someone said from behind him as he rummaged for more clean glasses. "Did you see that ridiculous pre-show routine of hers? She's a bigger diva than you."

"I am not a diva," came a woman's indignant voice. "I'm not the one who gets weekly facials."

"It opens your pores. Got to keep my face pretty for that starring role I'm sure to get."

"In your dreams."

Someone rapped on the counter top and Jamie straightened up.

"Barkeep," said the guy. "Three glasses of the red and don't skimp. It's gonna be a long night."

Turning, Jamie reached for the bottle but he stopped with his hand outstretched as he caught sight of the guy behind him.

The guy stood a couple inches shorter than him, slightly stocky but clearly in shape, with a boyish face, a dimple on his left cheek even when he wasn't smiling. Sandy-blond hair swept into his green eyes purposefully and he smiled when Jamie paused a second too long.

"Red," Jamie repeated quickly, grabbing the bottle and glancing at the two girls next to the guy instead. The woman with long, wavy brown hair crossed her arms as she watched him, and the other dark-skinned girl gazed across the room.

It wasn't often that Jamie froze when presented with good-looking guys, but maybe he'd just gotten over it considering he lived with Drew. Though this guy wasn't exactly traditionally good-looking—he looked more like an exceptionally-tall hobbit with good hair—he reminded Jamie of a Disney prince somehow. It was probably the hair, or maybe his green-ish-blue eyes. Whatever it was, it made Jamie's hand shake slightly against the glass as he finished pouring.

"Here you go."

The guy smiled, handing the glasses around to the girls. He turned back to Jamie, who had made to put away the bottle.

"You do this often?"

"What?"

"Serve private parties?"

"No, uh, I work at a bar down in Brooklyn. Don't normally make it across the bridge." He didn't usually get chatted up by hot industry guys either.

"You should. Manhattan is a great place to be."

The brown-haired girl next to him shook her head and took a sip of her wine. "Come on, Roman. Stop playing footsie with the bartender. Jenna wants to talk about the 'In the Treetops' number in the second act."

"That can wait for rehearsal." He waved her away.

Jamie felt the flush on his neck at the girl's words. He put away the bottles on the counter instead of meeting the guy's eyes. Considering he worked in a bar, he should have been used to people hitting on him, but most of the people who did were women, and they were usually drunk. It wasn't quite the same.

The girl rolled her eyes. "Come on, Sidney. I'd rather not watch a train wreck." She grabbed the other girl's wrist and tugged her away into the crowd.

Jamie found himself glad that the guy didn't go with them, swirling the wine in his glass and smiling at Jamie. It wasn't exactly the contact he'd hoped he would make, and he didn't stop his mind when it wandered to dark rooms and groping hands as he watched the guy finger his glass.

"What?" Jamie asked finally. He should stop thinking about tongues and fingers and heat pressing against his skin. It had been a while since he'd thought about that. The few times he'd hooked up with guys since coming here, they'd been at dim clubs, in dark, dirty alleyways that always left Jamie feeling unclean, but it wasn't like he wanted a relationship from any of those people, any of those interactions.

"Just wondering why I've never seen you before."

"Because I live in Brooklyn?"

The guy smiled, flipping his hair from his eyes. "I just meant, with such a pretty face. Feel like I would have noticed you anywhere."

The flush grew and Jamie coughed awkwardly. "Do you use that line on every bartender?"

"It is an open bar. Gotta tip you somehow." He winked. "I'm Roman, by the way."

"Jamie."

Jamie wasn't sure if asking if Roman wanted to hook up in a closet was a good idea. The last guy who'd shown any serious interest in him had been David, and Jamie had absolutely no desire to repeat that relationship. Even as his mind flit back to the drugs, and David's nagging voice telling him he'd never make it in New York, he hesitated to say anything else to Roman, scratching the back of his neck instead and glancing around the room.

Lots of unfamiliar people milled around, sipping wine and congratulating each other on an opening night well done. The furniture here cost more than Jamie's whole month's salary, he was sure. There were no tears or rips or dents in anything. It was pristine.

Sometimes he felt so out of place.

"I take it you're part of the show?" Jamie said at length. Roman wasn't David, after all. It didn't have to be like David. They could just hook up. Of course, this was all in his head. He didn't even know if Roman was interested in that kind of thing. "Let me guess, stage crew?"

"Oh," Roman said, clutching his chest with fake hurt. "Ouch. Surely I'm not that unattractive."

Jamie shrugged, though he couldn't hide his smile. "I don't know any stage crew so I can't really make a fair comparison." Roman was, in fact, one of the most attractive people Jamie had seen in New York, and he wasn't completely sure why Roman was still talking to him.

"Let me assure you that stage crew are no match for me," Roman said, leaning over the bar.

Jamie smiled slightly as he uncorked another bottle of wine and poured a glass for a woman who came up beside Roman. When she left, he set it on the bar top. "Sorry, but I'd have to see it to believe it."

"I am insulted that you don't believe me."

"Well, I just met you," Jamie pointed out. "For all I know, you could be stage crew and you're just lying so I'll like you more."

Roman's smile grew wider and something fluttered in Jamie's stomach at the sight. "So that means you like me already?"

Jamie didn't know what to say, fiddling with the hem of his vest. Could he take it back? Did he want to?

"Well, I mean, you don't seem as strange as some people I've met," he said because honestly, how can you know you like someone after five minutes of talking? He certainly liked the way Roman looked, and there went his mind again with the dark corners. It had been too long.

"What bar do you work at?" Roman asked when Jamie got too distracted wondering if Roman was as strong as he looked.

Jamie shook himself sharply. "It's the one on Fifth Avenue, right near the —"

"Alright, I'm back. Let's serve some more self-important assholes." Drew stepped in behind him, smelling strongly of cigarettes and making a face at his vest as he grabbed it off a box of wine glasses. As he pulled it on, he grumbled to himself. "When we get home, we're ordering pizza and I'm getting you drunk." He buttoned the last button and caught sight of Roman. "Who are you?"

Couldn't Drew have taken five more minutes? Just five, Jamie thought woefully. Instead, Roman was glancing between them as if gauging how to respond.

Roman smiled instead, though, at Drew. "I was just leaving. It was nice to meet you, Jamie." He grabbed his wine glass and headed into the crowd.

"Who was that?" Drew asked as he left.

Jamie didn't reply, watching Roman leave. Roman glanced back for a second, meeting his eyes and smiling. Something tugged at his gut, and Jamie paused. He probably shouldn't—he was supposed to be working after all—but he wanted to. He wanted to go after Roman. Drew did it all the time, so why couldn't he?

"I'm gonna take my break," Jamie said instead, yanking off his vest and leaving Drew rolling his eyes behind him.

Jamie wasn't sure what he was doing. He didn't even know if Roman was interested in him. His heart hammered as he scanned the room; he saw the girls Roman had been with but no Roman. Great. He'd lost him.

As he looked again, his eyes lit on the staircase by the wall. Roman was climbing it, alone. Without stopping to question what insanity had taken hold of him, Jamie followed. He wasn't even sure what he was going to do once he got up there, but Roman was the first person in a long time that he'd even thought about talking to. Lately, the work of dating or even hooking up had seemed monumental and certainly not worth it.

At the top of the stairs, he almost ran into Roman, who was coming out of the bathroom. He paused when he saw Jamie, a small tilt to the corner of his mouth.

"Just washing my hands," he said, holding them up as proof. "Did I forget to return my glass?"

Jamie didn't do this a lot, and definitely not at industry parties where he should have been more worried about making an impression on people who could help his career. Instead, he was standing outside the bathroom with a hot actor and debating the best way to say this. "I was just thinking about what you said," Jamie said, words tumbling ineloquently from his mouth.

"What did I say?"

"That you're not stage-crew pretty."

Roman smiled. "I'd like to think I'm dancer pretty, soon to be lead actor pretty."

"I think you're right."

"Do you use that line on all the actors you meet?" Roman asked with a cheeky grin.

"Just the nice ones."

They still stood alone at the top of the stairs. No one else had come up. For a moment, a palpable silence fell between them. Drew was downstairs, complaining about working, and Laurel expected him to be the responsible one and keep an eye on him. He felt like that was all he did lately—keep Drew in line. So much for that one.

"And how nice are you?" Roman asked after a minute.

The last time Jamie had done something like this, it had led to six months of utter hell, but David had been over a year ago now. It was long over. He wanted to do this, to have a tiny bit of release from the stress of his life. It didn't have to be a big deal. It could just be fun. It was with that thought that he pushed Roman inside the bathroom and locked the door behind them.

"What about the boyfriend?" Roman asked as his back hit the sink, rattling the items sitting on top.

Jamie's fingers stilled on Roman's zipper and he frowned. "Boyfriend?" Glancing up, he caught Roman's gaze on his face, Roman licking his lips as though he wasn't too concerned with the answer. Arousal stirred in Jamie's stomach at the sight, along with a flicker of unease at how much he'd missed doing this with someone who wasn't a drunk fling. They were both sober.

"The guy downstairs who's going to get you drunk later," Roman replied, slightly breathless.

"Oh, that's, that's just Drew." Jamie shook his head. Drew wasn't who he wanted to think about right now. Drew wouldn't care he was doing this. He probably didn't even notice he was gone. "He's not—we're not—"

"Just checking. I'm not into helping people cheat."

"No," Jamie said swiftly. His hand rested on Roman's zipper, and if he took too much longer, he might talk himself out of this.

Leaning into Roman, he kissed him first, almost tentatively, but Roman's hand moved to his jaw, kissing back and Jamie's worries melted away for a moment. This was something he could do.

Getting the zipper undone, Jamie slid his hand under Roman's waistband, curling around his cock. The first time Jamie had done something like this, it had been in high school and he'd been terrified the whole time of being caught. He had never spoken to that kid again.

Roman's mouth was soft but firm against his, insistent but not sloppy, and Jamie pulled away when he got Roman's jeans over his hips. Sliding to his knees, he didn't stop to second-guess himself. It would have been entirely too easy to do. Instead, he licked the palm of his hand and slid it over Roman's cock, hearing the soft change to Roman's breathing.

Stroking quickly, he leaned in, licking up the underside slowly. His heart beat hard in his chest, partially out of nerves. He didn't even know Roman, but between the Book and trying to keep Drew from getting fired, he felt like he had no control. This was something he could control, something that he wanted.

Roman wasn't loud, biting his lip as Jamie took his prick in his mouth and sucked. He kept his hand pressed to the sink, fingers curling against the porcelain. He seemed to be trying to keep quiet, and since there were people not twenty feet away, Jamie was glad. After all, he was supposed to be working, not sucking off strangers in the bathroom.

Still, he didn't hold back, sliding his hand in time with his mouth and getting a rush of satisfaction when Roman bit back a groan and squeezed his eyes shut. Roman was even hotter like this, with his neck stretched back, and Jamie could stare at the sharp line of his jawbone, the smooth skin of his neck, unmarred by tattoos unlike Jamie's.

"Shit," Roman cursed a minute later. "Shit, Jamie, I—"

He moved faster, holding Roman's hips still and sucking. His own cock throbbed in his jeans, but he liked the way Roman gasped for breath, biting his lip to keep quiet when he strained against Jamie's grip. This was how it should be—Roman actually focused on him, running a hand through his hair, not too high on drugs to forget what was happening.

Jamie pulled back just as Roman came, grabbing a handful of toilet paper to clean them both off. He watched Roman's face, a wave of satisfaction coming over him as Roman leaned against the sink, breathing hard. If there was one thing he knew he was good at, it was this. Even David had agreed there.

Jamie sat back on his heels. In the moment, he hadn't thought about what he would say now, how he would explain this, but Roman didn't ask for an explanation. Instead, he let out a long breath when Jamie rose and tossed the toilet paper in the trash.

"I knew there was a reason I let Merryn drag me to these parties," he said, pushing back his hair. He smirked. "That was not quite what I expected."

Jamie didn't know what to say. If he let himself think about it, he could come up with a million reasons why it had been a bad idea, but he didn't. He'd wanted to do it, so he did, but he did wonder for a second as Roman pulled his pants back up if he should have. Who said Drew was the only one who got to hook up with random people? Laurel probably would have said it just wasn't in Jamie's nature, but he'd done it before. It hadn't always ended well enough, but not much did in life.

"I don't know about you, but that's not the kind of tip I usually give to bartenders," Roman said and reached for Jamie, sliding a hand in his back pocket. For a second, Jamie was too surprised to react, but Roman pulled out Jamie's phone instead. Typing something in, he smiled. "You should call me."

"Gonna prove me wrong about the stage hand thing?" Jamie asked, taking the phone Roman handed back.

"Sure as hell gonna try," Roman replied, stepping around Jamie and opening the door. Jamie remained for a moment, catching himself smiling stupidly at Roman's name in his phone. It had just been a blow job. Nothing to get too excited about. He forced the smile off his face. He had to get back to work and back to Drew, who'd probably insulted half the guests by this point.

Tucking the phone away, Jamie checked his reflection in the mirror, rubbing at his reddened mouth. He hoped Drew wouldn't notice, but then, these days, Drew barely noticed anyone but himself.

Chapter 3
Taking Chances

Jamie's mind wasn't on the customers scattered around the bar. Instead, it was stuck on the book. Whoever had invented editing had to have been some kind of masochist. Sometimes Jamie wondered how he had ended up here, wiping down tables night after night in a bar then going home to stare at the blank screen on his computer for hours at a time, willing some sort of words to come out of his fingers.

It was the guy, his protagonist, who had no real ending. Jamie knew what was supposed to happen, but getting there was starting to become impossible. Drew had been right when he said the best friend needed work. Jamie just couldn't make it happen. Coma boy needed to take charge of his life, prove he wanted to live more than he wanted to die. Right now, he was stuck in a rut with only clichéd ideas left to mine.

Really, what was so hard about waking up from a coma?

"Don't let Drew scare off the customers with his songs," Laurel said as she pulled on her coat, eyeing where Drew sat at the piano, running his fingers over the keys.

"I won't," Jamie promised. There weren't many customers anyway though it was late.

"Mhm," Laurel murmured, checking her watch. "I won't be back, so lock up when you leave."

Jamie knew she was gone the minute Drew started to play. He never played when Laurel was there.

A familiar melody, one of the songs Drew had been working on for a while, filled the bar. The few people scattered around at tables looked up at the sound, then continued on with their conversations.

Drew's playing had always made Jamie feel calmer, and Drew always seemed much more relaxed when he played. Jamie had always felt that way ever since he'd found Drew playing in the empty band room sophomore year of high school. For a long time, Drew wouldn't acknowledge he was even good, but Jamie had encouraged him so much that Drew had ended up studying music in school. Getting him to come to New York had taken a little more convincing.

Moving to the piano, Jamie leaned against it, watching Drew's fingers dance across the keys.

"That sounds almost done."

Drew didn't look up but made a vague noise in return. "It's coming along."

"Coming along as in you've actually written down the music somewhere?" The bits of napkins littering the apartment with scribbled notes on them made no sense to Jamie. Drew had always been scattered, but lately, it was getting out of control.

Drew made another noise, his hands falling from the keys. "Where'd Laurel go?" he asked instead of replying, but Jamie wasn't fooled by the abrupt change of subject.

"You know that's why we came here," Jamie pointed out. He didn't need to remind Drew of that fact, but he did anyway. His dreams didn't involve pouring shots for the rest of his life or living in a way-too-expensive-for-its-faults apartment. He saw people performing his shows under the glittering lights of Broadway, or even off-Broadway. Anything to get his writing out there. He couldn't do it without songs, though.

"Yeah, I know," Drew replied under his breath. "Jamie, you gotta get out more."

"What do you mean? I get out plenty," Jamie argued. Oftentimes, he just didn't see the point of going to another bar after working all night in one. Plus, he didn't make enough money to go see any of the Broadway shows he loved so much. He didn't want to go out every other night like Drew did and bring home yet another nameless girl to the apartment.

"Yeah, okay," Drew said, but Jamie bristled at his tone.

"I do!"

"Working a party doesn't count as going to a party." Drew shook his head. "How are you going to make your show happen if you don't meet people here?"

"Our show, you mean?" Jamie crossed his arms as Drew shrugged.

"You can't rely on me for everything," Drew said, rising from the piano. "I mean, when was the last time you got laid? If you can't remember, it's been too long, man."

Jamie frowned as Drew headed for the bar. First of all, he had met Roman the other day, although he'd conveniently forgotten to mention that to Drew. He didn't need everyone knowing his business, and he didn't need to bring guys back to the apartment to prove anything. Secondly, he did not rely on Drew for everything.

Jamie followed him to the bar, leaning on the counter as Drew grabbed a bottle of vodka from the shelf.

"I go out," he insisted, receiving only Drew's rolled eyes in response. "Just because I don't sleep with every person who looks at me doesn't mean I'm alone."

Drew tilted his head to the side, with that pitying look that Jamie hated on his face. "Look, we both know David fucked you up but you don't have to be a monk. There's more to life than writing and watching black and white movies on TV. This is New York. You're the always the one praising it so much. Go do something in it and stop riding me about the book."

"It's not like you're working on it," Jamie shot back, but he felt the sting of the David remark more painfully. He wasn't the walking wounded.

"I gave you a song last month," Drew said. "Isn't that working on it?"

"And before we came here, you wrote five songs in one month. Since we got here, you've done two and those took you five months to write. It's not like we have less time here. If anything, we have more." Jamie didn't understand what had happened to cause the sudden drop-off in production. There was no way Florida was a better place to write. There was no inspiration there.

Drew moved down the counter to mix drinks. "Florida was just better."

"That's ridiculous," Jamie scoffed. "Florida was awful. If I never go back, I'll be perfectly happy."

Drew didn't respond to that, shoving his hair back and watching the alcohol pour.

"Your songs are great," Jamie said instead. "If you'd just write them down."

"Do some more editing and maybe I will," Drew replied, grabbing the glasses and leaving Jamie at the bar.

He hated to admit it, but Drew did have a point about the book. It had been years and he was still halfway through editing. At what point would he become one of those people lamenting their wasted dreams?

The thought was terrifying and Jamie shook it away. He wasn't even twenty-two and he was already worried about becoming a Broadway failure.

Fuck Drew for putting that thought in his head, he found himself thinking as he leaned against the back counter. He wasn't going to be that person, and he didn't need Drew to have fun.

Jamie stared at the page on his laptop, the cursor blinking steadily. He'd tried everything he could think of to make this easier—printing it out and marking it with red pen, rereading it from front to back, even taking entirely too long showers to attempt to force his brain to work better and come up with fixes. Every time he edited a draft, something else seemed to go wrong. He felt stuck, and the cursor only made him angry.

His problem was the ending. It had been plaguing him for months. His main character was in a coma, but in his head, the world continued to turn like normal, but how was he supposed to get out of the coma? The plot had seemed simple enough when he thought of it, so long ago, but the logistics of two realities was more difficult than he'd guessed. It wasn't just that but also getting the character across. Owen had lost everything, so what was he fighting for?

Sometimes, Jamie just wanted to give up on editing. Staring at the pages, unable to come up with a solution, made him want to cry in frustration some days. It seemed so easy but was so incredibly hard.

As he sat on the fraying couch, he found it difficult not to keep checking the clock on the wall as it ticked later and later. A half-empty box of Chinese food sat on the coffee table in front of him. He should have been focusing on the book instead of listening to the tick of the clock and stilling every time he thought he heard footsteps in the hallway.

Drew never told him where he went on nights like these, but Jamie knew what he did. It was pretty obvious when he'd wake in the morning to an unfamiliar woman making coffee in his kitchen. Jamie wondered what Drew would say if he ever had a guy stay over. He never had, but that didn't mean he couldn't.

Sometimes, he wondered why Drew even bothered going out, considering what he'd left in Florida. They never talked about Kristin except when Drew was too drunk to care. The texts and phone calls, which had used to come every day, had slowed significantly. That was totally normal, though, right? They'd broken up when Drew and Jamie moved to New York. Drew had been excited about coming. "A brand new adventure, Jai," he had said. "Maybe you'll sleep with a famous director. And maybe I'll run into Billy Joel and get a few tips. Wouldn't that be awesome?"

Jamie wasn't sure where that enthusiasm had disappeared to, but Drew didn't have many good things to say about New York these days.

He needed to work on the book, Jamie told himself firmly, not get distracted with whatever Drew was doing.

Typing a few sentences was all he got done before his eyes strayed to the clock again. It was incredibly easy to distract himself from writing, as much as he *knew* he needed to keep editing. All it took was a click to the internet and he would be lost in a cycle of email and social media checking. Pulling out his phone, he opened up the contacts folder, scrolling through the names. Most of the people in his phone, he hadn't called in a while.

He stopped as Roman's name scrolled into view.

He hadn't told Drew about the other night, his momentary lapse of sense—it wasn't often that he followed guys to bathrooms to suck them off and even less often that he called them afterwards. What did he have to lose? Just his dignity, and how much could be left of that these days? Calling Roman didn't have to be a big deal.

Pushing the laptop away, he curled up in a corner with his phone, holding his breath as it rang.

"Hello?"

Jamie sat up sharply. "Roman? It's Jamie."

"Jamie?"

Jamie could barely hear Roman over the background noise. Music and talking poured into the speaker.

"From the party the other day?"

"Oh!" Roman said loudly. "Hey! What's up?"

"Is this a bad time?" He could barely hear Roman over the noise.

"No, no. Just my call's coming up."

"I was just, just wondering if you wanted to do something." Jamie cringed to himself. He probably should have taken a moment to think through what he was going to say instead of sounding so incredibly lame.

"Do something?" Jamie could hear the grin in Roman's voice. "What are you doing tomorrow? I'm having a thing at my place after the show. You should come."

"I have to work until ten."

"That's perfect. I'll text you the address."

"Okay—"

"You can bring your friend if you want."

"No, Drew won't want to come," Jamie said quickly. That was a train wreck he didn't want to witness. Besides, Roman seemed nice. He didn't need to be subjected to Drew's new disdain for everything New York.

"Then I guess I'll just see you. Oh, shit, that's me." Jamie heard him fumble the phone. "I gotta go. I'll see you tomorrow, right?"

"I-yeah, yeah," Jamie said, but Roman had already said goodbye and hung up.

He lowered the phone, now feeling the thudding of his heart, his palms sweaty again. There was no need to be nervous, he told himself. It was just a party, just a group of people he didn't know and a guy he'd met twice. He'd be fine, and he didn't plan on telling Drew anything about it.

Glancing at the clock again, he shook himself finally and grabbed his laptop, snapping it shut and disappearing into his room. When Drew came home hours later, Jamie pretended to be asleep and not to hear the way he ran into the furniture on his way in or dropped his keys in the hall and the feminine giggle that followed.

Chapter 4
Jamie in the Bronx

Jamie wasn't sure he'd ever been this far north, almost to the edge of the Bronx, but the tall buildings of Manhattan had fallen away slightly, giving a little space between streets. A streetlight flickered as he passed beneath it and stopped at the steps leading into a tall, brick building. The directions on his phone told him to ring number six-seven-one, so he shook away his nerves and stepped up to the box.

"Yeah?" A woman's voice came through the crackling speaker box.

"Uh, I'm looking for Roman?"

"Sixth floor," the woman said, clipping him off at the end. The door buzzed loudly and he pulled it open.

The old elevator rumbled dangerously as it went up, and Jamie began to regret not taking the stairs, but he made it to the sixth floor in one piece. Moving down the hall, he found Roman's apartment easily. The door stood open a crack, music and voices leaking out. He knocked lightly and the door swung inward.

Inside, people he didn't know barely glanced at him as he stepped in and shut the door behind him.

Roman's apartment wasn't any bigger than his and Drew's, though it was much better decorated with matching throw pillows on the couch and a rug spread over the hardwood. It was crammed with people and Jamie maneuvered himself around. He hated big crowds, especially big crowds of strangers.

Drew hadn't asked where he was going when he'd asked Laurel if he could leave early. He doubted Drew cared where he went.

For a moment, he lingered awkwardly near the wall, but that wasn't why he'd come. He'd come to see Roman, and speaking of, Roman appeared a second later, smiling widely, his dimple even more pronounced, making him look like an adorable chipmunk as he bounced up to him.

"Jamie, you made it."

"Yeah. I didn't know there were affordable places up here."

Roman laughed. "There aren't. This place keeps me squarely in the poor bracket."

Jamie felt less awkward now that he wasn't standing alone like a loser at his first party. "I get that. People warned me New York would be expensive but I think I might have overestimated my ability to earn money. My bartender charm doesn't get me as many tips as I'd hoped."

"It certainly caught my interest," Roman said with a smirk.

Jamie flushed at the reminder. "Well, it was a party, right?"

"Yes, it was," Roman agreed and the pause lengthened between them. "Hey, I want you to meet some people," he said, grabbing his arm and saving Jamie the embarrassment of saying something stupid like that he liked the way Roman's hair fell in his eyes.

Roman led the way through the crowd to two girls Jamie recognized from the party before. The girl with the long brown hair sipped her drink, standing by the wall, and nodded at something the dark-skinned girl sitting in the chair said. She raised an eyebrow as Roman led Jamie to them.

"Jamie, this is Merryn." He nodded at the brown-haired girl. "And Sidney."

The other girl smiled at him briefly. "Nice to meet you."

"You were the bartender," Merryn said, setting her glass down on a nearby table. "Are you working this party too?"

"I invited him," Roman replied before Jamie had to, although he felt a flash of embarrassment. "Stop being a bitch."

"Just asking a question," she said, inspecting her nails. "If I went home with half as many bartenders as you do…"

"Then maybe you'd be a little happier."

Merryn made a face but didn't reply.

Roman's arm slid around Jamie's shoulders, and Jamie's mind flashed back to that moment at the party, Roman's hands curled against the sink. It was enough to distract him from the moment at hand, thinking about the way Roman had kissed him back, soft and insistent.

"Merryn and Sidney are in the ensemble too," Roman said, drawing Jamie out of his memories and forcing him to stop thinking about Roman's mouth.

"Dancer number two," Sidney chimed in. "A glamorous role in which I get to ask, 'And what did he say?' in the third act."

"At least you have a line." Merryn grabbed her glass again and crossed her arms. "And you don't have to deal with Christina's dirty looks. How she got the lead, I'll never know."

"Slept with the director," Sidney replied.

"Don't they all," she muttered.

"And this is what I want to get myself into," Jamie joked. It wasn't as if he hadn't known about theater drama but he'd hoped that stopped after school. Apparently it was just the same in the real world.

Merryn glanced over sharply. "Are you an actor?"

"Writer. My friend and I are working on a show."

Merryn didn't seem too interested, making a noise and leaning back against the wall. Sidney, on the other hand, leaned forward, elbows on her knees.

"What's it about?"

"Yeah, what's it about?" Roman echoed. "Maybe we can play the leads."

"You wish." Merryn snorted but Roman ignored her.

Jamie shoved a hand into his hair, something to distract him from the way Roman's fingers curled into his shoulder. He could feel the warmth of Roman's body close to his side. He couldn't think about that or he'd get hard right there, and that probably wouldn't be the best first impression on Roman's friends.

"It's this kid who gets in a car crash and he's in a coma, but in his head, life has gone on just the same. His best friend steals his girlfriend and his mother has a mental breakdown and leaves the family. In the real world, though, everyone thinks he's going to be in a coma forever and the doctors are telling his parents they have to decide what to do. So Owen, the main character, has to fight his way out of the coma or he could die forever."

Merryn drained her glass. "Didn't they make that movie a few years ago?"

Roman shot her a look as she shook her empty glass at him.

"You know, Jamie, you don't have a drink," he said instead of acknowledging Merryn. "Let's fix that."

"It's not that bad, is it?" Jamie asked as Roman led him away from Merryn and over to the counter filled with bottles of alcohol.

"It sounds awesome," Roman replied sincerely. "Merryn's just high-strung, but I think she's still pissed about losing the lead to Christina. She had it in the bag, but 'Stina's got a little more of this going on." He gestured at his chest. "Not hard to see what Nathan was looking for. What's your poison?"

"Nathan?" Jamie repeated, eyes widening. "Nathan Stuggart? The guy who has directed more Tony award winners than any other director ever?"

"That's the one. Everyone knows it should have been her, but you can't change a director's mind. Or she could just be pissed because I didn't take out the trash this morning. Who knows." When Jamie didn't answer the drink question, Roman grabbed a bottle of vodka and began pouring two drinks.

"You live with her? And I thought Drew was bad."

"That's the bartender guy? He doesn't exactly seem like the sunniest." Roman handed over a cranberry cocktail. "How do you put up with that?"

"He isn't always like that. He's usually really outgoing, but lately..." He shook his head. He didn't know what was going on with Drew lately except that he seemed to be annoyed at everything. "I've just known him for a long time." Jamie didn't really want to talk about Drew, not with Roman this close to him, close enough that he could smell his aftershave, soft and breezy like a summer's afternoon in the park.

"Plenty of those in everyone's life," Roman agreed. "Come on. I'll intro you to some of the other people in the ensemble. I promise they're not as prickly as Merryn. Some are even nice."

"Does that mean there's a stagehand here?"

Roman sighed, as though put-upon. "You're just not gonna believe me without proof, are you?"

Jamie smiled. "You started this."

"Fine. If you insist on comparing my beautiful face to that of a stagehand's." Roman said it as though Jamie had asked a big favor, but he slid a hand to the small of his back and led him to a group of people. Jamie smiled behind his drink and tried to remember the names of the people Roman introduced him to.

Jamie emptied his third glass, leaning sideways into the couch as Roman sat across from him. He didn't know what time it was or how long he had been there. The party was still going strong, but Jamie declined when Roman offered to get him another drink.

"I think I've had plenty."

"As long as you can make it to the subway in one piece, you're good." Roman grinned. "I've been meaning to ask, where did you get your tattoo done?" He reached out, brushing his fingers against Jamie's neck before Jamie could do much more than blink. Warmth blossomed over his skin at Roman's touch, and he watched the way Roman's eyes flickered over his skin.

"Oh, I got it done in college," he said, but he wasn't thinking about the questionable studio he'd gone to when he was nineteen, determined to be someone other than the too-skinny, nerdy kid he'd been in high school. The black and blue lily flower crept halfway up his neck with a trailing stem running down his collarbone. He was watching the way Roman's tongue wetted his lips and he raised his gaze to Jamie's.

"Let me guess: NYU?"

Jamie shook his head. "Uh, no. Drew and I just went a local community college. Didn't really have money then. Still don't have money."

"And where's local?" Roman asked, scooting forward on the couch until their knees were almost touching. Around them, groups of people chatted and laughed. Merryn stood at the counter pouring herself another drink and arguing with a tall guy about something.

"Florida."

"You're kidding." Roman laughed, but Jamie didn't.

"No."

"But you look so New York. You don't even have a tan."

"I didn't when I lived in Florida either. I hated it there." He twisted the glass between his hands. High school wasn't something he liked to relive, and these days, he usually didn't have to. The only thing that had made Florida bearable had been Drew. People in New York understood him. They were like him. "When you're not tan and you don't want to go to the beach constantly, you're weird."

"You're just creative. Creative people get a bad rap." Roman shook his head. "All my friends in high school were drama freaks, but it just prepared me for Broadway." He shrugged. "I bet your show is awesome."

Jamie laughed down at his lap. "Maybe when it's done, it will be."

"Would you let me read it?"

Jamie's head snapped up, meeting Roman's sincere gaze. "Read it?"

"Yeah. I love reading new stuff."

For a moment, Jamie didn't know how to respond. He hadn't shown the show to anyone. Jamie barely had half the songs and the editing process was making him want to tear out his hair most days. It wasn't ready for consumption by other people.

"I don't think it's ready."

"Think about it. I'd like to read it." Roman's hand rested against his knee, a warm, heavy weight.

The touch was so easy, natural, but Jamie's heart pumped faster and he couldn't stop himself from focusing on it. He wasn't sure what this was, with him and Roman, but it was different. He just hoped entirely different from David.

His eyes fell on the clock behind Roman. It was after midnight already. "It's getting late."

"Early start tomorrow?"

"Yeah, I should get back," Jamie said, but it was reluctant. He'd rather stay there with Roman, leaned in close to him, talking about things that didn't matter, things that did. He'd promised himself he'd finally get Drew to commit to a timeline, if that was even possible.

"I'll walk you out," Roman offered, rising first and grabbing their coats from a pile on a nearby table.

Jamie smiled at the offer, taking his jacket from Roman. Together, they left the apartment and headed for the stairs. Jamie was glad; he didn't trust that elevator.

"You know what I like about you?" Roman said as they descended and Jamie glanced over, pulling his jacket tighter as they went down and the air grew colder.

"What?"

"You're not what I expected."

Jamie wasn't entirely sure if that was a good thing. "What am I?"

"You're a realist," Roman said, pushing open the door to the street and letting Jamie go first. "You get that New York isn't a dream factory. You'd be amazed how many people I meet think they'll just move here and get famous like that. But you're writing and you're working for it."

David would have called him delusional, moving to New York even though he knew how hard it would be. But Roman didn't. Roman thought it was a good quality to have. It surprised Jamie slightly, more than it should have.

Roman bumped Jamie's shoulder as they walked, heading for the subway entrance around the corner. Jamie smiled to himself but it wasn't visible beyond the darkness surrounding them, the orange streetlights and the flash of a cab's headlight that passed on the street.

He paused at the steps, looking up from the ground finally. Roman was still watching him and he smiled as Jamie met his eyes.

"I'm glad you came."

"Me too." Jamie's breath clouded in front of him and he shivered in the cold. He wasn't sure the way his hand shook in his pocket was from the cold or from the nervous rush that spread through him as the moment lingered.

Roman stuck his hands in his pockets and rocked forward on his feet, a smile at the corner of his mouth.

"So I'll see you later?"

Jamie smiled at the way Roman asked, as if Jamie might say no. He leaned forward, hands sliding from his pockets as the distance closed between them and their mouths connected.

Roman's mouth was warm compared to the chilly night, lips pressed against Jamie's. From down below, Jamie heard the rush of a subway car and a gust of lukewarm air came up from behind him.

Roman's hands rested gently on his waist as they stood there, mouths pressed together in an easy kiss that could have easily led to more if they weren't already standing outside in the freezing cold.

Exhaling slowly, Jamie pulled back, licking his lips. "Yeah," he said, pushing his hands back in his pockets and smiling at Roman.

Roman returned the grin before turning on his heel and heading back for his apartment.

Jamie watched Roman until he disappeared around the corner then turned finally, taking the stairs into the subway. It hadn't been the night he had expected, but that had been a good thing regardless.

Chapter 5
Subtle Invitations

"This is what New York is all about," Drew said as he pushed open the door to a small café. The smell of coffee and pastries practically smacked Jamie in the face.

"Over-priced coffee?" he asked with a grin, following Drew inside and plopping down at a table by the window. They'd only been in New York for two days, but already, Jamie could just feel that it was where he should have been his whole life.

The café was small but on a busy street, tables set up outside for people to enjoy the breezy summer day. Drew pushed his hair back and grinned at Jamie, gesturing around them.

"This is what you wanted, right? You're gonna make New York your bitch."

Jamie wouldn't have gone that far, but he couldn't help the excitement coursing through him. New York was going to change everything, and Drew was with him to make it happen.

"We need to find jobs," Jamie said instead, and Drew shrugged.

"How about a piano bar? I could get discovered as the next great talent and you can ride my coattails to the top."

Jamie snorted despite himself, laughing and shaking his head.

"What?"

"I was just remembering that time in high school when you threatened to punch me if I told anyone about you doing music."

Drew nodded thoughtfully. "I didn't want to be different. It's harder to be yourself in high school, though you never seemed to have a problem."

"Maybe, but it got me shoved into plenty of lockers." Jamie was so glad to be done with school, done with Florida, done with David, for good. This was a fresh start for both of them. Nothing holding them back. "I'm glad you admitted you're a great musician."

Drew smiled. "I'm glad you made me."

"Did I do something to piss you off?" Drew grumbled into his oversized mug of coffee, brows furrowed heavily.

Jamie jerked out of his thoughts, watching Drew twitch back upright as he tipped sideways in his chair. "Why?" He grabbed a packet of sugar from the holder in the middle of the table and shook it to the bottom.

Around them, the café was dotted with people, the smell of scones and muffins wafting from the back. Out the window, grey sky peeked through the gaps between tall buildings, reflecting silver in the windows.

Drew glowered across the small round table at Jamie. "Because you fucking dragged me to a café at nine in the morning on my day off. Is this about me saying you don't go out? 'Cause I didn't mean get up earlier. I meant, go out later."

"We need to talk about the show," Jamie said, noting the way Drew immediately seemed to tense up at the mention. He didn't used to do that.

Drew looked barely awake, clutching his coffee like a lifeline, inhaling the scent like it might act as a reviver.

He was dressed haphazardly, in a wrinkled tee shirt and jeans that probably hadn't been washed in weeks. Jamie purposely didn't stare at the way the collar hung loosely over his collar bone. Instead, he turned his own coffee mug around in his hands and glanced out at the sidewalk.

"What about it?"

"Well, we've been working on it for almost two years now, and you've only given me half the songs, if you count scribbles on napkins."

"Don't worry about it." Drew took a fortifying sip.

"If it's not finished, we'll never find a producer." If they never found a producer, they would just end up working at the bar forever, and Jamie wasn't sure he could do that. "We need to keep working on it. I'm still editing, but if you could just get another few songs..."

Drew set down his mug, pushing a hand through his hair and rubbing the bags under his eyes. "I can't write anymore."

"What do you mean? Of course you can write," Jamie scoffed. Drew had written a song just last month.

"No, it's, it's hard," Drew said slowly, holding onto his mug tightly, and Jamie frowned.

"Writing is hard, but I still do it. You're just tired. If you didn't go out so much, you could work on it more." If Drew spent half the time he did on dates working on songs, they'd be done by now. He'd seen Drew sit at the piano at work, staring at the keys, almost as if willing notes to come out of his fingers, but they didn't. It wasn't that hard. If Jamie could do it, so could Drew.

Drew had agreed to come, to move to New York and work on the show, but since they'd gotten there, they'd done less work than ever. Drew wouldn't have agreed to come if he didn't want to. He was a great songwriter but he spent his time out of the apartment, away from his notebook. Distracting himself wouldn't get anything done.

"What does it matter anyway?" Drew said finally. "We don't have a producer."

"Because at some point, we want to get one. I don't want to work in a bar the rest of my life." Jamie hadn't come to New York to spend the rest of his life working as a bartender. He could have moved to Miami and done the same thing.

"Neither do I."

"Then you should write the songs down on something other than cocktail napkins."

Drew shook his head, frowning at Jamie. "Why are you so adamant all of a sudden? Is that guy you went out with a producer?"

Jamie stopped with his mug half-raised to his mouth. "What guy?" His throat went dry when Drew scoffed.

"The one you left work early for. I've known you for six years, Jai. I know when you go on dates."

Jamie didn't know what was worse—that Drew had known the whole time or that he didn't care. Not that Drew should care. Jamie could go out with whomever he wanted. He hadn't told Drew because it was just a date, just a simple date. He could be a casual dater. After David, it sounded like a much better option than coming home to Oxy pills scattered around the apartment and unfamiliar clothes tossed over the couch.

Jamie set down his mug, hating the flush on the back of his neck. "He's not a producer. He's none of your business."

"Whatever." Drew drained the rest of his coffee. "You keep working on the book. That's the most important part, right?" Standing up from the table, he grabbed his jacket off the back. "I'm going out tonight. Don't wait up."

"Drew!" Jamie turned as Drew stepped past him and out the café door. Drew didn't come back, though, and Jamie shivered in the cold air coming in through the door. So much for a timeline.

He knew what "going out" meant and he didn't want to think about it. He shouldn't even care who Drew went out with. They were just nameless, meaningless girls. It had been years since Jamie had had his stupid crush on Drew. He was completely over it, except that nagging twinge when Drew brought home yet another girl. Shaking his head, he forced the thought from his mind. He was over it.

The truth was, that of all the time he'd been in New York, Jamie hadn't met very many people. When they'd first moved there, Drew had wanted to explore, to go out and meet people, but as time had gone by, he'd only gone out to pick up girls. Jamie wasn't sure Drew even enjoyed that.

Jamie worked too much to make friends aside from the bar regulars like Trisha, the girl who worked in a ridiculously expensive boutique, although she hoped to design her own clothes someday, or Ken, the intern in the mayor's office who could barely afford his rent let alone to go out. Jamie slipped him free drinks sometimes as he complained about the rest of the interns.

Finishing his coffee, Jamie pulled on his jacket, leaving a few crumpled dollar bills on the table. He would have to find his own distraction tonight.

When Jamie had texted Roman earlier, just to see what he was doing, he hadn't expected to end up backstage at a Broadway show. Drew had already left for his "date" and Jamie didn't think he could stand sitting around waiting for him to get back. He needed to get out, go somewhere, just stop thinking about what Drew was doing.

Backstage was a rush of people in glittery costumes hurrying around, girls rushing to their places and people yelling for marks and cues. Jamie stood off to the side, trying to stay out of the way, but entranced by the view, the performers on stage twirling around in their elaborate dance numbers.

He could just see it. Someday he would be standing there as the writer, having jumped through all the hoops to get it done. Drew would have finally finished his songs and some beautiful actress would be singing them as guys in tight pants danced around her.

Roman came off the stage, sweat glistening on his skin as he grabbed a towel and grinned at one of the other guys.

"Hey, Jamie," he said breathlessly, wiping off his forehead and checking the stage. "How's it look?"

"It looks amazing." Jamie couldn't suppress the grin on his face as he stared out at the stage. "You're amazing. It's..."

"Amazing?" Roman laughed, tossing the towel away.

Jamie nodded uselessly. David would never have invited him to something like this. Well, David would never have wanted to go anywhere where there wasn't a thudding bass and tons of drunk people.

"I'm glad you're so easily impressed with me. Most New Yorkers are perpetually jaded."

"Oh, sorry," Jamie said quickly, stomach sinking. David had used to call his enthusiasm for Broadway nauseating.

"No, it's nice." Roman smiled at Jamie in a way that made Jamie think of candle-lit bedrooms and rose petals. It was a strange feeling.

Jamie caught himself staring at Roman a second later, at the red bowtie around his neck, brown pinstriped pants, the way his chest moved quickly as he tried to catch his breath, straining under his white shirt. Looking away, he crumpled the program he'd snatched earlier.

"Oh, look," Merryn said as she breezed by in a dress so sparkly it was almost blinding. "The bartender."

"Hi, Jamie!" Sidney chirped as she whipped past as well, in the same dress.

Someone shouted something and Roman's head lifted sharply. "That's me. Don't move. I'll be back."

He gripped Jamie's arm for half a second before flitting off again. Jamie moved out of the way of the stagehands. Roman stepped out on stage for another number and Jamie bit his lip, leaning against the wall and watching the curve of his ass in those pants as he danced.

"So be honest," Roman said as he unbuttoned his shirt and Jamie didn't look away, catching a glimpse of Roman's taut stomach. Roman tossed the shirt over the back of his dressing room chair. Other dancers changed as well, but Jamie kept his gaze on Roman's station. "Too many costume changes, right? I can barely keep track every night."

Roman grabbed a tee-shirt from off his station and pulled it on.

"Quit complaining, Roman," one of the other guys said, smacking him on the head as he passed. "You know you love taking your clothes off."

"Fuck off." Roman laughed, shaking his head and turning to Jamie. "You have to get going or do you have some time?"

Jamie met Roman's gaze. "I've got time."

Roman smiled as he grabbed his jacket.

"Roman?" Merryn's voice came from around the corner of the door. "You decent?"

"Like you care."

She stepped inside, barely acknowledging Jamie. "I'm going out with Sidney. You want to come?"

Roman glanced at Jamie. An excited flutter raced through his body at the glance, and Jamie ducked his head, fiddling with the zipper on his jacket.

"I think I'll pass," Roman said after a second.

"Fine. I'll be back later." Merryn breezed away, leaving the two of them alone in the dressing room.

Roman pulled on his jacket. "Apparently my apartment is going to be empty, if you're interested in a nightcap."

Jamie smiled and followed Roman out of the dressing room and towards the street.

"It must take a lot to get you drunk," Roman said as he handed Jamie a beer and sat down on the couch next to him. "Being a bartender and all."

"I guess," Jamie said with a shrug. He was acutely aware that they were alone—not just alone like in the bathroom at a party, but *alone* alone. "How long have you been a dancer?"

"Professionally? About five years. I moved to New York as soon as I turned eighteen, but I've been in classes and programs since I was six years old." He shifted closer to Jamie. "And how long have you known you were a brilliant writer?"

"I wouldn't say brilliant," Jamie protested into his drink. "Mostly I started because I didn't have anyone to talk to as a kid, but when *Phantom of the Opera* came out, it became an obsession. I must have watched it a thousand times. My mom may have hid it a couple times. I think I was in love with Gerard Butler."

Roman smiled. "You knew all the way back then, huh?"

He shrugged and took a drink. "Hard not to when all the other kids could sense it. They were like crocodiles after blood."

"Kids are cruel," Roman agreed and Jamie nodded. He had a million stories of being shoved into lockers, pushed down in the hall, called names. Luckily, school was long over.

He watched Roman for a minute. A few weeks ago, when he'd pushed Roman into that too-fancy bathroom, he hadn't expected to end up here. Drew never saw his one-night stands again. Jamie hadn't thought he'd see Roman again when he'd started it, but now that he had, he wasn't sure what to categorize it as. Roman was certainly good looking and funny and a sharp contrast to David, who would never have asked about his writing.

"Why'd you give me your phone number?" he asked suddenly, unable to stop himself.

Roman paused. "Despite what Merryn says, it's not every day I get a blow job from a bartender, especially in a renowned director's bathroom. Aside from the fact that it was awesome, you were cute, and obviously, I had to redeem my honor and prove you wrong about the stagehands comment you so grievously made." He smiled and Jamie felt a flutter of something unexplainable under his skin. "But that's not why I keep calling you."

"And what is?"

"I like talking to you," Roman said seriously. "You're not caught up in the drama of the industry. You've got an actual head on your shoulders. You're smart. And you aren't afraid of Merryn."

"Only sometimes," Jamie pointed out but he smiled when Roman scooted closer.

"I want to ask you something," Roman said, setting his beer on the table.

"If it's about the show; yes, I admit fully that you are much hotter than the stagehands."

"No." Roman smiled. "Though you're completely right. I was actually wondering about your roommate."

"Drew?" The question caught Jamie off-guard. They hadn't really talked about him much, and he didn't see what he had to do with anything.

"You said he was straight, right?"

"He is."

"Are you sure?"

"Why?" Jamie asked. "You want to date him?" It was a joke but the thought of Roman wanting to date Drew over him was off-putting.

"Of course not," Roman said, shaking his head. "You just seemed close."

"He's my best friend." Jamie shrugged. He guessed what Roman was getting at, but he didn't really want to have a talk about Drew or his previous relationships. He really didn't want to bring up David, of all things.

"So when do I get to meet him? I mean, you've met Merryn and we both know what a pleasure she can be."

Jamie hesitated. It was a little soon for that, wasn't it? "You don't want to meet him. If you think Merryn is bad..." He smiled slightly, but he could see Roman about to ask why, so he did the only thing he could think of in the moment and kissed him. It wasn't that, eventually, Roman might meet Drew. He just didn't see the point so soon. Besides, Roman meeting Drew would probably be all sorts of awkward.

Roman let Jamie kiss him, his lips soft pressed against his, mouth opening to kiss him back.

Jamie's heart hammered loudly as he kissed Roman, leaning in towards him, feeling the warmth radiating off his body. It had been a long time since anyone had reached for him, warm hands sliding over his back and pulling him in closer.

Roman's fingers dug into his back as they slid down on the couch, Jamie on top for the moment. His hands hit the couch on either side of Roman's head and he broke the kiss, staring down at Roman's reddened lips, the way he licked them slowly and tilted his chin up as he smiled.

"Come here," Roman murmured, pulling Jamie back by his neck, and their mouths collided.

The warmth of Roman's mouth combined with the slide of his other hand down his back, pushing under his shirt, fingers grazing up his lower back, sent a shiver through him. He sucked in a short breath at the press of their bodies, Roman's hips pushing into his.

"Mmm," Roman hummed against his mouth, tongue sliding in against his slowly, sucking on his bottom lip. His hand slid into Jamie's hair, and Jamie exhaled shakily a second later.

His eyes were closed, and he concentrated on the feeling of Roman's fingers digging into his waist, the way Roman's mouth slid down his throat. His body felt like it was taut like a string, ready to spring apart at any moment. It had been so long since he'd felt like this with anyone. He didn't care if they fucked or if they just kept doing this.

His skin burned and he sought out Roman's mouth again.

It wasn't until Roman's hand slid down over his ass and pulled him forward that he felt it, the hardness growing in his jeans, the heat rushing down, and his eyes widened.

He pulled back sharply, pushing himself up onto his arms. Roman's hands stilled on his body, and Roman blinked up at him, mouth gently parted.

"What? What's wrong?" he breathed. His eyes flicked down Jamie's body for a second.

Staring down, blood pounded in Jamie's ears, a loud rush that seemed to obscure any other noise. A momentary panic had taken hold, completely unrelated to anything he was feeling. His mind flicked to Drew and the girls Drew brought home. They meant nothing to him as far as he could tell, but he kept bringing them.

"Are you okay?" Roman asked a second later, trying to push himself up, but Jamie's weight held him down. "Jamie?"

Jamie blinked down at Roman beneath him. Roman wasn't like those girls, a one-night kind of thing. This was different. The longer the pause went on, the more concerned Roman looked, trying to shift up, but Jamie stopped him, hands on Roman's arms.

"If you don't want to," Roman said finally, "you can say—"

"No," Jamie said quickly, shaking his head. "I do. I do want to."

Roman arched an eyebrow. "Okay," he agreed, drawing him in for a soft kiss. "How about we move this somewhere more comfortable?"

Jamie smiled, his heart beating faster when Roman's hand closed around his wrist and tugged him off the couch.

Chapter 6
Productions

Roman grabbed Jamie's wrist, pulling him past the coffee table and back towards one of the doors off the living room.

If Roman hadn't been leading him, Jamie would have assumed they were in Merryn's room. The walls were plastered with various Broadway posters, a few of Marilyn Monroe and Bernadette Peters, and one very prominent photograph of Andrew Rannells. The bed sheets lay wrinkled, as though Roman hadn't bothered to make it that morning. CD cases lay open and scattered next to an old CD player on top of the dresser.

Jamie entered behind Roman, who shut the door and flipped on a small lamp next to the CD player. Jamie picked up one of the albums on the dresser.

"Guys and Dolls soundtrack?"

"Oldie but a goodie." Roman reached over and took it from his hands, setting it back down. "But you didn't come here to judge my music collection, did you?"

"Not exactly," Jamie admitted, a rush of excitement flooding his stomach as Roman toed off his shoes and pulled his shirt over his head, dropping it on the floor.

For being somewhat short and stocky, his body was as fit as any dancer Jamie had ever seen. He itched to touch his flat stomach, to run his fingers over the definition of muscles that spread up to his chest.

Roman took a step forward, reaching for the hem of Jamie's shirt, moving slowly, and Jamie let him as he tugged it up and over his hair, leaving it mussed.

"See?" Roman asked as he tossed the shirt aside and ran his hands up Jamie's chest to his neck. "Not so bad, right?"

"I suppose you look good without a shirt on," Jamie admitted, though it wasn't grudgingly. He'd gladly spend more time watching Roman undress.

Roman pressed a kiss to his cheek, a hand sliding over his shoulder. Jamie leaned into the touch, bare skin against bare skin when Roman shifted forward.

Roman's mouth slid down his cheek, over his jaw and near his chin. "Normally, guys jump at the chance to be with a dancer." His lips brushed against Jamie's and his hand slid over his lower back, rubbing against the bare skin, the slight rise before the waistband of his jeans.

"I'm not normal," Jamie muttered, holding his breath as Roman's hand crept lower, fingers gliding along the waistband.

"I know." He pressed a kiss to Jamie's lower lip.

Jamie felt his warm breath against his skin, the slight pressure of his hand against his back, nudging him towards the bed as Roman took a step backward.

"That's why I like you."

Roman sat down on the bed, smiling up at Jamie as he waited.

Jamie gazed down at Roman, at the trail of hair leading under his jeans, the way he leaned back on his hands, head tilted to the side, waiting. Roman said nothing, though his eyes were on the crotch of Jamie's pants. He smiled up at him, though, after a second.

Jamie didn't want to second-guess himself. He didn't want to start thinking about Drew or David or anyone else from the past. He wanted Roman, and Roman sat on the bed, half-naked and with a smirk on his face.

His hands reached for the button on his jeans, pulling it apart and sliding down the zipper. Roman's eyes widened interestedly, following the movement as he pushed the waist down an inch or two. He pushed his jeans down completely and stepped out of them. In only his underwear, he felt slightly exposed, but Roman's eyes traveled upward slowly to his face.

Roman smiled, still leaned back on his arms and shifting in his jeans. Jamie could see the rising bulge under the fabric and it sent a thrill through him as he stood there.

Jamie stepped forward, climbing on the bed over Roman and sinking his weight down on his hips. "I like you too," he murmured as he leaned down to kiss Roman.

Roman's hands slid to his waist immediately, grabbing onto his torso, and before Jamie had a chance to react, Roman rolled them over, pressing him to the mattress. Roman's kiss left him panting for air, hands bunched in the sheet and gasping as their hips pressed together.

Roman pushed down against him, the rough slide of fabric against Jamie's cock sending a shudder through his body. Heat flooded his lower body and he exhaled slowly against Roman's mouth.

Roman's mouth never left his even as things sped up. He heard the pull of Roman's zipper, felt him kicking off his jeans, but Roman's concentration was on him, on his mouth, his lips, his tongue, Roman's hand curling around the back of his neck.

Their legs slid together, Jamie's locking around Roman's. Any nerves vanished as they moved together, bodies pressing against each other, hands gliding over bare skin.

Jamie's eyes closed as Roman slid down, tongue curling around a nipple and hot mouth closing around it as his hands smoothed over his stomach. His prick thudded with blood as Roman moved closer, tongue leaving a cool trail over his skin. He felt each brush of Roman's fingers, the way his nails scraped over his hips, tugging the waistband of his underwear down, his cock coming free.

At the first lick, Jamie bit his lip hard, the heels of his hands digging into the mattress. Roman's tongue slid up the underside of his cock, taking his time as his hand stroked Jamie to a full hardness.

"Oh, shit," Jamie breathed when Roman moved in completely, taking his cock in his mouth and sucking until Jamie's toes curled and he had to stop himself from pushing his hips into Roman's mouth.

Roman moaned around him, the reverberations shivering up his skin. His hands shoved Jamie's legs apart, moving in faster and harder. Jamie's cock slid against the inside of his cheek as he pulled away, licking his lips and glancing up.

Jamie swallowed hard at the darkness in Roman's eyes, the sparkle of mischief there as he leaned back in, tongue sliding over his cock and pulling away repeatedly until Jamie could only pant for breath and reach for Roman's shoulder. His fingers dug into the flesh as his hips pushed up, thrusting into his mouth.

Roman let him, moving with him, and he seemed to know when Jamie was close, but it might have been because Jamie let out a whimper, his body stiffening under Roman's mouth.

Roman was quick to pull away, though, leaving Jamie panting beneath him.

Flushed, Jamie's eyes fluttered open and he licked his lips quickly. He couldn't remember what it was like to just let go, but he wanted Roman to do anything he wanted to him.

Roman palmed himself for a second, adjusting his hard-on as he moved back up Jamie's body to bite at his jaw before groaning into his neck, muffled against the skin.

His hips pushed into Jamie's insistently now, and Jamie could definitely feel his cock through the fabric of his underwear, the wet spot on the front.

"I want to fuck you," Roman whispered into his neck, grinding his hips down. Jamie felt a rush of heat over his skin, his hand reaching up to grip Roman's back as he pushed down again. "I want to be inside you."

Jamie wasn't going to protest, not when his cock strained against Roman's. He wanted to be fucked, to be fucked so hard that he didn't question anything anymore. He wanted the stretch, the burn that came with a good fucking. It had been so long since he'd wanted it like this, since it didn't feel like it was a job, like a distraction from other things in his life.

He nodded in response to Roman, too far gone to form actual words. He dragged Roman's mouth to his for a sloppy, biting kiss, breaking only when Roman pulled away to stretch up to the bedside table. Lying with Roman's body pressed to him, he heard the crinkle of plastic, and Roman came back with a condom in hand.

"Fuck," Roman muttered as he shoved off his underwear, and Jamie stared down at his thick cock, shiny with precum and curving up his stomach.

Roman rolled the condom on and flipped open the tube of lube he'd taken out with it.

Jamie watched him prepare himself, hand sliding over his cock until it was slick and his fingers were coated in lube. For a second, he worried how this would feel considering it had been a while since anyone but himself had gotten him off. He didn't voice his concerns, though, tilting his head back as Roman scooted in closer and spread his legs.

The first finger pressing against his entrance sent a wave of unease and excitement through him, and he sucked in a breath as Roman pushed inside. It was just as he remembered it, however, a tight pressure that only built when Roman added a second finger and worked through his muscles.

Sliding up, Roman hooked Jamie's legs over his shoulders as he positioned his cock at Jamie's entrance.

Jamie's eyes blinked open at Roman's mouth covering his, right before the sharp shock of pushing in hit him.

"Oh," Jamie breathed, mouth falling open and barely responding to the kiss. Instead, he took several panted breaths and tried to adjust to the thick pressure inside him, the feeling of Roman's prick sliding deeper into his body.

Roman said nothing, hands pressed against Jamie's thighs, digging into the flesh to keep his legs up as he drew back and pushed inside.

Jamie's body felt like it was burning up with each movement of Roman inside of him. Each movement sent a new prickle over his skin. Bed sheets crumpled in his fist, and the headboard knocked against the wall as they moved together.

It had been so long, he thought, as he heard Roman's panted breath above him, heavy and rhythmic with the thrust of his hips. So long since he'd felt this desperate need to press closer, to get his hands on any skin he could, so long since anyone had let him.

Roman's hand reached for Jamie's cock, still slick with lube, sliding against him and squeezing.

"R-Roman," Jamie panted as he felt the pressure building, blood pounding under Roman's grip. His words were lost to Roman's groan.

His legs slipped from Roman's shoulders as they moved faster. Jamie bit his lip against the flush on his skin, the tightening in his stomach as Roman jerked him off faster and faster.

"Oh, oh, shit," Jamie breathed a second before he came, hot and wet on his stomach, slipping with Roman's hand. His stomach clenched and a wave of relief crashed over him as his whole body seemed to unwind.

Roman watched him, eyes glued to his cock, sliding up his chest slowly, but he kept moving.

Lying there, Jamie swallowed thickly, remnants of his release sparking against his skin like static electricity. His body moved with Roman's, pushing back and riding with him until Roman cursed under his breath and came, hips pushing into Jamie's body erratically until they slowed and stopped.

Letting out a breath, Jamie rubbed his forehead, wiping away the sheen of sweat gathered at his brow. Come cooled uncomfortably on his stomach, and Roman pulled out slowly, flopping down on the bed next to him.

Roman laughed slightly but said nothing, stretching widely.

For a few minutes, neither spoke. Jamie didn't want to go, but it was already late. He sat up finally and made to slide off the bed, but Roman grabbed his wrist before he could get too far.

"Now don't try to sneak out of here like some college party morning-after scene," he said, sounding completely comfortable as he lay there naked.

"I wasn't, I—"

Roman tugged him back, turning his head to smile at him. "At least give me a proper goodnight."

Jamie smiled, but he reached for his shirt on the floor.

"Hold on a sec," Roman said, rolling off the bed and padding out of the room.

Roman came back a second later, hopping on the bed next to Jamie and handing him a towel to clean up with. He took it, wiping off his stomach.

"Figured a graceful exit at least required you to clean up," Roman said easily.

"Thanks," Jamie said, setting the towel aside. His underwear was still on the floor, along with the rest of his clothes.

Roman smiled in response, reaching up and brushing Jamie's hair from his eyes. "No problem. So do I at least get an, 'I had an awesome time' before you go?"

Jamie laughed. "I had an awesome time," he said, lifting his gaze to Roman.

"Good." Roman leaned in and kissed him easily. "Maybe next time, we can go to your hood. I haven't been to Brooklyn in a while."

"Oh, uh, sure, maybe," Jamie replied, but if he was honest, he'd rather keep Roman separate from that part of his life.

"I'll text you later, yeah?"

"Okay." Jamie nodded, smiling as Roman kissed him again, longer this time.

"Okay," he said as he pulled back. "You can sneak out now."

"I wasn't sneaking."

"Uh huh." Roman grinned as he leaned back on the bed. "Lock the door on your way out."

Shaking his head, Jamie pulled on his clothes and hid his smile as he grabbed his pants off the floor.

"I'm done with men," Laurel said, slamming down the bottle of tequila on the counter. "You with me?"

Jamie glanced over from where he was tapping a beer for the couple at the end of the bar. Laurel flashed him a sarcastic smile as she grabbed a handful of shot glasses and lined them up.

"What happened to the blind date?"

"I wish I was blind," she replied, pouring the row of shots. Jamie finished up the beer and handed it off to the guy.

She passed him a glass when he returned.

"Why don't you tell me why men are such piss-ants? Why do they think we all owe them something? I went to dinner with you and now you think I should get down on my knees and thank you with a blow job in a back alley?"

Jamie cringed. "Laurel…"

"Don't be sensitive. There is no man like a gay man to make comments like that. Why can't straight men be more like gay men?"

"Sleeping with guys?"

"They listen. You listen. Drew, Drew doesn't even listen to himself. Where is he tonight anyway?"

"He's, uh—"

Laurel scoffed, taking another shot and pushing another at Jamie. "Never mind. I don't want to hear your excuse for him this time. That boy needs to get himself together or he won't have a job."

Jamie frowned but didn't reply. As far as he knew, Drew had skipped out half an hour ago for a "date," though if hooking up with a new girl every other night counted as a date, Jamie wasn't sure. When he'd asked, all Drew had said was, "If they're not better than what I left behind, what's the point in seeing them again?"

"I should just become a lesbian," Laurel went on, tossing back her third shot. She refilled the glass. "Pierce my nipple and go to Lilith Fair."

Jamie downed the glass she forced into his hands. It was better to get tipsy than to listen to her rants about men. He wasn't sure that he had any new views on the subject.

"What about you?" she asked suddenly, brushing her hair off her shoulder. "Why no boyfriend? This city is crawling with hot gay guys."

"I..." Jamie thought of Roman; he wasn't sure what they were yet or even what he wanted them to be.

"Oh, right, Drew," Laurel said, waving her hand and taking another shot. "Drink more." She nudged another glass at him but he didn't take it.

"Drew, what?" he asked instead.

Laurel half-laughed and gave him a look he was obviously supposed to understand. "Come on, Jamie. Don't lie to yourself."

A wave of unease swept through his stomach at her words, and he took the shot, tossing it back. It burned his throat, but he needed the numbness right now. He didn't like what she was implying.

"Drew and I aren't like that," he said, and she shook her head.

"He is pretty." She sighed slightly. "But a horrible employee. Although, the other day, after you left, he surprised me."

"He did?"

"He smiled, talked to the customers, was even nice to the hipster guys that come in here. You know, the ones he usually avoids talking to at all costs unless there's a pretty girl with them."

"That's..."

"Strange? I thought so too, but I'm not complaining. Maybe you need to take some more time off so I can get the good Drew at work."

Jamie frowned. "Are you saying I'm the reason Drew's been such a downer?"

Laurel shrugged with a look that clearly implied she thought so. "I'm just saying he was a different person the other night."

Since when was Jamie responsible for Drew's mood swings? He couldn't control Drew. That much he'd learned over the years. Could she be right? Was Drew acting like a jerk because of Jamie? It sounded ridiculous, but something deep down worried Jamie. Drew had changed over the past few months, and Jamie couldn't help but wonder if it had something to do with him.

No, he told himself firmly. That really was ridiculous. Drew was an adult. He could take responsibility for his own problems. Jamie didn't have to feel guilty, but still...

Pouring himself another shot, he grimaced as it burned his throat.

Laurel patted him on the back. "People are capable of change, Jamie, for better or worse."

Setting down the glass, Jamie wiped his mouth and didn't reply. Drew was definitely changing, but it wasn't for better.

Chapter 7
Letting Go

Jamie scribbled on the notepad propped against his knees. His laptop sat open on the coffee table and the low glow of a lamp cast a shadow over his pen. The song changed on the laptop and Jamie didn't even look up at the slow slide of the front door opening.

Drew's keys dropped with a clink on the counter and Jamie heard the flump of his jacket on the chair that followed.

"Are you actually working on the book?" Drew asked, leaning in over Jamie's shoulder.

The pen stilled in his fingers. "Yeah."

Drew stepped back a second later, rounding the couch and flopping into the chair instead. He brushed his hair from his eyes and cracked open a beer, tossing the cap at the table where it bounced off and rolled somewhere on the floor.

Jamie watched him, biting his lip. He kept thinking of what Laurel had said. In fact, he couldn't get it out of his head. He'd been sitting there for over an hour, trying to edit, but frustration at the difficulty of it all had set his mind wandering to other, even less pleasant, thoughts.

"Have you done any more songs lately?" he asked instead of giving into the nagging voice that demanded to know if Drew was acting this way because of him.

Drew took a swig of his beer and stretched, legs splayed out before him, and Jamie looked away from the stretch of his jeans over his crotch. Sometimes it felt like Drew did things like that on purpose, and he hated the way his heart beat faster as he thought about it. He should have been long over those feelings.

"Haven't I told you not to worry about that?" Drew asked, kicking off his shoes and sinking into the chair.

"I am worried about it. Since we got here, all you've done is avoid working on the book. I thought you wanted to come?"

Drew rubbed his forehead for a second. "I did. It seemed like a great idea at the time."

"And it doesn't now?" Jamie wasn't sure he wanted an answer to that question, fearful he already knew it. They'd come to New York together, to work on the book, to be somewhere new. "You just need a break. Let's go to a concert or something. It'll help give you inspiration."

"I don't have anything to write down," Drew said, but Jamie shook his head.

"Yes, you do," he insisted. He'd seen the scraps of paper, the fragments of napkins. He'd heard the choruses on the piano.

"Just because you want to believe something is true doesn't make it true, Jamie."

"What are you talking about?"

"You're the one who wanted to do this, you know," Drew said, sitting back in the chair. "To move to New York, write a show, get on Broadway."

"You didn't?" Jamie knew Drew didn't care so much about Broadway; he cared about the music, but he'd been just as excited to come as Jamie, despite leaving Kristin behind.

Drew set his beer bottle on the coffee table with a slight thud. "I like writing music, and I'm good at it, but I'm not in it for the fame. I couldn't care less what some producer says about my stuff."

Jamie huffed, pushing the notebook off his lap. "If we can't finish one show, how do we expect to actually become playwrights?"

Drew scrubbed his face with his hands. "That's what you want."

"It's what you want too," Jamie asked, staring at him, but Drew didn't meet his gaze.

"Why don't you let me know when you have a producer, okay?"

"I still need the songs." Jamie frowned as Drew rose from the chair. "Drew? Drew, we're not done!"

"I am." Drew vanished into his room before Jamie could argue anymore, the door shutting with a click.

Huffing, Jamie sank back into the couch. Jamie wanted to make a name for himself here, to make a life, but Drew was resisting every step of the way.

Rubbing his face, Jamie groaned to himself. He wished life could be simple. Or at least, simpler.

"Did you always want to be a dancer?"

Roman lifted his cup to his lips and took a sip. It was warm in the café, the low hum of chatter from others surrounding them, and the whistle of wind whenever the door would open and shut.

"No," he replied. "When I was five, I believe I went up to my mother and told her that I was going to be a cheerleader. Of course, when I got into school and being a cheerleader got me picked on by the other boys, I quickly changed it to firefighter until my mom signed me up for jazz dance after school."

"And they stopped picking on you?"

Roman scoffed. "They called me all sorts of names all through school until I finally punched Trevor Davis in the mouth; knocked out two teeth. They stopped after that."

Jamie laughed. "I wish I'd done that, but…" He shook his head. Physical violence wasn't really his go-to response. "Drew did once. In high school, he broke this guy's nose 'cause he called me a fag." Drew had also punched David the last time he'd seen him, but that wasn't something Jamie liked to bring up. He'd rather forget about it.

"That was nice of him," Roman said, tilting his head to the side. "What does he do exactly?"

"He writes music." Jamie tore open a sugar packet and stirred it into his coffee. "For the show. I mean, well, really, he writes it because he likes to write it. He's really good, too. The first time I heard him play, it was like—this is going to sound stupid, but it was like finding an arm you'd been missing but hadn't realized. You'd just gone through your whole life without an arm without noticing and then there it was." He shrugged, rubbing the back of his neck. It was hard to explain. Becoming friends with Drew had changed Jamie's whole world.

Roman didn't respond for a moment, twisting his cup in his hands. Jamie cringed mentally. He shouldn't have been talking about Drew so much. It made it sound like… He shook away the thought. Maybe Roman hadn't noticed.

"Maybe we could all hang out," Roman said after a minute. "I'd like to meet him."

Jamie hesitated. He hadn't even really told Drew about Roman, not directly anyway, and that meeting would probably be a lot of general disinterest from Drew. Besides, things were finally going well in his life, and he didn't need to change that.

"He's not that interesting," Jamie said finally. "And he'd probably say something insulting."

"I live with Merryn," Roman pointed out with half a smile. "I can handle insulting."

Merryn and Drew were two different leagues, Jamie found himself thinking as he fiddled with a sugar packet. Together, they'd probably be a force of bitchiness that no one could stop.

He didn't want to keep talking about Drew, but Roman was watching, waiting for him to agree to hanging out. He cast around for something else to talk about, anything else to distract from the idea of bringing two parts of his life together. Things were better when they were separate.

"I've been working on the book," he said, and Roman seemed to frown for a second at the change of subject.

"Yeah?" he asked, though, swishing what was left of his coffee in the cup. Outside, snowflakes began to fall, dusting the sidewalk in a flurry of white.

"Yeah," Jamie said, his heart beat picking up speed as he tried to get his words in order. "I was wondering, if you were serious, if you meant it when you said you wanted to read it?"

He couldn't believe he was doing this, but if he ever wanted to get anywhere with his writing, he had to put it out there. At least with Roman, it was someone who understood Broadway, someone who might be able to give him valid feedback and probably wouldn't crush his dreams too hard if it sucked.

Roman's eyebrows rose in surprise but he smiled. "Of course. This means I get to play the lead, right?"

"You'd have to kiss a girl."

Roman shrugged. "I've done worse."

"How many girls have you kissed?" Jamie asked curiously, and Roman grinned.

"Wouldn't you like to know?"

"Was it a lot?"

"It was all acting," Roman assured him, stretching over the small table to lean into his mouth. "I'd much rather kiss you."

Jamie's smile barely surfaced as Roman kissed him softly.

"Besides," he said, sitting back. "Guys are much better kissers."

"You would know."

Roman laughed into his coffee. Jamie felt nervous now, but it was a good kind of nervous, and he sat back to watch the snow flutter past the window.

"Editing again?" Drew asked, emerging from his room in only his boxers and padding into the kitchen.

"I think I finally figured out what Owen needs to do to escape the coma. It's really important that he has a reason to live, because inside his head, he doesn't have anything. He's lost everything, so why would he want to keep fighting, right? He has to choose to live. There needs to be a moment when he chooses to live." He watched Drew yank open the fridge. "What are you doing?"

"Natalie wants a drink," he replied, rummaging in the fridge.

Jamie couldn't help glancing back at the closed bedroom door and frowning.

"Well, what do you think?" he asked instead. If he was going to let Roman read this, it needed to be more done than it was.

"Sounds fine," Drew said, kicking the fridge shut and coming over to the couch.

Jamie had been hoping for something a little more enthusiastic. "You're going to have to write the last song differently now."

"Yeah, sure, I'll get right on that," Drew said, the words laced with sarcasm.

"Seriously," Jamie said, but Drew cut him off.

"Seriously, Jamie. There's a girl in there who's a hell of a lot more interesting than this conversation."

Jamie scowled as Drew vanished into his room. He didn't have time to wait on Drew anymore, though he'd hoped Drew would help. After all, it was his show too.

Grabbing his laptop, he pulled it closer and began typing. It was time to finish this.

"Is that it?" Roman asked, rounding the couch with two drinks in hand and settling in next to Jamie as Jamie clutched the book to his chest.

He couldn't explain the anxiety he felt at even the thought of letting someone else read his work. Why had he thought this was a good idea? Because no one ever got a show done by sitting on the book. That was why. If he wanted to get better, he had to let go of the control and let someone else look at it.

"Okay, but," Jamie said as Roman set down the drinks and held out a hand expectantly. "It's not done, and it's not perfect."

"They never are." He smiled and waited, but when Jamie hesitated, he scooted closer. "I'm not a judgmental producer. I just want to read it. I promise to say many gushing things about it."

"What if it's awful?"

"It won't be. Now, come on."

It was just Roman, Jamie told himself. Just Roman who wanted to read it, Roman who liked him and wanted to get closer to him. Roman had studied these kinds of things, knew a lot about theater. Who better to read it? It was with that thought that he loosened his clench on the book.

"Shouldn't you two be making out or something?" Merryn asked as she breezed out of her room wearing an over-sized sweater that hung off her shoulder over a spandex top and sweatpants.

"Where are you going?" Roman asked as she grabbed her bag from the counter and checked for her phone.

Jamie was glad for the interruption, the moment to gather himself.

"Midnight yoga in the park," she replied, shoving her keys in her pocket. "It helps to center yourself."

"It's freezing out."

"Also gets me out of the apartment for an hour or two," she went on, ignoring him. She shot them both an obvious look. "Though maybe if you and the boyfriend went somewhere else, I wouldn't have to freeze my tits off. Don't you have an apartment in a shitty part of Brooklyn?"

Jamie halted. "I—"

"Goodbye, Merryn," Roman interrupted, and Merryn rolled her eyes, flipping her hair over her shoulder. The door snapped shut behind her. Roman looked at Jamie. "Why don't we go to your place sometime? It would definitely get Merryn out of our hair, plus you wouldn't have to come all the way up here."

"But you'd have to go all the way down there."

"What's the difference?" Roman asked. "I like Brooklyn. Lots of good bars."

Jamie shrugged awkwardly. "It's nothing special. I like your apartment. It's got much better furniture than mine."

"Jamie," Roman said in that tone that made him feel like a chastised five-year old.

"Here," Jamie said, holding out the book. "Take it before I change my mind."

Roman took it from him, staring at the cover page for a moment. Jamie knew they hadn't left the subject of his apartment behind. Couldn't things just stay the way they were? He liked seeing Roman. He liked that it wasn't a big deal. After David, anything that wasn't filled with drug-fueled rants and days-long disappearances was a good thing.

"Do you not want me to meet your friends?" Roman asked after a minute, and Jamie shook his head.

"No. Of course not. I just like this, what we have now." Why did things have to get complicated?

He could tell Roman wasn't satisfied with his answer from the way his mouth twisted. His life wasn't anything special. They didn't need to make it difficult. They could just enjoy being together without all the extras that came with complicated relationships.

He was distracted from his thoughts as Roman moved in closer, crawling over him and forcing him back.

"You know what I like about you?" he asked, adjusting his knees so that he was straddling him on the couch.

"I am delightfully quirky?" Jamie wasn't exactly sure they'd dropped the subject of Drew.

Roman shook his head. "You're not like other industry people I know. You don't want to gossip about who's fucking who. You just wanna get shit done, and that's a great quality to have." He paused. "You also give really good head."

Jamie laughed despite himself. "Glad that's on the list."

Roman leaned into Jamie's neck, brushing a kiss against it. "I've dated a lot of guys who think it's the most important thing."

"What happened to them?" Jamie shivered at Roman's tongue sliding down his neck, his hand pulling at the collar of his shirt so he could get at his collarbone. This was better. They didn't have to talk about him or his life anymore.

"It turns out it wasn't the most important thing," Roman murmured, kissing him slowly and slipping his tongue against Jamie's, lifting his hand to Jamie's hair.

The comfort of the moment was nice, Jamie thought as they kissed. Outside, the black sky lit up with yellow city lights and the occasional rush of sound passed by out the window. The snow from the few days before had become ugly black slush alongside the roads, but the clouds forecast more to come.

Roman stretched out on top of him, lips lingering against Jamie's for a moment. "I want someone who knows what they want, who doesn't get bogged down in stupid backstage drama, and who isn't going to run off with the first hot guy in tight pants that they see."

Jamie felt a flutter of hesitation as Roman kissed him. Things were moving quicker than he'd expected. What Roman wanted he could do, but how serious did that make this?

Roman's mouth pressed against his, his tongue sliding over Jamie's bottom lip, a slight nip as he shifted up. Roman's hand carded through Jamie's messy hair, tilted his jaw up, smoothed down the line of his cheek.

"I don't think that's gonna happen," Jamie said finally, leaning into the way Roman's mouth slid down his throat again, mouthing at the soft patch of skin behind his ear, his tongue sweeping over his tattoo.

"I hope not," Roman replied, and his hands moved slowly, sliding down Jamie's torso to the waistband of his jeans.

Closing his eyes, Jamie let out a slow breath and stretched under the hands enclosing on his hips. He didn't have to think about what this was right now. Right now, it was fun and he'd like to keep it that way.

Roman didn't push his shirt off, just rucking it up enough to get a good look at Jamie's stomach as he pressed his mouth to the pale skin.

Biting his lip, Jamie said nothing, enjoying the slide of Roman's tongue down his stomach, teeth brushing against his hip sending a shiver through his body.

"When I first moved to New York," Roman said quietly, hands moving to the button on Jamie's jeans, "I stayed with this guy who would bring home a different guy every night..." He pulled down the zipper slowly, the sound loud in the otherwise silent apartment. "And I thought, if I could be that good at what I did to get a different guy every night, then I'd really have made it."

Jamie frowned slightly, but then sucked in a breath as Roman's hand slid under his jeans to curl around his cock.

Roman smiled up at him. "I changed my mind."

With his free hand, Roman yanked down Jamie's jeans to his thighs, licking the palm of his hand before stroking him slowly. He closed his eyes against the way Roman squeezed his prick, a rough slide against his skin that erupted goosebumps on his skin, made him suck in a breath and squeeze his eyes shut.

Roman's mouth slid down, sucking on his inner thigh while his hand worked his cock, jerking until the blood rushed downward, prick hardening in his grip.

"Oh," Jamie breathed at the slow slide of Roman's hand, the way he flicked his tongue against the underside before licking a stripe up to the tip and sucking.

The warmth of Roman's mouth slipped over him as Roman sunk down, Jamie's cock gliding in against his tongue, grazing the inside of his cheek.

His lips were red from being bitten, and Jamie licked them as he let out a breath and opened his eyes to stare at the low ceiling above him. Roman's mouth on him moved quickly now, warm and wet, sinking down until Jamie could only feel the prickling rising on his skin, the heat building in his stomach.

"God, you're good at this," he muttered, gasping slightly and reaching for Roman's hair.

He didn't mean to push him down, but he couldn't help it as his hips lifted up, jerking into Roman's mouth. Roman didn't stop him or hold him back. Instead, he slid his fingers under his cock, smoothing against his balls and rolling them in his palm.

It wouldn't be long, Jamie knew, not when Roman ran his mouth over his cock, tongue sliding against the hardened length, hand gripping the base and tugging.

"Oh, shit," Jamie gasped when Roman pulled away, sucking at the base as he jerked him off. His hips jerked in Roman's grip, heat pricking at his skin, stomach tightening into knots as he dug his hand into the couch cushion.

Roman didn't stop jerking him off, not until Jamie's sharp breath as he came hard, stickiness landing on his shoulder, some in his hair.

"God," Jamie said finally as he let out a long breath and felt Roman climb back over him.

"I'll take that as a compliment."

"It is." Jamie smiled briefly, passing a hand over his forehead and feeling the lingering warmth.

"I can think of a better way to thank me," Roman replied, kissing Jamie long and hard this time. He grabbed Jamie's hand, guiding it down to his crotch and the bulge there.

Jamie pressed a short kiss to Roman's lips, squeezing his hand gently and reveling in the sound Roman made in his ear. "I could do that."

Roman grinned into the kiss as he pushed Jamie back down and Jamie reached for his zipper.

Roman arched into his touch as Jamie pushed his hand inside, not taking the time to get his jeans down or even give himself much room to jerk Roman off. Roman didn't seem to mind, his fingers digging into the back of Jamie's neck.

Roman's breath was hot against his temple as Jamie shifted, pushing a leg between Roman's, edging them apart as he jerked him off, hot and fast, Roman's cock stiff under his palm.

Roman kept Jamie close, close enough that he could hear every pant of breath, the way Roman cursed under his breath and groaned when he came, still wearing his jeans.

Slowly, Jamie pulled his hand out and Roman let out a long breath. Definitely better than a grope at a dark party.

"Was that enough of a thank you?" he asked as Roman rolled off him and onto the couch.

"Just being around you is one," Roman replied and Jamie's stomach flipped over nervously but he said nothing. It had been a long time since he'd dated anyone seriously and it made him nervous that someone cared about him like that. After last time, after David, he hadn't been sure dating had even been worth it. Now, with Roman, things were getting more serious and he wondered if that was what he wanted.

He didn't say anything about his thoughts. Instead, he let Roman slide his arm around his waist and flip on the TV. It was his own problem to deal with and he'd have to do it soon.

Chapter 8
Changing Tides

Jamie looked up as Drew plucked a few notes out at the piano. He hesitated a second, then set down the glass he'd been cleaning, leaving the bar and crossing the room.

Laurel had only been there for a couple of minutes, earlier before she headed off to some meeting or other. She had just told Jamie to lock up when he left.

"Is that new?" Jamie asked as he reached Drew.

Drew didn't look up, gliding his fingers along the keys in a melody Jamie knew this time. "Just messing around." He paused. "This is usually the part where you ask if I've done any work lately."

Jamie frowned. He didn't *want* to be the slave driver, but partnerships were supposed to be partnerships.

Drew's phone vibrated on top of the piano before Jamie could respond to Drew, and Jamie glanced at the screen.

"Kristin," he said, handing it to Drew.

Drew snatched it from his hand and immediately hit "ignore" on the screen. He shoved it inside his pocket and turned back to the piano.

Jamie frowned at his reaction. "Why'd you do that?"

"Do what?"

"Ignore her." Drew always answered Kristin's calls. He dropped whatever he was doing to talk to her, or at least he had. Now that Jamie thought about it, he couldn't remember the last time he'd heard Drew on the phone with her.

"Why shouldn't I?"

"Because you—" Jamie stopped himself abruptly. They both knew what he was going to say—*because you love her*—but saying it meant he couldn't ignore what he'd been trying to for so long.

"Look, Jai, it's none of your business," Drew said instead, rising from the bench and heading for the bar.

Jamie followed. "What happened?" He wasn't sure he really wanted to know, but if Drew was ignoring her, it couldn't be a good sign.

"Nothing happened. Just drop it." Drew turned his back on Jamie, rearranging bottles on the back wall.

"But—"

"Fuck, Jamie, just stop!" he snapped, setting down the bottle in his hand with a loud clunk against the counter. "I don't want to talk about it. So stop asking questions."

Jamie could do little more than watch as Drew pulled off his apron and tossed it down on the counter.

"I'm going home."

He stalked from the bar, leaving Jamie alone to clean up.

The apartment was dark as Jamie unlocked the front door and pushed it open carefully. He didn't really expect to find Drew there. He suspected he was blowing off steam somewhere far away.

Stepping inside, he shut the door and tossed his keys on the counter. They hit with a clink and slid a few inches on the surface as he tugged off his jacket and tossed it over the chair, jumping when the lamp clicked on unexpectedly, revealing Drew on the couch, facing the dark window.

"What are you doing?" Jamie asked, his heart pounding.

"She got a boyfriend," Drew replied instead of answering the question.

"Who?" Jamie stepped around the couch, frowning at Drew, his legs propped up on the table and three empty beers next to his feet.

"Who do you think?"

Jamie sat down on the table facing Drew, but Drew kept his gaze out the window. "Well," he said finally when the silence dragged on. "I thought you guys broke up."

"We did."

"And you've slept with a hundred girls since then."

Drew didn't reply, grabbing one of the bottles and draining what was left.

Jamie watched him for a moment. He didn't know what to say. He'd never been very good at comforting others. Most of the time, he had never been comforted himself, forced to keep his own thoughts and feelings to himself lest he get picked on for it.

"So she got a boyfriend. Big deal," he said instead, shrugging slightly and biting his lip as Drew sighed in return.

Drew set the bottle on the floor and pressed a hand to his forehead. "I think I want to go back to Florida."

"What?"

Drew stood abruptly and went to the kitchen. There, he yanked open the fridge door and grabbed another beer out. He cracked it open and stood with the fridge door ajar for a long moment, his face illuminated in the light from inside, frowning down at the bottle.

Jamie stared after him. He wasn't serious. There was nothing in Florida, just overly-tanned grandparents and theme parks.

"You're drunk," he said. It was the only explanation.

"I'm just trying to tell you the truth, Jamie."

"But you can't want to go back to Florida. Florida was awful."

"For you, yeah," Drew agreed. "But I'm tired of being here."

"That's impossible." Jamie refused to believe this. Drew was just upset about Kristin. And he was drunk. Not the best combination. There was no way he would go back to Florida.

"You can't just believe what you want to believe, Jamie," Drew said, shutting the fridge door. "I want to go back." He headed for his room but Jamie caught him by the arm.

"You can't leave," he said, but Drew merely shook him off, taking a swig of his beer and disappearing into his room.

Sinking back onto the coffee table, Jamie put his face in his hands and shook his head. What was he going to do now? Things never seemed to go well for long.

"Fuck," Roman breathed, his hand splayed over the back of Jamie's head as Jamie slid down his stomach, licking around his belly button and sucking a hickey onto his hip bone. It hadn't taken much to get Roman like this, spread out naked beneath him. With the apartment empty, they'd gone straight for the bedroom. Now, Jamie had Roman prostrate to his touch, encouraging him with groaned words, hips straining upward.

He didn't want to think about Drew or his recent proclamation. Jamie hadn't brought it up the next day, though he was sure Drew remembered from the way he'd avoided talking to him. He just wanted to enjoy some time away from all of those problems.

Roman's cock stood erect, hot and heavy in his hand when he slid down and smoothed his palm over the ridges and listened to Roman's appreciative moan. He was mostly naked except for his boxers, but his prick throbbed beneath the fabric, eager to be touched.

Slipping out of his boxers, Jamie moved slowly. He let his fingers glide up Roman's thighs, shifting up to straddle him. Roman's eyes opened and he watched silently. They hadn't gotten this far yet, but Jamie wasn't going to take the time to second guess himself.

Without a word, Roman reached over to the bedside table and pulled a condom from the top drawer along with a tube of lube.

A part of Jamie felt unnecessarily nervous as he took control, plucking the condom from Roman and rolling it on Roman's prick. Roman popped open the lube and slicked it on his fingers. As Roman slipped the first finger in, Jamie was acutely aware of the way Roman moved his fingers in and out, stretching him, giving him time.

Jamie was too impatient to wait, pushing at Roman's hand and reaching for his cock instead.

"Yeah," Roman murmured, pulling his fingers out, shifting and reaching for Jamie's hips to help steady him as he lowered himself. "Fuck, Jamie."

The first press was always more than he expected, a flush spreading over his skin. The feeling of Roman's prick inside him made him close his eyes, the stretch and fullness filling him in a way that nothing else ever did.

As he started to move, he cursed to himself. His cock throbbed as Roman pushed up inside him, matching his movements easily, hips thrusting up, his prick sliding inside him. Everything was too hot, even in the chill of the apartment. For a moment, he could only hear the rush of blood in his ears, their panted breaths, and Roman's occasional moan of encouragement as they moved faster and everything became a blur.

"God, Jamie, yeah, let me fuck you, just like that," Roman breathed, jerking his hips up, pressing his cock inside Jamie. Jamie groaned at the tightness, the spark of pleasure pricking his skin as they moved. "You're beautiful."

Jamie shut his eyes, rocking up and down with Roman, hands on Roman's stomach to steady himself. His own prick pulsed eagerly, and his eyes jerked open as Roman's hand reached for him and stroked slowly. It was too slow in comparison to how they were moving.

In between whispered curses and gasps, Roman groaning beneath him, and Roman's hand tugging on his cock, he didn't last long. As he slid down on Roman's prick harder than before, he came, a shudder wracking through his body.

He still moved as he came down, panting for breath, meeting Roman's thrusts until Roman groaned, hands tightening over his hips. It took a minute to slow to a stop, and Jamie pulled off Roman carefully and rolled over onto his back.

"Shit," Roman said, a grin spreading over his face as he melted into the comforter and slid his hand around Jamie's neck, tugging him over and kissing him slowly. "You're not too bad at that either."

Jamie smiled against his mouth and rolled onto his back, hands on his bare stomach and eyes on the *Hello, Dolly!* poster on the opposite wall.

Next to him, Roman sighed contently. "I finished your script."

Jamie's eyes widened but he didn't move. "Already?" A crawling sense of fear entered his stomach. That was quick. It must have been awful. Immediately, he didn't want to hear anymore.

"It's been a week."

"Yeah, but—" Jamie paused. He hadn't expected Roman to finish it so quickly. He honestly hadn't expected him to read it at all. Most people who said they wanted to read it only said it to say it.

"I liked it," Roman said, rolling onto his side and propping himself up on his elbow. "The characters were believable and engaging. The songs were good. Merryn thought so too."

"Merryn?" Jamie pushed himself up and Roman gazed after him. "You let her read it?"

"No, well, she stole it."

"Liar!" came Merryn's voice from the living room. "You left it lying around."

"How long has she been home?" Jamie demanded, feeling extremely precarious, completely naked, even though the door was shut.

"Who knows," Roman replied flippantly, sitting up and sliding his arms around Jamie's stomach, pressing his mouth to his shoulder blade. "But she liked it too. And she's picky."

"Really?" After all this time and all that editing, Jamie wasn't even sure if it was good anymore. He'd become so blind to any changes that it all felt like laborious work. A weight came off his chest at Roman's words. Maybe he could make it after all.

"I'm ordering pizza if you two are done in there!" Merryn called through the door.

Roman ignored her. "Really."

"Does she have to do that?" Jamie asked, slipping off the bed and grabbing his boxers off the floor. He'd feel better once he was dressed. He wasn't like Drew who didn't care who was home when he brought girls home. Jamie never brought guys back to the apartment.

"It was so good that I gave it to Nathan."

Jamie stumbled up from the bed, heart racing again as his eyes widened. "What?!"

Roman had given it to Nathan, Nathan Stuggart, one of the best directors in all of Broadway.

"If he likes it, that could mean big things for you and Drew."

Jamie nodded, thoughts racing. This could possibly have been the biggest break of his life. His thoughts went to Drew. Drew couldn't leave now. Not when they might finally have their shot. "What if he hates it?"

"He won't hate it," Roman replied. "You're lucky. Most directors don't even listen to people in the ensemble unless they're sleeping together."

Jamie paused, glancing at Roman, who shrugged.

"It was a hand job, like three years ago. Everybody does it with someone."

Shaking his head, Jamie didn't want to think about what Roman may or may not have done to get a part. He sank down onto the foot of the bed. "You really gave it to him?"

"You're welcome," Roman said, pressing a kiss to Jamie's temple.

"If you two don't mind, I'm trying to watch a movie," Merryn called from the living room.

"Come on," Roman said, squeezing Jamie's thigh and pushing himself up.

Jamie pulled on his jeans, and Roman threw on an old shirt and faded jeans before padding out to the living room. Merryn sat cross-legged on the couch, debating between two DVDs.

"Musical or action flick?"

"Action. I get enough of musicals at work." Roman took the DVD she held out and slipped it in the player. "What did you order?"

"Pepperoni, but we're out of drinks."

"I'll get some real quick," Roman offered. "Jamie, any preferences?"

"I'm fine with whatever," Jamie said; he was less worried about the type of drink Roman might get and more at the prospect of being alone with Merryn. He wasn't sure she particularly liked him.

"I'll be back," Roman said, grabbing his keys off the counter. As the door shut behind him, Jamie hesitated. His only choice of seat was the couch with Merryn as the chair was piled with laundry.

"Do you live in a condemned building?" Merryn asked not a minute after Roman left.

"What?"

"It's just you guys never go there. You know, this is my apartment too, and I don't really like spending my free time listening to you fuck."

Jamie's neck reddened at her frankness. "Sorry."

"Don't be sorry. Be considerate." She paused, silent for a moment as she contemplated the home screen of the DVD menu. "Roman's dated a lot of people."

Jamie wasn't sure how to respond to that. Was she trying to scare him?

"But he's got this thing with you." She glanced at him, almost as if doubtful. "He seems to think you're worth more than a week or two of fun." She straightened up on the couch. "Now, I find your bright naivety about the industry grating, but Roman. Roman values enthusiasm and earnestness and being genuine."

"Well, I do too," Jamie said slowly, but he didn't miss her comment about their relationship in the long-term. He wasn't very good at long-term relationships if his last was any indication. He'd come away from David bruised and battered, and he wasn't sure he wanted to try that again.

"Good," Merryn said pointedly. "Because Roman gives far too many people the benefit of the doubt, but I don't."

Jamie didn't reply, and he was infinitely glad when Roman came back a few minutes later, though Merryn's words echoed in his head through the entire movie that followed.

Chapter 9
What a Guy Wants

"Hey, pay attention," Laurel said as she passed behind Jamie, glancing at the shot glasses he was pouring. "Jamie? Jamie!"

Jamie jumped, golden tequila spilling over the rims.

"Sorry," he said, grabbing a towel and mopping up the spill. He set the shots on a tray and shook the wetness off his fingers.

"What were you thinking about?"

Jamie rinsed out the towel in the sink. "Nothing, just nothing."

Laurel watched him clean up, hands on her hips. "The only things I know that can cause distractions like that are either men or family."

It wasn't either really. At least, not in the way Laurel was thinking. He kept thinking about Nathan Stuggart reading his book, about what that might mean. It could be just what he needed to snap Drew out of his ridiculous notion of moving back to Florida.

"You've both been acting strange," Laurel went on when Jamie didn't reply. "Drew isn't even talking to you, and you're all over the place. What gives?"

Jamie hadn't realized it was that obvious, and he turned away. "It's nothing."

"Lying to me is one thing, but lying to yourself is another," Laurel said. "Drew actually seems better, if that's possible. He didn't scowl when he came in this morning. You guys finally work out your issues?"

"We don't have issues," Jamie argued, but Laurel rolled her eyes.

"You're probably a great writer, Jamie. You know how I know?"

Jamie wasn't sure he wanted to.

"You're great at pretending."

Jamie frowned after her as she left. Things weren't great with Drew right now; that much was true. Okay, things hadn't been great for a while now, but he could still fix it. He just needed Drew to stay in New York.

The sound of the tap clicking off made him look up. Beside him, Drew set three beers on a tray.

"I have good news," Jamie said, watching for Drew's reaction, but Drew merely glanced up then back to the tray. "You know Roman?"

"No," Drew said simply.

"The guy from the party, the dancer."

"The guy you've been secretly dating," Drew said, grabbing a towel from the sink and wiping down the counter.

"It's not a secret, it's..." This wasn't the point. This wasn't about Roman. This was about Drew.

"If no one's met him but you, it's a secret. Are you afraid I won't like him? Anyone's gonna be better than David, so I promise not to punch this guy, okay?"

"No, it's, this isn't about him. It's not serious anyway. You don't need to meet him. I don't get why everyone wants to meet everybody else. Can't things just be fun without expectations? Why does everybody have to want something?" Things were stressful enough without Roman pushing for more in the relationship and Drew backing him up.

"Whoa, relax," Drew said, frowning at him. "I was kidding. You know, it's not like this guy *is* David."

"What's that supposed to mean?" Jamie immediately bristled and Drew shrugged.

"Just saying not everyone is a douchebag." He threw the towel in the sink. "What was it you wanted to tell me?"

Jamie knew that Roman wasn't like David. They were completely opposite. Where David had been callous, Roman was understanding and encouraging. Roman actually thought his writing was good.

It took a second to push Drew's comments away and focus on the point. He hadn't brought up Roman to get in an argument.

"I gave Roman the book and he liked it so much he gave it to Nathan Stuggart."

He waited a second for that to sink in, but Drew looked less than impressed, furrowing his eyebrows.

"Who?"

Jamie sighed. "He's an award-winning director. He could make this happen for real, Drew! Everything we came here for could happen!"

Understanding flitted over Drew's face but he didn't seem any more excited. Instead, he leaned against the counter and sighed. "I already told you I want to go back to Florida."

"But you can't go," Jamie insisted. "This was the whole point of coming here. We finally have a shot, and you're just gonna leave?"

If Drew left, it would be walking away from a golden opportunity. What could possibly be better than this?

Drew shook his head, not meeting Jamie's gaze. "I don't want to do this anymore."

"Yes, you do. You wanted to come here too, remember?"

"You're not listening to me," Drew said abruptly, turning to Jamie. "Yes, I wanted to come here. I thought it would be fun. But I miss Florida. I miss Kristin. I miss writing because I want to and not because I have to."

Jamie felt queasy as he listened to Drew. This couldn't actually be happening. Drew had to stay. He needed him to stay. Without Drew, he'd be just another sad writer in the city chasing success.

"This could be our shot," Jamie insisted, staring at Drew. His heart thudded loudly in his chest, the nerves in his body on edge.

"*Your* shot," Drew corrected him. "You're the one who wants this, not me."

"Then why did you come?" Jamie demanded, and Drew shoved his hair back.

"I have customers."

"Drew!" Jamie wasn't going to let him walk away.

"I don't know," Drew said loudly. "I was young and stupid and I thought it would be fun, and it was for a while, but I don't want to do this. I don't want to be a Broadway person. It's not who I am. Right now, I just wanna leave."

Grabbing the tray, he left Jamie staring after him. This wasn't how Jamie had imagined their first big break. What would happen if Nathan actually liked the script? What if he wanted to meet? Drew wouldn't go. That much was clear. He didn't even want to be there with Jamie anymore.

There was a sinking feeling in the pit of Jamie's stomach as he turned from the bar. They were ruining their chances. Drew was ruining his. Jamie didn't know what to do. He needed Drew to stay, but so far, all he'd done was push him further away. Without Drew, he wouldn't have anything.

The apartment had gotten dark around Jamie, leaving him mostly in darkness but for the one lamp he could reach from his position on the couch. The apartment was otherwise empty and silent except for the occasional siren out the window. He didn't know where Drew was and his texts had gone unanswered. He wasn't even sure what he could say anymore.

When his phone buzzed, he snatched it from the coffee table, but Roman's name flashed on the screen instead of Drew's. He felt a tiny flash of disappointment.

Guess where I am, the text read.

Hard Rock Cafe? Jamie typed back, sliding down on the couch.

Brooklyn.

Jamie's fingers froze above the keyboard.

You home? came another message.

Jamie wasn't sure why he hesitated. He knew what Roman wanted—a relationship, a real relationship that wasn't just hooking up. The thought made Jamie's stomach bunch up into a big knot. He liked Roman, but they hardly knew each other. It had only been a few months. Why did things have to change? They were fine the way they were.

Finally, he typed, *yeah but Drew's here and he's sick so probably not a good idea to come over.*

It was a lie, completely and totally. The moment he sent it, he stuffed the phone away. He just wasn't ready for that.

As the minutes stretched on, Jamie's unease grew when Roman didn't reply. He pulled the phone out again, checking, but there was no message. He didn't want to stop seeing Roman. They just didn't need to make it a bigger deal than it was.

But we can hang out later, he texted, staring at the screen after he sent it, willing Roman to type back.

OK.

Jamie's stomach sank at the two letters on the screen. Never a good sign. But he didn't have to feel bad about not giving in to pressure. If he didn't want Roman over, it shouldn't be a big deal.

Putting away the phone, he told himself he'd text Roman later. Tomorrow, or maybe the next day.

Keys rattled behind the door and it swung open as Drew came in. Drew glanced at him on the couch but said nothing as he passed by.

"Where were you?" Jamie asked before Drew could get to his room.

"Went out for a drink."

"Right, because you hate New York so much," Jamie scoffed.

"Jamie," Drew said warningly, but Jamie was tired of being the understanding one, the one who made sure Drew didn't do anything stupid when he was drunk, that he showed up to work on time. "Don't do this."

"No. I know you hate it here, and you want to go home, but you can't just give up on everything. What if Nathan likes the book? What if he wants to produce it? Would you still leave?"

"You can do all those things without me," Drew said, turning to face Jamie. "It's your story."

"It's our story."

"No, it's *your* story," Drew snapped. "You're the kid. The kid in the coma and you have to make a choice. Do you wanna live or do you want to keep using me as an excuse?"

"That is not true at all," Jamie argued. His heart pounded against his ribcage, a flush rising on his skin. "If it wasn't for me, you'd still be pretending you don't play."

"And if it wasn't for me, you'd still be in Florida," Drew retorted, glaring at Jamie. "I don't want to write Broadway musicals or hang out with lookalike club girls or prostrate myself to some asshole director. I want to go home."

Jamie wasn't sure his heart had ever been broken before, but it felt like it now. This was everything he'd been working towards since he was twelve years old. All he felt was a slicing pain in his chest, welling up in his throat as he shook his head.

"Fine," Jamie snapped, too angry to think of anything else. It was a complete waste. This whole time. "Then just go. Go back to Florida. I don't need you."

His heart pounded as Drew disappeared into his room, slamming the door behind him. As he stared at Drew's closed door, the anger began to ebb, replaced with a pit in his stomach. Drew wouldn't actually leave, right?

Roman held open the door for Jamie as they stepped out of the coffee shop and into the brisk morning. The sky above was overcast, clouded in grey, threatening snow again. Jamie breathed in the scent of his coffee, warmth bleeding through the paper cup to his hands.

They walked towards the park, along streets that Jamie usually never walked down. Brooklyn was different than Central New York, more homey with brick buildings and crumbling stairs. Everything downtown was shiny, silver and black, cars moving at a glacial pace and wearing out their horns.

He'd invited Roman down there, not to meet Drew or visit his apartment, but hopefully as a kind of peace offering. It wasn't like Brooklyn was off-limits. Though the afternoon had gone well so far, Jamie couldn't help his thoughts dwelling on Drew. It had been a couple days since the fight and neither had broken the silence yet. Jamie was afraid to. What if he said something that pushed Drew even further away?

"Everything okay?" Roman asked as they entered the park.

A dead leaf blew across the path in front of them and Jamie forced himself to perk up. He didn't want Roman to know about Drew or else he'd start asking questions. "Fine. It's just the cold weather. Not really used to it yet."

Roman slid an arm around Jamie's shoulders. "You better hurry up because more is coming. You're not in Florida anymore, Toto."

That was certainly true. Florida was probably seventy-five and sunny right now, palm trees decorated for the holidays. Jamie much preferred New York's brand of winter, with actual cold weather and snow.

"Did you really give Nathan Stuggart a hand job?" Jamie asked a minute later and Roman smiled at the ground.

"You do what you have to to get the part sometimes," he replied. "It's easy to get sucked into what the industry wants you to do."

Jamie didn't really like the thought of Roman sleeping with people to get parts.

"Would you sleep with someone to get the lead?"

Roman paused a moment. "I wouldn't cheat on you, if that's what you're asking. I've had it happen too many times for the exact same reason. In this business, people will get ahead any way they can."

They walked down the path towards the lake, late-fallen leaves scattering the ground, soggy from snow.

"Have a lot of people cheated?" Jamie asked, holding his coffee close, trying to breathe in the warmth. David had cheated, more than once, and Jamie had always felt awful when he found out, like he hadn't been good enough.

Roman didn't reply for a second, kicking aside a wet leaf stuck to the path. "It's hard dating people in the industry because you're never sure if they want you or if they want something you have."

Jamie didn't know what that was like, but he imagined it wasn't a good feeling.

"Relationships can be hard," Roman went on as they meandered down the path. "But just because something is hard doesn't mean it isn't worth the effort. Don't you think?"

Roman was talking about him. Jamie knew it. He took a sip of his coffee to give himself a second.

"Right," he said finally. A relationship was something much more complicated than Roman was making it, at least for Jamie. He wasn't sure it was something he even wanted right now.

"So are we close to your apartment?" Roman asked, glancing around at the buildings beyond the trees. "I still haven't been there."

Jamie took a drink, burning his tongue when he swallowed too much. He wiped at his mouth as they kept walking, hoping Roman hadn't noticed.

"It's a mess," he said quickly. "Drew's been sick and I've been so busy at work and everything. Really, it's a hazard zone."

Roman's mouth twitched. "I'm starting to get the feeling you're getting a lot more out of this relationship than I am."

"That's not true," Jamie argued.

"I haven't even met Drew, the infamous songwriter." Roman tossed his empty cup in a trash can. "We've been dating for over a month and you've met all my friends. I just want to know yours. That's usually how these things work."

Jamie chewed on his bottom lip. The whole idea made him uneasy. It had been a long time since he'd actually *dated* someone, and a part of him wasn't sure how this had even happened. He felt as though he had barely met Roman, but now they were in a *relationship*.

"I like how things are," Jamie said at length.

"Yeah, but I don't want to stand still."

"We're not. See? Walking." Jamie gestured at the path and ignored Roman's unimpressed expression. He didn't want to have this discussion.

"You know what I mean," Roman said, tone impatient. "I'm not interested in fucking around just because I can anymore."

Jamie felt a headache forming behind his temple and he sighed. Just because they'd been dating for a few months didn't automatically make them married.

"Do you get what I'm saying?" Roman asked, watching Jamie carefully, and it took a second, but Jamie nodded down at his hands. He knew what Roman meant; he just wasn't sure if it was what he wanted also.

Sitting in the semi-darkness, Jamie stared at his computer screen, the cursor blinking mockingly against the blank page. He didn't know what he was doing. Nathan had the script now. Making the tiny edits wouldn't change anything.

Sighing, he closed the laptop and set it aside. For a minute, he contemplated texting Roman, but since their walk in the park, he hadn't brought himself to. He'd said the wrong thing. He knew it, but how much did Roman want from him? He didn't have any answers.

Instead, he sat back on the couch and tried not to think about Roman.

The clock on the wall told him it was nearing midnight. He really should go to bed soon, but he was still up. He hadn't been sleeping well lately.

The sound of scratching keys in the door caught his attention and he lifted his head.

The keys scratched and fumbled, and it was another few seconds before the knob turned and the door opened.

Drew stumbled through the doorway, catching himself on the frame. He laughed to himself, struggling out of his jacket and flinging it on the floor as he came inside, not bothering to shut the door.

He ignored Jamie on the couch, gazing around the apartment as though looking for something. At length, he went to the kitchen and opened the freezer door, pulling out the bottle of whiskey.

Pushing himself up, Jamie shut the door and frowned at Drew unscrewing the cap.

"You want a drink?" Drew asked, shaking the bottle at Jamie.

Jamie watched Drew pull out a glass and pour himself a large dose of whiskey. He tossed back half with a grimace.

"I've been thinking about the book," Drew said, a slur to his words as he came over to the couch and saw the closed laptop. "About the girlfriend, the one who cheats with the best friend."

Jamie didn't reply, lips pressed together. Drew hadn't talked to him in days and he wasn't in the mood to stop him from falling over drunk tonight.

"She's a real bitch," Drew said, flopping onto the couch, whiskey spilling out of the glass. "And I was trying to think why she would do something like that to the guy that loves her. 'Cause, like, he's never done anything bad. I mean, he almost died and he's in a coma, but he's still *there*. Isn't that enough? He still loves her even though he's gone."

"It's enough," Jamie muttered, and Drew nodded, finishing his glass. This wasn't about the book at all. Something deep in his chest twinged painfully as he watched Drew.

"*I thought once that it would be you and me against the world,*" he sang to his empty glass, and Jamie sank into the couch, pressing the heel of his hands into his eyes. "*But you smashed my heart into a million pieces and threw it in the ocean to sink.*" He sighed. "Fuck."

Jamie didn't like it when Drew was like this, and he'd been like this more and more since coming here. Maybe he was right; New York wasn't the place for him. It pained Jamie to think it, but Drew hadn't been like this before. He'd been happier.

"I'll get you some water," Jamie said, taking the glass from Drew and going to the kitchen.

Drew slid down in the chair, eyes half closed. "I miss her. I miss Kristen."

"Here," he said, shoving the water at Drew. He knew Drew missed Kristen. Why else would he sleep with a hundred girls that looked just like her?

Drew took it but didn't drink, waving a hand at Jamie instead.

"D'you remember David?"

Jamie rubbed his temples. He didn't want to think about David.

"You should go to bed," he said, standing up and reaching for Drew's arm to pull him up.

"David was a douchebag," Drew slurred, letting Jamie drag him upwards and support his weight with his shoulder. "The cheating and the drugs, and all that shit he said about your writing."

"Come on." Jamie tried to ignore him, not to listen to everything he constantly remembered. Florida only held bad memories for him, and bringing it up again didn't make him feel any better, not when he thought about Roman and their last conversation.

"He was just jealous of your talent," Drew said as he stumbled through the bedroom door. "That's why nobody liked you in high school."

"Thanks." High school hadn't been much better, as Drew knew full well considering Drew had ignored him for the better part of it.

He pushed Drew onto the bed, and Drew fell easily. Jamie slipped off his shoes. Drew didn't protest, making a muffled noise against the pillow. Jamie grabbed a blanket from the bed and tossed it over Drew, then moved to the door.

He stood there a moment, watching the easy rise and fall of Drew's breathing. He didn't want Drew to be like this anymore, and as much as it terrified him, he knew there was only one solution. Turning from Drew, he switched off the light and shut the door behind him.

Chapter 10
Light and Dark

"Hey!" Roman greeted Jamie over the loud music filling the unfamiliar apartment. He pushed through the crowd to the door where Jamie stood, glancing around at the people he didn't know.

Roman already had a drink in his hand and Jamie thought he definitely needed one. He'd texted Roman hoping they could be alone, but a party was better than sitting in the apartment and pretending he wasn't waiting for Drew to come home so they could spend the night avoiding each other.

Jamie didn't know what to do. He couldn't talk Drew out of leaving. He'd tried and failed miserably. Every time he thought of it, his stomach twisted into knots. The whole time they'd been in New York, he'd never imagined that Drew would actually leave. There had been times, moments, when the idea had crossed his mind, but he'd always pushed it down. It was the only way to make things right, though.

"Hi," he replied when Roman reached him and ushered him further inside.

"How's Drew?" Roman asked as they headed for the drinks on the other side of the room.

Jamie's head jerked up. "Why?"

Roman was watching him closely and took a sip of his drink. "You said he was sick."

"Oh." Jamie forced himself to take a breath, but the memory of his lie welled up inside him and he didn't meet Roman's gaze. "He's better."

"You don't want me to meet him, do you?"

"I need a drink," Jamie said, pushing past some people and grabbing a bottle. He didn't care what kind of alcohol it was; any kind would do.

"Jamie," Roman said, coming up behind him and placing a hand on Jamie's waist as Jamie made his drink.

Taking a large drink, Jamie didn't know what to say. "I do," he said finally, though his chest seized up. "But he was sick. He's not usually in a great mood, but when he's sick, I mean, it's just awful." He was rambling but he couldn't stop himself. He took another long drink.

He didn't want to talk about Drew. Drew was leaving him. Turning, he scanned the room.

He didn't really know who was throwing the party, only that it was people from the show, other dancers and ensemble people. He thought he spotted Merryn across the room, but he didn't have any real desire to talk to her.

The music felt too loud, thudding in his eardrums. He wished they were somewhere quieter, but that would mean answering Roman's questions.

"Who is everyone?" he asked, hoping to distract Roman from asking about Drew and why he didn't want them to meet, and why they still hadn't been to his apartment.

Roman's eyes narrowed but he took a sip and answered the question. "Mostly cast members, some design people. Merryn and Sidney are around somewhere. Sidney just landed a supporting role in a show."

"That's great." Jamie clutched his drink, watching the people mill around the room.

They looked happy, all of them. They looked as if they didn't have any problems.

"Yeah," Roman replied, not sounding very enthusiastic. He seemed to hesitate for a second before leaning in closer. "I got some news. About your book."

"You did?" Jamie took another sip, a flutter of nervousness tingling under his skin. He wasn't sure what kind of news would be best.

"He likes it," Roman replied. "Nathan, he wants to meet with you guys."

It took a second to sink in, and he stared at Roman, waiting for him to say he was just joking. When he didn't, Jamie shook his head.

"What? No, but—"

"Yeah," Roman interrupted.

"Are you serious?" Jamie asked, heart battering in his throat. "You're serious? He wants to meet us. Nathan Stuggart liked my book?"

"He said it had 'great potential.'"

A wave of emotions crashed over Jamie as he tossed back his drink. From excitement to disbelief to dread. Drew wouldn't. He wouldn't meet with Nathan. He'd made it clear he wasn't interested in doing anything like this. What was Jamie supposed to do now?

Roman watched him closely. "Aren't you excited?"

"Yeah, yeah," Jamie said, feeling like he couldn't breathe. This wasn't happening to him. Something finally went right and he couldn't enjoy it, not like he should.

Roman tilted his head to the side. "We should celebrate."

"Yeah?" he asked, glancing at Roman. A part of him wasn't sure what he should be celebrating. This was a huge deal, but all he could think about was that it wouldn't be enough for Drew to stay.

"Let's go." Roman took his hand, and Jamie barely had time to set down his glass before they left the apartment.

The air pressed in heavy against his skin as Jamie panted for breath, fingers digging into Roman's shoulders as Roman pushed inside him. Though the room was dark, he could make out the outline of Roman above him, but more than anything, he could feel him. He could feel his body, strong and warm, pressed against his. Jamie's legs wrapped around Roman's back as Roman thrust in.

Roman leaned into Jamie, nose pressed against his cheek, warm breath ghosting over his cheek as his rhythm stuttered a second.

"Nathan's gonna love you," Roman whispered in between the soft noises Jamie made whenever he moved, whenever Roman's hips jerked into his, the wide stretch of his cock through tight muscles.

Jamie only gasped brokenly, clinging to Roman's bare back, swallowing against the flush on his cheeks, heat rising on his skin wherever Roman's hands brushed, gliding up his sides. His hair stuck to his forehead and Roman brushed it aside.

"This is gonna be great for you."

Something in Roman's tone made him pause, but the sharp thrust of his hips brought him back. His eyes met Roman's for a second, things blurry and hazy this close up.

Something unrelated to Roman's hand sliding to his prick knotted in his stomach as he stared at Roman.

Instead of replying or letting Roman go on, he dragged Roman's mouth to his, biting his bottom lip and sighing at the slow slide of Roman's hand on his cock. He didn't want to answer Roman and he didn't want to think about what his look meant.

"R-Roman," he panted against his lip as his hips jerked, pressure building in his prick with each stroke of Roman's hand.

"Shh," Roman hushed him, drawing him into another, slow kiss, and Jamie let himself fall into it.

"I'm gonna—" He gasped seconds before he came, cock jerking in Roman's hand. His mind went blissfully blank for a moment as Roman groaned and pushed into him, his rhythm losing its smoothness until he cursed and came.

Jamie sighed, long and loud, and Roman slid down on top of him. He didn't feel as good as he should have, though. He kept thinking about Drew, about Nathan, about Roman. None of them made him feel as good as they should have.

Roman rolled over at length, propping himself up on his elbow. "So when should I tell Nathan you can meet?"

A pressure settled on Jamie's chest as he lay there, staring at the poster of *The Book of Mormon* on the wall.

"I can't," he said as the pause lengthened.

"What?" Roman asked, staring at him as though if he looked close enough he could find the reason. "Of course you can."

"Not without Drew." He couldn't even believe he was saying this, but without Drew, he was just another writer. They'd been working on this book for so long that doing it without him would be like losing half of it.

"Well, make Drew come," Roman said as though it should be obvious. "I thought this is what you wanted."

"It is. I—" Jamie didn't know how to explain it. Roman wouldn't understand anyway. Sitting up, he reached for his shirt and pulled it on.

"You what?" Roman asked sharply from behind him. "Is this something else you're not going to tell me?"

"What are you talking about?" Jamie rose from the bed, searching for his jeans on the floor and ignoring the nagging feeling of Roman's eyes on him. It had already been a bad week. He didn't need another fight on top of it.

"I tried ignoring it for a while," Roman said, grabbing his shirt as well. "I mean, we don't know each other that well, but that's the problem." He pulled his shirt on, movements jerky and short.

"What's the problem?" Jamie asked impatiently.

"You won't let me in."

"That's not true," Jamie scoffed.

"I still haven't met Drew," Roman pointed out, snatching his jeans from the floor. "I haven't been to your apartment. I don't know anything about your life here because you won't let me."

Jamie floundered for a minute under Roman's accusing gaze. "There's nothing to know. I live in a shitty apartment in Brooklyn. I serve drinks to people who don't tip. I'm not hiding anything."

"I'm not saying you're hiding something," Roman said, running a frustrated hand through his hair and rising from the bed. "I'm saying, you won't let me in."

This was ridiculous, Jamie found himself thinking as he stared at Roman. They'd been dating for barely two months. How fast did he want this to move?

"I don't know what you want me to say," Jamie said finally. "We've been dating for two months. Does that mean we have to get married?"

"I guess meeting your friends was just too much to ask," Roman replied sarcastically. "God forbid you give me one inch of your life." He shook his head. "I just did something *amazing* for you, not because we're dating, but because I think you have real talent, and you won't even give me the courtesy of integrating me into your life. I'm always adding you to mine, and that's not how relationships work."

Jamie stared, unable to form proper words as everything jumbled in his head. Between Drew and Roman, he couldn't make sense of anything. Everything was his fault somehow?

"I'm not gonna be some perfect boyfriend. I don't even know what that is," Jamie said, frowning at Roman. "Did you even ask if I wanted a relationship? You just assumed I did."

"You're right. I didn't ask." Roman shrugged exaggeratedly. "I got caught up in the idea that you weren't using me for my connections, that you were being sincere when you said you liked me. I've dated too many guys who just wanted to get ahead, who just wanted a one-night thing. I thought you were different."

Jamie didn't know what to say. His heart was pounding, thudding in his ears as he stood there. "Sorry I disappointed you," he snapped. It seemed to be a pattern lately, one he couldn't escape, but he didn't feel bad. He never said he wanted anything more than what they had.

"You did," Roman replied, staring at him. "More than I imagined. You're not even going to meet with Nathan, someone who could change your life, because your friend won't go with you."

"You don't get it." Jamie scowled. Roman couldn't understand his and Drew's relationship.

"I don't!" Roman agreed, throwing his hands in the air, "because you've never tried to explain it to me. Every time I try to get closer, you pull away. Are you so dependant on him that you're willing to give up everything?" He shook his head, a disbelieving twist to his mouth. "I just don't have time for it anymore."

Jamie stared for a long minute as Roman's words hit him. Disappointment and anger curled in his chest, but he couldn't decide if he was more angry or annoyed. "So that's it?"

Roman threw up his hands. "I don't know what else there is to do. I'm not gonna be in a relationship with someone who can't be bothered to include me in their life. I'm not a sidekick, okay? I'm the main character."

If that was how Roman felt, maybe they were better off breaking up. Jamie didn't have to prove himself to Roman. He didn't have to defend his relationship with Drew and why he couldn't meet with Nathan.

"Okay, good," he said, grabbing his jacket off the floor. "I don't have time for someone who just assumes they know what I want anyway. You can tell Nathan I won't be meeting with him."

Roman scoffed as Jamie yanked open the bedroom door and crossed the living room. "I figured there was something weird about Drew, but I never thought you'd throw away your dreams for him."

Jamie didn't turn back, though Roman's words stung in a way he hadn't expected as he burst into the hallway and took the stairs instead of waiting for the elevator. He jogged down, feet pounding each step until he burst out the door into the swirl of snow falling from above.

His heart thudded loudly, blood rushing in his ears as he headed for the subway, his pace slowing until he reached the entrance. Taking a deep breath, he leaned back against the railing and closed his eyes. Just because he wasn't ready to introduce Roman to everyone he knew, which so far amounted to two people in New York, didn't mean he was pushing him away. Ever since David, he'd had to be more careful about who he let into his life. The only person in it who he knew wouldn't hurt him was Drew. Though lately, he even doubted that.

Snow settled in his hair and on the shoulders of his jacket as he stood there, hands shaking and knees weak.

There was nothing he could do, and he wasn't even sure he wanted to do something, so he turned and headed down the stairs, leaving Manhattan behind.

Chapter 11
Sober Realizations

Jamie frowned at the counter, stiffening as Drew passed behind him to grab a bottle off the back counter and pour shots for the table by the piano. He said nothing, keeping his gaze on the scratched bar-top and waiting until Drew moved away before letting out his breath.

He hadn't talked to Drew in days. The apartment was perpetually silent and neither of them had bothered to break it.

Jamie wasn't sure who he was supposed to be more upset with—Drew or Roman. He hadn't talked to Roman, and he didn't figure he would anytime soon, not after everything that had happened. It had only been a few days, but he kept thinking of Roman and how that had ended. Not his finest moment.

Roman's words still came back to him at the most inconvenient times, however, and he frowned at the counter as he wiped it down.

I never thought you'd throw away your dreams for him.

Jamie had been hurt plenty of times before by plenty of different people, but nothing stung quite like that. He resented the assumption that everything he did was related to Drew. He'd dated Roman, hadn't he? He hadn't even really told Drew about that.

Drew wasn't a safety net, he told himself firmly.

"You two have a lover's spat?"

Jamie jumped at Laurel's voice behind him.

"It's like the arctic tundra in here," she continued, grabbing a lemon and a knife, slicing it on the counter. "Someone forget to pick up their dirty underwear?"

Jamie really didn't want to talk about it, and he hoped she would just go away, but his hopes were unfounded as she stared at him for a minute or two.

"Seriously. You two have been nothing but little rain clouds for months. You ever think maybe this isn't working out?"

"What are you talking about?" Jamie muttered, putting away the glasses under the counter.

She rolled her eyes. "You're like a dysfunctional married couple, one that needs a divorce. Sometimes divorces are good. If people aren't happy in a situation, it's better to let go, you know?"

Jamie frowned and didn't reply. He and Drew weren't a couple. Drew had his own life and Jamie had his. Except that Drew's was back in Florida and Jamie had just ended his… whatever, with Roman.

"Shit," he muttered under his breath and Laurel scooped up the lemon.

"Growing up sucks, doesn't it?" she said before breezing away.

Jamie's gaze drifted to Drew across the room. There was a pit in the bottom of his stomach, one he hated and couldn't seem to get rid of no matter what he did. Drew didn't want to be here. There was nothing for him, nothing that he wanted, no matter how much Jamie tried to convince himself that Drew wanted the same things he did. They were very different people, even more now than when they'd first come.

Standing behind the bar, he sighed to himself and turned away from Drew when a customer called for his attention. He couldn't deny it any longer.

When Jamie had first moved to New York, he hadn't been disillusioned about fame and being "discovered" by someone famous or someone important. He'd spent most of his life back in Florida being ignored, picked on as the weird artsy kid who ate lunch alone and spent too much time scribbling in a notebook.

Now, he was still alone except he was alone in a giant city and he couldn't even talk to his best friend. Drew had pretty much been the only one he could talk to for years now.

Maybe he did cling to Drew for something to ground him, but it wasn't an excuse. He had dated Roman because he liked him. He couldn't be blamed for wanting to be cautious. That thought only made his stomach grumble in protest, a queasy feeling when he thought about Roman and how he'd left things. Maybe he should have tried harder.

Sitting on the couch in his apartment, he curled up and set his chin on his knees. He didn't know how to fix anything.

The doorknob rattled and twisted as Jamie sat there. It had to be Drew. He didn't know what he'd say. Every interaction they'd had in days had been stiff and oddly formal.

He didn't look up as the door opened and Drew stepped inside. He could tell it was him from the weight of his steps and the way he dropped his keys on the counter.

He expected Drew to pass by him without a word, and was surprised when Drew remained by the door for a moment then moved over, sinking down into the chair.

Jamie looked up, unsure what to do, so he remained silent as they sat there. The moment lingered and he wondered if Drew was going to speak at all.

"I bought a ticket home."

Jamie nodded at his knees. He'd figured it was coming. "When do you leave?" Knowing didn't help the ache deep in his chest. Now he'd really be alone.

Drew shifted, leaning forward. "Couple of days."

For a moment, Jamie didn't say anything. "You're really going?"

Drew sighed, sitting back. "Jamie, I'm not doing this to be a dick. Clearly, this isn't working. You want to be a writer, and you'll be a good writer. I just, I just don't want it the same way you do. I'm tired of random girls to fill the loneliness. I'm tired of serving idiots at a bar. I want to go home. I want to go be with Kristin."

"I know." Jamie couldn't pretend any more that Drew wanted to be here. He'd be happier in Florida. It just worried him what he'd do without Drew. Drew had been his best friend for so long. "But what about everything?"

"You don't need me," Drew pointed out. "You have the book and half the songs. There are a million other songwriters in this city who would love to work with you."

"What if I can't do it alone?"

"Come on, Jamie, you know you can. I know David shit on your dreams and I haven't really helped much since we got here, but you have to do it without me."

Jamie wasn't sure he could. Drew had always been the one to believe in him. When David had been running around getting high constantly, Drew had kept Jamie from being dragged down with him.

Drew shook his head. "I shouldn't have come with you in the first place."

"That's not true."

"I didn't want to disappoint you. You're the first one who ever thought I could do something with my music. You were the first person who actually knew me, and I wanted to be that person for you, but this past year, the past couple months, ever since David, you haven't been yourself."

"David was..."

"A douchebag." Drew nodded. Jamie didn't need reminding. He'd been the one in the relationship after all. He wasn't sure what David had to do with any of this anyway. "But you changed."

"I don't know what you're talking about," Jamie said, frowning. "David and I broke up over a year ago, way before we came here."

"Yeah, and since we came here, you've been using me as an excuse for everything."

"I have not," Jamie argued, indignant. Drew leaving he could accept. After all, Drew was right. He'd just been ignoring the signs for months, telling himself that if they could just get the show produced, it might make things better, but there was no point lying to himself anymore. He hadn't used Drew as an excuse, though.

Drew tilted his head to the side. "How many friends have you made here?"

Jamie opened his mouth then scowled. That didn't prove anything. He worked too much to do anything other than work on the book.

"And that guy you're dating—"

"We broke up," Jamie interrupted, but he wished he hadn't when a knowing look crossed Drew's face. "What?"

"Why'd you break up?"

"I don't know. He was going too fast. He was mad 'cause he hadn't met you or something." Jamie hadn't tried to do it. It wasn't his fault that Roman thought two months of dating equated to knowing everything about the other person including seeing where they slept.

"Why didn't you let him meet me?"

Jamie pressed his hands to his face, letting his feet fall to the floor. This wasn't about Roman. "On your good days lately, you haven't exactly been friendly. I wasn't going to toss him to the wolves."

"Why not?" Drew pressed. "The worst that happens is I don't like him. Or were you afraid that I would like him? You know, 'cause anyone that's not David is a step-up."

"Can we stop talking about David?" Jamie asked, pushing himself up from the couch and going to the fridge. He wasn't hungry or thirsty, but he opened it and stared inside anyway. Roman wasn't David. He knew that. Roman didn't abandon him to do drugs with total strangers or come home reeking of beer and unfamiliar cologne.

"I get it," Drew said from the chair. "David fucked you over and now you're scared of any relationship."

Jamie slammed the fridge door shut. "That is not—" He couldn't finish, shaking his head. He sighed. "Roman and I just don't want the same things."

"Oh, so he didn't want to get close to you, meet your friends, didn't care about your passion? Like you do?"

"You don't even know him," Jamie said, returning to the living room.

"No," Drew agreed, "but I know you. You're a hopeless romantic. You dream of moving to New York City and becoming a famous playwright. But you're too scared to get close to anyone. Except me, because I'm safe. I'll never dump you, right?"

Frowning, Jamie sank onto the couch again. Drew had been his longest relationship with a guy, all things considered. "This would be a lot easier if you were gay."

Drew smiled for the first time in days. "We probably *would* be an old married couple by now."

Jamie huffed down at the rug. "Laurel thinks we should get a divorce."

"She's probably right. If I stay here, we'll end up hating each other, and I don't want that to happen. You have to stay here and I have to go home."

Jamie was silent for a moment. Maybe he'd known all along that it would end like this, but he hadn't wanted it to. He'd had visions of the future, of success and bigger apartments and no more working in a bar.

He nodded, though. "Where are you gonna stay?"

Relief broke over Drew's face, and Jamie felt a weight come off his chest. They'd tried so hard, but it wasn't working out. Laurel was right. Drew leaving didn't have to be the end of the world.

"I called Kristin yesterday. I'm gonna stay with her."

"What about her boyfriend?"

"Turns out it was just a couple of dates. Nothing serious."

This was it then. Once Drew left, Jamie would be on his own to make things happen. He thought of Roman, of Nathan's request to meet him. He'd probably ruined that. It wasn't Nathan so much that bothered him but how he'd treated Roman. Roman *wasn't* David. He shouldn't have treated him like he was.

"If she gets sick of you, you can always come back," he said, and Drew laughed.

"I'll keep that in mind," Drew assured him, hitting his knee. "And Florida isn't all bad if I'm there, right?"

"Maybe, yeah."

"And if you like this Roman guy, maybe you should tell him. You can't run forever." Drew said seriously.

"I suppose," Jamie agreed because he didn't really have another answer. He didn't know how to stop pushing people away. It was second nature these days. He'd pushed so hard that Roman had given up, and for good reason too. Jamie almost couldn't blame him.

"This is gonna be good for both of us. I promise," Drew said, pushing himself up from the couch. "I'm gonna start packing."

Jamie sat back as Drew left for his room. The question now was whether Jamie had completely ruined any chance he had with Roman or if there was a way to fix it. For too long, he'd let the memory of David mar his relationships, and he didn't want Roman to be a casualty anymore.

Drew left four days later and Jamie stood at the line to security, watching him weave through the people and disappear on the other side. He took the subway home alone, clutching a bar and jostling around with the train. At home, he stood for a moment, staring into Drew's room, all the furniture still there, but no clothes on the floor, no mess to clean up or complain about.

He'd spent just a minute feeling sad, but Drew had seemed so much happier when he'd left for the plane, like he was his old self again. Jamie hadn't realized how much he'd missed that Drew.

Pulling out his phone, he scrolled through his messages, pulling up Roman's thread. It had been over a week and he hadn't heard a thing. That was his fault, he supposed. It was all his fault, but how was he supposed to fix it? A simply sorry wouldn't be good enough, not after what he'd done.

Hey, he texted finally. Lame, but it was a start.

No response came and he sighed, sticking the phone back in his pocket.

At the bar, there was already a new girl who cleaned up and spent no time bothering with the piano in the corner.

"At least no more moping, huh?" Laurel said, coming up behind Jamie and clapping him on the shoulder.

Jamie smiled briefly. "Don't think he'll be moping much in Florida."

"See?" Laurel asked, handing him a shot of tequila. "Divorces are good for everyone involved." She clinked her own glass with Jamie's before tossing it back.

Jamie hesitated, twisting the shot on the counter. Though Drew was gone, he was less sad than he'd expected. His more pressing concern was Roman. He'd been a pretty shitty boyfriend, or whatever he'd been. As much as he would have liked to blame it all on David, he'd been the one to do it.

He knew what he had to do, but the thought scared him, made his stomach twist and tighten until he felt as though he was going to be sick.

"Hey, Laurel, you've dated a lot of guys, right?"

"Oh, yeah," she agreed, pouring another shot. "Way more than I care to admit to, young grasshopper."

"So you've probably fucked up a few, right?"

Laurel set the bottle down and shot him a look. "If you're trying to ask for advice, you're not exactly going about it the right way."

"It's just, I was seeing this guy and I kind of completely screwed it up," he admitted. With Drew gone, all Jamie had to think about was Roman. Had it been so hard to let Roman meet Drew or come to his apartment? Or talk about something other than Broadway? Why couldn't he have just done it?

"How badly screwed up?" she asked, nudging his full glass towards him. "Like didn't call him back screwed up or slept with his best friend screwed up?"

Jamie frowned, taking the shot. "Somewhere in the middle?"

"Well, first thing, you've gotta apologize. Doesn't matter what happened or whose fault it was. If you want him back, you have to take the first step.

"What if that's not enough?" Roman hadn't ever responded to his text, although it had been a pretty shitty text, but still. Jamie didn't think just saying he was sorry would do it. He didn't know how to prove anything either, or exactly what he was trying to prove.

"You like him?" she asked, pouring them both another shot.

"Yeah."

"Then you gotta do whatever it takes so he knows you mean it. And whatever you did, don't ever do it again." She raised her glass and waited for Jamie to do the same.

He wasn't exactly sure how to do that, but she was right, and Drew had been right. He couldn't make excuses for not getting close to someone. He wanted to be with Roman. He just had to figure out how.

Raising his glass, he let Laurel clink them together.

"To not screwing up," she said, and Jamie tossed his shot back in one gulp.

I'm sorry.

The words felt completely underwhelming when Jamie sent the text. A text message was the equivalent of sending a carrier pigeon and hoping the person you sent it to wasn't afraid of birds. He wondered if Roman was even reading his messages or just ignoring him completely.

There was only one way he knew for sure to talk to Roman. That was how he talked Laurel into letting him off early on Thursday and taking the train up to the Bronx. Snow fell in thick flakes as he headed straight for Roman's apartment.

Every step up the stairs was heavy with anticipation. He hadn't really thought through what he would say. He just hoped that Roman wouldn't slam the door in his face.

At the door, Jamie hesitated, taking a deep breath to calm his pounding heart. He could do this.

He forced himself to knock after a minute, stepping back and waiting. Every second that passed with no answer made him more nervous, and by the time it did, he was sure his heart was about to explode.

It wasn't Roman at the door, though, but Merryn in her oversized sweatshirt and leggings. Her face immediately twisted with dislike as she caught sight of him.

"Merryn, hi," he said, taken aback slightly. He hadn't considered that she might be home.

"Don't you 'hi' me," she replied, leaning against the doorframe and blocking the rest of the apartment. "Because of you I've had to listen to constant bitching for over a week."

"I didn't—" Jamie started but she cut him off.

"You don't do that shit to someone who's been nothing but amazing to you," she snapped, poking him painfully in the chest. "You've got issues? We've all got issues, but you don't drag someone like Roman along with you."

Jamie winced and took a step back, out of poking range. "Is he here?" He'd rather have this discussion with Roman since Merryn was definitely scarier.

"He's not," she replied shortly. "And to be honest, I'm not happy you're here either."

Jamie's heart sank. "I need to talk to him."

Merryn scoffed, flipping her hair over her shoulder haughtily. "You're going to have to have a lot more than that to get past me. He liked you and you strung him along. That is not okay."

"I know," Jamie said desperately. "I was stupid. Can you just tell me where he is or when he'll be back?"

"You know, I can't," she said, shaking her head. "Because he deserves someone who won't take him for granted. In the meantime, I hope you get Chlamydia from your next fuck, and I hope he's a complete jerk. You'd deserve it."

The door slammed shut in Jamie's face and he couldn't say he blamed her.

Chapter 12
Breaking Through

Jamie didn't know what to do. Roman wouldn't talk to him—he hadn't been able to get a hold of him at all, not through calls or texts, and he knew Merryn wasn't on his side. She probably hadn't even told Roman he had come by.

"It's your night off," Laurel said as Jamie sat at the bar, head in his hands. "You shouldn't be here."

"And where should I be?" he asked. He couldn't even get Roman to answer the phone. How was he ever supposed to apologize if he couldn't talk to him? Maybe he should just accept defeat. Except that he didn't want to. Roman was the first person in months that he actually cared about, the first person who hadn't laughed at his dream of becoming a Broadway writer and actually thought he was good enough to do it, aside from Drew that was.

"Out!" She gestured toward the windows. "There's a whole city filled with guys that would be more than willing to turn your frown upside down. What's so special about this one?"

Jamie sighed, pushing around the drink he'd ordered half an hour ago but hadn't actually drunk. "For six months, I dated this guy who spent most of his time getting high and cheating on me, and now there's Roman who is the exact opposite. He's nice and smart, and funny, and I can't even get two minutes alone to tell him how sorry I am. I shouldn't have pushed him away. I should have appreciated him."

"Just ask yourself this," Laurel said, leaning over the counter. "What did he want and how are you gonna give it to him?"

Jamie didn't reply, frowning at his drink. What had Roman wanted? The answer was obvious, but Jamie wasn't sure how he could even get Roman to listen to him long enough to try.

His phone rang before he could come up with a response and Laurel waved a hand at him as she left.

"Hello?"

"Hey, Jamie!" came Drew's voice on the other end.

Jamie turned from the bar, heading to a table in the corner and smiling at Drew's voice.

"Hey."

"How's New York?"

"Same as usual." Jamie sat down and glanced out the window. It was dark out, the streets lit only by yellow lamps, reflecting off the slushy snow on the ground. "I assume Florida is sunny as hell?"

"As usual," Drew replied, and Jamie could hear the grin. "Kristin says hi."

"Hi Kristin." It didn't hurt as much as Jamie would have guessed, talking to Drew. He sounded much happier.

"How are things going with Roman?"

Jamie sighed. "They're not."

Drew paused. "Sorry about that. But listen, your parents keep asking when you're coming to visit. Maybe you should come down, take a break from all that laborious bartending. Some sun would be good for you."

Normally, Jamie would have balked at the idea of going back to Florida so soon, only eight months after leaving, but considering everything that had happened, maybe getting away was a good idea.

"Yeah, maybe," he agreed.

"Think about it," Drew said seriously. "Your parents miss you. And, you know, I do too."

Jamie smiled. "Thanks."

"Seriously. You can't stay away from Florida forever. It sucks you back in."

"Clearly." Jamie laughed. "I'll call you later, okay?"

"Sure thing, and Jamie, don't give up yet."

Jamie hung up a minute later and set the phone on the table. Maybe it was time to pay a visit home.

Jamie took the subway across the bridge, bundled up in a thick coat but still shivering when he got off and climbed the stairs to the street. The lights of Broadway lit up the night's sky as he walked underneath the tall buildings towards the cluster of theaters. He shoved his hands in his pockets and maneuvered between the crowds of people.

Stopping at the theater near the end of the row, he stared up at the flashing sign and took a deep breath. His watch told him the show had started a while ago. Instead of going to the lobby or the box office, he stepped out of the way of the main street where yellow cabs honked their horns at the pedestrians crossing the street.

Down the dim alley, he found the door to the back and stood back to wait.

By the time the door finally opened, he couldn't feel his feet and he had to walk around in circles to keep them from going numb. A rush of people poured out, slowing to a trickle after a minute or two. Dancers laughed and he heard something about going out for drinks, but he waited, keeping his eyes on the door, feeling the tingle of nerves on his skin.

Roman emerged finally, tying his scarf around his neck and tossing his bag over his shoulder. Jamie took a step forward, but Roman saw him before he could say anything.

For a second, no one said anything, and Jamie bit his bottom lip.

"Hi," he said finally, breath clouding before him, and he licked his chapped lips.

"Hey," Roman replied, hunching his shoulders against the cold.

"Um," Jamie said slowly, swallowing down his heart as it rose in his throat. This was the only way he could think of to actually talk to Roman without making some sort of big spectacle. He wasn't the grand gesture type, at least not in the typical movie way. He didn't think he could handle the public scrutiny that came with it.

Roman didn't help him at all, shifting from one foot to the other as they stood in the freezing cold alley. He glanced down the alley as though he'd rather be anywhere but there at the moment.

"You were right," Jamie said finally.

Roman merely glanced at him, puffing out a cloud of air. "That's… great. It's cold, so I'm gonna—"

"Wait, no." Jamie reached out his hand but stopped, pulling it back and looking away. He wasn't cut out for this kind of thing. "I'm sorry. I know it's not enough just to say it, but I mean it. You were right about me pushing you away, not letting you in."

Roman turned back to him slowly. His nose was already red from the cold, and he sniffed as he waited.

Bracing himself, Jamie took a step forward. He could do this.

"I've had really bad luck with guys. Most of the time, they're assholes. It was just easier to keep my distance." He huffed out a breath as he said it. "I've made a lot of mistakes, and I thought I didn't want a relationship. I thought you were going too fast, but you weren't. I was just slow."

There wasn't much he could say except to apologize. He'd been a monumental jerk and he wouldn't have been surprised if Roman didn't forgive him. He really hoped he would, though.

Before Roman could reply, the door behind him burst open and Merryn stepped out.

"You didn't have to wait for me," she said, stepping up beside Roman, but she caught sight of Jamie and her eyes narrowed. "What the hell is he doing here?"

"Merryn, don't." Roman stopped her.

She shot him a look but then sniffed. "I'll see you at home." She swept past Jamie with a dark look and disappeared around the corner.

"Guess she hasn't forgiven me either. But she's right. I was a douchebag."

Roman didn't reply, but his expression told Jamie that he agreed completely.

Nerves prickled Jamie's skin, though it might have been him losing feeling from standing in twenty degree weather.

"I know you're not like my last boyfriend. I *know that*," he said, more to himself than anything. "I was just afraid if I let you in, it would turn out the same." He took a fortifying breath, fingers trembling as he reached in his pocket. It was now or never. "Here," he said, pulling a piece of paper from his pocket and holding it out.

Roman didn't take it, eyeing it suspiciously. "What is it?"

"It's a plane ticket." Jamie swallowed down the lump rising in his throat. This might have been one of the stupidest things he'd ever attempted. "To Florida. For you."

Roman's eyebrows furrowed and he didn't speak for a long minute. "What?"

"I want to try again," Jamie said, shifting as he started to lose the feeling in his feet. "I didn't mean to keep you out of my life, and I don't want to again. I'm going to Florida, and I want you to come with me. Drew moved back, so you can meet him and my family and see where I grew up. I mean, it's not very impressive but it's home."

"Jamie," Drew said slowly, but Jamie shook his head.

"Flight leaves in a couple days. You don't have to come but I really want you to."

He had nothing else to say. It was all he could do. He hesitated a second, but Roman was staring at the ticket.

Turning, he headed for the street.

It could have gone worse. Roman could have yelled. He could have said that he deserved everything he got and that he wasn't worthy of his attention in the first place. He'd never thought he would end up like the guys he had dated before, the ones he had hated afterwards.

He went with the flow of the crowd, only stepping out when he reached the subway entrance. He'd done all he could and now he just hoped it was enough.

"I thought you hated Florida," Laurel said, tossing the rag at Jamie. He caught it gingerly and left it in the sink.

Jamie knew it would be hard explaining something like this when he'd spent the past eight months talking about how much he hated Florida.

"I just need to get away for a few days." He paused. "Thanks, by the way, for giving me that advance."

She laughed to herself. "You'll be wiping down tables for a month to make that up, but what can I say? I'm a sucker for happy endings."

"I'm just going to see family."

"And friends?" Laurel asked slyly, and Jamie frowned.

"If you're talking about Drew, he literally just left last week."

Laurel turned, leaning against the counter. "Yes, I am. It took you guys months to work things out and I don't want you running off to Florida with some slow-motion beach scene in your head."

"Laurel!" Jamie admonished. "I'm not going for Drew."

Her eyes lit up. "Does this mean you fixed things with the secret boyfriend? Is he coming with you? Because I could get behind that beach scene."

Jamie didn't roll his eyes at her, instead joining her against the counter. "I don't know if he's coming." He hadn't heard from Roman despite giving him the ticket two days ago. The flight left in the morning, and every moment that ticked by made Jamie more nervous that Roman wouldn't show up. After all, what did he have to offer but making up for his mistakes?

"Did you apologize?" she asked seriously.

"Yes."

"Did you mean it?"

"*Yes*," Jamie repeated. "I don't know what else I can do. Either he'll give me another shot or I guess I'm back to square one."

"Not quite square one," Laurel pointed out. "You've learned that some people are worth fighting for."

Jamie smiled slightly. "I thought you gave up on men."

She poked him in the chest before shoving the rag into his hand. "I haven't given up on you. Just make sure you come back, okay?"

"Nothing could stop me."

Standing before the security line at JFK, Jamie stared up at the flight list. The 10:45 to Orlando was on time. Checking his watch, he couldn't help but feel nervous as he looked around and didn't see Roman anywhere. Maybe he'd been hoping too much. Maybe he'd screwed up things too much to fix it.

He really needed to get in line if he didn't want to miss his flight, but still Jamie waited. He didn't know why he was waiting. Roman wasn't going to come. Even if he wanted to, Roman had work. Roman had a career that he wouldn't walk away from, not for Jamie. He'd done too much wrong.

Shaking his head, his heart sank as he turned towards the security line. Though he wasn't entirely surprised, he was still disappointed. He'd hoped maybe…

The airport bustled with people, tourists doing last-minute shopping in the shops, people drinking in the bars at ten in the morning.

At the entrance to the line, Jamie turned and scanned the crowd one last time. The large room was filled with parents and children, teenagers and college students, businessmen and women, and airport employees. As he started to turn, he caught sight of someone coming towards him, someone who looked just like Roman.

"Are you getting in line or not?" a man asked as he stood there, and he stepped out from in front of the entrance, eyes on Roman. The man pushed past him with a huff.

It took a minute, but Roman reached him finally, the ticket clutched in his hand.

"You came," Jamie said, hope rising within as Roman straightened up.

Roman shoved his hands in his pocket. "I did."

"Why?" Jamie almost couldn't believe it.

Roman paused. "Despite all your flaws—and there seem to be a lot—I still like you."

Jamie couldn't allow himself to get too excited. But Roman was here. He'd come.

"Here's the thing," Roman said finally. "I get it about guys being assholes. I've dated my fair share. It's especially hard to find someone here who isn't using you to get something."

"I would never," Jamie interrupted. "Is that what you thought? That's not why—"

"I know," Roman said, cutting him off. "I'm just worried that you're not ready. Whoever you dated before, I'm not him, and I don't like feeling excluded."

"You're completely right," Jamie assured him. "David was awful and I, I didn't give you a chance."

Roman nodded and Jamie's stomach twisted nervously. "I also really don't get the Drew thing. I just can't understand why you wouldn't want to meet with someone like Nathan because of someone else. I thought you were more ambitious than that."

"I was scared," Jamie admitted, "of doing things alone, of being alone. Drew is really the only person I've trusted completely for a long time. Without him, I just felt like I couldn't. I know it was idiotic. I've kicked myself a thousand times for it since he left."

He should never have hinged his happiness on someone else, but it was something he'd have to learn to manage in the future. He'd done it with David, and now Drew, and he didn't want to do it again.

"So I guess the bottom line is that I still like you, and maybe we both have issues to work out," Roman said at length.

"Yeah?" Jamie asked, something fluttering in his stomach, halfway between terrified fear and nervous excitement.

Roman ran a hand through his hair and nodded after a second.

"Yeah."

Jamie let out a breath in relief, smiling at Roman as the word sunk in. It couldn't really be happening. He rarely got second chances.

He couldn't help the tears of relief that gathered in his eyes, emotions overwhelming him, and he couldn't stop himself from wiping them before they could fall. "Shit. I promise. I promise I won't be stupid." The elephant on his chest was gone and he could breathe easily again, even when Roman pulled him into a warm hug and held him close. He smiled against his chest, brushing aside any lingering wetness.

"Everybody's stupid sometimes," Roman murmured into his hair.

Jamie pulled away a minute later, suddenly aware of everyone around them. So much for non-public gestures.

"I guess we're going to Florida," he said, glancing at the clock again. He hesitated, looking back at Roman. "What about the show?" They really needed to get going if they were going to make the flight.

"We have understudies for a reason. I think they can manage for a day or two, though I can't stay too long."

Jamie smiled. "I'm just glad you're here."

"So, Florida, eh? I've never been," Roman said, turning with Jamie to get in line.

"I never liked it much, but maybe it'll be better this time."

Roman smiled slightly and they shuffled forward.

Jamie frowned a second later as he remembered. "I guess you told Nathan I didn't want to meet him."

Roman slid a hand around his waist. "Actually, I told him I couldn't get a hold of you. He's getting impatient that you're keeping him waiting."

Jamie stared, searching for the lie in his face, but there was none. "You —" he said, and Roman simply shook his head.

"Honestly, I was pretty mad. I was going to tell him but then I thought, if it was me, I wouldn't want to miss out. Just because you were an idiot didn't mean you should lose your shot."

"Thanks you" he said, and he was grateful, especially when Roman smiled, his dimple even more pronounced than usual.

"You're welcome," he said seriously. "Now, the question is, have you ever joined the mile-high club?"

Jamie smiled at the scandalized look they got from the old woman in front of them. Roman bit back his laugh as the line moved slowly forward. Things may not have gone as Jamie had planned, but that didn't mean they hadn't worked out for the better.

About the Author

E. E. Grey started to write fresh out of high school, but the hobby grew over time. Now Grey has completed six novel-length works and over three hundred short stories. When not writing, Grey enjoys traveling, having visited over twenty countries already, and baking for friends and family.

About the Series

Olympic Passions

It isn't easy to win both love and gold. To be an Olympic athlete requires incredible passion. There are other passions, however, which rise in young men training in such close quarters. When these passions swell, an athlete's dedication can waver. It's hard to keep your eyes on the prize when your friend's finely muscled back is so distracting...

Will it be love over gold? Will these young men choose each other over the Olympics? Or can they find a way to win it all?

Works in this series:

1. Vaulted

2. Tumbled

3. Backstroke

About the Publisher

ForbiddenFiction.com is a publisher devoted to writing that breaks the boundaries of original erotic fiction. Our stories combine intense sexuality with quality writing. Stories at Forbidden Fiction.com not only arouse readers through sensations, but also engage them emotionally and mentally through storytelling as well-crafted as the sex is hot.

ForbiddenFiction.com is also designed to be a social reading environment. You'll have fun even if just reading the latest post each day, yet you will have the chance for so much more. Readers and authors can be part of ongoing discussions of specific works and individual authors as well as more general topics.

Sign up for a FREE Membership today at ForbiddenFiction.com

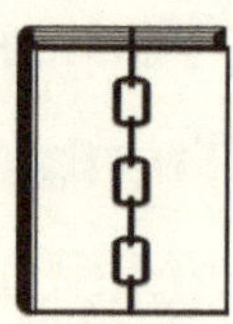

Also recommended...

You may also enjoy these other ForbiddenFiction works:

Breaking and Entering, by P.L. Ripley

P.L. Ripley wrote about gay men in trouble, and how they changed their trouble for something a bit more to their liking. These aren't tales where love heals all, but you can be certain that sex changes things.

In *Breaking and Entering*, ForbiddenFiction.com presents all the stories P.L. Ripley published with us, collected in one volume as a testament to his life and work. Here you will find tales of thieves who found an unusual—and erotic—way to escape the law, of how one man gave his life for love, of how another learned to let loose and live, and even one story where pursuit of the man of his dreams leads out of fear and into love.

Rest well, P.L. Ripley. You will be missed.

Bring the Love

There is something about the love of men for men that speaks to the heart. Masculinity in passion is more than muscle and attitude. It's in the mix of hardness and tenderness, the burning gaze and the soft caress. The struggle with expectation to be tough and the need to be vulnerable. There is something about these stories that show men opening–sometimes eagerly, sometimes reluctantly–to love.

For your pleasure, we offer you men who reclaim lost love, men who find themselves in the love of another man, and men who defy oppression for the sake of love. These are stories that show that an ending is not necessarily the end and that softness is not the same as weakness. In all, eleven stories of love and romance between men from ForbiddenFiction's top authors, including award-winners Julian Keys and Lynn Kelling. To you, our readers, we bring the love

www.ingramcontent.com/pod-product-compliance
Lightning Source LLC
Chambersburg PA
CBHW060426030726
47495CB00003B/758

9781622343508